1/19/17

A MARBLE HEART

TRAVIS GULBRANDSON

Copyright © 2017 by Travis Gulbrandson
Cover design by Travis Gulbrandson
All rights reserved.
ISBN 978-1-365-57895-3
No part of this book may be reproduced in any form or by any electronic or mechanical means including information storage and retrieval systems, without permission in writing from the author. The only exception is by a reviewer, who may quote short excerpts in a review.

For more information, visit www.travisgulbrandson.com.

A Marble Heart is a work of fiction. Apart from the actual people, places and events in the narrative, all characters and incidents are used fictitiously. Any resemblance to living persons or places is entirely coincidental.

The performance began at eight. It was the third day of December, and the opera house was cold all through, from the lobby to the backstage area where the children huddled together in a mass of shivering. Their unfamiliar new clothes were not made for winter wear. There were ten boys and girls here and ten times that back at the Home in Kansas City. Rev. Litten was on the stage, and the children watched him from the wings as he quoted complex figures about the number of orphanages operating throughout the country. At the end of his talk he introduced Marie LeWald as the youngest woman working in the charitable field today. She left her place in the wings, wading through the crowd of children, and walked onto the stage, first bowing to the audience and then curtsying to Rev. Litten before he took her former position.

Flora stopped listening as her Aunt Marie began to speak. She had spent all of her twelve years listening to some version of this talk. The cruel adoption laws, the broken families, the lost little children who often never again see their parents. Marie spoke with sobs in her throat and with hands clasped in a prayerlike vise beneath her chin. From behind Flora came a sound like a loud purr, and she took a half-step back into a boy and stayed there as if to warm him. She was right. It was the growling of his stomach. As Flora stood there an object brushed against her thigh, and without looking she reached down and took it in her hand. It was Celia's tiny palm. Celia was seven years old, the youngest child at the opera house. She had thick strawberry blond hair that was cut very short, above her ears, with a straight line across the bangs. It was the first time she had touched Flora by her own choice in weeks. She was sweet, like a stray dog that follows a stranger for blocks after a single friendly word or a kind look. Under her other arm Flora held her brother Joseph. He was ten. He was trouble. He was sweet, too.

Mrs. Baker's speech was last and the longest by halves, and the children did their best not to move when she was onstage. She had a pointed nose and pretty lips, and dark hair that she piled on the top of her head. Her eyes were her most striking features, in particular when they were hit by any kind of light. They were like smooth jewels whose radiance grew more intense as she spoke outdoors or lighted by candles, or as now, in the amber glow of the stage.

"The luckiest children in the world are those that have a family," Mrs. Baker told the audience. "They have parents to love them, and brothers and sisters, too. Apart from proper food and clothing, the love of a family is the most important thing a child can have. It is a very sad thing, then, that in this world of ours, with all of its people and with all of its homes, not all little children can be so lucky.

"You may ask, 'What about the children's homes? What about the orphanages? Are they not able to provide everything these little dear ones so sorely need?' I am ashamed to say they are not. Most of the little ones in these places have at least one parent. How, then, do such institutions come into being?

Oftentimes a parent is unable to care for their child. Perhaps they have had a series of misfortunes – they have lost their means of employment, they have succumbed to a sudden illness, they are unable to pay the rent – or perhaps only one tragedy has befallen them. This is when the orphans' homes swoop in. The unlucky parents will be served with what is called an order of the court and will have their children snatched away. There is a term for this. It is called kidnapping. And, not unlike a bandit that grabs a child off the streets, the courts will invoke a ransom of some kind. In addition, the homes also will take in funds from the county. Those places are paid off per child – per head, if you will. Like cattle.

"Once a child is placed in one of these homes – although I hasten to call them such, for how can it be a true home where there is no love? Once the child is placed there, it loses its identity. He is no longer little Johnny, she no longer pretty Jane. They are nothing more than one of the many holy little beings to which a numeric figure can be attached. Think of it – our laws are set up to aid in this business. For that is all it is. A business."

Mrs. Baker's head bowed as if she were in mourning.

"That is why I embarked upon my mission. It is why I founded the Joseph Walter Home. This name holds a special meaning to me, for it is the same as that of my own son. The poor little thing, he died in infancy."

Confused, Celia arched her neck to look at Joseph, who continued to stand next to his sister. Opening her mouth to speak, Celia pointed a stubby finger at him.

"But he's right–"

Before Celia could finish, Flora motioned for her to be quiet, a look of panic flashing across her face. The girl stopped speaking.

From the stage Mrs. Baker squinted into the wings to ascertain which of them had done it. No one from the audience seemed to have heard, and after a few seconds she turned back to the crowd and resumed her talk.

"As I worked to raise my young daughter without the help of a husband – he disappeared after the death of our son, and I heard later that he himself had died, too – I saw the need for a different kind of home, one that not only provides the food and shelter each child needs, but also the love they need just as much. Since I first opened that home in Kansas City, I have helped to raise hundreds of children. I have been a mother to them. Indeed, that's what they call me. 'Mother Baker.' Nothing makes my heart gladder.

"And of course, for those children who still have at least one parent, they are returned to their former homes once conditions there improve. This is not possible under the terms of a normal orphanage. Once those poor children are taken in by the county, they can be adopted, after which time they never see their true parents again. They are robbed of their families, their names and, I repeat, their identities. I guarantee you that nothing of this sort ever happens at the Joseph Walter Home. In addition to food, clothing and shelter, our children are given love, and they retain a sense of who they are. You cannot receive this guarantee from a county orphanage. The only guarantees those places can provide are broken homes and broken hearts. These things, dear friends, are forever."

Mrs. Baker looked again to the wings and broke into a smile that showed as many of her teeth as possible.

"It is difficult work, and costly, too. But I am glad to do it so that children like these can get all the love and comfort they so need and deserve."

She lifted her right arm with the palm out, and the children began to file onto the stage as they had rehearsed. Some held hands, while others stood close together in groups of two or three. All of them smiled and faced the darkened opera house as the applause boomed out like a hailstorm from the audience. The children formed a half-circle behind Mrs. Baker, who held up both of her hands until the clapping died down.

"And now, my children will favor you with a hymn whose meaning is so very important to us at the Joseph Walter Home. Thank you very much."

A small band played the opening strains of "No, Never Alone" as she left the stage. The performance went well, with each of the adults joining the children at the conclusion of the song. They took in the last of the applause and went back to the wings together, waving and smiling at the audience. The sound gave no sign of diminishing as Mrs. Baker turned to the children.

"Which one of you did it?" she snapped. "Which one of you interrupted my speech?"

She walked up and down the line of children, staring into their faces. Although she was near the far end of the group, Celia began to whimper. Her face went red and her eyes stung. Flora squeezed her hand. Celia shut her eyes and hoped her tears would not be seen.

"I did it, Mother."

It was Joseph. Celia squinted in time to see Mrs. Baker haul off and slap the boy hard across the lips with the back of her hand. Then Mrs. Baker returned to the stage to give a final joyous wave to the crowd.

She kept to herself. All the other women said so. Whenever they sat in the main room of the house talking with one another and tending to their children, she would plant herself in the corner and stare at them with her sharp eyes and whisper to her baby, a girl no more than five months old. Watt, she called herself. Mrs. Watt. She was a bit older than thirty. She was peculiar. The women sat across the room ignoring her and cooing at a baby boy the same age as Mrs. Watt's daughter, tickling his full pink cheeks and laughing when he smiled at them and exposed his toothless gums. He had been sick an entire week but was now well again thanks to some medicine the matron, Mrs. Pascoe, had acquired from the drugstore.

"It was a miracle," his mother said as she cuddled him. "I thought I'd lost him, sure."

She put her face to his scalp and inhaled the sweet aroma of his flaxen hair and soft skin as the other women murmured their agreement. The mother raised her eyes in time to notice Mrs. Watt curl her pointed nose in distaste. Raising her head the mother fixed Mrs. Watt with a cold look.

"Is something the matter?" the mother asked.

Mrs. Watt paid no attention, and moved to whisper into her baby's ear.

"Mrs. Watt," the mother said in a loud voice.

Mrs. Watt finished what she was saying, and then turned her head to view the other woman with an expectant look on her face.

"Have you something to say, Mrs. Watt?"

She remained quiet, and a slight smile played upon her lips.

"What is it?" the first woman said with growing hostility.

Mrs. Watt demurred with a shake of her head.

"No," the first woman said in a firm voice. "When somebody looks at my son that way I want to know what they're thinking. I have a right to know. Now tell me."

Mrs. Watt blinked a few times and continued to smile.

"I was thinking," she said, "that if your child has a poison, you can do much better for him than to give him more."

Out of reflex the woman kissed the top of her son's head and began to quickly rock him in her chair.

"I would never poison my son!" she said as her complexion began to darken.

"You did give him medicine," Mrs. Watt said.

"Yes..."

"What else is medicine, then, but a poison? The pharmacist sought a stronger poison than the one that was making your child ill. Supposing the poison you gave him affects his liver or his kidneys? What will you give him then? Another poison? Something even stronger? How would that affect him?"

Tears began to pour down the first woman's face, but the strength of her voice was unaffected.

"How dare you! I never gave him poison in my life. What do you think I should've done for him? Nothing? Would you rather I just let him die?"

"You should have prayed over him."

"I did! You know I did, you saw me. You all saw me, and I know most of you prayed for him, too."

"All infirmities can be cured through the love of God. But before this can take place one must repent one's sin."

"My son isn't even half a year old! What in the world could he have done wrong? He's got nothing to repent for."

"Perhaps *he* doesn't," Mrs. Watt said quietly.

The first woman stood, panting with rage, while some of the others attempted to calm her and the rest surrounded Mrs. Watt, berating her with angry voices. Soon they all were talking over one another. The babies started crying, and the room became so loud that nothing could be understood. The only one to remain silent was Mrs. Watt, who turned her baby until its head was resting on her shoulder, and patted its back with the palm of her hand.

Not thirty seconds had elapsed before Mrs. Pascoe appeared in the doorway and banged her hands together three times. Large with white hair, Mrs. Pascoe could be intimidating, despite her age.

"That's enough!" she shouted.

The women all turned to look at her, and there was a brief silence. Then they all began talking again, attempting to explain the situation, but Mrs. Pascoe raised her arms and told them all to leave the room but Mrs. Watt. A flurry of footsteps like rapid beats on a wooden drum filled the air until the two women, one holding her baby, were the only ones who remained. Mrs. Watt had yet to acknowledge the other's presence. Mrs. Pascoe scowled for a moment, but as she watched Mrs. Watt her features softened. In spite of everything it was hard to dislike her. She was so genuine, even if she was misguided.

"I heard what you said," Mrs. Pascoe told her. "Why did you talk to her that way?"

"She asked me to."

"You couldn't have spared her feelings? You could see that she was upset."

"I never said anything that wasn't true."

Mrs. Pascoe shook her head in fascination. She kept her eyes on Mrs. Watt and picked up a chair by its backrest, bringing it closer. Mrs. Watt whispered again to her baby as Mrs. Pascoe sat, continuing to watch her.

"Do you mind if I ask you a question?"

"Of course not," Mrs. Watt said.

"What are you, exactly? I mean in terms of religion."

Mrs. Watt did not answer.

"It makes no difference to me," Mrs. Pascoe went on. "As long as I've run this house I've helped all kinds of people. It's the Christian thing to do, you know. So what are you? I'm curious."

As if by way of answering, Mrs. Watt smoothed her baby's hair. It was filled with static and popped back up after she brushed it.

"Are you a Christian Scientist?"

"Not quite."

"It sounds very similar."

"That may be your impression, but it's not correct. Christian Science is not the same as Divine Healing."

"Then what does it make you?"

Mrs. Watt blinked rapidly as she spoke.

"Back in Minneapolis we – my husband and I – we attended the Zion Mission. We were Dowieites."

"Are you still?"

Mrs. Watt looked away again and she nodded.

"And what about him?" Mrs. Pascoe said. "Where is your husband?"

"I told you when I came here," Mrs. Watt said, sounding ashamed.

Mrs. Pascoe sighed. "Some women change their stories after they've stayed her a bit. When they first arrive, they think I'm going to judge them for what they tell me, but I don't do that. All I want to do is help." She paused a moment. "You don't know where he is, though?"

Mrs. Watt shook her head.

"Is he still living?"

"Yes."

"But you've no idea where he might be?"

"No."

"I'm sorry," Mrs. Pascoe said. "But I want you to know that you and your daughter can stay here with us just as long as you need to. All I ask is that you please try to get along with the others. Can you do that for me?"

"I'm not going to lie to them."

"I don't expect you to."

"If they don't want to hear the truth, then they shouldn't speak to me. I always speak the truth."

He stood looking at the house all morning. He was tall, with long limbs and a thick dark mustache. He kept almost completely still, with his arms crossed, staring and waiting. Mrs. Pascoe saw him first, but said nothing in case his presence might upset any of the women. This happened often. Sooner or later a husband would show up, if he was still living, and expect to be able to collect his wife regardless of what might have happened between them. It was easier to close off the house in the fall and the winter, but a hot summer day required all the windows and doors to be open to capture any hint of a breeze. Before she left the house Mrs. Pascoe took an umbrella, a heavy one, from the stand by the door. The man's expression did not change as he watched her approach. He squinted at her until she could not see his eyes, and his mustache moved right and left as if he were sucking a piece of candy.

"May I help you with anything, sir?" Mrs. Pascoe said.

The man seemed indifferent to the punishing temperature, and much of anything else. There was an arrogance in the way he carried himself, as if he expected the entire world to fall in with whatever his present whims might be.

"I'm looking for my wife," he said. "Mrs. Baker. Is she in there?"

"No, we have no Mrs. Baker here at this time, sir."

"Sure you do. She has a little daughter about half a year old. Mrs. Baker."

"No, sir. There is no Mrs. Baker here."

The man thought a moment, smirking.

"Mrs. Thorp, then. Or how about a Miss Walter? That's her maiden name."

"Sir. We have no one here who goes by that name. By any of those names."

"Anything that sounds like one of them? Walt? Welt? Whet? Whit?"

Mrs. Pascoe rapped the pavement with the tip of her umbrella.

"If you don't leave now, sir, I will be forced to report you to the authorities."

He snorted. "For what?"

"For harassment."

"Harassment, nothing. I'm not doing anything wrong. My wife's in that house and I've come for her. Now, if you'll go along and fetch her I'll be off and you won't have to worry about me anymore."

"Sir, please leave now, or I'm sending for the police."

He laughed and shook his head. "All right, if that's the way you wanna do it. I'll be back, though." He tipped his hat to her, revealing a high widow's peak. "Good day," he said in a sneering voice.

Mrs. Pascoe watched as he walked away. There was a certain grace in the way he moved, but a cheapness, too. He carried himself like an actor from a low-class theatre troupe. Pure snake oil. As he reached the corner the man turned back to Mrs. Pascoe and made a deep bow, waving his arm as if he were flourishing an invisible cane.

Most of the women were talking in the sitting room when Mrs. Pascoe returned. Mrs. Watt sat nearby, facing out the front window, a dark strand of hair wafting before her face. Mrs.

Pascoe stepped into the room and waited a moment. Then she spoke in a loud voice so that she would be heard over the others.

"Mrs. Baker."

Mrs. Watt laughed to herself without looking at anybody.

"Mrs. Watt, would you join me in the kitchen for a moment?"

Shifting the baby in her arms, she left the window and she followed Mrs. Pascoe without speaking to the kitchen, which was at the rear of the house. When they arrived there Mrs. Pascoe pulled out a chair from the table and invited Mrs. Watt to sit. Mrs. Pascoe did not join her. She stood and stared at Mrs. Watt, whose attention was focused on her baby.

"What is your name? What is it really?"

"Mrs. Baker," she said without looking up. "You just said it yourself."

"Then why did you tell me differently?"

Mrs. Baker gave no answer and showed no concern. Mrs. Pascoe let out a deep sigh as she got another chair and sat. She tried to catch the other woman's eyes.

"Why are you here? You told me your husband left you. Was that true?"

"It was, and it is."

"He's back now. I suppose you saw him outside."

Mrs. Baker said nothing.

"That was him, wasn't it?"

Mrs. Baker looked up for the first time since they had entered the room.

"How much does it take to run a house like this, month-to-month?" she asked.

"What does that have to do with anything?"

"I'm curious. It can't be easy to keep this place going. It's important, but people take charities for granted, and they can't always continue on."

"Is that what you'll be doing now? Continuing on?"

Mrs. Baker eyed her as if she did not understand the question.

"That man," Mrs. Pascoe said. "The one who claims to be your husband."

"He is my husband. In the eyes of the Lord he is my husband."

"Will you be going with him when he comes back?"

She shrugged, then looked away once more.

Mrs. Baker left with the man two days later. Mrs. Pascoe watched as they made their way to the end of the block, he carrying a suitcase and she holding the baby. One of the girls joined Mrs. Pascoe on the stoop, and pointed.

"Was that Joseph Baker?" she asked.

"I know him only as Mr. Baker," Mrs. Pascoe said. "Is Joseph his name?"

The girl nodded.

"You know him, then," Mrs. Pascoe said.

"Yes," the girl said, "and a bigger scamp never walked Tower Avenue."

The Bakers opened their home by the time summer was over. Mrs. Baker's aim was simple and pure, she said. In addition to providing a place for widows, orphaned girls and unfortunate young mothers to live free of charge, she would equip them with the tools necessary to become self-sustaining. Other shelters were merely that. Shelters. Once a certain amount of time had passed or there were no longer enough resources to provide for them, these poor women would be forced back out into the street. She had seen such cases herself, she said. Her home was different. The women and girls who came there would be taught useful skills – dressmaking, needlework, housecleaning – so they could support themselves once they were on their own again. A girl who spent no time at her home might be lucky enough to acquire a job, Mrs. Baker said, but would she be able to keep it? Without training, how would she be able to satisfy her employer? A girl like this was doomed to failure and must resort to money-making ventures that were not only dangerous, but quite often illegal. Donations allowed Mrs. Baker's home, which she called Sacred Refuge, to remain open, and thus save other women and girls from suffering similar fates.

Mrs. Baker was rarely turned down for a donation. She had a dramatic voice that was pleasant to listen to, and she could hold anyone's attention so that time became irrelevant to them. She would stare with her bright eyes, which appeared to gleam as she continued, like those of a hypnotist, with a silent plea for the listener to stay just one more minute, one more minute.

"God save you," she would tell each donor as she took their offering. Then, with a smile, she would put the money in her bag and move on.

The house was located in Duluth, Minnesota, on 628 West Second Street. Mrs. Baker ran it herself while her husband attended to his business interests out of town, including short trips every couple of months to observe the progress of Zion City in Illinois. While not enormous, the home was large enough to comfortably shelter four young needy women and their children, along with Mrs. Baker and her daughter Flora, as well as an overseer, Miss Lizzie Stevenson. The mothers and their children shared sleeping quarters upstairs.

When she was not out collecting donations, Mrs. Baker most enjoyed spending time in her office, which was situated near the front of the house. The room was bare apart from the rough-looking but sturdy desk in the center of it, and the two simple chairs on either side. There were no pictures on the walls, no decorations of any kind, but there was a handsome fireplace.

Mrs. Baker adjusted her chair and spoke through a delicate grin to the woman seated across from her.

"I'm sorry, would you kindly repeat your name, please?"

"Hoyt. Mrs. L. M. Hoyt."

"And what leads you to seek us out today? Do you know of somebody we might be able to assist?"

"Not through personal relation, no."

"Then have you come to help us?"

Mrs. Hoyt had trouble answering. She could not pull her attention from Mrs. Baker's dress. The material was black, but was so worn that she could make out the hue of Mrs. Baker's skin beneath it. The cuffs and buttonholes were frayed, and small bits of material were missing from the elbows. Mrs. Hoyt also noticed the dark ratted blanket that hung from the back of

Mrs. Baker's chair like a motheaten shawl. It made her feel overdressed. Indecent, even.

After a few seconds had passed Mrs. Hoyt found her voice, although she did falter a bit.

"I've heard of your work, and I was impressed at the number of endorsements you've gotten."

"Yes," Mrs. Baker said, continuing to smile. "People know our case is a just one."

"I feel that way."

"That's because you're a good woman."

Mrs. Hoyt shifted in her chair.

"Do you have children of your own?" Mrs. Baker asked.

"I do," Mrs. Hoyt said, beginning to relax. "But they're getting older. They don't need me like they used to."

Mrs. Baker nodded.

"It's a mother's curse."

"Yes. And so I was thinking I might be of some assistance to you. Around the house, or anywhere else. I know practically everything about sewing and housework, and I would be more than happy to share what I know with your charges for a few hours a day. I still have my own home to attend to, you understand."

"I am sorry, but we do have someone taking care of that instruction already."

"I see."

"Miss Seaverson. She's a good girl. Very efficient."

"I understand. What about the general running of the place? I'm quite good with figures."

"I'm afraid I do most of that work myself, along with my assistant Mrs. Lovejoy, and Mrs. Craig, my secretary."

"I'm seems you have all the help you need."

Mrs. Baker chuckled and leaned forward over the desk.

"If only that were true. Why, we're always in need of help. Mrs. Lovejoy and Mrs. Craig are out working in town right now." Still leaning forward, Mrs. Baker tilted her head. "Perhaps you could assist me, too."

Mrs. Hoyt found it difficult to contain her eagerness.

"With what?"

The smile still on her face, Mrs. Baker got up and paced about the near-empty room and spoke with a sense of deliberation.

"As you said, it was our endorsements that brought you here. We're always looking for more. From prominent citizens, you understand. We like to meet with them and present our aims to them, and then ask if they would like to lend us their names as a sign that our work is good."

She stopped walking and braced her hands on the back of her chair.

"And it is good work."

"I believe it is," Mrs. Hoyt said.

Mrs. Baker let go of the chair and began to walk again.

"But beyond that, what we truly need are donations. Monetary donations. Endorsements are perfectly wonderful, but they don't feed and clothe our young women and children."

Mrs. Baker sat back down and folded her hands as if she were going to pray.

"If people are able to help, they should do so. Do you believe that?"

"I do."

"I knew that you would. There are many others like you, too, praise God. I've been on collecting tours all over the place and I've always found those who are willing to help. Minneapolis, Superior – Alma, Wisconsin, my hometown. I've been all over this area, and there are people everywhere who believe in what we're doing."

"Where do you want me to collect?"

"I think we should go out together to start you off. Just so you get a general idea of how we do things. I have some business to attend to here, so I won't be going out again until next Wednesday. Does that fit into your schedule?"

"Yes, it would be fine."

"I can see, though, that you would like something to do before then."

Mrs. Hoyt nodded.

Mrs. Baker put her head back and gazed at the ceiling as she thought.

"Well, then," she said after a few seconds. "Why don't you try getting a couple of those endorsements we talked about? They might be a good way for you to get started off."

"Whom shall I ask?"

"Anyone you think might be sympathetic to our cause."

Mrs. Hoyt nodded again.

"Now there's just one more thing to go over," Mrs. Baker said. "The matter of money."

"I could certainly spare something."

"No, you misunderstand me. I don't expect you to go out and work for me without any kind of compensation for yourself. That wouldn't be fair, would it? You have your own household to maintain."

"That is true..."

"Yes. I know how difficult it can be. All of the women who collect for me earn the same rate – twenty-five cents of every dollar they bring in."

Mrs. Hoyt thought she had misheard.

"That's quite a lot," she said.

"It can be difficult work."

"But twenty-five cents for every dollar–"

Before Mrs. Hoyt had a chance to finish a man's voice broke in. It was loud and irate, and it caused both she and Mrs. Baker to jump.

"We don't pay any more than that," the man said.

Turning in her chair, Mrs. Hoyt saw him standing in the entrance to the office. He was tall, and had a mustache and a grim scowl. Mrs. Baker's voice was unchanged when she addressed him.

"Joseph, hello. Mrs. Hoyt, this is my husband Joseph. Joseph, this is Mrs. Hoyt. She's interested in working for the home."

Baker entered the room and Mrs. Hoyt stood and extended her hand. He did not take it, and stopped less than a foot from her, glaring into her face.

"We only pay twenty-five cents on the dollar, and that's it," he said.

Mrs. Baker did not get up.

"No, Joseph, Mrs. Hoyt thinks twenty-five cents is too much. I was just trying to explain that the rate is warranted because the work is so difficult."

Baker's features relaxed at once, melting into a seductive smile. He took Mrs. Hoyt's hand and gave it a gentle shake.

"It *is* difficult work, ma'am." His voice had become softer, smoother. "Especially with my wife in charge," he added with a laugh.

He released Mrs. Hoyt's hand and wandered behind the desk.

"Joseph sells butter and eggs out in the Iron Range," Mrs. Baker said. "He's out of town usually, and when he's in town he has a room someplace else. It wouldn't be proper for him to live here with all these young ladies. In fact, I didn't know he would be with us today."

Baker shrugged, said nothing.

"I suppose you'll want to speak to him, then," Mrs. Hoyt said. She had not sat back down. "What day did you say you'll be going out?"

"Next Wednesday. I'll be leaving around nine."

"Good," Mrs. Hoyt said. "I'll be here to meet you. And until then I'll work to get some more endorsements for the home."

"Bless you," Mrs. Baker said.

"Until Wednesday, then."

As Mrs. Hoyt turned to go, Baker came around the desk and stood by the door.

"I'll show you out," he said.

Mrs. Hoyt nodded and passed through the door, with Baker following.

"Thank you for your help," he said as they moved down the hallway.

"You must tell Mrs. Baker I'm thankful she's giving me this chance. I only hope I'm able to do well."

"I'm sure you will, if she's helping you," Baker said when they reached the front door. He put out his arm and turned the knob, and pulled the door open for Mrs. Hoyt. He followed her out to the front porch but kept his hand on the door.

"She's real good at what she does," Baker said.

Mrs. Hoyt turned and smiled at him.

"I'm sure she is."

"And you will be, too, I'll bet. You just have to work hard at it is all. When Mrs. Baker started she pulled in maybe thirty to sixty dollars a day."

"That much?" Mrs. Hoyt asked.

"Heck, that's nothing compared to what she can do now. Sixty dollars would be a bad day for her. Now she can get over eighty. I've seen her bring in a hundred and thirty once. That's no lie, ma'am. The others are good at it, too, but none are as good as my wife. Mrs. Craig's good. She gets as high as thirty-six some days."

"My goodness. It's a wonder you need me at all."

"Sure we do. Times are hard for these women."

Lizzie Seaverson entered the room upstairs where the girls sat waiting around a large oak table with the material and the sewing things. In her hands she carried a stack of patterns, which she proceeded to distribute to the four women. They were young, none of them older than twenty, and all but one not yet seventeen. They looked much older, though, with deep lines of worry at the corners of their mouths and thick fat calluses on their palms. Each of them claimed to be either a widow or simply unsure of where her husband had gone.

"This may look difficult at first," Miss Seaverson said, "but it'll get easier for you as we go along."

"I already know sewing," said one of the girls, who called herself Mrs. Davidson.

"I'm sure we all know how to darn," Miss Seaverson said. "But what about proper dressmaking?"

"Sure I do."

"Me, too," said a woman called Mrs. McDonald.

Miss Seaverson set the remaining pamphlets on the table.

"Then maybe you both can help me teach the others."

"It don't make sense at all," Mrs. Davidson said.

"What doesn't? That you might help me teach the other girls?"

"No, that you'd think we'd have to be taught how."

"I don't understand," Miss Seaverson said.

"Dressmaking and sewing's the whole reason we came here, Mrs. McDonald and I."

"That's right."

"To teach it?"

"No, to do it."

"That's what the ad was all about," Mrs. McDonald said.

"What ad?" Miss Seaverson asked.

Mrs. McDonald pulled a small bit of paper from her pocket and handed it to Miss Seaverson. It was folded twice into an uneven square, and she stared at it without doing anything.

"Open it," Mrs. McDonald said. "The ad's on the inside part."

Miss Seaverson undid the folds and smoothed the paper with her thumbs, which came up black from the smudged ink. She scanned the text until she found a few brief lines.

"WANTED – DRESSMAKING and plain sewing, at Sacred Refuge, 628 West Second."

Miss Seaverson read the item three times, looking as if she were attempting to solve a puzzle.

"How odd," she said.

"I thought so, too, but I don't mind," Mrs. Davidson said.

"Yeah, a free room's a free room," Mrs. McDonald said.

Miss Seaverson kept still and silent.

"You want us to sew, anyway, even though we know how already?" Mrs. Davidson said.

Miss Seaverson jerked her head before she answered.

"Yes," she said as she refolded the paper and gave it back to Mrs. McDonald. "And help me show the other girls, both of you. That should make it easier for them."

She came around the table and watched the others as they set to work. Looking up, she noticed Baker standing in the hall, watching her. He was not standing in the doorway, but leaning against the far wall. His ankles were crossed and his thumbs were hitched in his front pockets. He smiled without parting his lips.

"Excuse me a moment," Miss Seaverson said.

She went to the door, Baker watching her all the time, and closed it.

Mrs. Baker beamed at Mrs. Pascoe from the front porch. She wore new clothes, and her hair looked almost red in the afternoon sun. Mrs. Pascoe took a surprised breath, but did not move to further open the door. She looked Mrs. Baker over, and noticed she clutched a sheaf of clean printed papers.

"Mrs. Pascoe, how well you look."

"And you, Mrs. Baker," she said, stumbling for a response. "How may I help you?"

"I merely wanted to stop and extend my thanks for the kindness you showed me and my daughter. We wouldn't be here today if it weren't for you."

"Well, now–"

"In fact, I appreciate your efforts so much that I'm endeavoring to do the same kind of work in Duluth."

Mrs. Pascoe's legs felt wobbly. She took a faltering step onto the porch and shut the front door behind her so that Mrs. Baker could not come inside the house.

"So soon? But you were only just here. Are you sure you can get everything organized, and so quickly?"

"Of course I can, when I'm following an example like yours."

She handed Mrs. Pascoe one of the papers, and Mrs. Pascoe looked at it long enough to see the two bold words – "Sacred Refuge" – that ran across the top. Her arms fell to her sides.

"But how can you manage it? You need money to perform this kind of service, connections. It's not something to go into with no plan of management."

"Oh, we get by, I can assure you."

Mrs. Pascoe shifted her weight from foot to foot as Mrs. Baker continued to stare at her with the same blank smile. Mrs. Pascoe glanced to the side to see if there were any chairs nearby.

"But Mrs. Pascoe?"

She looked back to Mrs. Baker.

"Yes?"

"There is something we need."

"Oh," she said. Although she was not aware of it, her voice was shaking. "My dear, I'm in no position to give any kind of–"

"It's not a financial request," Mrs. Baker said. "In one sense it is, I suppose, but not a literal one."

"I don't understand."

"Mrs. Pascoe, it would help us enormously if you could give us an endorsement of some kind. You have such a good reputation that it would be a great benefit to us if we could use your name."

Mrs. Pascoe let out a long breath that made it sound as if she were trying to laugh without making any noise.

"What do you mean?" she said.

"Well, if you would look at the sheet I've given you you'll see we have a list naming all the people who have given us endorsements. We share this list with others to assure them that we're a worthy cause. If we were able to take your name and put a mark next to it saying you've given us some money, you don't know what that would mean to us."

Mrs. Pascoe gave the list a brief scan.

"How much money?"

"I was thinking somewhere along the lines of fifty dollars."

Mrs. Pascoe's voice became firm and she folded the paper once down the center.

"No, absolutely not. I couldn't possibly."

"I'm not requesting that you actually give us that much," Mrs. Baker said in a placating way. "I only request that you allow us to say you did. For the sake of appearances."

Mrs. Pascoe was nonplussed.

"Appearances."

"Yes. Any cause that finds itself with your name attached to it is sure to succeed."

Mrs. Pascoe stared at Mrs. Baker, who returned her look with one of detached serenity. She showed not the slightest discomfort with the situation. She was such an odd person.

"No," Mrs. Pascoe said. "You don't seem to understand that if you go around Superior using my name to make a push for your own home that it might do me harm. I still have my place to run here."

"I understand completely," Mrs. Baker said with a nod. "I have no intention of using your name in Superior. I would never want to encroach on your home like that."

"Really?"

"Oh, I think what you do here is just wonderful. That's why I want to do the same thing across the lake. But I would never want to drive you out of Superior or hurt your work in any way. I would never use your name within the borders of this town. It would be unforgivable. If you hadn't been here when I needed you, I don't know what I'd have done."

Mrs. Pascoe stood, thinking.

"There are women in Duluth who need the same kind of assistance," Mrs. Baker said urgently. "You can only help so many. Let me share some of the burden."

"I need to give this some more thought," Mrs. Pascoe said.

Mrs. Baker waved as she opened the front door of the house. It was pouring, and the rain drummed hard against the roof.

"I've done it," she called to Mrs. Hoyt, who was climbing the porch steps.

"Done what?"

"I've got the endorsement of Mrs. Pascoe. It'll be a real help to us."

"I have some news like that myself," Mrs. Hoyt said, smiling against the wetness.

"Oh, come in and tell me all about it before you freeze."

Mrs. Hoyt stepped into the house and rubbed the cold from her hands. In an instant a puddle collected at her feet like melted snow that had been tracked in on her shoes. Mrs. Baker closed the door, and they stared at each other before they began to giggle like children.

"Don't you have an umbrella?" Mrs. Baker said.

"Yes, but I didn't think I would need it. The sun was shining when I left home, but the sky opened up when I was only halfway here."

She stretched out her arms and brought them close again, rubbing them against each other.

"Look at you, you're shivering," Mrs. Baker said. "You look like you just stepped out of the lake. Give me your hat and your wrap and I'll find a place for them to dry. You go to my office and I'll be there soon. I've got a fire going, and it should help warm you up."

Mrs. Hoyt stood near the hearth and let the flames thaw her skin. One of the logs was partway green and steam shot out the end of it with a loud hiss, as if it were a kettle spout. Mrs. Hoyt found the noise relaxing and she shut her eyes and turned around slowly, allowing the heat to move up her legs and back. She blinked several times and smiled, light-headed, like she had just awakened from a long nap.

On Mrs. Baker's desk she noticed an item that had not been there before. A decorative box about six inches wide, with a beautiful finish of black lacquer and a pair of golden hinges on the back. Mrs. Hoyt's eye had been caught by the firelight that danced and played on the shiny finish, and after admiring it a few seconds she stopped and thought how out of place it seemed with the rest of the house, like a bouquet of roses placed in a rusted can.

"I've brought you a towel for your hair," Mrs. Baker said as she entered the room. "We don't want you to catch cold. You better step away from that fire, too, in case your dress decides to shrink."

"I know. I only have to cast off the chill." She came forward and accepted the towel. Mrs. Baker's clothes were different than they had been. While they were not new, they were in much better condition than any Mrs. Hoyt had seen her wear before. There were no holes, and no obvious mending had been done to them. "Thank you," she said and began to dab at herself with the towel while she walked to the window.

Mrs. Baker folded her hands and watched Mrs. Hoyt with restless anticipation.

"I don't intend to rush you," she said, "but what was the news you mentioned?"

Mrs. Hoyt began to laugh.

"That's right," she said and wiped the back of her neck. "You told me to get some endorsements, and so I did. Well, one. But anyway, it's a big one."

When she finished speaking Mrs. Hoyt brought the ends of the towel to her face until it was completely enveloped.

"Who?" Mrs. Baker asked.

Mrs. Hoyt lowered the towel and turned to look at her.

"Mayor Hugo."

"Lord be praised," Mrs. Baker said and pressed both hands to her chest. "And bless you, my dear. This is wonderful news."

Mrs. Hoyt ran the towel over her ears, using her index fingers to dry them out.

"However did you arrange it?" Mrs. Baker asked.

"I simply went to his home and described your plans. I've been acquainted with the Hugos for some time, so it really isn't that much of an accomplishment."

"No, no, no, don't underrate yourself. Oh, the Lord knew you could help us. That's why He brought us together."

"The mayor did have one condition."

"Which is?"

"He doesn't like the name 'Sacred Refuge.'" Mrs. Hoyt held out the towel and looked for a place to drape it. "'Gush,' he called it."

Mrs. Baker took the towel from Mrs. Hoyt and rolled it into a bundle.

"I see," she said. Then, her tone brightening, she added, "Well, that doesn't seem too big a problem."

Soon it was Wednesday and Mrs. Hoyt arrived early in the morning to begin work. Mrs. Baker was waiting for her, wearing a clean starched black dress and hat. In her hands she clutched two stacks of pamphlets, one of which she gave to Mrs. Hoyt. Mrs. Baker also gave her a jar identical to one she herself carried. Each had a slit on the lid into which money could be dropped, and they were wrapped in black paper so that nobody could see how much or how little was inside. With a final call of goodbye into the house the women set off for the day's work.

They spent the morning roaming the streets of Duluth, where Mrs. Baker would describe their mission to everyone she could. She asked that Mrs. Hoyt not speak that first morning, so as to educate her in the best way of eliciting donations. Mrs. Baker spoke very well, with real passion, and it was difficult for Mrs. Hoyt not to be affected by the things Mrs. Baker described, no matter how many times she heard them. Sometimes she even found herself shedding a tear for those young women who found themselves forced to "get whatever work they can" due to a lack of proper training for honest jobs. It was a tragedy, if a common one. The people with whom Mrs. Baker spoke recognized this, too, and none of them failed to give what they could spare. As the morning drew on, the collection jars became heavier, coins clanging and paper rustling with each step the women took.

After lunch it was Mrs. Hoyt's turn to spread the message. It was daunting, but as long as she stayed close to Mrs. Baker's words she was met with success.

"Don't worry, dear," Mrs. Baker said after Mrs. Hoyt received her first donation. "The more you do this, the more comfortable and confident you'll become – and the more they'll give."

Toward the end of the day they met with a Mr. F. A. Patrick, who gave a full twenty dollars to the Refuge on the spot.

"Who runs this place, exactly?" he asked.

Mrs. Hoyt looked to Mrs. Baker, who replied after she finished slipping the money into her jar.

"I run it, sir. Mrs. Julia A. Baker."

"I understand that, ma'am, but what I mean is, do you answer to anyone?"

"I answer to our Heavenly Father."

"I was thinking more of something in the way of a board of directors."

"No, sir, not at this time."

Mr. Patrick nodded. "I suggest you give it some thought. I trust what you're doing – it's an excellent cause – but I feel a board of directors would give you an added credibility. That's all."

Mrs. Baker nodded and gave him a warm smile.

"Yes, I was thinking that myself, sir, and I plan to organize a board just as soon as I get matters on the proper basis. We've only just started the work recently, you see."

"Of course."

"Thank you, sir, and God save you."

"Yes, and thank you, Mrs....?"

"Walter."

Mr. Patrick nodded and smiled. "Yes. Mrs. Walter. Thank you so much."

The women walked for a bit after they left him. Then Mrs. Baker spoke.

"I suppose that's enough collecting for the day. Would you be free to join me again tomorrow? I think you've gained enough confidence to do most of the talking. You'll be able to go out on your own soon."

"Mrs. Baker?"

"Yes?"

"Why did you introduce yourself as Mrs. Walter just now?"

The women stopped walking as they reached the curb, and waited for a horse-drawn cart to pass through the intersection.

"Did I?"

"Yes."

"That's funny. Walter is my maiden name. I suppose it was just a slip of the tongue. That's common enough – especially after the long day we've had. It can be easy to make those little mistakes. How do you think it went?"

"Very well."

"I agree."

The cart now out of the way, they walked into the street.

"Mrs. Baker? Forgive me, I have another question."

"What is it?"

"What about Mr. Baker? Where does he live?"

"Wherever his job takes him. Throughout the state, into Wisconsin, Illinois…"

"That must make things difficult, not having him around all the time."

"We manage. His work helps to subsidize my work."

They stepped onto the curb and continued down the sidewalk.

"Even if we aren't together we are still helping each other," Mrs. Baker said.

The young women and their children had to leave Sacred Refuge once Baker came there to stay. It might not look right, both he and his wife said. The Bakers rented a place for the women on Dodge Block where they could continue to learn and work with Miss Seaverson. It was a better environment to teach dressmaking, the Bakers said. As for Sacred Refuge, it now was occupied by Mr. and Mrs. Baker and Flora, as well as a nurse who took care of the baby, and a girl who did the cleaning. When asked by Mrs. Hoyt if the move was necessary, Mrs. Baker replied that it was. She needed her husband in the work, she said. It was not as if the women were suffering, she added, since through her husband's connections the place at Dodge Block was provided with as much fresh butter and as many eggs as they needed.

Baker liked it at the house. He enjoyed sitting in the office in the big new carved chair behind his wife's desk, and doing business over the telephone they had installed in the hall. He liked to meet visitors in person, as well, and teach them about the work and the need for collections. Each day they would come to ask questions about the Refuge, or to express interest in working for it.

"My husband tells me that your representatives collect up to fifty dollars a day," a woman named Mrs. Medric Perrault told him one afternoon.

Baker had been seated in a chair on the porch when she arrived. His eyes were closed and he smiled and inhaled the breeze that rolled in off the lake, and the smell of fish and oil from the boats going in and out of the harbor. Mrs. Perrault called to him from the walk and started in right away with her questions. Mrs. Baker was out.

"Fifty dollars seems like quite a lot," Mrs. Perrault said.

"We work hard for it," Baker said. "Some time ago my wife led a team of solicitors through the woods on a tour of the camps. They came away with five hundred dollars then, but it was so difficult I've had to think twice about letting them go back there."

"I shouldn't doubt it. Five hundred dollars."

Still smiling, Baker's voice became tense.

"What of it?"

"I'm sorry?"

"If people want to give, that's their decision. Those who do give will be blessed by God. Don't you believe that?"

"Of-of course, but–"

"You hesitated," Baker said as he stepped off the porch and came slowly toward her. "Why was that? Do you believe it or don't you?"

"I do."

Baker nodded, his eyes cast toward the ground.

"Hmm. Forgive my asking, but what church do you belong to?"

"I'm a Methodist. I go to–"

"That explains it."

Mrs. Perrault's cheek began to twitch and she blinked a few times to try and relax it.

"What do you mean?" she said.

"It comes as no surprise that you would question the works of a true Christian," Baker said and raised her eyes to meet hers. "Methodism is the faith of the Devil."

Mrs. Perrault opened her mouth to speak but Baker cut her off.

"As Dr. Dowie says, it is not a church of God. It's a church of people who are dead in trespasses and sin. Why else would it be losing members at such a fast pace? Thousands this year alone, their own records prove it. Methodism is dead. Let it be buried."

Mrs. Perrault stood with her mouth hanging open. Baker finished talking and folded his arms. A look of satisfaction crossed his face and he raised his heavy eyebrows as if to prompt a response.

"I came to offer my help," Mrs. Perrault said. "I'm a good Christian."

"Anyone who calls herself a good Christian and chooses to remain in the walls of the Methodist church is a hypocrite. Good day to you, madam."

With a polite nod Baker turned and climbed the steps of the porch, and entered the house without saying anything more.

Duluth was cold most of the time once November came. Even though she was bundled up and carrying a large roll of fabric Mrs. Hoyt shivered uncontrollably as she walked to the Dodge Block. Time had passed, but she had never visited there, being so busy collecting funds for its residents. She saw the building up the street and gave a relieved sigh when she noticed a white plume of smoke snaking out one of its chimneys.

Near the front door a smallish woman stood watch over several tied bundles of split wood while a trio of girls gathered up what they were able to carry and brought it inside. The air was still and bitter. The woman by the door hugged herself and puffed out her red cheeks, blowing out a cloud of fog, and stomped her boots against the pavement near what was left of the bundles.

"Excuse me," Mrs. Hoyt called as she drew closer. "I'm looking for Miss Lizzie Seaverson. Do you know where I might find her?"

"That's me," the woman said, continuing her movements. "May I help you?"

"Yes, I'm Mrs. Hoyt," she said as she came near. She lifted her arms a bit and added, "I thought this might be of use to you. For dressmaking, you know."

Miss Seaverson nodded, but did not look pleased.

"Did Mrs. Baker send you?"

"No. But I work for her. I received this fabric as a donation. It isn't much, but I thought you might be able to use it."

"Nobody sent you?" Miss Seaverson asked.

"No, I knew the address so I just came. I'm awfully sorry I didn't come before."

The front door opened again and the three women returned. On seeing them Miss Seaverson squatted to pick up one of the remaining bundles of wood, and let the other women get the rest. They worked quickly, without speaking, and when everything was gathered they went back inside. Mrs. Hoyt followed.

"What a big place," she said when she entered. She heard something like a cackle from one of the girls and Miss Seaverson looked back at her.

"You're not in it yet," she said.

In a line the women climbed the stairs. As she went up Mrs. Hoyt noticed how very little difference there was in the temperature inside and out. Once they reached the top the women went to a door at the end of the hall and filed in as fast as they could. Again Miss Seaverson looked to Mrs. Hoyt, who had lagged a bit.

"Hurry up!" she said in a voice more frustrated than angry.

Mrs. Hoyt broke into a trot that did not stop until she entered the women's quarters and Miss Seaverson had shut the door.

It was truly pathetic. A single room, twelve feet by sixteen, with one folding bed and one cot. Four small children huddled together on the bed wearing mittens, hats and thin coats. For heat there was a small Franklin stove, into which the women fed a single piece of food after the one that preceded it had burned down. The room's lone window was coated with a layer of frost that made it look like it was lined on the outside with a roll of thick white paper. Mrs. Hoyt watched slackjawed as the women piled the wood in the corner of the room, each of them continuing to move once she had finished, rubbing her arms or her sides, or smacking her hands together.

"Please don't breathe with your mouth open, not unless you're trying to warm your hands," Miss Seaverson said. "It'll only make more frost."

Mrs. Hoyt pursed her lips and stared a moment before she spoke.

"Do you all live here?" she asked with some timidity.

"I don't," Miss Seaverson said. "Not anymore. It was too crowded. I might end up moving back, though, because I can't afford my room. What did you want again?"

Mrs. Hoyt lifted the cloth.

"Material. I brought it so you could teach dressmaking."

"We'll get to it once my fingers aren't numb anymore," one of the women said.

"Put it by the door," Miss Seaverson said.

Mrs. Hoyt stepped back and propped it in the corner. She turned to face the others, who looked like they had already forgotten she was there. She felt ashamed, and looked down at her feet. The floor was bare, she noticed, and strewn with tattered strips of bark and clumps of dust, like the floor of a woodshop. Looking back to the women, she cleared her throat.

"What else do you need?" Miss Seaverson asked before Mrs. Hoyt could say anything.

Mrs. Hoyt opened her mouth, but all that came out was a sigh.

"I'm sorry," Miss Seaverson said, and approached her. "I don't know what to do, myself. We have nothing, as you can see."

"At least you have wood for your stove," Mrs. Hoyt said.

"And that we get from the county." Miss Seaverson lowered her voice, although the room was so compact the others could not help hearing everything she said. "When Mrs. Baker told me we would be getting our own place, I assumed it would be – well, different. A little house, a cottage, anything. Almost anything would be better than this."

"Maybe if you spoke to her."

"I have."

"I could speak to her for you."

"I don't think so."

"Or Mr. Baker. He seems like a nice enough man. Maybe a little coarse, but…"

Miss Seaverson shook her head. She leaned against the wall and pointed quickly to the room.

"They didn't even get us these beds, you know. We had to find those ourselves. More charity. More charity for girls who are here to learn how to be self-supporting. Does that make any sense to you?"

Mrs. Hoyt did not reply. One of the children was sitting up on the bed. It had large blue eyes and they were focused on her. Mrs. Hoyt stared back a bit and smiled. The child continued to watch her, no emotion on its face. It was like an automaton, giving the appearance of a living thing but none of the spirit.

"Do you have food?" Mrs. Hoyt said at last.

"Not enough," Miss Seaverson said. "You see that baby looking at you? Do you think it's staring because it thinks you're pretty? Maybe it thinks if it looks at you long enough you'll give it something to eat."

Mrs. Hoyt acquired the turkey as a donation from a woman named McCaskell not long before Thanksgiving. They had to eat it before that. There was no way it would keep, and no way for the girls to cook it in their room. Mrs. Hoyt brought it to Sacred Refuge with the idea that they would come there from Dodge Block, at which point she could help outline their problems to Mrs. Baker.

The wind was brutal the night of the dinner. It took Mrs. Hoyt more than forty-five minutes to get from her own house to the Refuge, but as soon as she saw the lights shining out the windows on the first floor she was glad she had made the trek. It was beautiful, like a print by Currier and Ives, with the house looking warm and happy.

When the door was opened for Mrs. Hoyt the smell of the food poured out and filled her head. It was so welcoming it made her forget how cold she was. Along with the turkey she could smell the fresh bread, the thick mashed potatoes, the rich gravy. She entered as if on a cloud and drifted toward the dining room, which rang with the merry laughter and delighted chatter of young women's voices. She lingered in the door a moment and scanned their faces before she entered. Mr. Baker was at the head of the table and Mrs. Baker sat at the other end. Toward the center of the room Flora was in her own little chair with a tray, and she was being tended by the uniformed nurse. Another uniformed woman continued to bring plate after heaping plate of food in from the kitchen. Mrs. Craig and Mrs. Lovejoy were seated at the table, as were a couple of other girls Mrs. Hoyt knew from her collecting trips. There remained a single unfilled chair. Nobody noticed as Mrs. Hoyt ducked back into the hall and made a quick survey of the other rooms. All were empty.

"Where are the girls?" she asked as she reentered the dining room.

Mrs. Baker saw her and stood, smiling as she approached.

"I'm so glad to see you," she said and grabbed Mrs. Hoyt's hand. "Oh, you feel just like ice! We have a fire going if you want to warm yourself."

Mrs. Hoyt did not return her smile.

"Where are the girls?"

Mrs. Baker released her grip and held up her arm as if to show off the room.

"Why, they're at the table, of course. You know–"

"I don't mean them. I'm talking about the girls from Dodge Block. Where are they?"

Mrs. Baker sighed. "Oh, it's awful. They couldn't come because of this foul weather."

"The other girls are here, though, I see," Mrs. Hoyt said.

"Yes, well, they live nearby. And, they didn't have any little ones to bring along with them. Can you imagine taking little babies out on a night like this? They're liable to catch their deaths of pneumonia! It would be too awful! I don't want that on my conscience."

"But they're the reason I acquired this turkey. It was for them. This whole evening was to be for their sake." She shook her head. "Mrs. Baker, we need to discuss a few things."

"Of course, dear," Mrs. Baker said and put her hand on Mrs. Hoyt's shoulder. As soon as she did, she removed it and clutched it as if she had been burned. "My goodness! You're even colder than I thought! Come with me, we'll go to my office and get you warmed up."

Mrs. Baker put both hands on Mrs. Hoyt's shoulders and turned her toward the door, then maneuvered her into the hall.

"We don't need *you* getting sick tonight," Mrs. Baker said as they walked. "Not after all you've done to help us. You're one of my best workers, you know. We need to keep you fit!"

When they reached the office Mrs. Baker positioned Mrs. Hoyt before the fireplace. The logs inside glowed bright and hot like forged iron, and the nearby rack was choked with cut pieces waiting to be tossed in.

"There," Mrs. Baker said. She rubbed Mrs. Hoyt's arms up and down as if to aid circulation. "That's better, now, isn't it?"

Mrs. Hoyt stayed quiet.

"Now," Mrs. Baker said. "I want you to stay in here a good five minutes – until you're properly warmed up."

Mrs. Hoyt raised her head and looked at the mantelpiece. Resting on top was a trio of ornamental glass bowls. They were clear, and cut in such a way that made them look like crystal. They were beautiful and they served no purpose.

"Will you promise me to do that?" Mrs. Baker said.

"Have you taken steps to incorporate yet?" Mrs. Hoyt asked without looking at her.

"Oh, yes, but that takes time, dear," Mrs. Baker said after a second's hesitation.

"What about changing the name from Sacred Refuge?"

A noise like a sigh passed from Mrs. Baker's lips.

"Yes, yes, we'll deal with all of that later on."

Mrs. Hoyt heard Mrs. Baker's footsteps as they backed toward the office door.

"You just focus on warming up right now," Mrs. Baker said. "Come out in five minutes – no sooner – and have something nice to eat."

Mrs. Hoyt said nothing, and stared into the flames.

"And Mrs. Hoyt?"

She turned to look at Mrs. Baker, who was leaving the room.

"Again, thank you so much. God save you."

Mrs. Baker left without waiting for a response.

Mrs. Hoyt returned to the house two days later. She went straight to the office, but was slow in walking there, peering into the open doors along the hall. In one room three women – all collectors – were chatting, while one of Mrs. Baker's uniformed employees sat in another feeding the baby. As Mrs. Hoyt came to the open door of the office she saw Mrs. Baker sitting behind her desk as if she were awaiting Mrs. Hoyt's arrival. Her posture was perfect, and her hands were folded in front of her. When she noticed her visitor, she gave a businesslike smile and nodded once.

"Mrs. Hoyt. Please come in and have a seat."

Mrs. Hoyt did as instructed, placing her hands in her lap.

"I thought perhaps we could talk about some things."

"Of course," Mrs. Baker said, the smile still on her face like a grim mask.

Mrs. Hoyt spoke in a clear voice without hesitation.

"I want to tell you that I think it's unfair how the women are living at Dodge Block. They don't have enough food and they don't have enough space. The room is cold and the babies need better clothing."

"Who gave you that idea?"

"No one. I've seen it for myself."

Mrs. Baker was no longer smiling.

"Those women have no business to complain. I know how to do my work."

"All right, then. When are you going to incorporate? I don't know how many weeks it's been since you said you would, but it still hasn't been done."

No reply was forthcoming.

"Mrs. Baker, the home ought to be put in the name of a company, which would then perpetuate the work."

"That's out of the question. The work will be done in my name, and mine alone."

"But you have no corner on life – who would continue the work if you should die?"

"My daughter."

"The infant daughter who's being nursed in the next room?"

"She will carry on the work."

"At this time? Now? Even if you die?"

"God would not let me die."

Mrs. Hoyt bit her lip. Then she opened her bag and took out a folded sheet of paper. She smoothed it out as well as she could, and then handed it across the desk.

"The women still need supplies. I've made a list of people who might be able to get some."

Mrs. Baker scanned the names and frowned.

"This Dr. Long you have marked down – is that Dr. Long the Methodist minister?"

"It is, yes."

"I've met with him," Mrs. Baker said, looking at Mrs. Hoyt over the top of the paper. "As I spoke to him I could feel God within me, and God told me that Dr. Long is not a pure man."

Mrs. Hoyt felt her pulse begin to rise.

"I am a member of his church, and I happen to think he's a very good man."

Mrs. Baker smiled and laid the paper on her desk.

"All ministers are the same," she said. "They are all bad."

It was their best day. They arrived at the site early in the morning, having taken one of the trains from Chicago. It was bright out, with a sky of purest blue and a soothing breeze coming in from the southwest. Thousands of people were there – too many to count – and all of them were filled with Christian love, and excitement that the time had come at last. There was Baker and his wife mixed in among the throngs of followers. Flora was about one week younger than five months, and she was in Wisconsin with Mrs. Baker's parents. It was a month before she went to Mrs. Pascoe's. The Bakers were on the first train, even though they had read there would be seating for more than three thousand at the ceremony. They had to be sure to get a place near the front. They had to see him.

As of yet, there were not many of the buildings that soon would make up Zion City, the site of which was located off the banks of Lake Michigan. It was just like Dowie's newspaper, Leaves of Healing, had said it would be. In the middle of the property was the Hill of Zion, which soon would be the home of the Zion Temple. Jutting up from the ground like a giant piece of ornate scaffolding was the Observatory Tower, glorious and decked in the Zion colors of gold, white and blue, and a banner that proclaimed, "Christ is All." From the top of the tower's four corners perched two Zion flags, the American flag and the Union Jack. The site of the temple, all three hundred fifty square feet of it, was roped off with a white cord, from which hung miniature Zion flags, with larger flags waving above the corners of the perimeter, each of them bearing the official crest.

To the west of the tower was the speaker's platform, which was flanked by one hundred seventy-five seats to accommodate the choir. In front of the platform lay a sea of white chairs, and

Baker corralled his wife to a spot that gave them both an up-close view of the stage. All around them people continued to arrive, laughing and talking, spreading out beneath the trees to enjoy their picnic lunches. Mrs. Baker dug into her bag and brought out the sandwiches she had prepared that morning, and split them with her husband, who said a few brief words of thanks before they began their meal.

As the lunch hour drew on the crowd became more excited. Word had spread that he was among them at the site. He left Chicago at ten forty-five that morning with the officials of the Christian Catholic Church of Zion. He also brought his wife Jane, who was about fifty, and his son and daughter, Gladstone, twenty-two and Esther, nineteen. All three of them were highly involved in his work. The seats in front of the amphitheatre filled quickly now with people whispering to each other in feverish anticipation. The stage was set in such a way that it was surrounded by sloping ground, allowing the spectators to see over their neighbors' heads without strain, as if they were sitting in a real auditorium.

"I wish I was you," Baker told his wife. "Seeing him for the first time. I know you've read the Leaves and seen his picture and heard me talk plenty about him, but it's not the same as being there. That's when you really feel his power."

A look came over Baker's face. His eyes were wide, and they sparkled in the noonday sun. When he spoke he had a calm smile, like a little boy tired from a long day.

"He can feel what you're thinking, too, that's the thing. If he feels somebody isn't listening or doesn't believe, he'll just stop what he's saying. He'll point at that person and he'll tell them to get out, and he won't say anything more until they do.

I've seen it. He sure can show those hypocrites up for what they are."

Mrs. Baker had heard the stories before, but she listened with interest as she finished what remained of her lunch.

"I saw him one time, it was in Omaha. There was an old woman there who couldn't hardly see. She was up on the platform with him, her and a bunch of cripples. He had a whole wall of canes and crutches there from the people he had healed already. And he came up to this woman and he took off her glasses. 'Get up and walk,' he told her. She stood there and stood there. And you know what happened? He went up behind her and gave her a push. She didn't walk, though. She fell right off that platform and broke her arm. We didn't feel sorry for her, though. Rev. Dowie said she must've committed some grievous sin and couldn't be healed. Otherwise she would've been. He said she wouldn't ever be forgiven for it. *That* I felt bad about."

Mrs. Baker glanced right and left for an indication of when the festivities might begin. Then, as if in answer, Zion's guard, choir and church officers began to assemble. A strong trumpet call blared out and the choir took its place on the platform, and Zion's orchestra began to play the notes of the processional. Then the singing began.

Forward! be our watchword,
    Steps and voices join'd;
Seek the things before us.
    Not a look behind.

Burns the fiery pillar
    At our army's head;

Who shall dream of shrinking,
  By our Captain led?

Forward, thro' the desert,
  Thro' the toil and fight!
Jordan flows before us;
  Zion beams with light.

Glories upon glories
  Hath our God prepar'd.
By the souls that love Him
  One day to be shar'd.

Eye hath not beheld them,
  Ear hath never heard;
Nor of these have utter'd
  Thought or speech a word.

Forward, marking eastward
  Where the heav'n is bright,
Till the veil be lifted,
  Till our faith besight.

Suddenly, there he was, standing on the platform before the choir. The General Overseer. The Rev. John Alexander Dowie. He wore the full bishop's vestment, with his long white beard spilling like a sheet of cotton down his chest. He was a big man, powerful and proud, with a full voice and a thick Scottish burr. The crowd was silent as it rose for him to give the invocation and lead them in the Apostles' Creed, and more hymns, and a prayer in which he called for Zion to be blessed in America, in Europe, in Asia, in Africa, in Australia, in all the islands of the seas.

How holy he was, how pure. Mrs. Baker could see it in his face. She could read it all. His boyhood in Scotland, then Australia. His preaching and his prayers for those who were sick and then became healed. She had missed him in Chicago, at the World's Fair. Thorp never would have taken her. In any case she did not even know the name of Dowie then. Baker knew. He saw, and he would tell her of it whenever it seemed she was losing faith. He spoke of how Dowie could hold the attention of anyone, no matter how long he spoke, and how when he stopped they wanted more. And at the times when Dowie would order the faithless out of the church and refuse to resume his speech, how the crowd would wait for him to recommence. As they waited they would sit, each of them, in perfect rapturous silence. He was in Chicago all these years now, Dowie was. But now at last he was home. Zion City.

It was an historic day, the anniversary of the fall of the Bastille, and being 1900, it was a Jubilee year. It was Dowie's job as a messenger of God's covenant, he said, to proclaim the Eternal Covenant of God, The Covenant of Salvation, Healing, Holy Living, Perfect Redemption and to proclaim Liberty through Faith in Jesus by obeying God.

"I therefore stand here today to proclaim that the rule of the people, for the people and by the people is not good, but that the rule of the people, by God and for God, is the right rule," Dowie said.

His followers responded without a prompt.
"Amen."

"We have learned that lesson," Dowie said. "We hold it dear in our hearts."

Dowie said that despite the day on which it shared its anniversary, the groundbreaking of Zion City was not a rebellion.

"We are, it is true, rebelling against the devil and the apostate churches. We are rebelling against a baptism which says that if you sprinkle a little water on a baby's nose, you will change its heart. You all know that that is a lie, because thousands of you were sprinkled on the nose and your hearts were not changed.

"We rebel against the idolatry of the Mass, which tells us that a priest can change a bit of bread into the body, blood and bones of Jesus Christ. We rebel against the dogma of the infallibility of the pope, and declare that only one is infallible, and that is God. We rebel against the world, the flesh and the devil. We rebel against false principles. We rebel against the wine cup and the beer pot, and the tobacco manufacturer who makes stinkpots."

Here the audience broke out in waves of laughter, and Dowie waited with a patient smile for them to finish.

"There are none here today, thank God," he said, continuing to smile.

"Amen," the crowd answered.

"We rebel against the gambler, the gambling hall, the theater and the unclean house. We rebel against sin, and against disease, and against death, and against every power of Hell. I thank God we are good rebels in rebelling against these things."

"Amen."

"This is not a revolution. We do not propose to cut off the heads of the Baptists. We desire to take them from the freezing house where the water in the baptistery has become sixty feet thick with ice. We wish to take people from the Methodist haunts of sin where the ministers have pledged themselves to the worship of Baal in secret, and have renounced their God. We desire to take them from these places where they have been falling under the power of the devil, and to bring them into Liberty in Zion."

"Amen."

"It is not a rebellion. It is not a revolution. What is it? It is a restoration of God and of all His crown rights. We claim that God in Zion is restoring the Christian church in its primitive beauty and glory and power. Therefore we claim the restoration of the kingdom of God. That kingdom must be within first. It is not here. It is not there, for it is – where?"

"Within you," the people said.

"It is within the heart that the kingdom must first be established. Your spirit must be free from sin. Your soul must be made pure, and your body must remain clean. We claim the right of God to rule in every home, in every business, in every store. Is that right?"

"Yes."

Dowie went on into the afternoon, laying out his hopes of seeing Zion temples in cities all over the world. And in Zion City itself the temple would be the center from which everything else spread. The buildings they would see – schools of all kinds – colleges, schools of industry, of training. There would be libraries and places where people could come and be blessed. There would be homes of divine healing and orphans' homes.

There would be a gigantic factory for lace-making, the money generated from which would go toward supporting the rest of the city.

Mrs. Baker absorbed it all. She felt charged by Dowie's words, capable and empowered, and began to formulate a plan in her mind. Dowie's voice faded as she continued to think, and she watched the scene with a quiet smile on her lips. She watched as the members of Zion's Guard made their procession around the site, circling it three times in their brilliant white and blue uniforms. Mrs. Baker saw Dowie scale the tower and salute them. She knew what to do, she thought, as she gazed up at his radiant face.

Baker peered out the window with one hand holding the drapes and watched the man outside. He had been standing there for some time in his heavy coat and dark bowler hat. He had a divided mustache, and every few minutes he would smooth both sides of it with his right index finger and thumb. He stood on the other side of the street, and sometimes he would stop passersby and point discreetly at the house, listening as they talked. Baker did not like him. He looked like trouble.

After a fourth person spoke to him the man started across the street, and Baker stepped away from the window. He went down the hall and called for his wife and then trotted upstairs, ducking around the corner so he would not be seen. Baker strained to listen as his wife opened the door to the man outside, who introduced himself in a deep voice as Detective Troyer. Baker closed his eyes and waited as the pair continued to chat.

Baker was calm. There was no reason to be nervous. He had nothing to hide.

The man stepped inside the house and Mrs. Baker led him down the hall to her office. She chatted the whole time. She had a musical voice, and Baker enjoyed listening to her even when the words were indistinct. When he was sure they had sat down Baker rose and crept to the room above the office, where he listened at the vent. She was something. Her speech never sounded forced. Depending on how receptive her audience was, she could even shed a few tears, like an actress. It was miraculous. And now she was doing it again, going over the same stale lines with the fervor of an evangelical. The detective spoke, too. He was moved, Baker could tell. His voice gave him away.

"Would you be at all interested in giving your endorsement to our work?" were Mrs. Baker's final muffled words.

"Yes, I certainly would."

Baker grinned and shook his head in wonderment. Then he went downstairs. He arrived in the office just as the detective finished his signature. Mrs. Baker smiled at the sight of her husband and took the paper from the detective.

"Joseph, there you are. This is–"

"Detective Troyer," the man said as he rose. He extended his hand to Baker, who grasped it and gave it a firm shake. "How are you today, sir?"

"Fine, thank you."

"Joseph, Detective Troyer has just given Sacred Refuge his endorsement."

"That's wonderful. We're so glad."

The detective cleared his throat.

"Now that you're both here, I suppose I can get started," he said.

"What do you mean?" Mrs. Baker asked.

"Mr. Baker?" the detective said. "Would you care to take a seat?"

"No."

Baker moved past him to stand behind his wife on the other side of the desk. The detective smelled of pipe smoke and Baker wrinkled his nose when he noticed it.

"Detective Troyer," Mrs. Baker said. "What do you mean about 'getting started?'"

"Well, Mrs. Baker, I've heard some reports about you and your husband and I'm following up on them."

Neither of the Bakers seemed nervous.

"What have you heard?" Mrs. Baker said.

"May I sit?"

"Of course."

He grunted as he resumed his seat and slipped his hand into the pocket of his coat, inside of which was his pipe.

"Forgive me, but I can only go on what I've heard from other people, so please don't take offence. The women you help, they don't actually reside at this house, do they?"

"They do not," Mrs. Baker said.

"I thought not. They live in a place on Dodge Block, is that correct?"

"Yes, it is."

"Have they done something?" Baker asked.

The detective shook his head and turned his pipe, still in his pocket, several times in his hand.

"Not that I know of. I'm only verifying some information."

Detective Troyer pulled his pipe from his coat and rested it on his knee.

"And you have four women and four children living there, correct?"

"Yes," Mrs. Baker said.

"And you pay their way through collections."

"Yes, and we train them to be self-sustaining."

Detective Troyer nodded. "These collectors in your employ, is there a finite amount each of them brings in each day?"

"No," Baker said firmly.

Mrs. Baker smiled. "That would be impossible, because you see, each day is different. Some days are good, some are bad."

"Like people," Baker said.

The detective lifted his pipe to his mouth.

"Now, I've heard some figures, and–"

"Don't smoke that thing in here," Baker said.

Troyer smiled and returned the pipe to his pocket.

"Excuse me, my apologies. I've heard some figures, and I want to know if they're accurate." He removed a sheet of paper from his vest and read it over. "It says here that you collected thirty to sixty dollars a day when you started out, but that now you get eighty to one-hundred thirty. Is that right?"

"That seems awfully high," Mrs. Baker said.

"What would it be, then?" Detective Troyer said.

"Lower than that."

Troyer glanced once more at the paper. "It also says here that you collected five hundred at the camps."

"No, that is definitely incorrect," Mrs. Baker said.

"What is correct, then? What are the numbers?"

"My wife already told you. Lower."

"How much lower? What do you bring in on a per-day basis?"

Mrs. Baker smiled again. "That would be difficult to say. As I told you before, those numbers fluctuate on a daily basis."

"I understand," Troyer said. "Of the money that *is* brought in – whatever the amount – how much of it goes into your operation?"

"All of it," Mrs. Baker said.

"Ah, well, you see, I've heard that you let your collectors keep twenty-five percent of whatever funds they bring in."

Bakers face grew darker.

"That's a lie."

"I can only report what I've been told."

"You've been told a lie."

"Then what is the truth? How much do you spend? How much do you give your collectors?"

Neither of the Bakers said a word. Detective Troyer leaned back in his chair and crossed his legs.

"How long have you been married?"

"I don't see how that's any of your business," Baker said.

"I'm asking a simple question."

"Who's been talking to you about our marriage?"

Detective Troyer grinned.

"I'm afraid that's confidential."

"We don't have to answer that line of questioning."

"That's right, you don't. I'm just curious. Well, if you won't tell me when you got married, could you tell me where? Was it in a church? Was it done by a justice of the peace? Was it in Minnesota? Wisconsin?"

Baker spoke through a clenched jaw.

"If you must know, it was over two years ago."

"And where–?"

"Minnesota. Minneapolis. August."

Detective Troyer looked into his eyes.

"Which means, Mr. Baker, that at that time you were still married to your first wife. Is that correct?"

Baker appeared to have stopped breathing for a moment. He blinked slowly and his mustache danced over his lips. Mrs. Baker gave no visible reaction.

"She had already filed for divorce," Baker said in a sour voice.

"Where–?"

"In Two Harbors!"

Detective Troyer continued to speak in his relaxed way.

"It's all right, you don't need to shout. Do you know if the divorce was finalized at the time of your second marriage?"

Baker worked his way around the desk, waving his balled fists in the air as if he were preaching before an enormous crowd. It was what he always did when he was angry, and it seemed to happen without his realizing it.

"No, I don't know, but she did file! But it doesn't matter even if it wasn't done, because me and Mrs. Baker are common-law man and wife! But you probably already know about it, don't you? You might turn your nose up at that, too, but God sure doesn't! He knows we're man and wife! He knows the truth!"

Mrs. Baker almost appeared to smile at her husband. Her cheeks were a healthy red and her eyes shone like lighted candles.

"I'm not here to judge you, Mr. Baker," Detective Troyer said, maintaining his comfortable posture and friendly attitude. "I'm merely verifying some reports."

"You've done nothing but judge us since you came in this house!" Baker yelled. "If we're so bad, if people don't trust what we're doing, we'll give 'em their money back. All of it! How does that sound to you, Mister Detective?"

As Baker spoke, Detective Troyer rose and slipped on a pair of black leather gloves. He did not shrink away from Baker, who continued his harangue until he was inches from Troyer's face.

"You're truly willing to give the money back?" Troyer asked when it was over.

"Yes. I always mean what I say."

Detective Troyer interlocked his fingers and pushed until the gloves were snug against his palms, but never broke eye contact.

"Forgive me for saying so, Mr. Baker, but isn't that how a mitt gang works?"

Baker took a step back. When he spoke, much of the force had gone out of his voice.

"Beg pardon?"

"You know what I mean," Troyer said. "I don't want to draw any odious comparisons, but that's exactly how they work. First the gang skins a sucker, and then if he squeals they pay him his money back. That is, if he promises not to say anything about it. Isn't that right?"

The bells of the telephone trilled at a painful level from the end of the hallway. Mrs. Baker emerged from her office and walked toward the machine with her mouth hanging open as a defense against the noise. She took the receiver from the hook and spoke in a loud voice.

"This is Mrs. Baker speaking from Sacred Refuge. How may I help you?"

A man's voice came through thick and hearty.

"Mrs. Baker. We've never met before, but I understand you're using my name in some kind of testimonial. This is Mayor Hugo."

"Yes, Mayor, we appreciate your endorsement very highly," she said through a smile.

"Mrs. Baker, I was led to understand that my name would only be used if the name of your institution were changed."

She opened her mouth as if to let out a gasp.

"Oh, my, I had no idea."

"Yes, ma'am, and I find it most perplexing that not only were my instructions not followed, but my name is being listed on circulars all over the state."

"You have my sincerest apologies. I can take your name off of them right away. Thank you very much for bringing this situation to my attention–"

"Mrs. Baker…"

"Yes?"

"While we're discussing the issue, I feel I should inform you that my office has been receiving some distressing reports about your work."

Mrs. Baker moved the receiver to her other ear and leaned closer to the mouthpiece.

"From whom?"

"I can't tell you that, ma'am, but suffice it to say that some people are raising questions about your methods – your means of acquiring funds, your spending of them and that sort of thing."

"All lies, I can assure you."

"I truly hope so."

Mrs. Baker heard the front door open and looked to see her husband enter the house. He was bundled in a thick coat and scarf, and he stamped the snow from his boots before he walked away. When he had gone Mrs. Baker went back to the conversation.

"If these rumors concern you so much, why don't you hold an investigation?"

"Are you sure about that, ma'am?"

"Of course I am. I have nothing to hide. Select some of your best citizens and let them ask me whatever questions they want. You'll find these reports are nothing more than rumors. They're lies, and that's all."

"Who would you suggest serve on this committee?"

"My attorney, Ingebret Grettum. You may choose your own representative."

"Are you familiar with Dr. Long, the minister?"

"Yes."

"I choose him. That is, unless you object."

"I do not. Although I suggest they pick one final member on whom they can agree."

Mayor Hugo clicked his tongue once and breathed through his nose.

"This may take a few days," he said. "May we call you again?"

"Of course. Thank you, Mayor."

"Thank you, Mrs. Baker."

Mrs. Baker returned to her office to see her husband warming his hands at the fireplace. His skin was red and he panted as he stood there.

"Who were you talking to?" he asked.

"Never mind," she said as she entered. "It's not important."

"Mrs. Baker? This is Capt. Pressnell. Can you hear me all right?"

She held the receiver a few inches from her ear and waited to answer.

"I'm calling in regard to the investigation you suggested to the mayor."

"Yes," Mrs. Baker said in a loud flat voice that was pitched more toward the hall than the mouthpiece.

"Mr. Grettum and Dr. Long have chosen me to join their committee and asked if I would contact you and find out when we can meet at my office. It's over in the federal building."

"Yes," Mrs. Baker said again, raising her voice even more this time.

Soon Baker appeared at the end of the hallway and came forward slowly with his head cocked.

"Would the twentieth of March work?" Pressnell asked.

Mrs. Baker looked at her husband and moved her lips as if she were speaking, but she made no sound.

"What's that?" Baker asked.

Mrs. Baker pressed close to the mouthpiece, her voice suddenly filled with apprehension.

"N-no. No, sir."

"How about the following day?" Pressnell asked. "Say about ten o'clock in the morning?"

Again Mrs. Baker looked to her husband and mimed speech.

"What are you saying?" Baker asked.

"That would work much better," Mrs. Baker said into the phone.

"Mrs. Baker, is someone else in the room with you?" Pressnell said.

Baker shrugged at his wife and shook his head. She placed her hand over the mouthpiece and spoke to him in a fervent whisper.

"Sacred Refuge is being investigated. They're selecting a committee, and they want my advice about who serves on it."

"No Methodists," Baker spat. He began to pace, moving his arms as if he were getting ready to throw a punch. "Absolutely no Methodists," he kept repeating as he stalked away.

"Mrs. Baker, are you there?" Pressnell said.

"Yes, captain," she answered in a calm voice. "I shall see you at ten in the morning on the twenty-first. Goodbye."

Capt. Pressnell's office contained a long table. The committee sat on one side, and there was a chair for Mrs. Baker on the other. In the open areas of the room more seats had been placed, many of which were filled by the time Mrs. Baker arrived. She came alone, and paused at the door. That Hoyt woman was there, and Detective Troyer, and even Mrs. Pascoe. From the table Grettum saw Mrs. Baker and stood, the other men on the committee following suit as he motioned for her to sit. After a few preliminaries Pressnell began the questioning.

"What is the financial condition of your institution?"

"We do well," Mrs. Baker said.

"How well?"

"Well enough to suit our needs."

"Could you perhaps elaborate a bit?" Dr. Long said.

"I shan't. This is hardly the proper way to conduct an investigation."

Bemused, Capt. Pressnell stroked his chin.

"What do you suggest we do?"

"I want you – all of you – to come to the house and see what the money is expended for. I didn't have proper notice of what your questions would involve, all this talk about money."

"What do you think we should ask about?" Pressnell said.

"The work itself."

"A great deal of your work seems to involve the collecting of funds," Dr. Long said.

Mrs. Baker curled her lips and shook her head.

"I've seen you many times myself, you and your women," Long said. "I've–"

"You've no right to pass judgment on me. I'm doing right. I'm doing what any Christian should be doing by trying to help these unfortunates. It's not your place to tell me it's wrong – you of all people. I should think a man of the Gospel should know better."

Mr. Grettum cleared his throat and raised his left index finger.

"Perhaps the committee *is* proceeding in the wrong way," he said. "This woman is in reality the defendant in this case, and she is presumed innocent until she is proven guilty."

"No," Capt. Pressnell said. "She is not to be considered as a defendant. She stands in the position of the plaintiff, for the reason that she has courted this inquiry. Complaints have been going about that she has wrongfully used money contributed to her, and she has courted this inquiry and asked for it in order that she may show the people what she has done with that money. It is for her to state what she has done with it."

Mrs. Baker could feel the stares of everyone in the room.

"I shall not," she said.

"Then how much have you collected?" Pressnell said. "Tell us that."

"Not so much."

"But how much?"

"It's hardly worth mentioning."

"Then you have nothing to worry about. You haven't, in any case. Please, just tell us."

"I don't know that I can remember exactly."

"Give us your best estimate, then."

Mrs. Baker sighed. "I would say it was between three hundred and four hundred dollars altogether."

"Thank you," Pressnell said. "And, from whom have you received endorsements?"

"I don't need to tell you."

"Mrs. Baker," Dr. Long said, "you've been using these names all over town. They've appeared in the paper."

"Then you must already have them," she said.

"Would you be kind enough to verify them for us?" Pressnell asked.

"Dr. Long was one."

"Good. Who else?"

"Mayor Hugo."

Grettum interrupted again, saying, "Now remember, Mrs. Baker is to be presumed innocent until she has been shown to be guilty."

"We have the right to enquire," Pressnell said.

"No, sir, you haven't," Mrs. Baker said. "I shall reveal what I wish, and what I do not wish to reveal, I need not."

"Have you used the endorsement of Bishop Morrison?" Dr. Long said.

"I have the endorsement of Mrs. Morrison, but I have not used her husband's name."

"What about Dr. Ryan?"

Mrs. Baker said nothing. She stared at her hands and worked some of her fingers as if she were pushing back the cuticle.

"Mrs. Baker?" Capt. Pressnell said.

"I think you gentlemen are taking advantage of me," she said without looking up. "If you were to come to the home I could show you all I have, and all I have done. What I have said all over the city has nothing to do here."

Grettum attempted to catch her gaze.

"Here we are again beginning at the wrong end," he said. "There is no issue here. There are no charges. If you would get your books you could show them to us and prove what you have been saying."

"I have no one to send to get them," she said looking at the floor.

"You can fetch them yourself," Grettum said. "I can accompany you to the Refuge, and we'll return here and set everything right."

"I can't allow that," she said.

"Mrs. Baker," Captain Pressnell said, "please look at the committee when you address it."

She raised her head quickly to stare at them. Her eyes flashed with hate and she held her lips tight. She did not say anything.

"Thank you," Pressnell said. "Now, why can you not allow it? We're giving you the opportunity to clear your name."

When Mrs. Baker spoke her tone was a mixture of sweetness and condescension.

"I can't bring you my books because I haven't any."

The committee members sat in silence for a few seconds. They seemed bewildered, all of them but Grettum, whose face was a picture of disappointment.

Mrs. Baker continued, "Even though I don't keep regular books, I can show that I have expended all of my funds properly."

Grettum placed his hands on the table and pushed back his chair a bit.

"We're going about this in the wrong way," he repeated. "We're getting nowhere, and we'll make no progress without official charges."

"This inquiry is being held at Mrs. Baker's own solicitation," Capt. Pressnell said. "As such, she should be willing to cooperate and answer our questions."

With a sigh, Grettum pulled his chair close to the table again, and the questioning recommenced. Mrs. Baker did not admit to much. She had a proper bank account, but refused to say whose name it was under. She admitted to having a nurse and cook living at her house. They were each paid fifteen dollars a month, she said. They were not the only ones at the house. Mrs. Baker said that at times there were as many as nineteen or twenty people there. Of her husband, she said his work often took him away from home. In any case, he had nothing to do with the running of Sacred Refuge. Of herself, she refused to say anything.

"That is none of your affair," was her refrain. At last she looked to Dr. Long with soft pleading. "Remember what Christ said of the sinful woman. He who is without sin, let him cast the first stone."

"We've no intention of doing anything but what is right," Dr. Long said. "But, if you have been soliciting the people of Duluth for money, they have a right to know if you're a proper person to expend it. You should be willing to answer questions about your marriage and your character. You do not come to us as a sinner, but as the person who is to save sinners."

"You are right in that," she said, raising her chin. "I am not a sinner, and because of that, I refuse to answer any more questions."

Capt. Pressnell was unperturbed.

"Mrs. Baker, have you ever passed under another name here in Duluth?"

No answer.

"Were you only just married this February?"

"I deny your authority to ask such questions."

Capt. Pressnell put on a pair of gold-rimmed glasses with rectangular lenses and read from one of the sheets of paper before him on the table.

"We have a report of your giving roast turkey dinners at your house, while the women you claim to be helping have scarcely enough to live on."

"Who told you that?" Mrs. Baker asked sharply.

"I cannot say at this time."

"Slurs, nothing more."

"Is your institution an incorporation?"

Mrs. Baker stomped the floor once with the heel of her shoe.

"Stop imposing on me!" she shouted.

Capt. Pressnell whipped off his glasses and glared at her.

"Mrs. Baker, it begins to appear that *you* have been placing a great imposition on the people of Duluth."

The woman crossed her arms and refused to say anything further. She and the captain spent a long while staring at each other across the table. Eventually Grettum looked Pressnell's way.

"And there are truly no charges against Mrs. Baker?" he asked.

"That's what I've told you," Capt. Pressnell said. "Repeatedly."

"And I repeat that this investigation is going on in the wrong way," Grettum said. Before the others could speak, he added, "You are construing the matter in your way, I'm doing it in mine."

Capt. Pressnell rubbed his eyes and gave a long sigh.

"Mrs. Baker, since it appears you are not willing to cooperate, I see no reason for questioning to continue. However, there are several others we wish to speak to, and we ask that you remain here so that you are aware of what they say."

Mrs. Baker rose from her chair and took another one, away from the table. Grettum raised his head and waggled his finger so she could see.

"Don't say a thing," he told her. "You have closed."

That was when they began to file up to the table, each of them telling the same outrageous stories. Some of them Mrs. Baker had never even met, like a certain Mrs. Perrault, who claimed that Mr. Baker insulted her. There was Mrs. Pascoe, and Detective Troyer, who said, "They were like the Irishman's flea. You could never get them to the point. They were dodging all the time." The worst of all was Mrs. Hoyt. It was she who contacted the police, and she who now sat before the committee proclaiming falsehood upon falsehood, all of which were accepted without hesitation by the men asking the questions.

Although she was given the opportunity to do so, Mrs. Baker asked no questions of her own. She sat quietly with a benign look on her face, as if she were in church. When it was over she stood and addressed the men at the table.

"I'm glad this investigation has been held. There have been lies told here against me, but I will meet them at the proper time. God is with me in this work, and I shall keep on with it. The poor people for whom I am working need me. No one understands them as do I. No one can give them the sympathy that I can. God is with me, and will comfort and sustain me and give me righteousness. To show you my cause is worthy of support, I promise to bring my records here the first of next week."

When Mrs. Baker came hauling an armload of ledgers and papers to the meeting on Monday she was accompanied by her husband, as well as Mrs. Craig and Mrs. Lovejoy. She seated herself before the committee, while the others took up chairs behind her. The women all wore the same look of hopeful expectation and sat with straight backs in the hard chairs. Baker was relaxed, seeming almost to sneer as his wife made her statement.

"The allegations that were made last week against my work and myself were the result of personal spite – in particular on the parts of Mrs. Hoyt and Mrs. Perrault. Everything Mrs. Hoyt talked about has a rational explanation. The women at Dodge Block were invited to the turkey dinner, but they were unable to come because of the weather. It was too stormy. The reason they carried wood upstairs was to save fuel in cooking."

Mrs. Baker heard more people enter the room and turned to see that Mrs. Hoyt and Miss Seaverson were among them. Mrs. Baker sniffed as if she detected something foul before she looked back to the committee. Opening her mouth to speak again, she faltered.

"Dodge Block," Baker said.

"What?" his wife asked.

"Dodge Block. Why they went there."

Mrs. Baker nodded and started again.

"Dodge Block. The women went to live at Dodge Block because the house was getting too crowded."

"Better place," Baker muttered and rubbed under his nose.

"And, it was a better place to do dressmaking. I hope this answers some of the questions that were raised last week."

"Thank you, Mrs. Baker," Capt. Pressnell said. "The committee now requests that you submit your financial records, as you promised you would do last week."

Before she could say anything in response, Baker answered for her.

"Are there any other witnesses?"

"I beg your pardon?" Pressnell asked, raising his head to better see the other man.

"Are there any other witnesses?" Baker said, stretching his words as if he were addressing someone who was hard of hearing.

"There are," Pressnell said.

Baker smiled. "This committee won't hear anything about my wife's finances until everyone else has been heard."

Pressnell put on his glasses before he spoke.

"Mr. Baker, perhaps it would be proper for your wife to make her full statement first, just to avoid confusing things?"

Baker rested one of his long arms on the back of his chair.

"The others will speak first, or we'll be leaving immediately," he said.

"Mr. Baker, for someone who has been represented as having no part in his wife's work, you do seem to be taking a pretty active role in it today."

"I'm just here to see that justice is done."

"Oh?"

"Last week you had your own witnesses, didn't you? My wife had no chance to get her own witnesses, so of course she came off looking bad. It was shameful. The whole thing was a conspiracy."

Capt. Pressnell fixed Baker in a sharp look.

"Mr. Baker, when I called your wife last week in reference to this matter, her answers over the telephone were prompted by a man whose voice I could hear in the background. I now recognize that voice as yours. In case you've forgotten, this hearing was called at your wife's request. Its purpose could not have been misunderstood, and the idea that she was in any case waylaid is simply ridiculous."

He looked to Mrs. Baker, his patience slipping.

"Now, please, ma'am, present your financial statement so that we can move on."

"Don't do it," Baker said.

Mrs. Baker did not move. The other two members of the committee glanced at Pressnell. He seemed very tired, and his face had begun to turn pink. He took off his glasses once more and wiped his eyes.

"All right," he said at last. "We have no power to force you into anything. Take a seat next to your husband if you will."

Mrs. Baker stood and left the table with a faint smile on her lips.

Mrs. Craig was the next to speak. She was about thirty-five, strong and attractive, with a big voice.

"Have you been collecting for the Refuge?" Dr. Long asked.

"I have."

"Are you paid for your work?"

"Yes, sir."

"How much?"

Baker gave an exaggerated sigh when the question was asked.

"Twenty-five cents on the dollar at first, and one dollar a day after that," Mrs. Craig said.

"Have you collected outside of the city?"

Baker seemed to growl like a dog, and he stood and began to shout.

"I object to all questions on the financial affairs of the home at this time!"

Dr. Long retained his patience, and refused to raise his voice.

"Mr. Baker, if you wish to answer our questions you may, but right now it's Mrs. Craig's turn."

Baker mutter a few words and sat again.

Dr. Long smiled. "Mrs. Craig, have you ever collected funds outside of Duluth?"

In an instant Mrs. Craig's voice had changed. She sounded quiet, almost fearful, and she could not refrain from glancing at the door.

"I'm sorry, sir. Mr. Baker thinks it is not necessary to answer those questions now, and I will not."

"Will you answer them later, perhaps?" Dr. Long said. "Will you be on call in case we ask you to return?"

"No, I'm sorry. My husband is sick. I must go home."

Standing, Mrs. Craig began to back away from the table.

"Mrs. Craig, will you come back if we send for you?"

"I don't know," she said, looking at the floor. "It depends on whether I can leave my husband or not."

Dr. Long continued to speak in the same even manner.

"Mrs. Craig. Please sit down."

After thinking for a few seconds, she obeyed.

"Now, where did you go collecting?"

Baker half-rose and spoke to the back of Mrs. Craig's head.

"I instruct you not to answer. This committee hasn't any authority over you."

"Did you collect five hundred dollars in Ashland?" Dr. Long said.

Mrs. Craig's voice regained some of its power, although she did not look at him.

"No, sir, I never did. Nothing like that amount."

Smiling, Baker returned to his chair.

"Was it one hundred?" Dr. Long said.

"If it was that much, I was doing well."

"What did you know of the Bakers before you began working for them?"

Mrs. Craig said nothing.

"Does Mr. Baker have anything to do with the work?" Capt. Pressnell said.

"Mrs. Baker said that he instructs her."

Pressnell nodded. "Do you know whether she was ever married before?"

"I object to these questions about the past of myself and my wife," Baker shouted. "They have nothing to do with our present work."

Mrs. Craig refused to answer all questions thereafter.

Lizzie Seaverson took her place behind the table. She folded her hands in her lap and stared at them as if she thought she might not be called upon if she did not look up. Capt. Pressnell watched her with a sympathetic look and waited for her to move. When she did not, he spoke to her in a soft voice.

"Miss Seaverson?"

She did not look up. "Yes, sir."

"Are you feeling all right?"

She nodded.

"You were in charge of the room at Dodge Block, is that right?"

"Yes, sir."

"Mrs. Baker has told us the women were sent there because the house was getting too crowded, and it was a better place to do dressmaking. Is that correct?"

"Yes, sir, that's what she said."

"How did you come to leave Dodge Block?"

Miss Seaverson looked up for the first time. Her eyes darted to the side, as if she thought she might be able to see who was sitting behind her.

"I refuse to answer."

"Did you not tell someone that you left because of Mr. Baker?" Capt. Pressnell asked.

Miss Seaverson shut her eyes. The awful empty room. The door opening. There he is, with his hands reaching out. He approaches. He will not be stopped.

"Yes, I did."

"How was it that he caused you to leave?"

His hands. The bruises on her flesh still tender but no longer visible. She drove the thoughts from her head.

"He told me to leave."

"You understood him to be the manager of the place?"

Miss Seaverson opened her eyes and blinked three times before she looked down once again.

"Well. He had to have his say."

Later in the afternoon Capt. Pressnell tried again.

"Let us have this financial statement. It is time for that."

"We will not," Baker said, still perched in his seat like a gargoyle. "You are here to obey. You'll have it when we get ready, and not before. If you don't like that you can quit right now."

"Mr. Baker, it's been a long day. Please."

Baker jumped up at that moment and began waving his arms as if he were trying to attract the attention of somebody across a crowded room.

"No, I object!" he said. "The evidence shows that this is a one-sided affair. We will produce those books at the proper time and place, but this is not that place. This is not a proper committee. The agreement we made when this started was that there be no Methodist minister on the committee. This whole thing is a black Methodist conspiracy! You've attacked Mrs. Baker's religion, called her a Dowieite and attacked her private character. You've already passed judgment. You passed it before this hearing commenced. There is no hope for righteous judgment from this committee."

Capt. Pressnell moved his head so that he could see Mrs. Baker, who remained seated behind her husband.

"Mrs. Baker, would you please put an end to this and produce your books?"

Baker took a step to the right, blocking the captain's view.

"I speak for her," he said. "The whole trouble is that we're getting a few dollars some of these other institutions want to collect."

"Well, Mr. Baker, let's talk to you a while, then," Capt. Pressnell said in a resigned voice. "How long have you been married?"

"That's none of your business."

"Have you lived at Two Harbors?"

"What business is that of yours?"

"Have you lived at Ashland?"

"It's none of your business."

"What did you do there?"

"None of your business."

"Did you run the Colby House restaurant?"

"What's that to you?"

"Do you know Chief Tanner of the Ashland police?"

"Say, who appointed you, anyway? What right have you got to ask me such questions?"

Capt. Pressnell smiled. "Well, you certainly didn't appoint me."

"No, I didn't. Long did. He's got you so he can do what he wants with you. Your whole committee is of the same kind."

"You said the whole committee," Capt. Pressnell said, continuing to smile. "Do I understand you to mean Mr. Grettum, also?"

"He's not, I guess," Baker said, backing down a bit. "But we still bargained that there would be no Methodist minister on the committee. This is nothing but a black Methodist conspiracy and a blackmailing scheme."

Dr. Long raised his hand before responding.

"I wish to call attention to the fact that no question pertaining to religious belief has come at any time during this investigation."

"That's right," Capt. Pressnell said and gave a nod.

"You might not have asked them yet, but I'm sure you're planning to do it soon," Baker said.

"You have no right—"

"This whole investigation is a conspiracy, and that's all it is."

Once he had completed his harangue Mrs. Baker jumped out of her chair and motioned for Mrs. Lovejoy and Mrs. Craig to join her, and the three of them broke out singing, their voices eclipsing all other sounds in the room. The members of the committee and the witnesses could do nothing but gape in astonishment as the women went on, their hands clutched at their abdomens, their mouths opened wide as they all but shouted the words.

> *I've seen the lightning flashing,*
> *And heard the thunder roll;*
> *I've felt sin's breaker's clashing,*
> *Trying to conquer my soul;*

I've heard the voice of Jesus,
   Telling me still to fight on;
He promised never to leave me,
   Never to leave me alone.

No, never alone,
   No, never alone,
He promised never to leave me,
   Never to leave me alone;
No, never alone,
   No, never alone,
He promised never to leave me,
   Never to leave me alone.

    The investigation closed shortly thereafter. Two days later it was announced that the Bakers had rented a house at Lakeside to be used as the new location of Sacred Refuge.

The committee's final report was given to Mayor Hugo and also appeared in the Duluth newspapers:

    "…(Mrs. Baker) was called on to produce books to show what money had been obtained and what disposition had been made of it. This she refused to do, but promised to do so at a future meeting. The committee called on any persons present to make statements for or against the institution, and a number of persons did make statements.

    "Mrs. Baker promised to be present at a future meeting, at which time she would produce the books and make a full statement of financial matters. March 25, at 2:30 o'clock, was subsequently fixed as the time of holding such second meeting, and Mrs. Baker was notified. She appeared, and brought with her what appeared to be books of accounts and other papers, and stated that her husband would conduct the proceedings on her behalf. We then called upon her to produce her subscription list and books of account and to make a statement of the financial matters as she had promised. Thereupon Mr. Baker objected to her producing the required information at that time, and stated that he wished to put in some evidence in opposition to statements as to Mrs. Baker's character that had been made at a previous meeting, and he failed to put in the financial statement at the proper time.

"They were permitted to introduce witnesses, and afterwards were requested by the committee to produce or make a financial statement. Whereupon they absolutely refused to comply, notwithstanding the committee repeatedly requested Mrs. Baker to make a statement. Each time she obeyed the order of her husband and refused to do so.

"The committee has worked under great disadvantage, as it did not have the authority to call witnesses or power to compel the managers of the institution to produce books showing the receipts and expenditures of the 'Refuge' and other information. Notwithstanding, some information was obtained which will be of considerable benefit to the public, a summary of which has already been published in the daily papers.

"The institution is supported by public subscriptions, but it has no board of control, and the management is responsible to no one. The money is banked in the name of Mrs. Baker. Witnesses testified that at least six paid collectors are employed, and one of the collectors said that in one day in the logging camps over $100 was taken in. Some of the collectors were paid a commission, the usual rate being 25 percent, and others were paid salaries. As to the total amount collected, or what becomes of the money, the committee could obtain no further information.

"The information as to the work done was incomplete and unsatisfactory. It was shown that four young women and four babes were supported for some time in the Dodge block. These all lived in one room, 12 by 16, which had one folding bed and a cot on which the eight persons were supposed to sleep. The cot was furnished by outside parties. It appeared that they had to furnish their own fuel. After all the explanations had been made, the fact remains that the treatment of these young women is enough to condemn the whole management as incompetent, if not cruel.

"It is a private enterprise living off the public, controlled not by Mrs. Baker, as the public believed, but by her husband. His spirit dominates the work, and the testimony showed him to be the controlling power. Although engaged in the work of the 'Sacred Refuge,' he bears a name which would unfit him for conduct or even have a voice in the management of such a work. Even the witnesses who defended the institution had not a good word to say of him. While evidence is not lacking to show that he is a bad man, a letter from the chief of police of Ashland was especially damaging to the reputation of the man who is engaged in the work of caring for unfortunate women.

"The committee considered the work of the 'Sacred Refuge' as it is conducted, the character of the management, the methods of collecting money, as unworthy of moral or financial support, and would recommend that the whole matter be referred to the police for immediate and thorough investigation.

"We have done what we could with our limited authority but if the public is to be protected, something more must be done at once. In the meantime the public will do well to cease further contributions to the institution, and firms will protect the men in logging and mining camps by giving them information concerning the work."

By the time the report appeared in the papers, the name of Sacred Refuge had been changed to Baker Orphanage. In January that next year, *The Bemidji Pioneer* told its readers, "The 'Baker Orphanage' people are working the towns along the Fosston Branch. Get your marble heart ready."

Her eyes were the first things I noticed about her. Anybody would. It was like they were lit from the inside, shined like candles in a dark room. I saw her around town a few times before I introduced myself, and that was what I thought every time I saw her. She was so pretty. I couldn't get up the nerve to talk to her for a long while, but once I did it wasn't so bad. She was real friendly. She would talk to anyone.

I wasn't what her parents hoped for. I know that. Both our parents had farms, but that place of theirs was so big. They weren't regular farmers. They were real well-off. Germans, too, born in the old country. Prussians, really. Both her mother and father were, just like my parents. Except for the money. Lots of brothers and sisters, too. I didn't have that. When I was growing up it was just my folks and me, but I can't tell you how many kids there were in her house. It seemed like every time I was over there to see her they had a new one. I heard one time her mother gave birth to eighteen in all. I don't know if that's true, but I'd believe it. Anything you tell me about them, I'd believe it.

I think maybe that's what she saw in me, a way to get out of that house, get away from all those other people. I was her ticket out of there. But where to, you know? She probably didn't think that far ahead. Or maybe she did, and I was the one that didn't.

She always had some kind of plan, even if I didn't see it at the time.

It was real nice at first – all the way through, really, as far as I knew. I'd go to work at the restaurant, she'd come in with me, takin orders and stuff. She was good at it, too. She was a talker. So was Joseph. He worked back in the kitchen with me and he could go on all day, never say the same thing twice. We'd all three grab a quick bite in the afternoon once the rush was over. We'd all talk then, but now that I think on it they never talked to each other when I was around. Just to me. Never a word to each other but hello in the morning and good night before we set out for home.

That's where she was the best. That's where she told me how much she loved me – on the way home each night. And she'd tell me how happy I made her. Said it so much it seems odd now, like she was trying to hide somethin. Sure, she was playin me for a fool, but how would I know that? Who doesn't like being told what they wanna hear? Nobody I know.

One day she was gone. Just like that. I get up in the morning and she's not there. I get to the restaurant and Joseph's gone, too. You'd have to be pretty stupid not to have that situation figured out in about three seconds.

I was real bitter about it for a long time. I couldn't even look at a woman, or a man and a woman together without wanting to do somethin stupid like start a fight. But I got over that. The census guys came a few months back, and I told them I was never married. Seems like it now, anyway, it happened so long ago. All that time I've just been doin the same thing. Go to work in a restaurant, or cook at one of the camps, and then come home to an empty bed.

I got cancer now. Most of the time it feels like I swallowed a hot coal and it's eating up my stomach from the inside. I can't work anymore. I don't have too much longer. I let go of all my hate now. It didn't pay to keep it. It's probly how I got sick in the first place.

I'm glad she's gone. I miss her.

The Chicago Auditorium was filled with an audience of five thousand, each member of which waited in tense anticipation for the announcement to be made. It had been discussed for weeks, but now was the time for verification. It was Lord's Day, and the crowds gathered at the doors starting in the early morning. Once they were allowed entry that afternoon they were greeted with the sweet voices of Zion's choir, who stood resplendent in their matching robes.

The atmosphere was electric. The people needed a day like this one. So did Dowie, as it came a single day after he was cleared of manslaughter by a grand jury. The incident that led to the charge had happened about two weeks earlier. Dowie was called to pray for the pregnant wife of Deacon Judd. She was in great pain, the deacon said. The calls continued from four in the morning until eleven at night, when Dowie at last left for the Judd home. The deacon was waiting with his wife, who was being attended by two maternity deaconesses. Mrs. Judd was unconscious. Placing his hand on her breast, Dowie prayed. Mrs. Judd lay quiet. She went into labor within the next half-hour. Dowie left. By morning Mrs. Judd was dead. So was the baby. Doctors later testified that if Mrs. Judd had been allowed basic medical treatment their lives could easily have been saved. Dowie was charged as being criminally responsible by the coroner's jury, but the authorities failed to convict him.

Dowie planted himself center stage as the music ended. He read scripture and took the offering, and then began the address everyone had come to hear.

"I shall not say what I have to say until I have read to you what God has said. More important than my speaking is God's word. I read to you what God said in the last verses of the Old Testament: 'Behold, I will send you Elijah the prophet before the great and terrible day of the Lord comes. And he shall turn the heart of the fathers to the children, and the heart of the children to their fathers, lest I come and smite the earth with a curse.'

"This prophecy was delivered four hundred and twenty years before John was born. John the Baptist, the son of Elizabeth and Zacharias, a priest, was born when Elizabeth was an old woman, beyond the years when women bear children. Zacharias had the announcement made to him when he was offering sacrifice in the temple. Gabriel, the angel, came to him with the wondrous message that he should be the father and Elizabeth the mother of a son who should be Elijah the prophet.

"Now John the Baptist, Jesus said, was not only Elijah, but that Elijah was to come again for a third time. One of the blunders that people make in reading a certain passage to which we shall come presently in the Acts is that Christ is to restore all things. What did Jesus say? 'Jesus answered and said, Elijah indeed cometh and' – what?"

"And shall restore all things," the crowd answered.

"'But I say unto you, that Elijah is come already, and they knew him not, but did unto him whatsoever they listed. Even so shall the Son of Man also suffer of them.' That is to say, they killed him. 'Even so shall the Son of Man also suffer of them. Then understood the disciples that He spake unto them of John the Baptist.' Was John the Baptist Elijah?"

"Yes."

"Was he right when he said, 'I am not'?"

"No."

"Who knew best, Christ or John?"

"Christ."

"Christ or Elijah?"

"Christ."

"If I were to say, 'I am not,' and God said, 'You are,' who would know best?"

"God."

"Well, I have said 'I am not' long enough about a number of things. I have been rebuked. I have said, 'Lord, I am not able to do this,' and I have been rebuked again and again by God, who has told me that He never expected me to be able to do it, for I was only at best a willing agent whom He could use as an instrument by means of which He would Himself do the work. I am not able to fight this battle with my own strength. God is able, is He not?"

"Yes."

"Is God able to give me strength?"

"Yes."

"And He will. That is the trouble with some of us. We forget that power belongs to God. That is the reason we have not done many things that we might have done. Now I desire to refer you to the ninth chapter of Mark, where we have the same story in three short verses: 'And they asked Him saying, The scribes say that Elijah must first come. And He said unto them, Elijah indeed cometh first, and restoreth all things. And how is it written of the Son of Man, that He should suffer many things and be set naught? But I say unto you that Elijah is come, and they have also done unto him whatsoever they listed, even as it is written of him.'

"All things were not restored by Elijah in his second coming. Did Elijah, in the person of John the Baptist, restore all things when he came?"

"No."

"Did even Christ Himself, during His earthly ministry, restore all things?"

"No."

"Then that must indicate another coming when all things are to be restored. Moses indeed said a prophet shall the Lord God raise up unto you from among your brethren. Whence was he to come?"

"From among your brethren."

Dowie nodded. "'From among your brethren.' He was simply to be a man of the nation 'from among your brethren, like unto me.' He was to be a man like Moses."

He stopped speaking a moment and lowered his head a bit, nodding.

"It is now more than two years ago since I was led to declare that I believed that God had called me to be the messenger of His covenant. That has been spoken, written, printed. The multitudes heard the message." Here he raised his eyes. "Multitudes received it. Thank God that the little white dove is carrying Leaves of Healing everywhere, and God has blessed my declaration that I am the messenger of His covenant. That covenant is a covenant of salvation, healing, holy living. Who else is preaching, and successfully demanding the practice of it?"

"No one."

"I say fearlessly today that the Christian Catholic Church in Zion alone holds up the banner of the everlasting covenant of salvation, healing and holy living in Christ our lord."

Cries of "Amen" were heard amidst the tumult of applause as the crowd rose to its feet. Dowie allowed himself a proud smile and waited a minute for the people to resume their seats.

"Thank God for that," he said when the auditorium was again quiet. "When long years ago somebody said that they believed that the spirit and power of Elijah were with me, I said, 'No! Do not let me get that in my head! No!' And I was angry.

"When God gets angry He is mightily angry, for it is a righteous anger. I thought mine was a righteous anger. 'No! Do not talk to me like that. All the good that ever I can do will be spoiled if I get that thought in my head.' John the Baptist never more earnestly said 'I am not' than I did. If anybody wanted to make me angry they had only to say I was Elijah. Then I said, 'Get away. Attend to your own business. Leave me to mine.'

"But friends, I saw it and I knew it not. I feared, perhaps, if I can ever fear like those who do not really know what fear is. At least I hesitated to acknowledge what I saw, even to myself. I do not think I ever was afraid. I have asked a good many people, when they said they were afraid, how it feels to be afraid. I do not think I know. I do not want to know.

"If any man fears, he is not perfect in love. There is no fear in love, and I daily live a life of love – the love of God, which strips me of everything that produces fear, so that I love men all over this wide world too much to be afraid to tell them the truth, no matter what the telling may cost me. God forbid that fear should still my tongue or still the message on my lips which God has put into my heart, as well as into my mouth.

"When a man gets to the age I am, fifty-four, he naturally begins to think of letting up a little. But to my intense surprise – and I will not say other than delight – as I passed into my fiftieth year I found that a new spirit, a new life, a new strength had come. I saw as the century was swinging open before my sight that my personal ministry had begun, that the messenger of the covenant was also Elijah the restorer.

"John in his day was that messenger, for Christ declared it. Although the son of Zacharias and Elizabeth, he was the physical, physical and spiritual embodiment of Elijah. Then I saw the messenger of the covenant, when he came again, must not only be the embodiment of Elijah, but he must also be 'that prophet.' I saw that when the times of the restoration of all things, which must precede the coming of the Lord, had come, then Elijah must come. Moses had said it thirty-four hundred years ago. God had said it through Malachi twenty-three hundred and twenty years ago. Jesus said it nearly nineteen hundred years ago. Peter said it.

"Elijah's first manifestation was that of prophet in the reign of Ahab, king of Israel. His second manifestation was that of priest, as John the Baptist was. But of Elijah's final manifestation all the scriptures had said that the physical,

physical and spiritual embodiment of Elijah must take the form of prophet, priest and ruler of men.

"I say it fearlessly, that by the grace of God I am and shall be that."

In no time the people were on their feet, clapping and cheering so loud it all but shook the building. As the noise continued, Dowie stood nodding, smiling, taking it all in.

Essie Smith cupped her hands and blew into them. The days were always cold now, and her thin gloves did little to protect her skin, which felt prickly and stiff. Her nose leaked a constant transparent stream of mucus to her lips, and she wiped it before she lowered her hands back to her sides. Mrs. Baker did not seem to notice. She had been going all morning and never once seemed to register the fact that autumn had come, even though everyone she stopped on the road seemed to do the same frigid dance as they listened to her speak. She was something.

After the noon hour they went to one of the small restaurants in Sauk Centre's business district, and warmed themselves with hot tea and sandwiches. Near the end of the meal Mrs. Baker wiped her hands with a napkin and watched the younger woman. She was pretty, Mrs. Smith was, with a kind face, and she ate fast and ran her finger across her plate to get any missed crumbs.

"I've been thinking about your predicament," Mrs. Baker said.

Mrs. Smith said nothing in return. Her eyes were troubled, and the color rose in her cheeks.

"A young woman like you," Mrs. Baker said. "A young widow with a baby and a mother to support – you're just the kind of soul I wanted to help when I envisioned the idea of Baker Orphanage."

"Yes, ma'am," Mrs. Smith said in a tiny voice.

"I have a proposition. Once you start collecting on your own, why don't you send you baby and your mother to come and live with us?"

Mrs. Smith raised her head and began to shake it.

"I couldn't do that," she said. "It wouldn't be right."

"Why is that?"

"My son's no orphan. He's got me, doesn't he? And my mother, too."

"He certainly does, and he's a very lucky boy to have you both. But what if something were to happen? He's already lost his father."

Mrs. Smith opened her mouth and inhaled to ward off tears.

"I am so sorry," Mrs. Baker said. "I didn't mean to upset you."

She reached across the table and took Mrs. Smith's hand. She held tight to it and spoke as if she were saying a prayer.

"I'm trying to help you provide for him, and for your mother, too. I can't go on the road every week – I have a house to run. That's why I need good Christian women like you to help me. You're my angels, all of you, you're my angels. I thank God for you each day."

Now Mrs. Baker's eyes began to fill, and she let go of Mrs. Smith and dabbed at them with a lace handkerchief she took from her bag. When she was done she put it back and cleared her throat.

"What I propose is that you travel around getting donations, just like you've seen me do this morning. If you agree, I'll pay you ten dollars a day. Don't have a care about your inexperience. The more you do it, the more successful you'll be. I can assure you of that."

Mrs. Smith thought for a while, with her palm supporting the bottom of her chin as if to keep her head from wobbling.

"I'm sorry, but I can't do it. What about my son? I wouldn't be able to leave him. Or my mother."

"I already told you, I want them to come with me. We can take care of your little boy, and we always need help around the house. If your mother comes to help us there, I'll see that she gets six dollars each week."

"How much will you charge to care for my baby?"

"Nothing at all. What is the purpose of a charity if it won't be charitable?"

Mrs. Smith was smiling so hard it looked like she was about to laugh.

"What is your answer?" Mrs. Baker said. "Will you work with me?"

Mrs. Smith allowed herself one quick giggle.

"I will."

"That's wonderful. God save you."

Mrs. Smith continued to smile as she wiped her hands with a napkin. She looked at Mrs. Baker and shifted in her chair.

"Will you excuse me a moment?"

"Of course."

Mrs. Baker watched her enter a hall at the back of the restaurant. She knew it was going to work. She knew how people acted. Not just Mrs. Smith, but everyone. She knew what they would say and what they would do. When she spoke she would watch them and know what they were thinking, and marveled at how she could change their reactions by using a different inflection – or even by changing a single word. There was no such thing as an individual, she realized. People all were remarkably similar. It made no difference their age or their sex. They made the same comments, and asked the same questions. They behaved the way she wanted them to. She could look at them and know them. She would look at a child and know its value to them.

She sipped her tea and closed her eyes, thanking God for being so good to her.

The new house was located among a row of handsome places on London Road, number 4544. They had not stayed long in Superior before they returned to Duluth. The rent was good and it was close to Lake Superior – close enough that the smell of it was always present. It had a calming effect on her. Baker Orphanage was bigger than the Sacred Refuge and there were more residents, most of them children. Mrs. Baker no longer spoke of dressmaking or any other trades, and she had given up the room at Dodge Block. It was easier to keep track of things when everybody lived under her roof and nobody was asked any questions without her knowledge. To be safe, there was no more collecting in Duluth, either.

Laid out before her at her desk was a white sheet of paper and a pen that waited poised in a crystal inkwell. After a moment she looked to the window at her left. It was near a corner of the house, and the sun shone through it. With a smile Mrs. Baker got up, came toward the window and stared into the street. On the floor above she could hear the sound of footsteps and high-pitched chattering, but she kept her focus on the outside, and soon she was no longer aware of the noise.

Mrs. Baker returned to the desk, where she took up the pen and began to write in a clean, elegant script, "Baker Orphanage – Lakeside Branch."

"We need to think about gettin' some more help around here."

Mrs. Baker looked up to see her husband standing at her desk. Lowering her eyes, she redipped her pen and wrote some more.

"If we want to do this right, we'll need someone else to look after all the kids."

"Do you think so?" Mrs. Baker said without looking up.

Baker sat in the chair across from her with one leg splayed to the side.

"Yeah, I do. It's not like the other place. These kids are orphans, they won't have anybody to look after them."

Mrs. Baker finished the sentence she was writing and put her pen back in the inkwell. She looked at her husband. He was attempting to look serious, but there was a half-smile at the corner of his mouth and an unconscious arch to one of his eyebrows.

"What do you suggest?" Mrs. Baker asked.

Baker shrugged. "Oh, I don't know. Maybe you could place an ad or something."

"We already have a nursemaid."

"For Flora. That's different, she's ours. That old woman–" He stopped short. "You need someone else for when more kids start getting here. Someone a little bit younger, maybe. Someone that likes kids. Someone that can keep up with 'em."

Mrs. Baker said nothing.

"We wouldn't have to pay them as much that way, if they were younger. That's one thing."

Mrs. Baker watched him. His eyes danced as he stared at her. He adjusted his position in the chair so that his knees touched. Mrs. Baker took her pen and began once more to write.

"I'll send a letter to my parents," she said. "Perhaps one of my sisters can come."

Baker nodded and stood.

"Whatever you think is best," he said as he left the room.

The disappointment in his voice was palpable.

Rev. Savage stood and smiled as Mrs. Lloyd entered his office. She had no appointment, but he did not mind, and he held out his hand for a shake. When he saw her face he drew back. She looked as if she were ready to spit on him, her lips bunched into an angry scowl.

"Mrs. Lloyd," he said, trying to remain cheerful. "What brings you in today?"

She stopped in front of him and crossed her large arms. In one of her gloved hands was a sheet of paper, and it made a crackling sound when she slapped it against her hip.

"Is everything all right?" Savage asked.

Mrs. Lloyd spoke in a voice so angry it was scarcely above a whisper.

"I can't believe you would do such a thing," she said.

"I beg your pardon?"

"The Children's Home Society isn't the only charity worthy of assistance, you know. There's room for more than one, especially where children are concerned."

"I agree. What's happened? Please, sit down."

Mrs. Lloyd continued on as if she had not heard.

"I was downtown this afternoon when I was approached by a woman representing a place called the Baker Orphanage. She wondered if I might make a donation. I told her I was sorry, but that I only contribute to the Children's Home Society."

"Yes, and we appreciate it."

"That was when she told me that you personally said to her that there was no need of both the Baker Orphanage and the Children's Home Society in this state."

Savage lowered his eyebrows so that two creases appeared behind his glasses at the bridge of his nose. His lips parted but no air escaped until he began to speak.

"I never said anything of the sort. Who told you this?"

"The woman from the orphanage. She was one of their representatives."

He closed his eyes and shook his head.

"But that's preposterous. I've never even heard of it. Do you know this woman's name?"

Mrs. Lloyd grew calm, and she frowned, suddenly guilty and embarrassed.

"I'm afraid I don't. I am sorry, Reverend, she got me so agitated I suppose I wasn't thinking clearly."

Savage waved his hand. "It's all right," he said and turned one of his chairs so Mrs. Lloyd could sit. "These things happen."

Mrs. Lloyd straightened her sleeve as she got into the chair. "All the same, I feel awful for the fuss I made."

"Never mind, never mind."

He moved another chair so it faced Mrs. Lloyd. After he had sat he leaned forward with both his hands pressed flat against each other.

"Do you think you might remember who she was later on?"

Mrs. Lloyd shook her head. "No. She talked a good line, but I think that was the one thing she didn't tell me."

"What did she tell you, then? Where was she from?"

"She said the orphanage is in Duluth, but that they want to expand."

Mrs. Lloyd handed him the paper she was holding. Savage adjusted his glasses and let his fingers stroke his goatee. At the top of the page was written in capital letters, "BAKER ORPHANAGE – LAKESIDE BRANCH." Below this was a description of the institution's aims, and at the bottom was a list of eighteen prominent women named as "being associated with the grand work." None of these women were from Duluth.

It was unseasonably warm for late October – near seventy – and the men's faces had turned red by the time they arrived at the house on London Road, and they stood under a large tree patting their foreheads and the backs of their necks with handkerchiefs. Detective Troyer shook his head, smirking.

"If it were summer we would be telling each other what a pleasant day it is," he said.

"But it is a pleasant day," Rev. Savage told him.

Troyer raised his eyebrows and began to fold the cloth.

"It won't be in a few minutes," he said.

Cooled off now, the pair mounted the steps of the porch. Troyer knocked on the door, which was soon opened by a young girl. She looked about sixteen. Dark-haired, she had full cheeks and a pretty smile.

"How may I help you gentlemen?" she said.

"We would like to speak with the Bakers," Troyer said as he and Savage removed their hats. "Are they home?"

"Whaddayou want?"

Baker's voice blasted out from the end of the hall like a bark from a large dog. He stomped toward the door like a pugilist, his hands curled into fists and his shoulders twisting left and right.

Troyer wore a quiet smile. "How are you today, Mr. Baker?"

The girl stepped away from the door as Baker approached. He stopped an inch before the threshold and shifted his eyes first to Troyer, then Savage.

"I said, what do you want."

"We've come to ask you some questions," Troyer said.

Baker's mustache rose in a lopsided smile as he snorted.

"This orphanage is a private business. It isn't open to any investigation."

"If you don't want the public to know your business, Mr. Baker, why do you solicit contributions from them?" Troyer said.

Baker crossed his arms and leaned back on his heels.

"You'd be a fool not to take money from any place you could find it."

"How many children are living here?"

The young woman who had opened the door poked her head from behind it and smiled at Troyer.

"We have five orphans right now," she said.

Nearly chuckling, the detective looked to Baker. "Is this true?"

"Yes," Baker said, maintaining his angry tone.

"Are they home?"

The girl began to speak once more, but Baker shushed her.

"Go and get some work done, Selina, and leave me to talk with these gentlemen."

The girl nodded and walked up the hallway, disappearing into one of the rooms. Baker eyed her until she was gone.

"Are they home?" Troyer repeated.

"What?" Baker asked, turning back to the men.

"Are they home? Are the children at home right now?"

"Some of them are here. Some of them are at school. Three or four, I don't know how many."

Rev. Savage took a step closer and gave Baker a friendly nod. "How long have they been staying here?"

"None of your business."

Baker shut the door before they could ask anything further. The men stood there a moment, then placed their hats back on their heads, and left the porch in silence. There was nothing to say.

It had been a good day. Essie Smith smiled as she counted her ten dollars and set it on the bed away from the rest of the money. Even after she had taken it out there still was more than thirty-five left. It was up so much from the twenty or so she had managed to bring in when she started. She sat for a bit, staring at it all.

Soon she took out her bag, inside of which was an old blouse rolled up like a towel, jammed in with her other things. The blouse bulged as she lifted it out and made a crackling sound when she placed it on the mattress. It was full. She had never seen so much money, and the pile grew each day. She placed her ten dollars on top and stared. It was all hers. She continued to smile. It made her feel safe somehow. Protected. But as big as her nest egg looked, it was miniscule compared to the amount she sent back to the orphanage each week. Her eyes drifted to Mrs. Baker's share. She still had to sort it and count it again, and exchange it for larger bills that she could send to Duluth. There was so much of it. She had not exchanged any of her own money yet. The more bills and coins there were, the richer she felt.

Slowly she reached out her hand and picked up one silver dollar from Mrs. Baker's pile. It was so new that she could see her reflection in it. She turned it in her palm three times, feeling its weight and its smooth finish. She closed her fingers around it and paused, thinking. Then, with a sigh, she dropped it back onto the bed and picked up her bundle.

She resolved to work harder. The bicycle would help her cover more ground. It was too late to use this year, but it was marked down for the holiday, just short of fifty dollars. It was more than Essie had ever spent on anything. It was Christmas Eve when she had it shipped in Joseph Baker's name to Duluth. They could hold it for her until spring.

Later on when Essie arrived back at the hotel from dinner, a letter from her mother was waiting. Essie smiled as she took it, and all but ran up the stairs to her room. Once inside, she sat on the edge of the bed, still in her winter clothes, and hooked her finger in the fold of the envelope.

The news was unsettling. It turned out that staying at the orphanage was not without cost. The first charge was for the care of Essie's baby. Two dollars a week. The same went for her mother, out of whose salary the fees were applied.

Essie read the words several times. After the fourth reading she returned the letter to the envelope and put it on her bedside table. Perhaps she had misunderstood Mrs. Baker's offer. And anyway, her mother was earning two dollars a week more than she had been.

Baker took a huge bite out of his toast, which he shoved into his mouth corner-first. He had placed his egg on top, and when he bit down the yolk spurted out in a geyser that covered his fingers. Mrs. Baker looked up from her paper and watched as he stuck each of them into his mouth one at a time and sucked until they were partway clean. When he had finished he rubbed his hand dry with his napkin. Throwing it on the table next to his plate, he looked at her and smiled.

"Good morning," he said.

Mrs. Baker opened her mouth to reply, but before she could another voice came from behind her.

"Good morning, Joseph."

It was Selina. She entered the dining room and paused to give Mrs. Baker a kiss on the cheek. Then she went to her chair. Like her sister, Selina was pretty, but her eyes lacked that sparkle that so defined Mrs. Baker's features. Although Selina's face had a seriousness to it that made her seem older than her sixteen years, she acted like a young girl. Most of her sentences were finished with a giggle, and instead of walking she often would run from place to place, including inside the house. She was buoyant and chirpy, but she always got her work done.

"You have a good sleep?" Baker asked.

"I did," Selina said as she set her napkin in her lap. "Did you?"

"Like a log," he said and laughed.

Selina joined in while Mrs. Baker continued to watch in silence from her end of the table. Clumps of egg yolk clung like snot to Baker's mustache, and they jiggled as he shook his head.

"Wipe your mouth," Mrs. Baker said.

Baker flashed a grin and did as she asked, and then she began to read the paper again.

"How did you sleep, Julia?" Selina asked.

She turned the page. "Not well."

"That's true," Baker said, looking to Selina. "I don't know how your sister manages to keep going for as little rest as she gets."

"It's always been like that, Mama says. Ever since she was a baby."

"Is that right, Julia?"

Mrs. Baker looked at the paper, clenching her jaw. In her hand she held a fork, the tines of which were pointed in the air as if she intended to stab somebody.

Baker laughed again. "Now, Julia, that's nothing to get upset about. If you don't sleep, you don't sleep. It's not worth getting worked up over."

He laughed some more. Selina joined in, but their enthusiasm weakened when Mrs. Baker refused to acknowledge them. Baker cleared his throat.

"Julia? You all right?"

Mrs. Baker dropped her fork on the plate with a loud clang and took the paper in both hands.

"Listen to this," she said and began to read. "'Nature's Breakfast Food is the purest and most nutritious on the market. On sale at all grocery stores in this city. A percentage of all profits paid to the Children's Home Society of Minnesota, Rev. E. P. Savage, superintendent. Our agents will call at your home to sell you sample packages.'"

"Sounds like a good idea," Baker said.

Mrs. Baker shot him a look and he got quiet.

"'Our concern has no connection with Baker Orphanage or any other *fake* concerns.'"

She had hardly finished the sentence before she threw the paper on the floor.

Baker shrugged. "It's not as bad as it could be."

The temperature hovered around zero most of the day, and Essie Smith's feet felt as if they had gone to sleep as she walked to the orphanage with her bag under her arm. The soles of her shoes seemed harder in the cold weather, and louder, too, when they touched the sidewalk. The air was like breathing fire through her nose, and even her lungs felt chilled.

Baker had a kind, solicitous look as he opened the door for her and took her things.

"My wife is out of town," he said as he led her to the fireplace. "She's always working."

"She's a remarkable woman."

Essie took off her gloves and held her hands before the fire.

"Could you please get my mother and my baby? I want to see them."

Baker nodded and set down Essie's bag.

"They're busy with something right now, but I can get them in a few minutes."

He came forward slowly as Essie continued to warm herself, rubbing her hands against her face and breathing through her mouth, puffing out her cheeks. Baker saw a glistening between her nose and upper lip and he smiled.

"Could you use a handkerchief?" he asked.

Embarrassed, she covered her mouth.

"I suppose I could."

Baker chuckled and pulled a white cloth from his pocket and handed it to her. He stood a bit too close, as if he was waiting for something, and she took a step away from him.

"Thank you," she said and gave a few hard blows. Wiping now, she said, "Mr. Baker, where are you storing my bicycle? I would like to see it."

"What bicycle?"

"Stop joshing me, I shipped my new bicycle to Duluth on Christmas Eve. I did it in your name, for Heaven's sake, with your permission."

"I'm afraid I don't know what you're talking about," he said and crossed his arms.

Essie raised her eyebrows.

"Do people send you bicycles so often that you can't keep track of them?"

"No. I'm saying I don't know what you mean."

He was no longer smiling.

Essie was not intimidated and spoke in a firm voice.

"Mr. Baker. I have the receipts in my bag. If this is your idea of a joke I don't think it's very funny. Now. On Christmas Eve I bought a bicycle. I sent it to Duluth – express – under your name. What's become of it? Are you telling me it's vanished?"

"Don't you accuse me of anything."

"I don't think I have to. If you didn't do something with it, what other explanation is there?"

Baker gave a breathy chuckle and began to shake his head, but Essie cut him off before he could say anything.

"I didn't want to bring this up, but why are you charging my mother and son to stay here?"

"That was the agreement."

"Pardon me, sir, but it wasn't. Your wife told me they could stay for free as long as I collected on her behalf."

"So you claim."

"It's the truth!"

"There's no way to prove that."

"Your wife told me–"

"And I told you she's not here."

"Where is she?"

"Out."

"Out where?"

"Out on business."

"When will she be back?"

"I can't say."

"You can't say, or you won't?"

"I can't. Because I don't know."

Essie stepped away from the fireplace and moved to the window. She had grown hot and she moved her elbows to keep her sleeves from sticking to her skin.

"Whenever she does come back, I've got a few questions I'd like to ask her."

"You won't have that chance."

Essie looked back at him. Baker spoke in a voice devoid of feeling.

"I'm going to go get your mother and your baby, and then I want you to leave this house."

"In this weather?"

"Leave this house," he repeated. "And don't come back."

The detectives arrived the next day with a warrant for Baker. There were two of them, Irwin and Mork, and they waited in the cold three whole minutes before Mrs. Baker finally opened the door.

"He isn't here," she said after she glanced at the paper.

"When will he be back?" Detective Irwin said.

"I don't know."

"Where is he?"

"Chicago. And I don't know when he'll return."

Detective Mork took a step forward and gave a wary smile.

"May we please come inside a moment?"

"No, you may not."

"I'm sorry, Mrs. Baker," Irwin said. "We got to make sure he's not in."

"It's not that we don't believe you," Mork said. "We just have to make a search is all."

Mrs. Baker stepped onto the porch and closed the door behind her.

"On whose authority do you intend to make this so-called search?"

"The city's, Mrs. Baker," Irwin said. "You're holdin' it right in your hand," he added, pointing at the warrant.

"You have no call to investigate us. This is a private business."

"We don't care about your business," Irwin said. "We're just here to find your husband."

"He's not here."

"Then you have no reason to worry," Mork said.

With a dark frown, she let them in. The house was clean and warm, and the children who were there seemed happy and well-fed. There were girls, too, whom the detectives saw looking after the babies, sweeping the floors, dusting the furniture. But there was no Baker. There was no bicycle. The detectives checked each room with Mrs. Baker following, her eyes filled with hate.

Not long before they were through with their search, Irwin slipped into the dining room, away from Detective Mork and

Mrs. Baker. Inside there was a young girl returning a clean set of dishes to a solid oak hutch. She smiled when she saw him, and stopped her work.

"Excuse me, Miss, but do you know how many children live here?" Irwin asked.

The girl closed her eyes and shook her head.

"I couldn't say, sir. I'm not sure."

She picked up a stack of plates from the table and placed it on the top shelf of the hutch.

"More than I would have figured," Irwin said. "It's a sad thing, so many orphans in one city."

The girl returned to the table for some drinking glasses.

"They're not all from Duluth," she said. "They're from all over the place."

"I see."

The girl shrugged as she began to put the glasses on the shelf, going back and forth to the table carrying two at one time.

"But they're not all orphans, either," she said.

"Excuse me?"

The girl stopped a moment and looked at him with a smile that made him feel ridiculous.

"Only two or three of them are orphans," she said with a shake of her head.

"Really," he said, more as a statement than a question.

"Sure," she said and picked up two more glasses.

"Then who are all the others?"

"I don't know. But I do know that they have parents."

"How's that?"

"They're payin' their board."

She said it as if it were the most obvious thing in the world.

"What do you mean?"

The girl sighed and looked at him from the hutch, a glass in one hand. She spoke slowly, inserting pauses every two or three words.

"The parents – pay us money – to take care – of their children."

"How much money?"

The girl put the glass on the shelf.

"As much as they're willing to pay, I guess. They don't all pay the same amount."

"What *do* they pay?"

"I wouldn't know anything about that. I'm just here to clean and help with the other chores. All I know is what they tell me, and Mr. Baker said we have to take both kinds – ones that pay and ones that don't. He said it was protection against the law, takin' a few of the ones that can't pay."

"Is that his primary aim? To take the ones that do?"

"Like I told you, I wouldn't know. I'm only here to clean. Why do you ask so many questions?"

Mrs. Baker spoke from the back of the room, causing both of them to jump.

"It's because Mr. Irwin is a detective, Selina. But I'm afraid you'll have to say goodbye to him. He's leaving now."

It was a month before Judge Tuley handed down his decision and ordered a receivership for the Zion Lace Industries for a bond of seven hundred thousand dollars. The case had been brought by Samuel Stevenson, Dowie's brother-in-law and lacemaker. Tuley said Stevenson had given Dowie all of his assets, and that Stevenson was owed one hundred thousand dollars, either from Dowie or the lace industries. When he heard the decision Dowie sat back in his chair in what the papers described as "a picture of woe." His wife covered her face, and some of the women in the gallery cried out. Dowie clenched his fists with impotent rage, then stood and stormed out of the courtroom.

Despite the terrible news, Zion City was beautiful, Baker thought, with buildings grander than the ones in Washington, D.C. There was Elijah Hospice, the elegant hotel that contained more than three hundred fifty rooms and a dining area with a seating capacity of four hundred. The lace factory was massive, covering four acres of land and employing hundreds of workers. There were general stores and a fresh food supply, and the Zion Printing and Publishing House. There was the administration building, two storeys of solid granite that contained the bank, the Land and Investment Association and the Bureau of Securities and Investments, along with Dowie's personal office.

Dowie greeted Baker at the door. He had on a smart dark suit, over the top of which flowed his long snow-white beard. Baker stepped in and was ushered to the desk. It was almost the size of an automobile, and its surface shined like still water. The walls of the room were lined with shelves stocked with large books and volumes of bound magazines. There were ornaments and crystal and a telephone. At the back of the room stood a large man who neither spoke nor moved, and next to him in the corner was a tall machine with a clock face, almost like a timecard puncher.

Dowie sat down at the desk and motioned for Baker to sit across from him. He looked tired, but dignified. He would rebound.

"It's been a long time," Dowie said.

"I wasn't sure you would remember a person like me. I'm nothing but a follower."

"Followers like you have enabled me to accomplish all that I have. Good people and the good Lord."

"I've continued to follow you, and your teachings."

"I thank you for it."

"You've been an inspiration to me and my wife."

Dowie smiled and nodded, folding his hands over his stomach.

"We're running a home for children in Minnesota. We speak against the consumption of alcohol, and about the power of divine healing."

"That is not always an easy road," Dowie said. "You will be attacked, I can assure you."

Baker nodded. "We have been." Then, clearing his throat, he added, "I was at the final hearing. I'm so sorry."

Dowie waved his hand. "We will triumph, wait and see."

"I know you will."

Dowie smiled again. Baker looked from him to the large man. He was watching Baker with dark eyes, and Baker dropped his gaze.

"That's Robert," Dowie said. "When one reaches a certain level of prominence and success it becomes necessary to keep such men as him on hand at all times."

Baker looked up again. "Even a man of God?"

"Divinity makes no impression on those who disagree with you."

Baker nodded. "We're finding that, my wife and I. People feel we should run our operation according to their own standards. But we will never waver in our beliefs."

Dowie thought a bit and then stood and walked to the machine in the corner. He pressed a button, and a buzzing sound was heard for a second or two, then a click. Dowie bent over and pulled out a small white card from a slot at the base of the machine and brought it back to the desk, where he handed it to Baker.

Baker looked at the card. One side was blank. The other bore a simple message: "You were prayed for at 1.24 P.M."

When Baker grew tired of watching the passing scenery he took Grettum's letter from his coat and looked at it again. He already knew what it said. He knew before he read it the first time. Return the bicycle and you will not be arrested. It was more than a month since that business had started. The steady click-clack of the rails went on beneath him as he folded the letter and returned it to its envelope. He looked around. The light was beginning to wane. He stood and moved to the end of the car, opened the door and stepped outside.

The cold air invigorated him and he opened his mouth and let his warm breath pour out like steam. He held the letter to his chest as he turned back to the car, peering in through the window, and broke into a smile when he noticed who had just entered. It was that detective. Troyer, or whatever his name was.

Baker shook his head in wonder. Continuing to smile, he loosened his grip on the letter, allowing the wind to catch it and take it spinning into the trees.

A porter came to the table where Troyer was sitting and gave him a cup of coffee. Troyer took out his pipe and lit it, then sat idly stroking his mustache as he puffed and read his paper. He did not look up when Baker reentered the car. Nobody did. Baker did nothing to hide his presence. He whistled three tuneless notes as he approached the table, then spoke as if he had come upon an old friend.

"Good evening, Detective."

Troyer looked up. There was a hint of surprise on his face, but his voice was firm.

"Chief," Troyer said.

"I beg your pardon?"

"I've been made chief of police since we last met, Mr. Baker."

"Reverend," he said mimicking Troyer.

Troyer raised an eyebrow.

"I've been named a Reverend by Doctor Dowie. So it looks like we're both rising in the world."

A curl of smoke snaked out the side of Troyer's mouth.

"I wouldn't say that."

Baker stopped smiling. "I understand you're looking for me."

"That's right. I suppose Mr. Grettum has informed you of your options."

"Yes."

Troyer took another puff and aimed the smoke toward Baker's head.

"I take it you'll come see us at the station in the morning."

"I'll be there. You don't have to worry about that."

Troyer smiled now himself. "I'm not worried." After a moment, he said, "You don't mind that I'm smoking, do you?"

"It doesn't matter what I mind. I don't make the rules on this train."

"I'm sure it's killing you." Troyer took the pipe from his mouth and wiped his lips. "Thank you for informing me of your plans. I look forward to putting an end to this tomorrow."

"Don't worry about it," Baker repeated as he left the car.

He did not come the next morning. Troyer waited until late in the afternoon to telephone the Baker house.

"Are you coming or are you not?" he asked.

Troyer thought he could almost hear the smirk on Baker's face when he answered.

"Can you give me another day?"

"No, you've had more than enough time."

"You'll have to send out after me, then," Baker said and hung up.

Detective Irving arrested Baker without incident at the orphanage later that day.

Chief Troyer pulled on his coat and glanced around his office to make sure he had not forgotten anything before he went home. He was preparing to turn out the lights when the telephone rang. With a sigh he went back to his desk, picked up the mouthpiece and held the receiver to his ear.

"Hello?"

"I want to speak to Chief Troyer," said a woman's voice.

"This is he. How may I help you?"

"My name is Mrs. M. H. Mueller, and I'm calling to tell you I think it's terrible what you're doing–"

"Slow down, please."

"–to Mr. Baker. I think it's shameful. Mr. Baker has done nothing but good for his fellow man, and you're treating him shamefully."

Troyer took a deep breath.

"The only reason Mr. Baker is in jail is because he refuses to return a bicycle he stole, ma'am. I wouldn't call that good."

"And what you're doing to the orphanage! What right have you to give out false information? I'm trying to help them right now, and nobody wants to contribute because of the awful things you've been saying."

"There is nothing false in anything that–"

"If I had my way you would be tarred and feathered!"

Troyer's stomach growled. He was tired, and he wanted to go home. He began to loosen his coat.

"Ma'am…"

"Shut up! You're not paying for this call! I can say anything I want!"

"Ma'am–"

"If I were your wife I'd get a divorce from you in twenty-four hours."

"If you were my wife I would certainly insist on your getting one!"

Troyer slammed the receiver down so hard that he broke the hook off the body of the telephone. He held the pieces in his hands, staring at them in impotent fury. Someone knocked on the door and he looked up to see Grettum standing there balancing a bicycle against his hip.

"Mr. Baker is ready to settle," Grettum said.

Troyer watched him in silence and continued to hold the broken telephone.

"Mr. Baker will pay whatever costs are required to have this case dismissed," Grettum said. "I also would like to point out the costs your department would accrue in bringing in witnesses if you chose to prosecute."

Troyer sighed. Grettum smiled.

"I shall tell him we have reached a deal. Good evening."

He left the bicycle at the front of Troyer's office. When he could no longer see Grettum he dropped the pieces of the telephone on his desk and sat for a long time rubbing his temples.

Even before a new telephone had been purchased for Troyer's office reports came in at a steady clip. Baker Orphanage had thirty solicitors traveling the state, collecting as much as two hundred dollars each day. They were in New Ulm, where two of them were arrested. They were in St. Paul and Minneapolis, in Hibbing and Virginia. There was a girl collecting in Springfield, and more in Red Wing. They were everywhere, and by the time Troyer was able to inform the local police departments of the orphanage's true nature, the girls would have moved on to the next town.

Ultimately he decided to make a circular and send it to the postmasters of every town in the state to warn off potential donors. It was requested of the postmasters that they place the information in as conspicuous a place as possible. It was all he could do.

The Bakers left Duluth at the beginning of April. They did not own the land on which the orphanage was housed, and when the Duluth Trust Company demanded the one hundred twenty-nine dollars it was owed for the past four months rent the Bakers found it was easier to leave than to pay. They went to Wisconsin. The Duluth newspapers celebrated.

More than a year later, in July 1903, a young woman came to the police station. Her eyes were red and swollen, with fat purple bags underneath. Chief Troyer ushered her into his office and closed the door. She sat a while wiping her nose and trying to keep her mouth shut. When she was able to breathe she told him she had given her daughter to the Bakers in February and had not heard anything from them since.

"I'm sorry, but they don't live here anymore," Troyer said. "They haven't for some time, as a matter of fact."

The woman nodded. Her face began to turn as red as her hair.

"I know. I went to the address they gave me. The neighbors told me all about it." A gurgle came from her throat. "I feel so stupid."

"Don't," Troyer said. "They've fooled a lot of people. That's what criminals do."

"It's my fault."

"No, it isn't. It's their fault."

The woman looked at him, her face as wet as if she had dunked it in the sink.

"Do you know where my little girl is?"

Troyer found it hard to look her in the eyes.

"The Bakers are in Wisconsin now."

"Do you think they still have her?"

"I know that when they left town they had five or six children with them."

"Who were they?"

"I'm sorry, I don't know their names."

"What about now? How many do they have now?"

"I don't know."

"Did they take them all to Wisconsin?"

Troyer's expression gave him away.

"Tell me," the woman said.

After a moment, Troyer answered, "I've been told by my contacts that when they started their new place, they only had three."

Troyer stood for the next few minutes with his hand on the woman's shoulder, silent, trying in vain to comfort her as she fractured.

You do what you can. If somebody breaks the law you arrest him, and if you can't do that you can at least try to let people know what's going on. You tell them, This is what you've got to be aware of, be careful of this, this and this. After that it's out of your hands. People are going to make their own choices, whether it's the right choice or not. And if they make the wrong one, you've still got to help them. That's what this job is all about. It makes it tough sometimes. Folks act like we spend all our time eyeing everyone, waiting for them to slip up somehow, like we're just trying to stir up trouble. But I can tell you, if we weren't out there putting a stop to some of the things that go on – believe me, we'd hear about it. You should be glad we're out there.

I never understood that. People don't like it when they see you collar somebody, but they never stop to think did the guy deserve it. They get mad at us, but what they're really doing is sticking up for some crook. You think about that.

Even if we do arrest somebody that sure doesn't mean that it's over for them. They can always break the law again. The judge could rule in their favor. They can buy their way out of trouble. They can go on to the next town. Or on to the next state.

Find themselves a whole new group of people to fleece. It happens all the time. But that doesn't mean we want it to. That's why we send out that information. People aren't going to know something's wrong unless you tell them. Trouble is, there's only so much we can do. People will always think what they want to think. Sometimes truth doesn't matter.

It was just after six when Esther Dowie rose. The house was receiving special visitors in the afternoon and she wanted to be ready. After she got up from her bed she stretched and rubbed her eyes. She used the chamber pot. Then she went to her dressing table, poured some water from the pitcher and splashed her face with it. The water was cold and it gave her goosebumps, and she patted herself dry with a towel. She eyed herself in the mirror. She was plump and healthy-looking, with good color in her cheeks. Her thick dark hair was wrapped close to her head, and as she looked at it she thought how long it would take to prepare. With a sigh she opened the drawer of the table and took out her curling iron, which she set on top. Then she brought up her oil lamp and placed it next to the iron. She removed the chimney and set it on the floor and unscrewed the burner from the fuel container. From the drawer she took a small funnel and the forbidden bottle of oil. She inserted the funnel into the container and poured oil into it. She poured in short spurts and picked up the lamp after each nip to gauge how full it had become. The room was too dark for her to be certain. When she thought it was three-quarters full she closed the bottle and put it in the drawer with the funnel. She took her time so the wick would absorb as much oil as possible. Before she shut the drawer she got her matches. She struck one and held it to the wick.

Esther's screams carried like alarm bells throughout the entire building. Hannah Wold, the maid, was the first to make it to the hallway and saw the glow over the transom above Esther's door. She ran to it and attempted to turn the knob, but it would not move.

"Esther!" Hannah shouted. "Unlock it, please!"

The lock clicked and the door fell open and Esther stood there, a column of flame that swerved right and left as she tried to tear off her nightgown. Esther ran past Hannah into the hall, continuing to fumble with the buttons. Inside the room Hannah saw the lamp, which rested on its side at the foot of the table, burning like a campfire.

"Put it out!" Esther shouted. "In the room, put out the fire!"

Miss Anderson, the seamstress, scrambled in from a nearby room and held out her arms, tugging the burning garments from Esther's body. Soon they were off, and Esther peeled away what remained of her stockings and ran shrieking to Miss Anderson's room. She jumped onto the bed and lay there writhing and begging for something to cover herself. Hannah and Miss Anderson put a sheet on her, and jumped when they heard the sizzle of a hissing cloud of steam from the hall, which came spewing up when Mrs. Callahan, the cook, poured water onto the still-burning clothes. Then Mrs. Callahan went to Esther's room and doused that fire, as well.

Dr. Speicher arrived at twenty minutes after six. It was said later that the first thing Esther told him was, "This is my own fault. I have disobeyed my father."

The doctor examined her. He noticed her eyebrows were gone. There were slight burns at the sides of her face, toward her ears. Her hands were poised at the top of the sheet, preventing it from resting all the way against her body. The skin of her fingers was raw and there was a small burn on her left wrist.

"I need to pull back the sheet," Speicher told her.

Esther nodded, and took a breath to steel herself.

The doctor lifted the sheet. It was bad. From her right hip to her shoulder, under her arm and around her back the skin was black and peeling. It was the same on her left breast and spots of her right, and her entire right leg. Her left leg was burned, too, but not quite as bad. Her feet were the worst, with the skin of the heels cooked through and hanging loose like tender roasts. Three-quarters of her body was burned. The room was filled with the stink of it.

Esther received no medicine. Instead Speicher and Miss Anderson dressed the wounds with cloths and Vaseline and prayed over her. Dowie and his wife arrived from Zion City at a quarter after nine. Dowie also prayed, and it was reported that Esther apologized again. Her pain subsided as the day dragged on and the greased dressings continued to be applied. By one o'clock Esther's wounds were numb, although she felt awful tearing sensations in her stomach and chest. In half an hour her limbs went cold and her body shook with violent racking coughs. A bowl was brought to her face and she spat out a substance like unset black gelatin. Her vomit was black, too. Everyone continued to pray.

Near six-thirty another doctor was called, and he looked her over and said nothing could be done. She was again refused drugs. She declined further. Her breathing grew heavier, and she shivered like a frightened animal. At last she slipped into unconsciousness. She was gone ten minutes later.

It was nine o'clock at night.

Esther's casket was white and silver, and it lay for several hours in the hall of the general overseer's suite on the second floor of Zion Hospice No. 1. Late in the morning the casket was brought out and taken up Shiloh Boulevard to Elijah Avenue, with the Zion City residents following in silence as it reached Lake Mound Cemetery near Twenty-ninth Street. Nothing but footsteps could be heard as they entered, and then gathered around the gravesite, which was presided over by Dowie. His wife Jane was there, as well, and their son Gladstone.

"My beloved friends, I could not give this sacred task to another," Dowie said when everyone had settled. "How hard it is to keep my bitter tears from falling, God knows. It has seemed so many times these last two days as if this heart must break and I must go with her, who had twined herself about my heart, from infancy up through the lovely, sweet Christian maidenhood that had just passed into womanhood. Oh, I could not give the task to another, and therefore I came to do it myself. God help me to finish it."

"Amen," the people said.

"Your love is very precious to me, my sweet wife and son. What we would do without it, in this crisis, seems almost impossible to tell. Life would not seem worth living, but for life that I may yet live for you, beloved, and for those to whom I minister throughout the world, and for the fulfillment of the mission which God gave to me.

"I will not enter upon the details of the heart-rending incident which plunged my dear daughter from the midst of life to death. I will say this, however, that the message she sent to her dear brother, my manly son, who has been such a comfort to us, is the message that I will give you all. She said, 'Give Gladstone my love. Tell him to love God and serve Him always, and to obey those who have rule over him in the Lord.'"

As he said the words, Dowie looked at his son, who held his mother's hand and faced forward with hard eyes.

"Amen," the people said.

"That was her message," Dowie said before he turned back to the assembly. "When I saw her, after the deadly and horrible burns, the first word she said to me was, 'Papa, before you pray – I sinned in disobeying you. It is all my own fault. Forgive me before you pray.'

"I said, 'Have you asked God?'

"'Yes,' she said, 'and I know he has forgiven me. I have it in my spirit.'

"'Oh,' I said. 'You know Papa would do it before you asked him, almost, but I am glad to say, 'Yes.'

"And I kissed the lips within which the fire had entered. That was the dreadful thing. It had entered into her breast, and we did not know at first. But, oh, we had a most precious twelve hours! The pain was all taken away, thank God!"

"Amen."

"My own daughter was beloved as none can tell, for she was a part of my life. It will be so dark without her. I do not know sometimes how to live. But I must live for you, and for God, and for His work, and I am no coward. I desire to tell you, then, what I have told you often in Zion City, that we are now come to live on God's ground, and He will not suffer us to disobey. Not my wife, my son, my daughter, myself, nor anyone else. The time has come to obey God. I say to you as God's prophet, foretold by Moses, that if you will not obey the word of God, all there is left for you is that you will perish, for the time has come for a holy people in a holy city. God grant it."

"Amen."

"As you can see, it is a very worthy cause, Mister...?"

"Turner. Alexander Turner."

Mrs. Baker smiled and nodded. "Mr. Turner, of course. It's an important cause, and we need lots of help in making sure the little ones stay clothed and fed."

"I suppose you would," Turner said and scratched his chin. He shoved his hand into his hip pocket and brought out some coins. Mrs. Baker continued to smile as he counted them. When he was through he held out his fist, and she put her open palm beneath it.

"Here," he said as he dropped the money. "Twenty-five cents. I'm sorry it's not more, but it's all I have with me."

Mrs. Baker handed him a flyer and put the change in her bag.

"There's no need to apologize," she said. "You've done so much for us, Mr. Turner. Thank you, and God bless you."

Wisconsin was a nice place, she thought as she watched him. Especially Alma, where she grew up, with the river, and its green fields and rolling hills, so much like the old country, her parents said. It was why they had stopped there. And there was Hudson, too, which had people like Mr. Turner, who were always ready to help the needy. But it was not always that way anymore, thanks to Troyer and his poisonous words.

Before she closed her bag Mrs. Baker drew out her watch. It was early yet. The hearing was not scheduled to begin until after lunch. Mrs. Freel and Mrs. Murphy were waiting for her in jail. They had collected twenty-nine dollars under false pretenses, the authorities said. She put her watch back in its place and took a deep breath. The work was difficult enough without this ridiculous interference.

Mrs. Baker went to the nearest building and braced herself against it. The baby had been stirring all morning, and she clenched her stomach muscles in the hope that it might stop the movements, if only for a little while. It had been like this the entire day, and she knew it would be at least three more months until it was born. She gritted her teeth.

Both women were waiting at Judge Arnquist's courtroom when Mrs. Baker arrived. Their faces were red, as if they had been crying, and when they saw her they did not seem relieved. Mrs. Baker took a seat and waited for the hearing to begin. The women made motions with their hands and flapped their lips at her, but Mrs. Baker could not understand what they were trying to say.

The sound of heavy shoes came up the aisle, stopping when they reached Mrs. Baker's side. She looked at them. They shined like mirrors, and she lifted her head to see a cleaned and pressed policeman's uniform. The man wearing it had fair skin and hair so blond it was almost white.

"Are you Mrs. Julia Baker?" he asked.

She thought before replying.

"I am."

"You're under arrest, ma'am," he said and reached for her hand.

Mrs. Baker did not move to give it to him, and raised her voice almost to shout.

"On whose authority?"

The officer was taken aback, and flinched as if he thought she might bite him.

"The city of Hudson," he said.

"And the charge, may I ask?"

The man seemed to regain his confidence, and reached for her again.

"Getting money under false pretenses."

"Ridiculous."

"Like it or not, that's the charge."

He took her by the wrist and raised her arm. With an exasperated sigh she stood and allowed him to lead her down the aisle.

"Who filed this charge, so-called?"

"Man named Turner. Alex Turner."

Mrs. Baker stopped moving, but the officer kept on and gave her arm a tug so that she came stumbling after him.

"I only just saw him this morning."

"I guess he heard about you since then," the officer said and pulled her out of the courtroom.

Mrs. Baker's father came up from Alma before the day was over and paid the bonds to get all three women released. Two hundred dollars each. During the hearing it was said each of Mrs. Baker's solicitors collected an average of ten dollars a day so that three babies could be cared for at the rate of seventy dollars apiece, each day. It was a lie, of course. Mrs. Freel was asked if she was the secretary of the orphanage, since that was what it said on the official stationery. "I may have been secretary, but I wouldn't know it," she said. Mrs. Baker was furious. Her own sister. It was beyond belief.

The baby came in August. It was a boy. He was named for his father, who was around less all the time. When he was home he never touched her. Mrs. Baker stood over her son and watched as he slept. He had full cheeks and thin blond hair that grew straight up from his scalp like stalks of wheat. He lay on his back wrapped in a blanket, lips moving as if he were whispering. He did not look like her, she thought. Or his father. His features were too fair, too soft. Yes, that still could change, and probably would. People might say he was cute. They would like him. She began to count dollar figures in her palm, scratching them with her thumbnail and moving her lips along with the baby's. She added them several times and stared and thought and tapped her finger with impatience on the bassinette. The baby gave his head a tiny jerk and blinked his squinty eyes. Mrs. Baker froze and watched him. He began to gurgle and fuss. He sounded like an animal, she thought as she watched him squirm. In a few seconds his skin turned red and he scrunched up his face and opened his mouth like an enormous gasping fish. No tears came, or sound, and his mother watched close as his lips parted farther and exposed his pink toothless gums. Then it began. His crying sounded like a stick being dragged across a piece of vinyl, squeaky and grating. Mrs. Baker stepped into the hall.

"Selina, see to the baby!"

Then she went downstairs to her office.

Mrs. Baker attended her trial in mourning clothes. It was April 1903, and the prosecutors said that after only three years in business she had accumulated more than twenty thousand dollars. When the guilty verdict was read, she wept and wailed for help from God. The judge gave her the choice of paying a three hundred dollar fine or doing six months' hard labor in jail, both of which she felt were outrageous punishments for the wrongful receipt of twenty-five cents. She called for a new trial. She was denied. She petitioned the state Supreme Court. While waiting for their decision she went to Iowa. She acquired new orphans. She recruited new solicitors. She raised more money. She saw little of her husband, saw little of her children. In December the court overturned her conviction because the trial judge had allowed evidence showing, the newspapers said, that "she was not of the best character, was a liar and a bad housekeeper." By that time she was already settled in Joplin, Missouri.

That same year the Hutchinson News of Hutchinson, Kansas, printed a letter about Mrs. Baker that was written to someone inquiring about her activities. "Dear Madam – You are just right. There is something very wrong with that Mrs. Baker. Arrest her and keep her behind the bars. But keep her in Kansas, because nobody wants to see her here. She has been tried and found guilty of collecting money on false pretenses several times but always has cash enough to pay her way out. Then she goes to another state and carries on the same work. There is a tumble-down old frame house way back on the hill of this town where a certain Baker, with strange women, lives. It is called the orphan's home, but any one would be more appropriate than that. To her can well be applied Matthew 7:10, 'For the hearts and homes she has made sad are legion.'"

Dowie arrived in New York City midway through October on his private railroad car accompanied by his wife and son, and the members of his staff. They were trailed by as many of his followers as could be packed onto the nine other trains leaving Chicago through the rest of the day. Dowie had been promoting the trip the past few weeks. Using Madison Square Garden as their base of operation, all three to five thousand of them would gather for the morning meal and then disperse to numerous points of the city to hold street meetings and demonstrations, and also visit people in their homes. Dowie would remain at the Garden during this time to host meetings used to spread the teachings of divine healing and tend to the ill and the injured. The followers would receive dinner at five, following which time the evening meeting would be held. By the end of their stay, Dowie promised, not one house in all New York would have missed the message.

Fourteen thousand people came to the first service, which was held on a Sunday afternoon. It began with a procession of all six hundred members of the Zion choir entering bedecked in their beautiful white robes, followed by the officers of the church, looking regal in their finery. Everyone ascended a platform, with the choir assembling behind the pulpit and the officers on both sides.

Dowie was the last to take his place. He looked magnificent in his robes of white and black as he gave the invocation and recited the creed, and then the commandments. Soon after he began to discuss disease as being the result of sin a man in the crowd raised his voice.

"What about animals?"

Dowie paused mid-sentence and squinted into the blurred mass of faces.

"What was that?"

"Animals, sir!" the man called. "Is it sin that makes *them* ill, as well?"

"You wish to know the difference?" Dowie said. "Men have got humanity. Humanity is staggering today under an awful weight. Doctors have got on the back of humanity and taken it by the throat. Doctors tie humanity down and try to inoculate it. They inoculate you against smallpox. They inoculate you against smallpox by putting the pox inside you, and you will not know where you are if you let these fellows get you by the throat."

"Inoculations don't give you the disease itself, no matter how it may look!"

Dowie stepped off the platform, nodding his head.

"There's one person who would like to make mischief," he said. "The police want me to hand him over to them. But you'll have to behave yourself if you want to stay here, even if you are a person and not an animal. I know who you are, you miserable one-eyed Judas, and I'll spank you properly."

Dowie abruptly returned to the pulpit.

"How glad we ought to be that we have an infinitely patient God," he said.

"But, sir, inoculations—"

"Shut up!" Dowie shouted, stepping down again. "Inoculation is not the only cause of disease. There are also people, such as when a woman with a thirty-eight-inch waist attempts to squeeze into a twenty-eight-inch corset. She may then be wasplike, but she is not a honeybee, and I wish to stay clear of her."

He pulled the front of his robe tight across his stomach and pranced back and forth across the stage.

"I may not be beautiful with my flat stomach. I may look like a bale of cotton with the hoop off, as a cartoonist has portrayed me. Anyway, my wife thinks I am good-looking and my people are kind to me."

The Zionists applauded a full minute as Dowie returned to the lectern and took up his Bible.

"The gates of healing are as much open today as they were nineteen centuries ago in the time of Christ," Dowie said when the applause had ceased. "Today you will hear testimony proving as much. Through prayer remarkable results are achieved, even from hundreds of miles away."

"Sir!"

Dowie remained still, breathing hard, and stared at the text. Then he dropped the book and stepped down again, pointing in the direction of the voice.

"What do you know of the Lord's ordinances?" he shouted. "How many in this audience have given the tithes of that which God has given them? A pack of thieves, the lot of you. Let all who are giving their tithes now rise to their feet."

The final word was not finished when the people of Zion rose en masse.

"Good, for I wouldn't have come to New York with a single thief. But now you see who *are* the thieves."

The Zionists sat as one and Dowie gave a proud smile. Then, suddenly, the sound of wood clapping against wood was heard, slow at first, then faster and faster until it stopped altogether. Dowie looked in the direction from which it came and frowned at what he saw. A man had left his chair and now was headed toward the exit.

"Stop right there!" Dowie called. "The police authorities will sustain me if I hand you over to them. We pay tithes, and that's why these four thousand friends and myself are willing to spend a quarter of a million dollars to come down to New York and get your impudence. By and by we'll go down to your hearts, and then we'll get at your pocketbooks.

"'Oh!' they said. 'He's come down to New York after our money!' Well, I don't deny the soft impeachment. Do you think I can get money, though, out of you stinkpots?"

Several members of the audience began to hiss, at which point Dowie motioned for the choir to begin singing. As the music continued, another loud clap was heard, this one from a different part of the audience than the first. It was followed by another. Then another. Dowie gave his arm a violent shake and the choir fell silent.

"If this is New York and this is a typical New York congregation, I am in the face of a new experience. I think some of the people who came in today must have thought that this was a Buffalo Bill show. I wonder if the congregations of the churches here enter and leave as they please." He forced a laugh. "I reckon we have learned something and will be prepared hereafter."

More clapping came, from so many places in the audience it could not easily be determined how many people were leaving.

"There will be no more going out of the front door," Dowie said, raising his voice in desperation above the racket. "If any remained outside let them in. It seems a shame they should not have the seats the Buffalo Bill persons have left."

By this point the upswinging chairs sounded like a violent hailstorm.

"You're a pack of thieves, the lot of you!" Dowie shouted. "You are slaves of the bottle, slaves to tobacco! Stinkpots! You're nothing but a noisy rabble, and I don't want your money, you thieves! If this noisy rabble continues this sort of thing, I'll issue tickets to people who want to stay. I'll get a quiet meeting if I have to keep you here all night! You can't get ahead of me, you slaves of the bottle! Your principal statesmen and politicians of this city are all sots, and these dirty sheets call upon the rabble. You all lie, you dirty birds! I'll give it to you! I'll clean the whole of you liars out!"

He watched the main entrance in vain, waiting for a new throng to come pouring forth. After a few moments passed, he let out a defeated sigh.

"Well, let us keep the quiet audience we have," he said.

George M. Shelley was one of the big men of Kansas City. Born in 1850 in Kentucky, he moved to Iowa with his parents and spent much of his childhood there. After he graduated high school he went to business college in Chicago, and later attended Princeton. He arrived in Kansas City in 1870, where he went into the wholesale dry goods business. He married two years later and with his wife had one son, James. He soon entered politics, and was elected mayor of Kansas City in 1878, the youngest man to hold the office up to that time. On completing his first one-year term, he was re-elected the next year. In his later life the *Kansas City Star* remembered him as "a fighting Democrat," the first mayor to lay out a park in the city, who established the first mayor's Christmas tree there and founded the first exclusive dry goods wholesale firm in the city. He pushed the development of the city, the paving of the roads. When he found the sewer system to be inadequate, he took the city council to inspect it firsthand. "Donning sou'westers and rubber coats, the party, headed by the mayor, entered a sewer at Third and Walnut streets and crawled on hands and knees to Tenth and Walnut streets. Mr. Shelley's recommendations were enacted," *The Star* reported. In 1884 Shelley was appointed police commissioner for a term that ended three years later. He then became Kansas City's postmaster, a job from which he was removed by President Cleveland in 1888. This move was later reported to have been connected with emergency expenses when the post office changed locations. In 1895 Shelley was again named a police commissioner, and later that year was named chairman of the Democratic Committee of Jackson County. It was later suggested Shelley retired as police commissioner over his dealings with professional gamblers. In 1901 Shelley was elected president of the Upper House of the Common Council and Board of Public Works. By late 1903 there was talk of his running for mayor again, and he made his candidacy official the next February. He was not the only Democrat on the ticket, however. William T. Kemper also sought the city's highest office, and two Democratic conventions – one for each candidate – were scheduled for the same day in halls three blocks apart on Twelfth Street.

M. J. Crowe was built more like a wall than a man, very tall with huge arms and legs in perfect proportion to his gigantic frame. This was one of the primary reasons he was chosen as sergeant-at-arms of the Kemper convention. Around noon the proceedings broke, and Crowe and some friends made their way outside to the front of Turner Hall. It had been cramped and loud and hot, despite being only midway through March, and the air in the street was refreshing. Without discussing it the men began to move toward the site of the Shelley convention. As they approached a man called from up the block.

"Crowe!"

He looked in the direction of the voice and saw a small gang of men headed his way with clenched fists and angry faces.

"The hell is that?" somebody asked.

"It's just Welch," Crowe said. "He's my friend."

"You know him?"

"Sure."

"You oughta knock his head off his shoulders."

"Better not. He's a deputy marshall."

Cassimer Welch stopped a few feet from Crowe, looking ready to spit in his eye. His cheeks were cherry red and his head jittered back and forth as if he were dizzy.

"Nice day, ain't it?" Crowe said.

"What the hell is wrong with you people?" Welch said.

"Dunno what you mean."

"What're you tryna do to us?"

"Just gettin' some sunshine."

"We've won the nomination, you sons of bitches, and you know it."

Crowe never stopped smiling.

"That isn't what the numbers say."

"Because your goddamned clerks won't sign the returns! Shelley's got two hundred more votes than Kemper, and you know it. If they're not counted he won't get on the ballot. Now make them sign the returns and let's be done with this."

"Dunno what you're talkin' about."

"I'm asking you to be fair, that's all. Just do what's right."

Welch muttered something under his breath and Crowe's smile fell, although he did not look angry.

"I am doin' what's right, you sawed-off little prick."

"If you were fair you'd have made them sign those returns."

Crowe shrugged.

Welch shook his head and gave a sickening smile.

"Why do you have to do this? Your wife's snatch all dried up? Is causin' problems the only way you can get excited anymore?"

Immediately Crowe punched Welch in the face, making him stumble on his heels. At once the two groups of men were on each other reigning down blows. Welch fell against a wall and before he could stand upright Crowe grabbed him and put him in a headlock while he served vicious jabs to Welch's kidneys. Soon he let go of Welch, who fell to the ground. Turning toward the others Crowe raised his arms and began to shout.

"All right, you men, break it up! It's done!"

A shot rang out and a window shattered. Crowe looked back to see Welch balanced on his elbow with a revolver in his hand. He fired twice more, hitting Crowe first in the left heel, then in the side. Crowe fell and looked with amazement at his wounds, which poured out blood like open faucets onto the sidewalk. Grunting, straining, he stood and hobbled into Cramer and Bell's Saloon, where he went to the bar and steadied himself against the rail.

"You all right?" the saloon-keeper asked.

"He shot me!" Crowe said. "The son of a bitch shot me!"

Crowe recovered from his wounds, but Shelley lost his bid for mayor. Instead he was named to the board of public works. Remembering him years later, a relative said, "He was a typical politician."

Joplin was a bust. Kansas City was a better location, anyhow, being near the state border and having access to a larger railroad line. It was so convenient that it could enable the home to exist without receiving donations from the people of Kansas City itself. Any resident who said they had been taken advantage of would have no case.

Mrs. Baker changed the name along with the location. The Joseph Walter Home. It fit. It was a bad idea to include her own name in the title, and it was not a proper orphanage, so it seemed right to her.

The house was better than the one in Joplin, too, large and white with a long open porch and no fewer than three chimneys. The front door opened onto a large hall and staircase. On the left side of the hall were the parlors, followed by the dining room and kitchen. On the right was a washroom and another empty room that could be used for play. The second floor had several more empty rooms and the third was a big open space which Mrs. Baker planned to use as the boys dormitory. The gas fixtures had a shining newness to them, and the wood of the floors was polished and smooth. Mrs. Baker would not live here, but rather a few blocks away on Askew Avenue in a place not quite so large. There was still plenty of room for her and the children. It was just the three of them now.

The house on Cleveland was dense with August humidity when Mrs. Baker entered. She left the front door open and set about quietly to raise every window in the building and remove the stale odor. After she had been working more than an hour Mrs. Baker stood at the top of the stairs with her hand on the rail and closed her eyes. She inhaled until her nose was filled with dust.

A sound like five hands knocking came at the front entrance, and Mrs. Baker opened her eyes to see the nurse standing there with Flora at her side in a blue dress and Joseph wandering about the parlor like an untethered dog. He had on a white shirt and black knicker pants, and while there was a clean part in his blond hair a fat cowlick stuck up in the back.

"What are you doing here?"

Starting, the nurse looked up and smiled.

"Excuse me, I didn't see you."

"I asked what you were doing here."

"It's time for the children's walk, and I thought we would come see how you're doing."

Mrs. Baker leaned over the banister and stared at her son. He had stopped walking and was violently turning his head back and forth, searching for her and whining. He was almost four and still he acted like a baby.

"I wish you hadn't," Mrs. Baker said. "I don't want them here. This is no place for them."

She continued to watch Joseph, who had spotted her and stretched out his arms as if she could reach down and pick him up from where she stood.

"Mama!"

Mrs. Baker looked back to the nurse.

"Now look what you've done."

Joseph waddled to the foot of the stairs and hoisted his leg to mount the first one. Mrs. Baker did not leave her spot. The boy began a slow climb using his hands and knees, making determined grunts as he moved along.

"I don't have time to fool with you now," Mrs. Baker said, sighing before she went into one of the nearby rooms.

Joseph heard her and lifted his head in time to watch her leave. Immediately his face darkened and he began to cry and shout for her, and when she did not return he rolled onto his back on the stairs and closed his eyes and let out a long loud scream. The nurse watched and cooed, telling him to be a little man, but her voice was as inaudible as a whisper under his continued raging.

Soon Flora left the nurse's side and went to her brother. She leaned over and touched his knee, rubbing and patting it. Joseph's cries subsided and he blinked his red eyes. He looked at her, continuing to gurgle, and sniffed. Without saying anything, Flora took his hand and he stood and walked with her out the front door, the nurse trailing five feet behind.

Mrs. Russell wrapped her scarf around her neck and pulled on her gloves before she said goodbye to the children. All four of them clustered around her, fidgeting. The older ones' faces betrayed no sadness, but Katie was only six, and she cried as if she had burned herself.

"I'm so sorry," Mrs. Russell said and wiped Katie's face. "You have to be brave. So will I. I don't like leavin' you here, either, you know. But you'll have Irene and the boys here with you to keep you safe."

"That's right," Mrs. Baker said from her place in the hall. "And there are lots of other boys and girls here. You'll make so many friends it will be like you have a dozen new brothers and sisters."

The girl looked only at her mother. She had stopped crying, but her face was dripping and she breathed like she had the hiccups.

"I'll be back," Mrs. Russell said. "I'll write you from the hotel, too, and I'll save up as much money as I can so we can all be together again. And I'll visit you whenever I can, too. Would you like that?"

Katie nodded. She was calmer now and she wiped her face on her sleeve. Mrs. Russell smiled and looked at her other children, who all remained outwardly calm, and then took each in turn by the cheeks and planted a kiss upon their foreheads. Then she placed her hands on the shoulders of Eddie, who was the oldest.

"Look after them, now," she said.

He nodded.

"That goes for all of you," Mrs. Russell said. "You all need to help each other as much as you can."

They said they would, and after another goodbye she left. The children waited for a moment and stared at the door in case she should rush back inside and beg them to join her. From another room they heard the chattering of little voices, and bursts of wind against the walls of the house, and they felt totally alone.

Steady footsteps came from behind and they turned to see Mrs. Baker moving toward them. She smiled and clasped her hands at the front of her waist.

"I'm sure you'll like it here," she said as she came to a stop. "Now, why don't you tell me again what your names are, and your ages, too."

"I'm Eddie. I'm thirteen."

"I'm Earl. I'm twelve."

"And who are you?"

"Irene. I'm nine."

Mrs. Baker looked to the youngest.

"I know who you are," she said. "You're Katie. And how old are you, darling?"

"Six."

Mrs. Baker ran her fingers over the girl's sandy hair.

"Well, I'm Mrs. Baker, and you'll be seeing a lot of me while you're here."

The children stood there, unsure of what to say. At last Earl looked to a spot near the door, where their things had been piled.

"Would you like us to unpack?"

"Not tonight," Mrs. Baker said, continuing to smile. "It's getting late, and you'll all be in bed pretty soon. You've eaten your supper, haven't you?"

They all nodded, and some answered, "Yes, ma'am."

"That's fine. Well, now. The other children will be getting ready for bed soon, so I suppose you had better join them. Come with me."

When Earl awoke it was still night. His brother lay sleeping in the bed next to him, and the room was filled with the sounds of breathing. Earl sighed and watched the ghostly white rectangle of light on the floor where the moon shone through the window. He was not tired. His stomach felt odd and fluttery and his scalp tickled as if he had used an anthill for a pillow. The sensation was maddening. Lifting his head Earl rubbed his hair until the feeling ebbed. It returned soon after he had relaxed again.

He sat up all the way and waited for a long while and agonized over that awful feeling, which was like the points of a hundred clipped fingernails being dragged over his skin. He put up his hands and took a few strands of hair in his fingers, pulling them straight until it felt like he had drawn something out. The object was tiny and smooth, like a bead, but it was also soft. He held out his hand and looked at the thing with curiosity. In the darkness he could not see much, but as his eyes became better adjusted he made out what looked like the glinting of tiny wings. He frowned and crushed the insect between his finger and thumb. He felt a slight crunch, and a squirt of grease against his skin. Then he wiped his hand on the blanket and lay back down.

The Joseph Walter Home children formed a line outside the kitchen, where they waited for breakfast. They kept as still as possible, none of them shoving to get a better place. They were quiet, too, and stood there without even whispering. At the rear of the line next to his brother and sisters Earl watched the other children. They were unclean, with greasy hair and a film of dirt and oil on their skin, and they wore clothes that looked as if they had never been changed. Despite the lateness of the year, only about half of them wore shoes.

 The kitchen door opened and the children froze. Two girls scarcely older than the inmates of the Home emerged, one of them carrying a tray piled with tin cups, the other with a bucket. As they walked up the line each child took a cup, all of which were filled with milk, and took a hunk of bread from the bucket. When the food was gone the girls worked their way back to the kitchen, collecting the empty cups as they went.

After they were gone the kitchen door stayed open, and the children could hear the sounds of silverware clinking against dishes, and muffled conversations among adults. And the smell. There was food in the kitchen – real food. Bacon and eggs. The children stayed where they were and inhaled what they could. Earl closed his eyes and thought of his mother, and of how much he hated his father. He had been gone four years now, and Earl's hatred of him never waned. He left their mother, left all of them, even though he had not died. He just left. Earl doubted Katie remembered him. If Irene remembered, she never mentioned him. Eddie was different. He never let Earl say what he thought, almost as if he maintained a hope that one day their father would return. It was a stupid idea.

After a few minutes a woman came out of the kitchen. She was old, with a stern face and white hair that looked even brighter because of the black dress she wore. At the tip of her pointed nose rested a pair of glasses with gold rims. When she looked through them she lowered her eyelids and raised her brows, which gave the impression that everything she saw was worthy of contempt. She walked slowly, looking all of the children in the face. She said nothing until she came to the four Russells at the end of the line.

"Everyone but you four go upstairs to your rooms. Wait there for further instructions."

The others filed past, quick and quiet down the hall until they reached the stairs. If they spoke as they climbed they were not heard.

The woman spoke again when the footfalls had ceased.

"I'm Mrs. Shaw. I'm the head matron here."

Her voice was deep but sharp, as if she were trying to suppress the urge to shout.

"You do what you're told and you'll be happy here. You all mind well, don't you?"

They nodded.

"That's good."

Katie lifted her hand, fingers out, until it was even with her cheek.

"She raised her hand," Mrs. Shaw said. "This girl knows how to behave. Yes, what is it?"

"Where is Mrs. Baker?" she asked in a small voice.

"She's at her own house. You won't be seeing much of her. She's always off talking to people, making sure we can keep taking care of you all."

Watching her, Earl saw a black crumb, either bacon or toast, at the corner of her mouth. It looked like dirt or a coffee ground.

"Mrs. Baker has the most important job of all," Mrs. Shaw said. "If she wasn't working every day traveling the country, you just think of where you would be. It should frighten you. You would go to an orphanage, get split up, maybe never see your mother again. It's not a happy thought, is it? When Mrs. Baker does come back I want you to thank her. I want you to tell her you love her. Tell her how happy you are to be here."

Earl stared at the crumb as she went on, and thought of how good it must taste. His stomach gurgled, and Mrs. Shaw pointed at him.

"If you're hungry now, young man, think of how hungry you would be without us. You just think of it."

As she closed her mouth she caught a taste, and shielded her face with her hand as she licked off the crumb. Clean once again, she straightened her back and addressed the two girls.

"Do you know anything about sewing?"

Irene nodded. "I do. A little."

"What about you?"

Katie shook her head and moved closer to her sister.

"That's fine. We'll teach you here. That's what you'll learn when you're not in school. You'll need to know so you can stitch the clothes when they get torn. We need to make them last. You boys won't be doing that, you'll be helping around the house. Then when summer comes, you'll all be working all the time. There is plenty to do, just wait and see."

"Will we still be here in the summer?" Katie whispered to Irene.

"Young lady, don't ever interrupt me," Mrs. Shaw said. "And I thought you were a good girl. Give me your hand."

Cautiously she held out her right hand, as if to shake. Mrs. Shaw grabbed her by the wrist and gave her a hard pinch on the tender skin between her elbow and shoulder until she yelped out in pain.

"That should teach you to mind," Mrs. Shaw said. "Don't speak unless I address you. That welt on your arm should help you to remember."

Katie grasped her sleeve and buried her face in Irene's shoulder. The others stood quiet, unsure of what to do.

"Be good, children, and always do what I tell you. Go upstairs now."

Mrs. Baker drank the last of her milk and set the glass near her empty plate. She looked across the table. The children were nearby, Flora chewing on a crust of toast and Joseph getting his mouth wiped by the nurse. Mrs. Baker's sister Marie was there, too, and so was Marie's husband, Leslie LeWald. Although she was more than ten years younger than her sister, Marie looked about the same age. She was like a drab version of Mrs. Baker. They had similar hair, similar skin, but Marie's features were less vivid. LeWald was about six feet tall, with the well-proportioned build of a laborer, and had light hair and clean hands with long fingers.

"What do you plan to do?" Mrs. Baker asked.

LeWald glanced her way and then swallowed what he was chewing before he looked at her more fully.

"I'll be working in a leather shop. I start first thing next week."

"That's wonderful," Marie said. "Isn't it, Julia?"

"Didn't you know?" Mrs. Baker asked her.

"I did, but I'm still very excited about it."

Mrs. Baker nodded. "I didn't know you had a hand for leatherwork," she told LeWald.

He grinned. "Yes, I have a few years experience."

"Is that what you did at the prison? Apart from your sentence, I mean."

LeWald's expression was frozen in the same good-natured smile, although it did grow a bit tighter.

"Yes, I did work in their shop, that is true. But I had the skill before I ever went there. I assisted my father when I was a boy."

Mrs. Baker wiped her mouth with a napkin.

"It makes me wonder why you ever became a forger when you had such a useful trade at your disposal," she said. "But, moving on, what will you be doing at this shop? Anything in the way of supervising?"

"No, I'll be working under a man."

Mrs. Baker shook her head. "That won't do at all."

"Julia..." Marie began.

"How won't it do?" LeWald asked. "What's wrong with it?"

"If you're going to be a member of this community, we'll need you to be more prominent. If people should find out about your past you'll need to show them that you can be trusted. Working in a position where you're subservient to another man won't do it."

"There's no reason for people to know what I–"

"And aside from that, it wouldn't be a proper reflection on us. With the help of your wife I run one of the most prominent charities in this city. We can't have you working at a place where you haven't any more status than one of our servants. How would that reflect on us?"

"I've already taken the job." LeWald's voice was hard. "I can't go back on my word. That wouldn't make you look too good, either, would it?"

"In this case I don't think it will affect us too much," Mrs. Baker said with a sweet smile. "I'd rather you not work at all than be somebody's helper."

"I don't have the money to open my own shop, if that's what you mean."

"You certainly haven't," she said, chuckling.

"And even if I did, I don't know anything about running my own shop."

"Don't be ridiculous, there's nothing to managing a business. All you need is money."

LeWald began to speak, but Mrs. Baker interrupted him.

"Yes, I know you don't have any. I heard you. Until you do have some, be patient."

"Where would I get it from?"

Mrs. Baker smiled again. "I think I can make some arrangements."

LeWald heaved a deep sigh and Marie gave him a sympathetic look. She loved him. He could tell. But he did wish she had told him more.

Flora took the last bit of food from her plate and put it in her mouth. Even though she was only six, she was very well-behaved. She chewed with her mouth closed and never filled the room with an avalanche of childish babbling. She had a calmness that made it easy to forget how young she was.

From his chair Joseph would growl and grunt like an ape, and the nurse would tell him to hush and finish eating, or tap his plate with a fork. Each time he made noise he would move his eyes to see if his mother was watching.

"Joseph," she said without looking up.

He grunted again.

"Mama…"

"Be a good boy, Joseph," the nurse said.

He turned his head and watched his mother. Near her plate a newspaper was opened to the middle section, and she stared into it so that he could not see her eyes. Looking back to the nurse

Joseph picked up a spoon and threw it over her shoulder. She scolded him and stood to fetch it.

"Joseph," Mrs. Baker said again. She still had not looked up.

The nurse brought the spoon back and sat down again.

"Behave, now, or you won't get to finish your breakfast," she said.

Joseph looked from her to his mother, who continued to read. He smiled and speared some egg with his fork, and his nurse smiled, too, as she watched him.

"That's a good boy," she said.

Joseph brought the fork to his mouth, but when it was within three inches of it he threw it as hard as he could at his mother. The fork twirled end over end two times before it landed square in the center of the paper with a loud clang. The egg left a splattered trail of grease across the newsprint, and the fork bounced onto the floor.

Mrs. Baker glared at him and got up from her seat. Joseph giggled as she came toward him and raised his arms so she could pick him up, but she bypassed his chair altogether and went to Flora, and brushed her hair with her hand.

"You're my good girl," she said.

Flora did not look at her mother. Instead she glanced at her brother's chair. His face was red and his eyes looked watery but he did not cry. His mouth was closed, and he sat very still. Although she was too big Flora soon felt herself being picked up and held close by her mother. She continued to look at Joseph. He watched them with complete sadness, but no jealousy.

"I'm going to take Flora to the parlor," Mrs. Baker told the nurse. "You bring Joseph upstairs and wash his face and hands.

Then you can put him to bed. If he's not going to behave I don't want him around." She addressed Marie. "Come with me, dear, so we can work out your schedule."

Marie obediently stood and followed Mrs. Baker out of the room. Flora turned her head as far as possible so she could continue to watch her brother. Great fat tears collected in his eyes but he made no sound until the nurse began to wipe the remaining bits of food from his face. Then he began to make a whine like the drawn-out cackle of a hen. The nurse slid her hands beneath his arms and began to lift him, but he struggled hard and she set him down again.

"Stop it, now," she said. "You've already got me in enough trouble."

She moved to take him again but he swung and hit her on the wrist with his open hand.

"Don't make me spank you."

LeWald stood and came around the table to Joseph's chair.

"Siddown," he told the nurse.

"I'm s'posed to put him to bed."

"I can do it."

"It's my job. I can't just sit around all day."

"Then go do something else."

The nurse scowled and went out the kitchen door, leaving the boy and the man by themselves. LeWald came forward and stopped less than a foot from Joseph, and stared down at him. Joseph chewed his lips, sniffling. After some time had passed, LeWald bent over and picked him up. He held Joseph in the air a moment. The boy was not afraid, and his tears had dried without spilling. They watched each other in the awkward silence.

Marie held tight to her husband's bare chest in the darkened room. She knew he was awake from the way his heart was beating. Strong and fast, as it always did when he was angry or upset. She felt awful.

"I'm sorry."

He did not respond.

"Les?"

She raised her head toward his face, but there was not enough light to see.

"Let's just go," he said at last. "We can go anywhere."

"With what?"

"I haven't given up that job. I could make a little money. We'll find a place to live. Or we'll leave. We can just leave."

"She wants me to go with her."

"Where?"

"Everywhere along the rail lines. Out of the city, out of state. She won't have me working in Kansas City. Nothing good can come of it, she said."

"What does that mean?"

Marie put her head back down, but continued to look in his direction.

"I don't know."

"Wouldn't tell you."

"That's all she said. Nothing good can come of it."

LeWald sighed and it made Marie's head bob.

"She paid for us to come here."

"I know."

"Do you want to go back to Wisconsin and live with Papa and Mama?"

"No."

"So what can we do?"

"I don't know."

They were quiet a full minute.

"We owe her now, you understand that?" LeWald said.

Marie said nothing else. LeWald felt moisture on his chest where her tears fell. He ran his hand through her dark hair and wiped her face with his thumb. She took his hand and kissed his strong fingers. The dark tangled hairs on his chest brushed her face. She liked the sensation of it.

"Don't think about it anymore," he said. "We'll stay. We'll make do."

She kissed his hand again, and slipped it below her nightdress until it touched her left breast. Smiling, she closed her eyes as he cupped it.

Mrs. Baker spent twenty minutes deciding which of the mufflers she would buy. She opted for one of the black ones. White would get dirty too fast, and the brown looked cheap, like raccoon. The fur was soft and she smoothed it with her fingers and wanted to brush her face against it but held back. She took it from the shelf and put it under her arm, squeezing it, so plush. In her hands she carried the jar of face cream and the pair of black gloves that fit perfectly and looked better than the ones in her bag that she had worn for the past two winters. It was good to have things.

On the second floor of the department store was a display of dozens of toys surrounded by decorations and artificial snow, on the edges of which was a wooden rocking horse. It had a beautiful painted white body with brown patches and a thick mane that spilled over its neck like curls of black frosting. Nearby was a rendering of the same horse being ridden by a smiling little boy with fat pink cheeks. Mrs. Baker thought a while, and continued to think as the salesman came by to ask if she needed help.

Mrs. Russell visited a few days before Christmas, and brought each of her children an orange and a new pair of shoes. They sat together in a room near the front of the house and Mrs. Russell tried not to cry as she watched them put on the shoes and dig into the oranges.

"My, don't they feed you here?" she managed to ask. She forced herself to smile, as if it would make her voice jolly.

Earl began to answer her, but Eddie cut him off with a forceful, "Yes."

Mrs. Russell reached out to touch Earl's hair and he flinched as if he thought she would strike him.

"I'm sorry, Mama," he said. "I don't want the bugs to get on you, too."

"Bugs?"

"In my hair. We've all got 'em."

Mrs. Russell looked at the other children. The girls were still devouring their oranges, and Eddie held what remained of his near his chin, slurping at the juice.

"There's not too many, don't worry," he said.

"But all of us still have 'em," Earl said. "Every boy and girl in this house."

"What does Mrs. Baker say?"

"She ain't hardly ever here. We haven't seen her three times since we've been here."

"She can't be here all the time," Eddie told his brother. "She has to go out and collect money. Otherwise we'd be out on the streets."

"I wish we were."

All the wind left Mrs. Russell's body. It was hopeless. The money was gone, and she had borrowed more so she could afford the shoes. She wanted to scream. Katie walked up and stood before her mother.

"Mama, do you have any more oranges?"

"I'm sorry, sweetheart, I don't."

She put her hand on her daughter's shoulder and rubbed her neck. She knew how much thinner the children looked than when she had last seen them.

"We get enough to eat here," Eddie said again.

Mrs. Shaw was in the kitchen when Mrs. Russell found her. She held a long wooden spoon, which she wielded like a riding crop. Nearby at the stove a girl worked stirring a mixture that looked like gray oatmeal.

"What do you feed my children?" Mrs. Russell asked.

Mrs. Shaw glanced over her shoulder a second, then turned to face the other woman.

"What did they tell you?"

"Nothing, really, just that they get enough."

"I should hope that's a sufficient answer."

"But it isn't. You didn't see how they ate those oranges I brought. I thought they were gonna eat 'em whole, peels and all."

Mrs. Shaw smiled. "Oranges are a treat."

"Don't you give them any fruit?"

"Yes, but they don't get oranges every day. And they're growing, too, you know – they eat everything so fast. I'm always telling them, 'Don't belt your food.' It's a miracle they don't choke or make themselves sick, they way they take it down."

On the second floor Earl and Eddie leaned against the wall. Eddie's head was down and he was smiling at his new shoes. They were black and shined like they were coated in varnish. Earl watched his own shoes with a sour feeling in his throat.

"I hate 'em," he said in a quiet voice.

Earl glared at him. "You shut up. Mama worked hard to get these for us."

"Spent all her money on 'em, too."

"She sure did."

"Now how long do you think it'll take before she can get us outta this place? We'll be in here 'til next Thanksgiving now."

"Don't say that."

"It's true."

"Mama's doin' her best."

"I know she is."

"Don't say nothin' to her about it."

"I won't, I'm not stupid."

"It's not her fault."

The boys said nothing for a minute, before Earl spoke again.

"It's Papa's fault."

Eddie grabbed him by the arm and pulled hard, dragging his brother so close that he felt his breath in his face.

"Don't you ever say that again. It's a lie."

"It is not. If he hadn't left us we wouldn't be here."

"It's not true!"

"If he was still here Mama wouldn't have to work, and she could take care of us instead of bringin' us here."

"Stop it!"

"He's a bastard, that's all he is. A goddamned bastard."

In a second the boys were on the floor, rolling and throwing punches until Mrs. Shaw was on them. She grabbed Earl, who was on top at the moment, by the collar and clubbed him over the head with her wooden spoon. When he refused to stop squirming she hit him again, this time three heavy blows across the face with her open hand.

By the time Mrs. Russell got to the stairs Earl had already been sent to bed and Eddie was going off to help in the kitchen. Mrs. Shaw followed close behind him, and shook her head as she passed Mrs. Russell.

"Stay as long as you like, but I'm needed in the kitchen," she said. "You understand. Boys."

Earl lay in a ball atop the thin blankets of his bed, crying and crying. Mrs. Russell came into the room slowly, until she saw him there and went to his side. His nose was bleeding, and the blood soaked into his pillowcase. Mrs. Russell sat on the floor so her face was even with his. She wanted to speak but found it impossible. Instead she put her hand on the mattress so her son would take it. When Earl noticed he closed his eyes and folded his arms around his chest.

"I'm sorry, Mama."

"Don't be. I'm sorry."

He opened his eyes again and looked at her.

"I hate it here so much," he said between gasps.

Mrs. Russell opened her bag and took out a handkerchief, which she gave to him. He took it and began to wipe his face.

Mrs. Baker took Flora in her arms and gave her a big hug as the girl clutched the new doll in her hand. The opened gifts lay in clusters around the room, with the LeWalds, and Joseph and his nurse sitting among them with nothing to do.

"My girl," Mrs. Baker said.

"Thank you, Mommy. She's beautiful."

Mrs. Baker set Flora down and looked at LeWald.

"Your gift may not be under the tree, but you have to admit it was the best one."

"Gift?"

"Don't tell me you've forgotten. Your business, of course."

He nodded. "Oh, yes."

"Oh, yes? That's all you can say? Most men work their entire lives for an opportunity like this, and here I've given it to you. I should think you would be a bit more thankful."

"I am, honest, but I'm nervous is all. I don't know anything about running a business."

"There's nothing to it – do what you know how to do. The only difference is that you'll be handling the money in addition to doing the labor. Do you know how much the supplies cost?"

"Yes."

"Do you know how much it runs to do the work?"

"Yes."

"Then you've nothing to worry about. All you've got to do is keep track of everything. Can you do that?"

"Yes."

"Then it's done."

Mrs. Baker looked at Joseph and gave him a big smile. As she opened her mouth to speak LeWald stood.

"But what if we can't make a go of it?"

Mrs. Baker rolled her eyes and waved her hand.

"Don't be such an old biddy."

LeWald began to say something but she cut him off.

"If it doesn't work out, I'll make another deal. I'm good at that."

LeWald did not say anything. Mrs. Baker frowned and put her hands on her hips.

"You've nothing to worry about," she snapped. "You live here, so you've not got any rent to pay, you've got no children of your own, you've got no real expenses to speak of. I am carrying you, do you understand? Stop worrying."

He nodded, then went to the far side of the room and leaned against the wall.

Mrs. Baker smiled again and turned her attention back to her son.

"I've got one more thing here for you," she said and disappeared into the next room.

Joseph stood on his chubby legs and waited for her to return. Soon she was back, carrying a large object wrapped in loose brown paper and tied with a white string. Mrs. Baker set it on the floor. Joseph walked over and pulled the knot loose and stepped back as the paper fell. It was the rocking horse. When he saw it he jumped up and down and shrieked at a glass-breaking pitch that caused several of the adults to cover their ears. In a second he was on the horse's back and rocking, laughing and smiling.

"Now, what do you say?" Mrs. Baker asked.

"Thank you!" the boy shouted, bounding off the horse straight into the arms of his nurse. She did not hug him back, and she looked away from the others' faces.

The sun had set, but everyone was still downstairs, and Earl listened to their muffled talk and laughter. His mother had been gone for hours, and he lay with his face to the window and watched the moon. Suddenly it was gone and he realized the light had been turned on. He rolled over and looked at the entryway. Mrs. Shaw watched him with an expression of disgust.

"Look at you," she said.

Earl did not answer.

"You look disgraceful," she said, taking a step forward. "Get out of that bed and come with me."

Earl was scared, but he obeyed. When she could reach him Mrs. Shaw grabbed him tight by the back of the neck and steered him out of the room, down the steps and into the second-floor washroom. She maintained her grip the whole way, with the nails of her thumb and middle finger digging into the skin beneath his ears. When they reached the bathroom she thrust him inside so that he stumbled and almost fell. She entered behind him and shut the door.

"Take off your shirt."

Earl waited a second, then pulled his suspenders off his shoulders. Mrs. Shaw watched him undo the top two buttons of his shirt, then slide it over his head. When it was off she took him by the neck again and positioned him in front of the sink. The basin was very deep, and it was filled three-quarters with water. Above the sink was a mirror, out of which Mrs. Shaw stared as she spoke to him.

"Look at yourself."

His face was not as stained as he had expected. There were only a few light red hints around his lips, as if he had eaten something with heavy tomato sauce.

"We can't have this," Mrs. Shaw said. "If you're going to stay in this house we can't have you behaving like a little monster. We expect so much more from you."

He nodded.

"Do you apologize?"

"Yes, ma'am."

"Say it."

"I apologize."

She pinched harder, making him wince.

"For what?"

"I apologize for fighting and being bad."

"Good boy."

Mrs. Shaw plunged his head into the water. It was freezing and the shock of it caused him to gasp and draw what felt like a gallon of it into his lungs. He choked and coughed and tried to struggle, but when he waved his arms he felt a sharp pain on his butt, where she had hit him. He tasted bile, and his eyes burned. He could hear nothing, and he began to feel nothing.

Suddenly he was free. Mrs. Shaw dropped him like a bundle of laundry on the floor, and he bulged his eyes at the ceiling and gulped the air like a beached carp. He looked to Mrs. Shaw and noticed she was holding a towel. She threw it on him and went to the door.

"Dry yourself and get back in bed," she told him.

The year 1906 was a hectic one for Kansas City's juvenile court. Dr. E. L. Mathias, chief probation officer, reported for that year how he and his fellow officers cared for eight hundred twenty-eight children. Although this was three times the amount seen in 1905, Mathias said that did not mean juvenile crime had tripled. It was because the juvenile court and its probation officers had become more efficient.

Mathias came to Kansas City in 1903, following his graduation from the Western Maryland College at Westminster. He was appointed a deputy probation officer by Judge McCune in January 1905 and a little more than a year and a half later was named chief. In addition to his work there, Mathias had a hand in establishing the Baby Home, the Juvenile Relief Association and the Juvenile Improvement Club. One of his biggest projects was the Boys' Hotel, which provided living quarters to boys aged fourteen to nineteen who had no other place to go. The boys were to turn over half their wages no matter how small for their board, not to exceed three dollars a week, an arrangement that enabled the hotel to be self-sustaining.

Mathias was a busy man.

He spent his final hours ranting. The newspapers said it was as if he had regained his former strength. The years had been hard on John Alexander Dowie. Around the time of his New York visit the creditors made their claims and the control of Zion City was given over to a federal receiver. Dowie embarked on a tour around the world and pleaded his case everywhere he went. When he returned six months later he proclaimed himself the First Apostle of the church. In 1905 he made plans to colonize Mexico and took an option on seven hundred thousand acres of land. It was after he returned to Zion City that he had his first stroke. After he had his second, he went to the West Indies for his health. He made Wilbur Glenn Voliva deputy general overseer of the church and the city.

Voliva stole it all. He said Dowie advocated polygamy. He said Dowie took advantage of his followers and stole their money, which Dowie spent on homes and business ventures that never came to anything. But Voliva was the real thief. First he transferred all the church's property from Dowie to Overseer Granger, which he could do because he had been given power of attorney. Next he called everyone to the Zion City tabernacle and pleaded his case against Dowie. He gave them a choice –

him or Dowie. Apart from about two hundred loyal Zionists, they chose Voliva.

Dowie filed suit, but it was useless. Everything that could have been done, was, and anyway, he was ill. His wife and son had left him. Zion City was a shell, with empty businesses and empty homes. It was all over.

Dowie sat in bed wearing his ceremonial robes, and began denouncing all of his betrayers at one in the morning. He continued until seven, when he finally began to grow weak. He lay back and looked around. Two assistants sat watching him. Neither of them had taken down what he said. In his last moments Dowie wondered if anybody would remember.

Mrs. Russell held the dress up to Katie's shoulders. It was not new, but it was clean, with a fresh looseness that comes from being recently laundered. Katie wore a proud smile as she looked at it, and her mother smiled, too. The other three children stood in an informal line behind her, each of them clutching the items their mother had brought. Earl was the only one who did not seem happy. He stared at his mother in a silent pleading way, but she seemed unaware of it. It was as if she had learned nothing. When she had finished handing out the clothes, she looked back at him.

"Don't worry so much," she said. "I didn't buy these. I got 'em from another lady works at the hotel."

"Where'd she get 'em?" Earl asked.

"I don't know. She gave them to me and I said thank you. That's all."

At once Earl felt ashamed and he looked at the floor. There was a gray clump of fuzz and hair near the toe of his right shoe, and he stared at it as if he were trying to memorize what it looked like.

"I'm sorry, Mama," he said. "Thank you."

"Yes, thank you," the others said and clustered around her, tugging at her sides.

Earl hung back. He continued to look down.

"Why don't we all go for a walk?" Mrs. Russell said.

Eddie walked with the girls about twenty feet ahead of Earl and Mrs. Russell, both of them running and dancing around him, letting out occasional delighted shouts and squeals. Earl looked like he was going to speak, and Mrs. Russell waited for him to start. He never did, though, and she took his hand and held it. She enjoyed the warmth of it, and the fact that she could smell him as she drew closer. The sun was out, and the birds.

"What's Mrs. Baker like?"

"I dunno," Earl said. "We haven't seen her but five or six times, and then not to where I could talk to her that much. She's out collecting money, Mrs. Shaw says."

"Yes, she told me. She asked if I would wanna do that, but I couldn't. It wouldn't work out, I wouldn't be any good at it. She asked me to think about it."

"She said she doesn't have nothing to do with the money."

"Who?"

"Mrs. Shaw."

"Oh. I'm talking about Mrs. Baker."

"Oh."

The two were quiet for a few seconds.

"She seemed nice when I met her. Mrs. Baker, I mean. She must be if she's always out workin' for your kids."

"That's where Mrs. Shaw says she is."

"She seemed nice is all I mean."

Earl watched his siblings as he walked on.

"I wouldn't know," he said. "I wasn't along when you met her."

Mrs. Russell felt like she was going to scream.

"Have you ever seen her children?" she asked.

"Didn't know she had any."

"Sure she does. Two, a boy and a girl. I think they're close to Katie's age. At least the older one is. They live right around here, not too far from where you do. On Askew Street, she told me."

"She must not be around much, then, if she's that close and we never see her."

Earl went out after his mother had left. It was no problem leaving the home. Most of the children did it at some point in the day. They only had to be back in time to get their evening bread and milk. Earl turned toward Askew when he reached the end of the block. It was not far, and he came to the street in less than five minutes.

The houses were nice, although smaller than the ones on Cleveland Avenue. Earl walked at a slow pace as he watched them, contemplating how he could find the right one. Ahead of him a block and a half he saw a young woman in a white uniform who led two children by the hands. Earl stepped onto the grass and leaned against a nearby tree. As the woman and the children came nearer Earl picked a fallen leaf off the ground and pretended to play with it. He waited for them to pass, but instead they turned toward a house a few yards away. The boy straggled behind, and the woman pulled his arm.

"Come on, Joseph," Earl heard her say.

Earl watched them from under his brow as they climbed the three steps leading to the front door, which they passed through. He did not move until it was shut, and then he dropped the leaf and crept along the walk until he stood in front of the house. It was clean and white, two storeys high, with no porch. He snuck up to it as if it were a sleeping animal, and peered through one of the front windows in time to see the uniformed woman taking the children up the stairs. When they were out of sight Earl moved along the wall of the house, looking on tiptoe into the windows, neither seeing nor hearing anybody.

He rounded the corner, continuing to spy until he came to a room toward the rear of the house. It was crammed with things: Pictures on the wall, shelves with little figures made of colored glass, books in cases and cabinets for papers. In the middle of the room was a huge desk that Earl thought looked larger than his bed. She sat behind it. Mrs. Baker.

Before her on the desk sat a beautiful polished box, the lid of which was open, and she dug into it with both hands without displaying its contents. Earl stretched as far as he could but it was impossible to tell what was inside. Around the corner of the house was another window, which offered a different view of the room. Running as quietly as possible he went to it and jumped up to get a better look, but the ground sloped down the farther into the yard he ventured, and he saw even less than he could before.

Earl looked around and saw a large rock near a tree in back of the house, and he ran to it and tried to pick it up. It felt like it weighed more than he did, but it gave some when he put his hands on it. Moving to one side he pushed it, causing it to roll, and he pushed it harder until it was more or less planted under the window sill. He placed his hands on the side of the house to balance himself and stood on the rock. As slow as he could he poked his nose over the sill of the open window and looked inside.

Mrs. Baker was closing the box. She took a tiny key from her pocket and locked it, and then put the key back and pushed the box forward on the desk. Turning her head she looked out the window and Earl ducked. The rock was dislodged, and he fell, landing on his back. The rock rolled across the yard until it hit the tree and stopped almost exactly where he had found it. Earl held his breath in the hope that she had not heard him. He lay flat on the ground, afraid to move, afraid to look away. Soon Mrs. Baker was perched over him with her head and shoulders sticking out of the window.

"What do you think you're doing here?" she said in an angry voice.

Earl raised his head and sat up, brushing his arms, trying to figure out what to tell her.

"Well?" Mrs. Baker asked.

"I guess I wanted to see your house."

Mrs. Baker sighed. It made her sound like a bull, Earl thought.

"Stand up," she said.

He did, and looked into her face. He knew from the way she watched him that she would tell Mrs. Shaw. He closed his eyes.

"Have you done this before?"

"No, ma'am."

"What did you see?"

"Nothing much before you caught me, ma'am."

"It was hardly worth it, then, was it?"

"No, ma'am."

It seemed like five minutes passed before she spoke again. Earl felt like he would vomit.

"Why did you choose my house?"

He considered how best to answer.

"Tell me this second, what is it that made my house so intriguing to you?" Mrs. Baker said. "And look at me when I speak to you."

He opened his eyes. She hated him. He could tell.

"I-I just wanted to see it, ma'am. I'm sorry."

Mrs. Baker moved her jaw.

"Do you live near here?" she asked.

Earl held his breath.

"Do you?" she asked again.

"Yes, ma'am."

"Do your parents know you like to go trespassing on other peoples' property? Do they know you go peeking into other peoples' windows?"

"No, ma'am."

"How do I know you aren't planning to break in the next time I leave?"

"I wouldn't do that."

"That's the road you're traveling down. If you continue on this way you'll become a full-fledged thief in the space of two years. Do you think a judge would show leniency because you're young? Or curious? They send boys to prison every day. I should grab you by the ear right this second and pull you home. Then I could tell your parents about what a bad little boy they're raising. Why are you smiling? Is this funny to you?"

Earl caught himself, and bit his cheek until he drew blood.

"No, ma'm."

"I should hope not. If my children behaved like you do I would have them sent away. Go along, now. Get home to your parents before I send for the police."

"Yes, ma'am. Thank you."

Earl ran from the yard. He stopped when he reached the end of the block. He paused, his chest heaving, and looked back at Mrs. Baker's house. He walked to it with an air of confidence, and did not slow his pace as he came before it. He just turned his head and spat onto the lawn.

The shop was not ready. Even after Mrs. Baker acquired a loan from Judge Hazell there still were not enough supplies. A jobbing house had been secured on Fifteenth Street but there were no finances with which to get it running. It was a nightmare, LeWald thought as he stared at the building from a corner on the opposite side of the street. It would be easy to run. He stared at his boots a moment and with a sigh stepped into the road. When he reached the other side he looked up to see that the door to the building was ajar. He ran to it and flung it open all the way. From inside the shop Marie looked at him and smiled.

"I've done it," she said.

"Done what? What are you doing here?"

She trotted over, gave him a kiss on the cheek and held his forearms.

"I've been to see Judge Hazell," she said.

LeWald broke free of her and moved further into the shop.

"Please don't talk to me about him, I feel sick enough already."

Marie went to the door, closed and locked it.

"No, this is good news," she said. "He's going to help us."

"He's already helped us. It's partly thanks to his help that we're in this mess – him and your sister."

Marie came back and took his arms again.

"You don't understand–"

"Marie…" LeWald held her plump face in his hands. Her eyes were clear and her cheeks were red as she smiled at him.

"I've been to see him," she said. "This afternoon, just now."

"We can't pay him. We simply can't. We can't even open our doors."

"I know, dear. And so does he. That's what we've been discussing."

LeWald lowered his hands to her shoulders.

"When?"

"This afternoon, I've just told you. Aren't you listening?"

"Yes. I'm sorry. I don't feel well."

"Perhaps you should sit down."

LeWald went behind the counter and brought out a stool, and sat without bringing it into the main part of the shop. Marie went to him after a moment, her smile somewhat muted now.

"Wouldn't you like to hear what's happened?"

He nodded. "All right."

"I went to visit the judge and told him how you were doing here, what's still needed and everything, and he said he's interested in it."

"I'd say he already has an interest in it."

"No, I mean that he wants to be a partner. He said once things get up and running he'll work with you. Not in the shop, but in the general management of things. Isn't that wonderful?"

"How's he ever gonna do that if we don't have the money to open?"

"That's part of it!" she all but shouted, and came right up to her husband so that he had to raise his head to see her face. "He's given me another loan, and he said you can use it to buy all the shoe findings and everything else you need to get a good start."

LeWald was afraid to ask.

"How much?"

"Six hundred dollars. Can you believe it?"

"So that's a thousand we owe him now."

She did not hear.

"This is an answer to our prayers. And then of course once the loans are repaid he'll be a partner. He'll get an equal share of the profits after expenses."

LeWald sat listening even after she was quiet.

"Don't you have anything to say?" she asked.

"This is something he *wants* to do?"

"No, he's already doing it. I just signed the paper at his office."

"Just you?"

"No, he signed it, too."

"What about your sister?"

"She wasn't even there. She set up the meeting, but she couldn't go. But the judge explained everything to me. It's all legal. He signed the paper himself, and so did I."

After she had completed her first sentence LeWald's head began to sink, and did not stop until it was even with her hip. When he spoke again he was in a daze.

"So you're accountable, then."

"Yes, we both are. Well, that's business, you know."

"I know."

He looked at her again. She was no longer smiling. She looked frightened, like a child who had done something wrong without realizing it.

"Les, I would never do anything to hurt us."

"I know that." LeWald smiled. "I'm sorry. I don't feel well. It's pretty warm today. I mighta been in the sun too long."

Marie smiled, too, and put her hand on his brow.

"You do feel warm."

"I'll be fine." He stood and kissed her, and led her around to the other side of the counter, and then to the door. "I have a few things to do yet, so you run along home," he said. "I'll be there soon."

"Will you be okay?"

"Yes. It's nothing too strenuous."

"Can I help?"

"No, it won't take long."

"If you're sure."

"I am. I'll be home soon."

He kissed her again, then let her out. When she had gone LeWald went back behind the counter. He sat on the stool and closed his eyes, holding his head in both hands.

Mrs. Russell waited almost five minutes at the front of the house before she saw any of her children, or any children at all. The girls were upstairs, Mrs. Shaw said, and started off to find them.

"Where are the boys?" Mrs. Russell called after her.

No answer came, and soon Mrs. Shaw was gone.

It was July, and the house felt like a sweatbox. It smelled like a gymnasium, a pungent blend of sweat and dirt. Mrs. Russell was glancing out one of the windows when she heard footsteps. Looking up to the railing she saw a small girl pass by. It was Katie, wearing her new dress.

"Hello, sweetheart," Mrs. Russell called.

The girl never stopped, and looked down at her with a combination of annoyance and confusion. It was not her daughter.

"I'm sorry, never mind," Mrs. Russell said as the girl disappeared.

Soon her daughters were rushing down the stairs, calling and laughing. Irene came first and Mrs. Russell picked her up and kissed her, telling her how big she had grown. Then she set her down and looked at Katie for the first time. The dress she wore was filthy, as if someone had used it to wipe soot from her hands. Mrs. Russell paused, then squatted and took the girl in her arms.

"I love you so," she said.

"I miss you, Mama."

"I miss you, too, Mama."

Mrs. Russell released her daughter and tugged at her dress.

"What is this you're wearing? What happened to the nice clothes I brought for you last time?"

Both girls stared at the floor.

"What is it? What happened?"

Katie turned so her mother could not see her face.

"They took them," Irene said.

"What do you mean? Who took them?"

"Mrs. Shaw and the other women. The gave our new things to the other girls."

"Why in the world would they do that?"

Irene shrugged and wiped her nose with the back of her hand. Katie continued to look away, and Mrs. Russell took her shoulder.

"It's all right, darling, don't you worry about it."

Slowly she drew the girl close and held her in her lap.

"I'm sorry, Mama," Katie said.

"I'm not mad at you," Mrs. Russell said and kissed her again. She opened her arms wider and pulled Irene near, too. After a moment she released them and stood.

"Now. Where are the boys? I need to talk to them."

"They're gone," Katie said.

"I can see that, but when will they be back?"

"Mama, you don't understand," Irene said. "They sent them away."

The first thing they did to Earl after he came to the farm was to shave his head. The man who did it used a pair of stiff clippers that made Earl feel like his scalp was being peeled like an apple.

The man had hands like canvas, and he gripped the back of Earl's neck as he worked, not to hurt him but to keep him from squirming too much. When he was finished he clapped Earl on the shoulder.

"There you go. You gotta wash good tonight, make sure you don't have none of them bugs left."

Earl's head felt cool, but good. For the first time in weeks the tickling had stopped. He put his hands on top of his head and rubbed his skin. He still had some hair, little clumps of it, and the occasional thin strip that stuck up like grass on a poorly-cut lawn.

"We'll find you a cap so your head doesn't burn while your hair grows back," the man said.

Earl looked at him. The way the man smiled almost made him look sad.

"Sorry, boy, but I hadda do it."

Earl slipped on the clean shirt he had been given and hooked up his new overalls. The man shook out the clippers and put them in his front shirt pocket, and motioned for Earl to follow as he began to walk. They went past a large white barn with a round roof to one of the outbuildings, which also was white. It was long, one level, with a row of even-spaced windows across one side.

"You'll sleep in there," the man said, pointing to the building. "There's cots in there. Most of 'em are bein' used right now, but we'll find you one. They're boilin' your old clothes and whatever makes it out they'll put on your cot. You can keep what you're wearin' now, too."

They did not stop, but continued on to one of the sheds. The man opened the door and stepped inside. Earl waited in front as the man rummaged around, and soon he came out with a brown cap. The bill had been folded to a forty-five degree angle, and there were old sweat stains around the edges. The man placed the cap on Earl's head.

"That fit?"

Earl nodded.

The man grunted and went back inside.

"You ever detasseled before?" he called.

"No, sir."

"Ain't much to it. Just take the top part of the cornstalk – it's sort of green and stringy-looking – and pull it off. Not in every row, though. I'll show you which. Just do what I do and you'll be fine."

He returned with a pair of work gloves and two burlap sacks, and gave the gloves to Earl.

"These fit?"

Earl pulled on the gloves and flexed his fingers.

"Yes, sir."

"Good," the man said and closed the door. "Come on."

They moved away from the shed toward the field. The man handed Earl one of the sacks.

"When you break off the tassel put it in there. Then they'll plant 'em next year. You got any questions?"

"Do you know where my brother is?"

"I didn't know you had one."

Earl said nothing.

"He ain't here, though," the man said. "Sorry. He could be nearby. There's lotsa places around. He's probably makin' money just like you."

"How much are they payin'?"

"I dunno what a kid your size would make. But they're fair here. Mr. Jones told me to let you know he's sendin' all your pay to your ma, so don't worry."

"He did?"

"Yeah. It's all goin' to Mrs. Baker, he said. Not like you'd be able to spend any of it out here, anyway."

They worked until after five, and then everyone went back to the building with the cots. In the main room was a long table with chairs around it, and they sat down and a large woman fed them stew, which she ladled from a big black pot. There were potatoes and chunks of meat in it, and carrots, too. Earl had three helpings. When the meal was over he took a bath in a galvanized tub, with hot water boiled in a big bucket. Then Earl spent time watching the sky and listening to the men talk and tell dirty jokes. Another man had a book about Alaska, and he read some of it to Earl. It all made him feel so good that when he went to bed he slept, and he did not wake up until morning.

It was rare for Mrs. Baker to sleep all night, or to fall asleep before two in the morning. Her mind was always active, formulating means of promotion and plotting different travel routes. It was a big key to her success. When the rest of the world was unconscious, she was still at work, and so was able to accomplish at least twice as much as the average person. Even with the continuous activity, the night grew long. Mrs. Baker lay in bed with her eyes open, noting how the lids were not even heavy. On the wall the clock chimed four and it almost made her smile. She had not slept, but nobody would ever guess. She was as alert now as she had been twelve hours earlier, and eight hours before that, and she thanked God for giving her such strength.

At four-thirty she rose and went to her closet with a lighted candle. It was so full that she had to bring out two or three dresses to be able to move the others on the rack. She never threw any of them out. No matter how worn they became, she could always make use of them. The worse looking the outfit, the more donations she often received. People liked to know they were needed.

She looked to the left side of the rack, where the poorer dresses were kept, and brought out one with holes on the sleeves at the elbows. It looked as if it would fall apart if someone pulled a loose string from it. She put down the candle and held the dress to her shoulders, turning to the full-length mirror at the corner of the room. A bit too dingy, perhaps, especially since she needed to make a good impression. This one made her look like a rag lady. She put it back.

On the right side of the rack were the newer dresses and the ones in better condition. She took one of them, a black one, and held it up. It was quite formal. She was not going to a party. One of the in-between dresses would have to suffice, but which one? So much time can be put into these decisions, she thought as she brushed her hand across them all, from one end of the closet to the other.

Earl was taken from the farm the first week of August and rode the train back to Kansas City with Eddie and a probation officer.

Mathias was his name, and he asked the boys questions the whole way, about the Joseph Walter Home and the farms where they had been staying. They answered his questions, but they did not speak to each other. Their mother had filed charges, Mathias said. Their sisters had been detained at the home, and their mother could not get a satisfactory answer about the boys. Mrs. Russell was charging the home with neglect, Mathias said.

Earl and Eddie met their sisters in the hallway of the courthouse, and Mathias led them to a large room filled with rows of benches. Their mother sat at one of several tables at the front of the room. She had not heard them enter, and she did not turn their way until Katie broke ahead of the others and shouted, "Mama!"

Mrs. Russell let out a cry that sounded more like pain than joy, and she got up from her chair with her arms opened wide. She had not stood more than two seconds before she fell over. Immediately the children were upon her, patting her arms and caressing her face. Soon she came to, and Mathias helped her back to the chair.

In the end, Judge Thomas J. Seehorne dismissed Mrs. Russell's charge. He was not moved by the story of Earl receiving a bloody nose from Mrs. Shaw. It was frequently necessary to punish children, he said.

Mrs. Baker stared from behind her desk as Mrs. Shaw entered the room. It was the first time Mrs. Shaw had been to the house and she felt good about it. It was a welcoming place with nice furniture and bright rooms, and was so clean it seemed almost like a hotel.

"Close the door, please," Mrs. Baker said after Mrs. Shaw had come in.

Mrs. Shaw obeyed, and then sat in the empty chair across from Mrs. Baker.

"You have a lovely home," Mrs. Shaw said.

"Yes."

Mrs. Shaw was unsure of what else she could say, so she waited for Mrs. Baker to speak.

"We've had quite the ordeal this week, haven't we?"

"Yes, indeed," Mrs. Shaw said. "But justice was served in the end."

"That's because I'm doing the Lord's work."

"You certainly are."

"Despite the efforts of that woman."

"Mrs.–"

"I refuse to speak her name, or have it spoken in my presence." Mrs. Baker shook her head. "Her lies notwithstanding, my work will carry on. It's what God intends. It's all part of His plan. That woman told her stories, but the name of my home has not been and will not be stained."

Mrs. Shaw sat straight in her chair and gave a proud nod.

"You were not as lucky," Mrs. Baker said.

"Newspapers print anything they want if they think they'll make a profit."

"I know that better than most. Still, even if the things they wrote about you weren't true, some people will still believe them."

"None of it was true. It was all a distortion. Newspapermen can take one tiny incident and put it in a different context to suit their own ends. They could make anyone look guilty."

"But they didn't do it to anyone. They did it to you."

"What can I do about it?"

"Nothing. If you came to them and tried to explain yourself you would only make things worse. I learned a long time ago that it's better to let these things pass. The more noise you make in your own neighborhood, the sooner you'll find yourself moving out of it. If these claims were made about you elsewhere it would be another matter entirely. As it is, all you can do is be silent."

Mrs. Shaw let out a sigh.

"I'm glad you're sticking by me," she said.

"I never told you that."

Mrs. Shaw felt her heart beating harder, as if someone were knocking on her sternum with a reflex hammer.

"I beg your pardon?"

"Mrs. Shaw, because of what the papers reported everyone thinks you're guilty. You told me as much yourself."

"But I'm not guilty – not in the way that they said."

"I'm sure that's true. Unfortunately, I cannot allow a woman of your reputation to remain on my staff. I will pay you through the end of the week, but you may consider your employment at the Home terminated, effective immediately."

"What do you suggest I do? This job is all I have."

Mrs. Baker gave her a look of the deepest sympathy.

"My heart bleeds for you," she said.

I have two children. We're alone in the world. I'm not strong, you can see that. My husband lives in Dudley. The county has been helping me to live with what light work I could do.

Some time back I had a hemorrhage of the lungs. Consumption runs in our family, so I was worried. I began to consider the frequent suggestions of putting my children someplace. I rejected the children's home idea and told Dr. Whitlock, my physician, that I would rather be in a place where I could be with them and work, too. The doctor said he had heard of such homes. He had met Mrs. Anna Baker, who represented such a home in Joplin.

On Friday morning Mrs. Baker came to see me. She said I could do light work, fancy work and some sewing and she would pay me a small wage until the baby grew larger, then she would pay better. I told her that I was not strong, that I had stomach trouble and could not eat everything, especially meats such as pork or bacon, but that fruits assisted my digestion so much. She told me about the home and said they had plenty to eat and that it was just the place I wanted. She said I believed just as she did about eating, anyway, that refined people did not eat meat. While we were talking another woman came to the door and

Mrs. Baker introduced her to me. She did not talk much and I do not remember her name.

She went away and I began to get ready. The county supervisor had already issued an order for groceries and I went to him and asked him if he would change it and give me an order for a few dry goods and a ticket to Joplin. He said yes, but stated that the county was perfectly willing to do all that they had done for me if I wanted to stay there. But I thought such a home would be the best for me and my babies.

I began to get rid of my things, poor as they were. At eight o'clock that night Mrs. Baker called in a cab and made arrangements for me to go to the station in a car which she would send at twelve-thirty to the hotel in which she stayed.

Mrs. Baker said, I know the train does not go until four o'clock, but I have an object in your coming so early.

When I went down on Saturday the first words she said were, Did anybody send anything?

I said, Send anything? No, what do you mean?

Did the doctor or supervisor send anything?

No, I replied.

Then she asked where both offices were, that of the doctor and also the county supervisor, and left. When she came back I asked her if she had success, and she said, Yes, I always do.

When the supervisor came to the hotel, she told him this was a grand work, just see, this was all for humanity's sake!

He replied, Well, I suppose it is.

After we got on the train Mrs. Baker told me in a confidential conversation that they had trouble with only one class of people at the St. Joseph's home, and that was with those who ate so much. She said people did not overeat anymore.

Some days at the home she stated they had a little piece of bread apiece which they ate and were thankful for it.

Before I started I bought a chicken and had a woman fry it. This, with some sliced light bread and butter and a few grapes quite filled a shoebox for a lunch for us. Mrs. Baker ate over half of it herself before we reached St. Louis and my child and I ate the rest. At St. Louis she asked me to loan her one dollar, which I did, and we went out together. At the lunch counter she bought me a cup of tea, herself a glass of buttermilk and my little girl a glass of sweet milk, and paid for it out of the dollar.

As we were getting on the train, one of the trainmen asked, Which goes to Kansas City and which to Joplin?

Mrs. Baker explained and he said it was impossible for us to go together, as the Kansas City coach would be switched off.

Mrs. Baker told me that she was so sorry she could not come on down with me but gave me the address of the home on a card and said the matron, Mrs. Brown, would pay my back fare when I reached the house.

I reached Joplin at eight-fifty Sunday morning and Mrs. Brown met me at the depot. She said she had received a message to meet a mother and two children and had met the early morning train. We walked to the home.

Mrs. Brown asked me for money to pay for having my trunk brought up, which I gave her. For breakfast we had three pieces of toast on a plate, a cup of tea for me and a shredded wheat biscuit in a small dish, one for myself and one for my child. There were three plates at the table and Mrs. Brown sat down with us. Before we were through some cold flour gravy was brought on the table. I did not eat any of it. My child ate some of the toast, as well as Mrs. Brown and her child.

I had no dinner and my children cried all day. Between three and four o'clock the other children were given bread and milk on a weather beaten door on the upstairs porch.

About four o'clock the matron asked me if I was hungry. I said, Yes, and so are my children. I am weak and have not much strength and my baby is strong. I need food for him.

Mrs. Brown said, Well, we have not got anything in the house to cook. We have two women in the kitchen, but they did not tell me we were so near out yesterday, and now the stores are closed.

I asked her if I could get something to eat at a restaurant and she said: Yes, if you have the money.

I told her I had a little and would have had more, but that I loaned Mrs. Baker a dollar in St. Louis, but that I must have some nourishing food to keep my strength up. She then asked me if I could eat fried potatoes. She said they might fix some for my supper. I told her I could eat almost anything good except greasy meats. She said they would give the baby some tea.

But I started out and inquired of a private family something about the place. They told me some things and gave a good meal for the child. There was plenty for both, but I did not eat.

I applied to the authorities and went back with a man after my grip. The matron met me. I said I wanted my things taken upstairs to the room they had given me. She followed and asked what was the matter. I said I did not have anything for myself and the children to eat. She said they had a plenty.

Well, I can't tell what you have had, but we have had nothing, I told her.

She said, You would better be careful what you say about us. I never told you we lacked anything for butter and I told you we could get some of that.

She had never mentioned butter at all.

I do not know what to do, as I have nothing to go back to. I may stop in St. Louis and put my children in an orphans' home and go to a hospital until I get able to work or die. It will be die, I guess. It seems as though I have had so much.

I hope my experiences may keep others from being taken in. The St. Joseph's home is clean. They had tables set with white cloths and cut flowers on them. But I do not think they ever ate at them at all.

From The Salt Lake Tribune, February 23, 1908:

Miss Juanita L. Sparling of Kansas City and Miss Panola DeVere Logue of Salt Lake are working here in the interest of Joseph's Home of Kansas City. They claim that their work should commend itself to all charitably inclined persons.

From The Deseret Evening News, Salt Lake City, February 27, 1908:

"WOMEN IN BLACK" YET IN LIMELIGHT
They Are Declared to be Frauds By People in Kansas City.
STATEMENT OF SEC. DAMON
Miss Sparling Characterizes Communication as False – Police Are Investigating.

The two women in black whom the "News" referred to a week ago as soliciting aid in this city for a Kansas City orphans' home, are further brought to public notice through Capt. M. M. Wood of the Salt Lake Associated Charities. The women are Miss Juanita Sparling and Miss Panola de Vere Logue. Prof. Tibballs, one of the directors of the association, also said last evening, that he had corresponded with Kansas City people about these women, and was told they were frauds.

REPLY FROM KANSAS.

In reply to a query from Capt. Woods, General Secy. C. F. Damon of the Kansas City Associated Charities wrote:

"The number of inquiries made of us concerning Joseph's Home has been so numerous that we have prepared and printed for distribution the following statement of the history and present status of the institution and its owner, Mrs. Anna Baker:

"Joseph's Home has been located in Kansas City since Aug. 1, 1906. It is owned and controlled by Mrs. Anna Baker; she is not accountable to any other person or institution, public or private, sectarian or non-sectarian. The institution is amply supplied with buildings and grounds to accommodate approximately 40 women and children. No appeal is made, so far as we know, to the citizens of Kansas City for funds to support the work.

"Mrs. Baker's career as a 'public benefactor' seems to have begun in Minneapolis, Minn., in April, 1899, when she solicited funds for 'Zion Mission.' On investigation by the Associated Charities of that city 'Zion Mission' proved to be nothing more nor less than a cheap restaurant in charge of one Joseph Baker, to whom Mrs. Baker was subsequently married.

"In 1901 Anna Baker and Joseph Baker established a home for fallen girls in Duluth, Wis., which they called the 'Sacred Refuge.' The manner in which this institution was conducted led to an investigation by a committee of prominent men appointed by the mayor of Duluth. The report of the committee condemned both Mr. and Mrs. Baker and the institution was closed.

"The Bakers then opened a children's home in Duluth, which they called 'Baker Orphanage.' It was in connection with this institution that Mrs. Baker inaugurated her present plan of employing women solicitors to travel over the country and raise funds. She employed as many as 12 solicitors at one time to travel through Wisconsin and the surrounding states to support her institution, which as a matter of fact not more than three or four children were being cared for at the home, and most of them were being paid for by friends or relatives.

WOMAN WAS ARRESTED.

"In 1902 she was arrested at Hudson, Wis., on the charge of obtaining money under false pretenses. In April of that year Mrs. Baker represented to one Alexander Turner that the 'Baker Orphanage' at Duluth was caring for a large number of orphans and that she was engaged in finding homes for them. Upon this representation Turner contributed a small sum. She was tried and convicted on the above charge. She was fined $300, and ordered to be committed to the county jail until it should be paid, not exceeding five months. She secured her release by filing a bond and appeal to the supreme court. On Dec. 11, 1903, the supreme court reversed the case and sent it back for a new trial on the grounds that the trial court had admitted evidence that was irrelevant to the issues in the case and very prejudicial to the defendant. For the full report of this case see the State vs. Baker, in volume 120 of the Wisconsin reports, page 135.

BRANDED AS FRAUD.

"Joseph's Home has always sheltered some women and children, the number varying from three or four to probably 30. In many cases we know that they were paid for. Notwithstanding these facts the institution was branded as a fraud, except at the very beginning, by the local press, by many representative citizens and by many persons who were inmates or applicants for shelter at the home.

"In a great many cases the citizens and authorities were obliged to furnish return transportation to women and children who had come to enter Joseph's Home and who had either been denied admittance or were treated so badly after being admitted that they refused to remain. A case in point is that of Mrs. Viola Summers, from Mt. Vernon, Ill., which was published in the Joplin News Herald on Monday, Aug. 31, 1903.

"Mrs. Baker employs solicitors to travel in the central states to secure funds for the ostensible purpose of supporting this institution. Judging from the inquiries that were received by Mr. C. Y. Lyon, mayor of Joplin, these solicitors have been working from the Gulf to the Great Lakes and from Colorado to Pennsylvania.

"It is impossible to ascertain the amount of funds collected by Mrs. Baker, or to know how they were expended. She has been requested to make a statement of her methods, funds collected, etc., to the Associated Charities of Kansas City, but she has failed to comply with the request.

"We submit that, judging from the foregoing history of Mrs. Baker she is not a fit person to conduct an institution of the sort that she appeals to the public to support. In addition, her method of collecting money is unscientific, extravagant and sufficient in itself to deny the institution the support of the public."

MISS SPARLING TALKS.

Miss Sparling characterizes the Kansas City communication as false, and says, "The Associated Charities aid only the children by finding them places in homes away from their parents. The charities object to us because we insist that the mother and child shall not be separated and assist destitute women to establish new homes where they can care for their offspring."

Miss Sparling offers letters from the Missouri State pardon attorney and representative men of Kansas City and other places highly indorsing Mrs. Baker, and in one of which the founder of the home is classed as "a grand women whose noble work is for Christ and humanity." An unusual report, in legal form, describes the finances of the institution, and shows that for a period of five months it housed from 31 to 50 inmates.

Chief of Police Pitt is investigating.

From The Salt Lake Herald, February 27, 1908:
SOLICIT FOR CHARITY HOME IN MISSOURI
"Two Women in Black" Collect Large Sums For Institution at Kansas City
RECORD OF JOPLIN SHELTER IN QUESTION
SALT LAKE ASSOCATION DECLARES EVERY DOLLAR IS NEEDED AT HOME

"Two women in black," who have been soliciting subscriptions in Salt Lake and throughout the intermountain regions for some time past for the Joseph's Home for Widows and Orphans at Kansas, City, Mo., have been allowed by Chief of Police Pitt to continue asking for contributions after having received orders to discontinue their activities in this city. They are Mrs. Julia Anna Baker and Miss Juanita L. Sparling of Kansas City. Since their arrival in Salt Lake, they have secured the assistance in their work of Miss Pauola De Vere Logue of 634 East Sixth South street. Mrs. Black and Miss Sparling have been stopping at the Wilson hotel, and while there met Miss Logue, who was a housekeeper at the hotel. When Miss Logue gave up her position at the Wilson three weeks ago, she was induced to assist the other two women in soliciting subscriptions to the Joseph's home.

Several weeks ago, complaint was made to the police of the operations of Mrs. Black and Miss Sparling, who were described as "two women in black." Objection was made to their soliciting money in the Dooly block.

Nothing was done at the time, as the policemen detailed to investigate the matter were for some reason unable to find the two women. (…)

Chief Pitt Gives Sanction.

This printed circular was dated Dec. 5, 1906, and indicated that the soliciting for the Joseph's Home had extended over a considerable period. Chief of Police Pitt, learning that the operations of the women were questioned, ordered them to discontinue soliciting subscriptions here. He then telegraphed to persons who were mentioned in the printed matter distributed by the women, asking if they were representing a legitimate charity. He received a number of replies, some adverse, some favorable. This caused him to amend his order so that the women could resume the collection of money.

"I have written to the mayor of Kansas City," said Chief of Police Pitt last night. "Any future action I take will be based upon the reply I get."

Are Highly Successful.

Mrs. Baker and Miss Sparling are said to have met with great success in their efforts to raise money in Salt Lake, and in the surrounding country. It is said that several prominent Salt Lake men have subscribed $250 to the Kansas City institution. The two women recently made a trip to Nevada, which, according to report, was fruitful of contributions to Joseph's Home.

Mrs. Baker and Miss Sparling are intelligent, attractive women. They claim that the Joseph's home is a legitimate charity, and that it does not deserve the attacks made upon it by the Associated Charities of Kansas City. They claim that widows and orphans are sent to Joplin from all parts of the country. Six, they claim, were recently sent from Denver, and several were to be sent from Salt Lake.

Needed at Home.

Discussing the operations of the women, Superintendent Woods of the Charity association said:

"It seems to be an extravagant thing for women who are seeking money for an orphan's home to live at a hotel like the Wilson. Their quarters there cost them $5 a day. I do not know how much money they have collected here and in the surrounding country. But whether their Joseph's Home is a legitimate charity or not, conditions in Salt Lake are such that we cannot spare the money for outside charities. Every dollar that our people have to give in charity at this time is needed right here. We were never before face to face with the conditions of today.

"The circular from the Associated Charities of Kansas City shows that Mrs. Baker and her assistants have been soliciting contributions for a long time, and throughout the entire country. If we could get at the books of the Joseph's Home, we would probably find out that the total amount collected was very large. As these women stop at leading hotels, a considerable portion of the money taken in must be eaten up by their expenses."

For Associated Charities.

One of the results of the investigation into the Joseph's Home is the determination to organize the Associated Charities of Salt Lake. This will embrace every charitable organization in the city. An auditor will be employed by the Associated Charities to go over the books and accounts of each charity and report on the manner in which money contributed by charitable persons is expended. About six organizations have already signified their willingness to enter this new association. Their books will be immediately audited. After that the examination of every three months will be in order. It is believed that the Associated Charities will have the effect of driving out of this field all unworthy enterprises masked under the guise of charity.

Say It Is Worthy.

Miss Logue stated last night that she did not take up the work of the Joseph's home without investigation. Before joining Mrs. Baker and Miss Sparling she wired to Kansas City for information about the institution. In reply she received a telegram, signed by seven business men, stating that the Joseph's Home was a worthy charity.

Miss Sparling said last night that the Associated Charities of Kansas City had been issuing circulars condemning the Joseph's Home for three years. She said that the courts had not been appealed to in an effort to put a stop to the issuing of circulars because it would take money to bring suit and all the money collected was intended for widows and orphans.

Mother and Child Together.

"The Joseph's Home," she said, "is for mothers and their children. During the past three years, we have sheltered 400 children. Of that number, 90 per cent are now with their mothers, who have succeeded in finding work by which they could support their children.

"Other homes separate mothers and their children. Mothers who find that they cannot support their little ones are compelled to surrender their claims upon them.

"The Joseph's Home issued an annual statement, showing the amounts collected and the expenditures made."

Miss Sparling exhibited a copy of such a report, dated April, 1907.

"The statement that no reports are made is false," she said. "The Associated Charities of Kansas City condemns the Joseph's Home in Joplin, Mo. Mrs. Baker was formerly with that charity, but is now working on behalf of the Joseph's Home at 2610 Cleveland boulevard, Kansas City.

Charity Is Independent.

"The attacks of the Associated Charities are unjust and untrue. We do not approve of the methods of that organization and see no reason why we should submit to its rule. Our charity is independent and we intend to keep it so."

Miss Sparling had letters from Speed Mosby, pardon attorney of the state of Missouri, which were written on the governor's stationery, in which Mr. Mosby stated emphatically that the Joseph's Home was a worthy charity. She had other letters from other prominent men in Missouri.

From the Deseret Evening News, Great Salt Lake City, February 29, 1908:

NOT SO BLACK AS ARE PAINTED

"The Women in Black" Find Some Salt Lakers to Champion Cause

MRS. JULIA A. BAKER'S STORY

Something About Women Whose Agents Are Collecting Money Here To Send Back to Missouri

"The Women In Black" who are canvassing the town for subscriptions for an orphan home in Missouri are still operating in this city with considerable success and in the face of the apparently organized opposition to their mission are making a number of friends and incidentally gathering in the coin. Of the two solicitors the woman with the soulful eyes and winning smile is the more successful.

Several gentlemen insist that Mrs. Julia Anna Baker, founder of the Joseph's home in Kansas City, to which reference has been made, is a much maligned lady. In a lengthy communication handed in for publication, one champion explains how it is that these ladies made their headquarters at the Wilson hotel. Among other things, he says:

"The circular letter sent out by the associated charities Mrs. Baker characterizes as unjust and untrue. It is not new and a suit for libel has been prepared against papers that have heretofore published it. Charitable work begun by her husband in Wisconsin was not successful and she was brought prominently before the public by reason of things for which she was not responsible. Her husband, who was a minister, finally deserted her and her two young children, leaving her homeless and penniless in Joplin, Mo.

FOUNDING OF HOME

"It was then that the ideas crystallized which led to the founding of Joseph's home. Conditions that confronted her forced these ideas upon her. The duty of providing for herself and children led her to seek employment. Before she could get employment she must put her children out to be cared for. The orphan's home offered the only solution. But the contrast: The children must be surrendered entirely to be adopted out if taken at all, unless she could pay for their keeping.

"To think of signing away her children, who were dearer to her than herself, never to look upon them again, nor to know of their whereabouts, to have lost the parental name and cared for possibly by some woman whose cold formality makes home but a name, whose heart knows not the meaning of motherhood! Such a picture confronted Mrs. Baker. She saw here what, to her, was an evil greater than that which caused the Civil War, for but few of the inmates of orphans homes are really without parents. She resolved that the inhumanity of such separations should be shown to a candid world and to do what little lay in her power to correct the evil. She conceived the idea of founding a home for mothers and children. She would care for the children of the homeless dependant mothers and at the same time uplift the mothers and help them by some useful occupation to become self-sustaining. This home should be dedicated to maintaining and strengthening the family ties.

"Mrs. Baker was imbued with the thought that the case is rare, if indeed any exist, where a woman who has become a mother is entirely devoid of the motherly instinct. She believes that however depraved a mother may be when untoward circumstances are removed she will respond to reformatory help as surely as the flower turns its face to the sun.

HUMBLE BEGINNING

"A humble beginning was made, and the benevolence of the people appealed to her to sustain the movement. With a stout heart and a prayer of faith Mrs. Baker toiled and success has crowned her efforts. Goods boxes were first, chairs, newspapers, the table cloths and beds were made upon the floor. She many times went hungry and impoverished her own wardrobe that the destitute might have relief. She met opposition and was beset by difficulties. The lapses of her husband were brought up against her; but knowing the righteousness of her purpose, she did not falter. Once gaining the ear of the thinking men they gave her hearty support. Her story bore the stamp of truth and friends increased. The home was moved to Kansas City, a more central point, and property was purchased for the present home. It is the aim of the founder to establish similar homes in other localities where they are needed.

SCORNS ASSOCIATED CHARITIES

"Mrs. Baker does not hold herself answerable to the Associated charities, but to the public. A strict accounting is made and a committee of business men make regular examinations and reports. Expenses are guarded and regulated as wisely as possible. On entering a town for the first time representatives seek a good hotel until acquaintance gives assurance of accommodations above reproach, at cheaper rates, preferably in private families.

"To offset the manner contained in the circular that has been published against her, Mrs. Baker could give the best class of evidence to more than the whole issue of the 'News.' Those who speak adversely are either uninformed or biased in their views by reports of rivalry. Judges and business men of the highest standing have given unsolicited endorsement to the work. It is thought the success of the Joseph's home or homes, will in time draw attention to much uncharitable charity, as it has been promoted in the past and is carried on today.

"After a personal visit and examination of the home, a report was made by seven prominent business men of Kansas City, of which the following in the closing paragraph:

"'We are not only impressed, but profoundly impressed, with what appears to us in fact unqualifiedly the most human undertaking we have ever known.'"

From The Deseret Evening News, Salt Lake City, March 4, 1908:

WOMEN IN BLACK DEPART

Notified by Chief of Police to Cease Soliciting Funds They Quit the Wilson

The two women in black, who have been "doing the town" in the aid of the Joseph Home of Kansas City, gave up their elegant suite of apartments at the Wilson this morning, and departed for fresher fields and pastures new. Officials of the Salt Lake Associated Charities followed them up, until Chief of Police Pitt told them they must cease soliciting funds. So they left the city. According to all accounts the women harvested quite a sum here, as they did in San Francisco, by working on the sensibilities of charitably inclined people, and there are many such in Salt Lake.

Joseph had never seen the man before and kept a close watch on him as he entered the shop and took a slow look at things. Dignified and stout, there was a slight droop to his shoulders. He was old, but he did not carry himself that way. His clothes were fancy and he had new shoes. He looked important. LeWald waved to the man from behind the counter, where there was a line of three other customers.

"Be with you as quick as I can, Judge," he said.

"There's no hurry," the man said. He had a thick voice, loud and strong.

Joseph got up from the corner where he was playing and crept behind the counter to where his uncle was standing, and held the seam of his trousers. The big man smiled, and Joseph ducked behind his uncle's leg.

When the customers were gone LeWald and the man spoke like friends and used words Joseph had never heard. After a minute or two the man called out to him.

"Are you shy, boy?"

Joseph stepped further behind LeWald and both men laughed. It made him want to hide even more.

"I don't know why he gets like this," LeWald said. "If he knows you he's all right, but if you're a stranger you can't get a word out of him."

"Come on, son, I don't bite."

Joseph refused to move, and soon he felt his uncle's big hands slide under his arms to lift and deposit him on the counter. The man laughed and shook Joseph's knee so that his entire body rattled.

"There, now. See? I'm not so frightening."

Joseph slowly raised his eyes and looked closer at the man. He had a face like a pumpkin, with full cheeks and dark lips. It glinted with perspiration, and he smelled like some kind of sweet spice.

"Hello, there. How do you do?"

The man stuck out one of his hands and held it open for Joseph. Looking down a bit, Joseph put out his own hand, which disappeared as the man gripped it – a bit too hard – and shook.

"What's the matter? Can't you talk?"

"Won't talk is more like it," LeWald said. "Soon as you leave he won't stop."

"So you've said."

The man let go of Joseph's hand and took him by the chin, raising it until they were looking into each other's eyes. His touch was again too rough, although he did not seem to realize it.

"You need to learn to speak when you're spoken to, boy. People won't do business with a man that can't look them in the face, and that's the truth."

The man let go of Joseph and they continued to stare at each other. Joseph rubbed his chin and hoped the man would not notice.

"You think your daddy'd be able to run this place if he was scared to talk to his customers? He wouldn't stay open a week." The man smiled. "Do you like comin' to work with your daddy?"

Joseph nodded.

"What's that, son? I couldn't hear you."

"Yes, sir. I do."

LeWald patted Joseph on the back and the man smiled harder.

"That's right, that's how you answer a man. You look him in the face and say 'Yes, sir,' or 'No, sir.' That's just the way to do it. And that's the way I'll expect it every time I come here. Do you understand?"

Joseph began to nod, but caught himself.

"Yes, sir."

"Smart boy. I'll be here plenty, too, to keep an eye on your daddy."

"Actually, Judge, I'm not–"

"You should be proud of him," the man told Joseph. "He's doing real well here. Real well."

Joseph looked at LeWald and smiled.

Later on Joseph sat in the wagon fingering the reins as he watched LeWald hitch up the horse. The sun cast a deep orange glow across the streets, with long dark shadows jutting out everyplace. When LeWald finished he clambered onto the wagon and pulled the reins out of Joseph's reach. Holding them in both hands, he whipped them against the horse's flanks and clicked his tongue. As they began to move down the street Joseph watched their shadows, now flat on the ground, now raised up as they passed by buildings and carts and other things, waving up and down, forward and back. It was hypnotic and Joseph laid his head against LeWald's arm. LeWald made the horse stop as they reached the intersection, and held it back. He stared forward as he spoke.

"I'm not your father. You know that, right?"

Joseph nodded.

"I'm sorry," LeWald said. He did not sound angry. "I'm not your dad. I felt like I had to say it."

Transferring both reins to one of his hands, he put his other arm around the boy's shoulders. Joseph tried to move away but LeWald held him close. He kept him there after he took up both reins again, and held him all the way home.

All of Ada Brady's possessions fit into one suitcase. She preferred it that way. It allowed her to travel wherever she needed as fast as possible. It batted rhythmically against her leg as she walked to the Home. The neighborhood was a good one. Up the street she saw a pair of boys who looked quite out of place for the area. They wore filthy clothes and their hair was sheared to the scalp. When they saw her they came running and panted like excited dogs. Ada smiled and eased her pace, but as they drew closer it became apparent that they were not happy, but frantic. They appeared to be eight to ten years old, but it was hard to say for sure. They were so small, and scrawny, too, with bones that stuck out at their wrists and on their faces.

"Can you give us anything to eat?" the littler one said.

The bigger one frowned and gave him a smack on the shoulder with his tiny fist.

"I'm sorry, lady," he said. "My brother don't mean to be rude. We're so hungry, is all. You got any work we can do? We'll do that if you can give us some food."

"I'm sorry, but I've just come into town. I don't have anything you can do at this moment."

The boys nodded.

"Thanks, anyway, ma'am," the bigger one said. "We're sorry if we bothered you."

"Wait a minute, now." Ada knelt on the ground and turned her case on its side. Opening it, she took out a small green purse with a metal clasp. She found a few coins and handed them to the boys, who thanked her several times before they ran away.

Mrs. Baker was on the porch ready to greet Ada when she arrived. She came down the steps and held out her arms and enveloped Ada in a warm hug.

"I'm so glad you've come to work with us," she said.

Ada noticed the house was quiet.

"Where are the children?" she asked.

"They're on an outing," Mrs. Baker said as she released Ada. "We like to keep them busy. Busy and happy."

Mrs. Baker led Ada through the house and showed her all the rooms, including Ada's bedroom, which was located on the second floor.

"It's in the center of the house, so if you keep the door open you'll be able to hear everything," Mrs. Baker said.

There was nothing much in the way of space or furnishings. A small bed, a small dresser, a small washstand. Apart from the single window, that was all.

"I'm sorry it isn't bigger."

Ada put her suitcase on the bed and turned to the door, where Mrs. Baker stood.

"That doesn't matter a thing to me," Ada said. "I'm not here for fancy living quarters, I'm here for the children. If it helped them I would sleep in a cave if I had to."

"You understand us so well," Mrs. Baker said and stepped aside so Ada could follow her into the hall.

"This house serves an important purpose," Ada said.

"It surely does," Mrs. Baker said as they began to go back down the stairs.

"I knew it did before, but just now I was stopped in the road by two boys. It's so sad. They were begging for food."

Mrs. Baker clucked her tongue as they rounded the corner and went toward the kitchen.

"That's when I really knew I was doing the right thing by coming here," Ada said. "But I can't stop thinking about those poor boys. I gave them some money, but what about when tomorrow comes and they're hungry again?"

Mrs. Baker pushed open the door and held it for Ada.

"If you do see them some other time, why don't you tell them about us? Ask them where they live and see if you can talk to their parents."

Ada entered the room and folded her hands.

"Would that be right?"

Mrs. Baker remained where she was.

"Most of the people who truly need our help are much too proud to ask for it."

Ada realized for the first time that the kitchen was empty.

"Is there anyone here at all?"

"Just we two," Mrs. Baker said as she came in. "I like to give the girls a few hours off between meals so they can rest a bit and get some air. They'll be back soon. They'll tell you more about their schedules and how things are run. It's time for me to leave now, too, I'm afraid."

"So soon?"

"A house like this one doesn't pay its own costs. I have a lot of others helping, but it's important for me to go out collecting right along with them. These children need a voice, and I'm happy to provide it."

"I understand what you mean, but that can't be easy."

"Good work is never easy. My only wish is that I could reach more people. Even with all of my helpers, we haven't reached nearly enough with our message."

"There must be a solution."

"I have an idea or two. But I've also a train to catch, and so I must go."

She went to the back door and opened it.

"What shall I do first?" Ada said.

"You could take a nap, or have another look around to familiarize yourself with the place. The girls shan't be long. When they get here you can oversee them."

"I'll do that. Again, thank you so much."

Mrs. Baker smiled.

"Thank you, dear, and God save you. You're so kind to help us."

It took Ada nine minutes to put away her clothes. The suitcase she slid under the bed. She pressed on the mattress. The springs were flimsy and loud, almost like the snarl of a cat or a tight violin string. She sat, and sank in deep so that she could feel the frame holding the bed. She took out her watch and checked it. It was not yet two o'clock.

Ada inspected the boys' room first. The air was stale, and she opened the few windows, which were located on the far walls. The smell would not go away without getting all the sheets washed, possibly more than once, she realized. She went to the nearest bed and pulled back the blanket, and saw a smattering of tiny insects hopping like grease in a frying pan when the air hit them. She let out a disgusted grunt and stripped the sheets from the bed, dragging them to the window and giving them a hard shake over the yard.

Downstairs the front door opened and Ada pulled the sheets in so they hung over the window sill. She heard several sets of footsteps, and she went to the stairs and began her descent. When she reached the second floor she was met by a pair of young boys, who smiled when they saw her.

"Thanks again for the money, ma'am," the bigger one said. "We feel a lot better now."

"Juliana, why have you not gotten married?"

Mrs. Baker looked to the corner of the porch where her father sat. He gazed out past the yard to the first road that led away from the farm. The air was cool, and he flexed his fingers above the arms of the chair to keep up his circulation.

"I was married."

"That was years ago. Both of those men were years ago. You need a man for today."

"I haven't any time."

"Your children need a man in the house, also."

"They have their uncle."

"An uncle is not a father."

In the distance Mrs. Baker saw the corn had begun to sprout in uniform rows that stretched to the horizon. She rocked her chair.

"I have to attend to my work."

"You can do that with a husband."

"Papa, I don't need a husband to do my work."

"That is true. But it would help you. He does not have to do your work, Juliana. But people would think better of you. Your work is for families. So, you must have one. A full family of your own. A husband and wife, and their children. It is what people want to see."

"Mrs. Baker!"

It was the voice of a man, smooth and melodic. Mrs. Baker walked faster, but not enough to attract attention, or make it appear as if she was trying to escape.

"Mrs. Baker!" the man called again.

She heard quickening footsteps, and soon he was at her side. He looked about sixty and wore a well-tailored suit. Not a policeman.

"You are Mrs. Baker, are you not?" he asked as he removed his hat.

"I am," she said and stopped walking. "Forgive me, I didn't hear you."

"Think nothing of it," the man said and replaced his hat. "I thought perhaps when you heard me beseeching you that you had mistaken me for some kind of cad, but of course you heard me not at all. Permit me to introduce myself. My name is Osgood Phillips, commonly known both personally and professionally by the initials O. C. G. Phillips. I am a practitioner of the law – a judge, to be exact."

Mrs. Baker's smile froze.

"I wanted to inform you, madam, that I was amongst the lucky individuals able to attend your recent speech. I was both pleased and impressed by the fervor with which you delivered your remarks, and wish to offer my services in whatever stations you require."

When she was able to catch her breath, Mrs. Baker raised her arm as if to usher him further down the sidewalk.

"Perhaps we could discuss it over lunch."

They chose a café with white walls and small tables. Phillips was talkative and greeted – or was greeted by – almost everyone he saw. The one time he was quiet was when he ate, which he did with delicate bites, using a napkin to cover his mouth each time he swallowed. He ordered for both of them, and when he had finished his meal he ordered again for himself. When all the food was gone he was ready to discuss Mrs. Baker's work.

"I owe you an apology, for prior engagements necessitated my premature departure from your presentation. If she were here, my wife surely would join me in this sentiment, as she missed the event entirely. Ah, such is life, such is life. But perhaps, madam, you might find yourself amenable to answering one or two of my inquiries."

"I'll answer as many as you like."

"Excellent. How many children have you in residence at this time?"

"That would be difficult to say. They're always in and out, you know."

"An estimate would be sufficient."

"I suppose it's around forty-four."

"And you've the necessary provisions to keep them clothed and fed?"

"We can always use more."

"I am sure that you can," he said, nodding. "It's never enough, is it?"

"Sir?"

"Mrs. Baker, you must spend an inordinate amount of time traveling."

"Yes," she said, a bit uneasy.

"Then surely you know better than I how important a service such as yours can be. You are able to provide shelter and comfort to the needy children of Kansas City, but how many others have you seen in your travels that you've been unable to assist due to matters of geography?"

She shook her head, relaxing once more.

"I try not to think of it. The idea that I'm unable to help any child breaks my heart."

"I'm sure that it does. I should think there are many even within the borders of your own hometown who have been denied the warmth of your caring embrace."

"It's all too true, to my everlasting regret."

"To how many people are you able to impart your message each year?"

"I haven't any idea. Hundreds, possibly thousands if you consider the women I have canvassing on behalf of the Home."

"From the inflection you employ when you say that, I suspect you find this figure woefully inadequate."

"I do, but I do have one solution that would help us reach more."

"Which is?"

"A magazine. One that could explain our intentions. Each month we could run stories about the work we do, stories about our happy home and our happy children. We could run stories about unhappy children who need our help, and about the kind people whose donations have enabled us to keep our house. I call it Mother's Appeal."

"I think it's a wonderful idea."

"Thank you. Would you be interested in making a donation toward it?"

"Possibly. I do question, though, whether the success of such a publication would compound your problems. With the increased visibility it may bring to your work, it may also engender a sudden increase in children and parents wanting to make use of your facilities. I know you probably could stand to care for more youngsters, but just how many could you take in before you found your home filled beyond capacity levels?"

"I honestly don't know. Not very many, I suppose."

"Have you ever considered opening a second facility in a different region, while utilizing your Kansas City residence as your primary headquarters?"

"I don't know how I could."

"It's a matter of simple arithmetic, Mrs. Baker. In theory, an increase in visibility would mean an increase in donations. Utilize the revenue you acquire from your publication toward the purchase of another home."

"But where?"

"Why not here in Oskaloosa?"

"Do you think it's possible?"

"We're good-hearted people. If the cause is worthy, we would be happy to support it."

Mrs. Baker did not speak. Instead she nodded, unable to keep from smiling.

The judge rose and gave a little bow.

"I beg your pardon, Mrs. Baker, but I must leave you now. I have another engagement."

He took a business card from his pocket and handed it to her.

"Please relay your progress as to the publication of your magazine. And please do also consider what I've said."

"I will."

"That's fine. Goodbye for now, and I hope to hear from you soon."

"You will."

Phillips bowed again and left the table. Mrs. Baker read the card two more times before she secured it in her bag.

The nurse was sleeping. Joseph did not know her name. There had been so many he had stopped learning them. This nurse was young. She was pretty, he thought. He liked her, and Flora did, too. He hated school. Flora liked school. It was Saturday, and both of them liked Saturday. Mother and Aunt Marie were in the office, and Joseph and Flora played in the parlor with the nurse watching until she fell asleep. She did that quite often. It was easy, since neither of the children ever yelled or stomped around like elephants. All the adults they met said they were good.

Joseph had a ball. It was red and firm, and he rolled it across the floor to his sister. They sat across from one another with their legs spread and their feet touching. When Flora caught the ball she rolled it back. They smiled at each other, even though it was a game for babies. They played like that for a long time, and when they tired of it they stopped.

The sun was out. The windows were open and the house was comfortable. There was a breeze and it shook the limbs of the maple tree in the front yard and waved them like the arms of a dancer. Joseph and Flora watched them for several minutes, hypnotized. Joseph looked to the nurse, who continued to sleep. Then he looked to his sister and without saying anything left the house through the front door.

Flora watched her brother. She could hear her mother and aunt still talking in her mother's office, and the breathing of the nurse. If any of them saw, Joseph would get in trouble. He was always in trouble with their mother, even though he was good. Flora went to the door, which remained open, and stopped on the top step. Joseph stood in the grass. The sun illuminated his blond hair like the fluff on a dandelion and his white shirt made him look more pale than usual. He did nothing but stand, gazing completely transfixed into the tree. Coming out of the house a bit further, Flora followed her brother's line of sight to a branch about fifteen feet off the ground. Perched there against the trunk was a large nest, a bit smaller than a dinner plate, with jagged sticks poking out like the points of a crown.

"Joseph," Flora whispered.

He did not acknowledge her.

"Joseph!" she whispered again.

Still nothing.

Flora looked over her shoulder to the inside of the house. No one had noticed they were gone. Turning back to the yard she crept down the rest of the stairs and onto the grass where Joseph stood.

"Come on," she said and took him by the arm. "Mother'll get mad."

"Look," he said and pointed to the nest.

"You can see it from inside the house."

"I know, that's how I found it."

Flora pulled some more but he did not budge.

"You'll get in trouble."

"But I want it."

"You can't have it."

"Why?"

"If there's a mother bird in there and you touch her nest, she'll never come back again. It's true. Our teacher told us."

Joseph looked up at the nest.

"There ain't any birds up there."

"Aren't."

"There aren't any."

"How do you know? You can't see up that high."

Joseph freed himself from her grip. He walked to the tree and grabbed one of the lower branches with both hands, and put his bare feet against the trunk. Using them as ballast, he reached up and grabbed the next highest branch, and the next.

"Joseph, please come back inside," Flora said without much conviction.

He continued to climb until he was right beneath the nest. There was a gap in the branches, and no way for him to make it any higher.

"Be careful," Flora said.

Wrapping one arm around the trunk Joseph stood on his toes and stretched out his arm, and Flora watched as he fingered the rim of the nest.

"Is there anything inside?"

"Just feathers."

"Knock it down."

With a flick of his wrist he flipped the nest off its moorings and it fell, turning over several times on the way to the ground. When it landed four naked baby birds scattered a few inches from where Flora stood. She gasped and looked at her brother. He saw them, too, and began to scream.

"I'm sorry, I'm sorry," he repeated through his tears as he climbed down and gathered the tiny bodies and deposited them with care into the nest. When they were all back inside Joseph picked up the nest and mounted the tree a second time.

"What in the world is going on out here?"

Flora looked to the house and saw her mother barreling down the steps, followed by Aunt Marie and the nurse.

"Mother, I–"

"Hush, Flora, I know it isn't your fault," Mrs. Baker said as she stopped at the base of the tree.

"But Mother, I–"

"Get down from that tree right now!"

Still crying, Joseph ignored her and continued to climb. When he reached his former height he tried to put the nest back. He was not tall enough, and settled for placing it a bit lower.

"Joseph! Get down here!"

Joseph rested his forehead against the tree for a few seconds and wrapped his arms around the trunk as if he were embracing it.

"I'm not going to repeat myself, Joseph! Get down here this instant!"

The boy used his shoulder to wipe his nose and eyes, and then began his careful descent. His mother all but growled as she watched him come down, and once he was within reach she grabbed the back of his neck and pulled him off the tree.

"What is wrong with you?" she shouted. "Why do you do these things?"

Joseph barely got a word out before she pulled him over her knee and began to hit him as hard as she could. After that all he could do was cry.

"Mother, please stop," Flora said. She was crying now, as well.

"He has to learn," Mrs. Baker said over and over. "He has to learn."

When her arm grew tired she let him go and he fell in a heap at her side, crying and moaning. Breathing heavy, Mrs. Baker nudged him with her shoe.

"Get upstairs now and get to your room. I don't want to see you for the rest of the day."

Joseph did not move. Soon Flora began to walk toward him, but Mrs. Baker shook her head.

"No, don't help him. If he can climb a tree he can climb the stairs."

After giving a final loud sob Joseph quieted down, sniffed and stood. He did not look at his mother or sister as he went up the front walk. Mrs. Baker followed him, stopping briefly to talk to the nurse.

"Take off that uniform and get out of my house. This is all your fault."

Silent tears flew from the nurse's eyes. She said nothing, and gave a little curtsey as Mrs. Baker passed.

Joseph entered the house and began to go up the stairs. Mrs. Baker stopped at the landing and rested one hand on the banister as she spoke to him.

"I won't stand for this kind of nonsense. Any one of my children would be glad to take your place in this house. From now on you can spend your Saturdays at your Uncle Leslie's shop. He knows how to keep his eye on a bad little boy like you."

"I'm not going," Joseph said without looking at her.

"I beg your pardon? Do you want another whipping?"

Joseph reached the top of the stairs and looked at her from behind the railing.

"I don't like him anymore."

Mrs. Baker clenched her fists and climbed three steps.

"What did you say?" she asked in a threatening voice.

"I don't like him. He's not my father."

Joseph lay on his stomach and stared out the dark window. The lights were off in the house next door, and had been for some time. He was hungry, not having eaten since lunch, but most of all he was sore. It hurt when he moved his legs and he would not dare to roll onto his back.

The hinges of his bedroom door squeaked and Joseph turned his head and looked toward it. He lowered his nightshirt, wincing as he did. Flora was there in her nightshirt, and she closed the door again and crept to his bed.

"Are you awake?" she whispered.

"Yes."

"I brought this for you."

She held out her hands and Joseph saw she was holding a dark object in a vague square shape. He reached over and touched it. Bread. Still on his stomach, he took it from her and crammed as much as he could into his mouth. As he chewed Flora sat next to him on the mattress.

"Thank you," he whispered between swallows.

Flora smiled and ran her fingers through his silken hair.

"I'm sorry," she whispered.

"You told me not to."

"Does it hurt?"

"Mm-hmm."

"What's it feel like?"

"Like a whipping."

Flora's cheeks felt hot.

"I've never had one."

Joseph finished the last of the bread.

"It's like a bad burn."

"How long does it hurt?"

"A few days. It gets better a little bit at a time."

Flora scratched her knee.

"Can I stay in here a while?"

"Sure."

She stretched her legs and lay beside him. Neither of them spoke for two minutes.

"Flora?"

"Yes?"

"Do you remember Papa?"

"A little."

"What was he like?"

"Strong. He had a mustache. He was tall."

"Was he nice?"

"Yes."

"Mother told me he died."

"When?"

"When she put me to bed. How did he die?"

"I don't know."

"Why not?"

"I was too little. It was a long time ago."

"Was I alive?"

"You were a baby."

Joseph said nothing.

"What did Mother say to you?"

"You don't have a real father. He's dead."

"We do so have a real father."

"But he's dead."

"He's still our real father."

"What did he sound like?"

"I don't remember."

Joseph turned his head back so he faced the window.

"Did you sleep at all?" Flora asked.

"No. I was too hungry."

"What did you do?"

"Just lied down."

"Maybe you can sleep now."

"No."

"Why not?"

"I can't stop thinking. Mother won't tell me anything else. She already said so."

"You'll get to sleep."

"It doesn't feel like it."

"You will soon enough. Shut your eyes."

He said nothing.

"Are they shut?"

"Yes."

"Everything'll be all right. You wait and see. When we grow up we'll be happy."

"That's a long time."

"Things'll be better sooner than that. They'll be better tomorrow." Her voice picked up momentum. "I stayed outside after you went in. I watched the nest, and the mother bird came back. I saw her. She flew around the tree three or four times and then she went into the nest. She stayed there. I saw it."

"What about what your teacher said?"

"The mother bird came back. I saw her."

"I'll look for her tomorrow."

"No, don't."

"Why?"

"She won't like it. Animals can smell people, and if she smells you she'll know it was you that pushed her nest off the tree."

"I'll only look for a minute. I'll look from the front door."

"It won't matter. She'll smell you."

"Then how can I get in the house?"

"If you have to go past the tree, you just walk as fast as you can. Don't look at it. Pretend that you just don't even see it. Maybe then you'll fool her. It's the only way. You have to promise you'll do it. Promise me you won't look."

He sighed.

"Okay. I promise."

Mrs. Baker spread the butter across her toast. The dining car was full and its passengers spoke to each other in loud voices over the clacking of the wheels and the clattering of the silverware. Mrs. Baker sat near one of the doors with her back to most of the car. She took a bite. The door slid open as she chewed and a man stepped into the car. He was tall, with auburn hair and red cheeks, and he wore a gray suit with a black bowler hat. His long nervous fingers played with the buttons of his coat as he walked about looking for an empty chair. When he turned back and saw Mrs. Baker's table he gave an uncomfortable smile and removed his hat.

"Excuse me, ma'am, but there are no other seats."

Mrs. Baker put down her toast and made a motion with her hand.

"Please, be my guest."

The man smiled again and nodded and put his hat in his lap after he sat down.

"I appreciate it, ma'am," he said. "Thank you."

"It wouldn't be very Christian of me to refuse you."

"No, ma'am."

Soon a porter appeared at the head of the small table and asked the man if he wanted anything.

"I believe I'll have the same as this lady. But instead of tea or coffee, may I please have one glass of milk and one glass of orange juice?"

"Very good, sir."

"Thank you."

The porter left and the man smiled at Mrs. Baker.

"I don't care to drink either tea or coffee. They aren't good for my stomach."

"Do you have trouble with it?"

"Chronically."

"Why do you think that could be?"

The man thought a moment, then shook his head.

"It's one of those things, I suppose."

Mrs. Baker nodded.

"What's your name?"

"Julia Anna Baker."

"Mine is Enbody. Joseph Enbody."

"Did you say Joseph?"

"I did."

"I have a boy by that name."

"You don't say. Is he here?"

"No, he stayed at home."

"Where is that?"

"Kansas City."

"Is your husband here? Have I taken his seat?"

Mrs. Baker became subdued. She pursed her lips and looked for a moment at her plate.

"My husband has been gone for many years now."

Enbody sighed and shook his head.

"I am sorry, ma'am. You must think I'm such a heel."

She looked at him again. He seemed about the same age as she, but he appeared older somehow. There were permanent lines at the corners of his eyes and deep crevices in his forehead. Despite his constant smiles, he seemed ready to weep.

"Not at all," she said. "Don't worry a thing about it."

Enbody was heartened by her words and the smile returned to his face.

"You must be a very strong woman."

"Any strength I have is given to me by the Lord. I thank Him for it, for it enables me to continue my work for my children."

"Have you more than just your boy?"

"In a way of speaking."

"How do you mean?"

Mrs. Baker was halfway through explaining her work when the porter returned and set the plate of food and the two glasses before Enbody. He was turning to go when Enbody motioned for him to wait, and took some money from his billfold. Handing it to the porter, he said, "I will pay for both of our meals."

"Oh, but I couldn't impose–" Mrs. Baker said.

"I insist."

The porter left and Enbody unfurled his napkin, placing it atop his hat, which remained in his lap.

"You need all the money you can spare," he told Mrs. Baker.

Silent now, she smiled, too, and proceeded to eat what remained of her breakfast. Enbody cut off a small piece of egg and put it in his mouth. He chewed slowly, as if he were trying to avoid biting into a piece of shell. After he swallowed he took a sip of milk so small it was difficult to say whether the level in the glass had changed when he set it down again.

Mrs. Baker finished her food and the rest of her tea before Enbody was one-third of the way through his meal. She watched as he scooped some of the yolk from his plate with a spoon and dolloped it onto a piece of toast. He bit into it and chewed. After he swallowed his color changed to a whitish green, and his stomach rumbled like a handful of gravel rattling in an empty drum. He pushed his plate aside. He picked up his glass of milk again and took another small drink. The noise rang out a second time, and Enbody winced and briefly bared his teeth. When the noises stopped he set down the glass and watched it with a look of intense longing. Then he shook his head, wiped his mouth, and pushed the glass away, too.

"You poor man," Mrs. Baker said.

Joseph sat in the corner facing the wall and did not move no matter how many times he heard the bell ring when the shop's door opened. He heard footsteps. They belonged to a woman. He could tell. His uncle spoke in a surprised, happy voice, and his Aunt Marie answered. They said a few things and then they waited a moment.

"Is he being punished?" she asked.

"Nope."

"What's he doing, then?"

"Avoiding me, ignoring me, whatever you wanna call it."

"Whatever for?"

"Eh, you know kids." He spoke louder. "Right, Joseph?"

Joseph sighed and crossed his arms tight.

"See what I mean?"

"Joseph," his aunt said. "Come here and kiss me."

With a jerk he got up from his chair and walked to her. She stood on the other side of the counter and he had to walk around it to reach her. His uncle smirked as he passed and Joseph ignored him. Aunt Marie smiled a nice smile and bent over. Joseph pecked her cheek. She had a smell that was clean and sweet, like budding springtime flowers.

LeWald looked over to Judge Hazell's nephew, who was in another part of the shop.

"James?"

"Yes, Mr. LeWald?"

"Could you watch him while my wife and I go in back for a few moments?"

"Yes, sir."

When the door was closed LeWald kissed his wife and held her close, pressing his body into hers. She could feel him through his trousers, and she almost fell from the way he pushed against her.

"Stop," she said. "What if somebody comes in?"

Raising one of his hands, LeWald leaned over and soundlessly turned the lock.

"No," Marie said. "Not here."

"When, then?"

He moved his hands along her hips.

"Tonight. I promise."

"Please..."

"Tonight," she said in a more forceful voice. She took him by the wrists and removed his hands, then pushed him back until he reached an office chair. He sat and she released him, and he sighed in frustration and spread his knees to display the lump of his erection. Marie giggled and LeWald propped his hands on the armrests of the chair and gave her a playful scowl.

"You wait," he said.

"*You'll* wait, you mean."

He sighed again and she smiled.

"How were things when I was gone?"

"The same as ever. How was your trip?"

"Not as good as it should have been. It's better than when I started, but I'm still nowhere near as good as Julia."

"You got some donations, though?"

"Not many, but some."

"That's all that matters, then. Those kids need all the help they can get."

Marie raised her chin.

"How do you mean?"

"Come on. I've seen how your sister makes them live."

"How *she* makes them live?"

"She decides what happens with the money, doesn't she?"

"Les, it's a charity, there isn't a constant revenue source."

"Even with all the women she has working for her? She's got two houses, a cook, a maid, a nurse, two kids of her own – what do you think she pays for all that with?"

Marie came toward her husband as if she was preparing to strike him.

"My sister is not a thief. She has nothing but the best intentions in everything she does. Why would she take in so many children if she didn't truly believe in what she was doing?"

LeWald stayed in his chair.

"I really don't know."

"I can't believe you."

Marie relaxed her posture and walked a few paces around the desk, fingering the leather protector that lay over the top of it.

"Listen, I'm sorry," LeWald said. "I don't know anything about it. I saw those kids, I didn't think they looked good, that's all. I didn't mean anything by it."

"Of course they don't look well. They're charity cases."

"Fine. That makes sense to me."

"Think how they might look if it weren't for my sister. They would be living on the streets."

"I'm sure they would. I never thought of that."

"No, you didn't. You just said the first thing that came into your mind, as usual. Why do you have to be so suspicious all the time?"

"I don't know. I'm sorry."

She looked at him again, her eyes flashing.

"Don't ever say anything about my family. They're good people."

"I know they are. I'm sorry."

Marie looked at the desk again. LeWald leaned forward and rubbed his hands together.

"Did you see her this time?" he asked. "You cross paths at all?"

A curious smile formed at Marie's lips, and she turned to him.

"I did see her."

"How is she?"

"It's funny. She says she has a beau."

Good lord, LeWald thought. He did not say it out loud.

Flora's new dress was as stiff and as white as a clean sheet of butcher paper. She wore a white bow in her hair, as well, and a blue sash around her waist. Joseph wore a navy blue sailor suit, and with it he had on knee-length white socks and black shoes. The pair of them waited on the settee, where the nurse had told them to sit. Mrs. Baker was returning today with a surprise, she said, and then went off to get some work done.

"Whatchoo think it is?" Joseph asked.

"I don't know," Flora said. She kept as still as she could and spoke in a quiet, measured voice. It was impossible for Joseph to tell if she was nervous or afraid. It made him uneasy.

Some time later they heard the front door open, accompanied by their mother's voice, along with that of a man. The man's voice was unfamiliar. Flora stood and motioned for

Joseph to do the same. From the hall came the rustling of coats being removed, and footsteps scuffing against the floor, and always their mother's uninterrupted chattering. There was a lightness in the way she spoke that neither Flora nor Joseph had ever heard before. She carried on like a girl of sixteen. Soon she was in the doorway, facing them. Her cheeks were red from the cold air outside, and her smile made them look like fat ripe tomatoes.

"Here you are," she said. She spoke in a singsong manner, and at a higher pitch than usual.

Flora went to her and Joseph followed, and each of them took turns pressing their lips against her cold face.

"I suppose the nurse has told you I've brought a surprise."

"Yes, Mother," they said in unison.

"Would you like to know what it is?"

"Yes, Mother."

Continuing to smile, Mrs. Baker stepped into the hall and motioned for someone to come forward. She moved aside to allow a nice-looking man to enter the room. He stopped near the door and Mrs. Baker put her hands on his arms and poked her head from behind his back.

"Children, this is Mr. Enbody. He's your new father."

"Hello," he said and smiled.

"That's Flora," Mrs. Baker said, pointing.

"Oh, my, aren't you pretty?" the man said. "How old are you?"

The color rose in her cheeks.

"Nine."

Mrs. Baker pointed again.

"And that's–"

"Oh, I know who that is," the man said.

Joseph looked at him. His skin was smooth, and faint dimples appeared at the corners of his mouth when he smiled. There was a sharp but pleasant smell about him, like peppermint, either on his skin or his clothes. Joseph squinted as the man watched him.

"Who are you?"

"Who are you?" the man said.

Joseph said nothing, just continued to eye him.

"My name's Joseph," the man said.

The boy nearly gasped.

"That's my name."

"Are you sure?"

The boy nodded.

"I guess we'll be friends, then," the man said.

Joseph nodded again and smiled, his mouth hanging open in astonishment.

"I'm sure Julia's probably told you her idea," Enbody said.

He and LeWald sat by themselves in the parlor while the women and children remained in the dining room. The meal was long over and the men had been sent out to talk and get acquainted. They sat in fine armchairs separated by a small table with a full rubber plant on top, and let several seconds elapse before each answered the other.

"Yeah, she has," LeWald said.

"It *was* her idea, I hope you understand that. I never would have suggested it myself."

LeWald smirked and nodded.

"I can believe she thought of it on her own."

"How do you mean?"

LeWald shook his head, saying nothing.

"I don't want you to think it was any kind of presumption on my part," Enbody said. "I know that's probably how it seems. A man marries a woman and the first thing he does is to insinuate himself into her brother-in-law's business. That's not the kind of man I am."

"I thank you for saying that."

"Julia seems to think it would work, that's all."

"You know the man we're in business with. He's a judge."

"I know, she told me."

"If you came on board we'd probably end up shutting him out."

"Those kinds of exchanges are made every day. One partner buys another's shares. That's business."

"I've heard it put that way."

LeWald cleared his throat.

"It's only there's the – I don't know you."

"I understand."

"What else she tell you about that judge?"

"Just a few things."

"She tell you about the money?"

"She said he helped finance the business, but she thinks he wouldn't mind being bought out if you and I were to form a partnership."

LeWald said nothing.

"Was that not true?" Enbody said.

"No, it's true."

"What's wrong?"

LeWald sighed.

"You seem like an honest guy. I just don't know what I can tell you."

"Anything. Be as honest as you like. I prefer it that way. If you don't want to go into business with me, I don't blame you. We've only known each other a few hours, for Heaven's sakes."

LeWald was silent again, and Enbody leaned toward him and spoke in a quiet voice.

"If you think that whatever you say is automatically going to get back to Julia, I want to assure you, it isn't. I assume some of the things I say won't go back to your wife, because we both know that if they did, they would soon get to Julia. Believe me, I know how sisters are. There was a pair of them in my hometown, twins they were. They fought about everything. They were spinsters and they lived in the same house their entire lives. They both wanted their way, so when it came time to paint the house, they ended up putting two different colors on it, one on the first floor, one on the second. It was ridiculous. But if you said anything about the first one to the second one, believe me that the first one would hear about it within ten minutes, and they would both go after you as fast as anything. I know sisters. What we say in a room by ourselves has no business being transmitted to either one of them."

LeWald leaned close to where Enbody had stopped, and when he began talking it was close to a whisper.

"Did Julia say anything about the furniture?"

"What furniture?" Enbody asked, just as soft.

"We're sittin' on it."

In addition to the chairs and table, there was another table, long and closer to the floor, a settee and one footstool. All were done in the same elegant style, with soft red fabric and mahogany. Enbody shrugged.

"There's more than just this. But that judge? He paid for it. And he wants his money, too."

"How much is it?"

"Two hundred an' fifty. It was Julia's idea to get a loan from him, but she ain't said a damn thing about getting him paid back. He's not mad – not yet – but he does want his money. I don't blame him. We've got his nephew working at the shop now, to pacify him, I guess. I shouldn't be tellin' you this. Marie would kill me if she heard. But that's the way it is."

"I can help you," Enbody said. "We'll get this figured out."

LeWald's eyes drifted to the entryway. He leaned back in his seat and smiled.

"Look who's here," he said.

Enbody turned and saw Joseph standing in the door, hugging the frame of it and sucking his bottom lip.

"Come on in," Enbody said with a smile, and sat back, too.

Joseph approached with great care, as if he were trying to keep from making any noise. He stopped a few feet from Enbody's chair and fidgeted as he watched him. Enbody glanced at LeWald and then stood and picked up the boy, laughing as he tossed him in the air and caught him, then sat in the chair again with Joseph in his lap.

"When's the happy day?" LeWald asked, smiling, too.

"We haven't settled on one. It's Julia's idea to visit Wisconsin and then stop somewhere and get it done on the way back. Nothing ostentatious."

Joseph looked into Enbody's face as he spoke, unable to keep from grinning.

"What you think of that, Joseph?" LeWald asked.

Joseph stopped smiling and looked at LeWald.

"This is my father," he said. He all but spat his words.

The partnership with Judge Hazell was dissolved the first of December, with Enbody making a deal to purchase his interest over time. Mrs. Baker married Joseph Enbody on the sixth. The ceremony took place in Worthington, Minnesota, at the Worthington Hotel. It was a simple affair. There were no attendants, and it was performed by the justice of the peace, Judge Coy.

"I've been doing this for seventeen years," Judge Coy told the couple afterward. "Yours is the eighty-ninth marriage I've performed. I have another tomorrow, so that'll make ninety in all."

"Congratulations," Enbody said.

"Thank you," the judge said. "I must be making a good job of it. In all that time I've only had two divorces. Bodes well for you two, wouldn't you say?"

A new partnership in the Co-Operative Leather Company was made on the twenty-second. It was signed by both of the LeWalds, as well as Enbody, but not Mrs. Baker. The shop on East Fifteen Street continued as the base of operations.

Joseph waited at the door to his parents' bedroom for a long while. It was a few days after Christmas. It was time for breakfast and neither Joseph's mother nor his new father was up yet. They were awake, he knew that. He could hear them. They would talk – or his mother would. He heard her most of all. She never sounded that way before. Desperate, even scared, as if she were being hurt. Joseph put his ear to the door, but he could make nothing out. They were trying to be quiet.

Even though he was straining to listen Joseph still did not realize how close to the door his mother was, and he almost fell into the room when she opened it. She jumped when she saw him there, and swatted his face with the back of her hand so that he stumbled back and away from her. Coming forward, she closed the door and moved to strike him again, but missed by two inches.

"What is wrong with you?" she said, less as a question than as an expression of frustration.

"I wanna see Papa," Joseph said from against the wall.

"You can't see him now. Come down to breakfast."

"Why can't I see him?"

"Because you can't. You'll see him later. Now get down there or you'll be sorry."

There were pancakes and sausages on the table, and everyone but his parents were already there when Joseph came in. He went right to his chair and soon a plate with three cakes and three sausages was set before him, and he began taking big bites, which he only half-chewed before he swallowed.

Mrs. Baker entered soon after Joseph, adjusting one of the pins in her hair.

"Mr. Enbody isn't feeling well this morning," she said as she sat. "He hopes to be down a little later on."

"What is it?" Marie asked.

"He has a weak stomach, you know. Poor man, he awoke in the night because it pained him so, and he didn't get much sleep after that."

Joseph continued to eat as fast as he could, with enormous bites almost too big for his mouth.

"Don't wolf your food," Mrs. Baker said. "You'll end up with chronic indigestion. Like your father."

Joseph swallowed what was in his mouth, and panted after it went down.

"If you make yourself sick, so help me," Mrs. Baker said.

Joseph set his fork next to his plate and caught his breath. The food he had eaten seemed to expand in his stomach like cooking rice until it felt heavy. There was so much left to eat. He stared at his plate, willing his stomach to somehow empty itself, and the adults talked about work and church and other boring things. He was sleepy and leaned his head on the back of his chair.

"Oh, you're tired now?" Mrs. Baker said. "You won't get much sympathy from me. I knew that would happen, but of course you wouldn't listen to me. But you'll clean that plate even if you have to stay there all day."

Flora's plate already was clean and Mrs. Baker excused her from the table without being asked. Marie finished eating, too, but she stayed in her seat. Mrs. Baker ate quickly – one piece of toast – and kept her eye on the door. When her plate was clear she stood and looked at Joseph and smiled.

"Were your eyes too big for your stomach?" she said and let out a fluttery laugh.

LeWald sighed and wiped his mouth. He shook his head as he stood, and his chair scraped against the floor. He stepped behind it, and then put his hand on it and pushed it back to the table.

Enbody stood in the doorway, weaving slightly. It was as if he had just appeared there by magic. His face was red like he had been holding his breath, and he had a smile that seemed almost unsettling to Joseph.

Mrs. Baker noticed him and inhaled.

"Joseph, go back to bed right now."

The sentence came out fast, like one long word. Enbody looked at her and took a wobbling step forward. It was then Joseph realized his father wore only a nightshirt, and that it jutted out in front like there was a wooden spoon hidden at his waist.

Marie noticed, too, and gave a little gasping cry, shielding her eyes with her hand as she fled from the room.

"You comna bed," Enbody said. He sounded like his tongue was paralyzed.

"Mrs. Baker looked at her son.

"Joseph, you may leave the table now."

He took his time getting up, as if he thought the floor might shift under his feet. His mother kept looking at him. There was a smile on her face, but it made her look more frightened than happy. Enbody came toward her and took her by the arm, pulling it.

"Come on," he slurred. "Come on, now."

"Stop. Get back to bed," she said and raised her hand so that he would let go.

Startled, Enbody stumbled back, and then his face darkened. His lips curled into a scowl and he pushed Mrs. Baker hard enough so that she lost her footing and fell against the wall, and then slid into a sitting position. She shrieked as her behind hit the floor. The table rattled from the force of it. LeWald stood frozen near his chair.

Joseph watched the three adults for what seemed like a full minute. None of them spoke. Then Joseph began to shout. He ran to his father and slapped his bare legs while roaring a series of indistinct syllables. Enbody seemed bemused for a moment, and then hauled off and hit the boy hard on the ear. It sounded to Joseph like the popping of a balloon, and he fell to his knees and put his arms over his head for protection. He shut his eyes tight and soon felt a series of vibrations on the floor near his head, and a covering of some kind draped across his back.

It was his mother. He recognized her smell. She was holding him and saying that it was okay. She kept saying it. He opened his eyes. In the doorway his uncle straddled Enbody and punched him in the face until his nose looked like a squished piece of fruit. Soon Joseph's eyes were blocked by his mother's strong fingers, and he felt her warmth as she made a shield all around him, and he realized that, somehow, he loved her.

"Come on, you two," LeWald said. "It's time to set out for home."

Flora and Joseph laughed and talked as they followed him through the back of the shop to the wagon, which they climbed without his help, and waited while he brought the horse around. It was spring and there were just a few traces of snow remaining, mostly the deep puddles like small lakes on the side of the road.

"I wish it was summer," Joseph said.

"I don't," Flora said. "It gets too hot."

"But there's no school."

"I like school."

Joseph grimaced.

Soon LeWald was back with the horse, and started hitching it to the wagon.

"Uncle Les?"

"Yeah," he said without stopping his work.

"Do we have to go to church tomorrow?"

"Joseph," Flora said, a little shocked.

"Why not? Mother's gone the next couple weeks. Don't tell me you like church, too."

"It doesn't matter if I like it or not, we still need to go."

"Do we have to, Uncle Les? I won't tell."

"I know *you* won't," LeWald said. He looked at Joseph, then at Flora, not moving until she spoke. Joseph looked at her, too, keeping as still as if he were posing for a photograph.

"Oh, all right," Flora said. "I won't tell. I promise."

Joseph threw his arms around her shoulders and squeezed. LeWald smiled and finished with the horse.

"But we should go next week," Flora said as LeWald climbed onto the wagon. "In case Mother asks about it later after she comes home."

"That's not a bad idea," LeWald said. He jostled the reins and clicked his tongue.

"I guess not," Joseph said.

They pulled into the street and all their talk ended. Joseph looked to his side and watched their reflections in the shop windows as they wheeled past, then lowered his eyes to peer over the edge of the wagon. He held out one hand so that his fingers extended over the side and he stared a bit past them. In a moment or two it looked like the entire wagon was spinning in a circle, with his hand as the pivot point. He smiled. He had done the trick before, and closed his eyes when he became dizzy. It was a warm feeling, and it made him happy.

Joseph opened his eyes again just as the wagon really did begin spinning. He heard his uncle swear, and Flora shrieked, and Joseph looked in time to see the wagon collide with a grocery cart that was being pushed into the intersection they were crossing. Frightened, the horse began to run and would not stop no matter how hard LeWald pulled the reins. Flora grabbed her brother and held him as they careened down the street.

Up ahead were several workers making repairs to the track for the street railway company, and they saw the wagon approach and raised their arms and shouted so the horse might stop. He kept running, and soon they were passing through the workers, who had to dodge out of the way to avoid being trampled. Some of them threw their shovels but the horse went on as if he were galloping over an open field. It all seemed to move so slowly to Joseph.

At the edge of the worksite one of the men dragged a wheelbarrow into the path of the wagon. Everyone saw it and braced themselves for impact. The horse saw it, too, and made a quick swerve. The wagon hit the curb and a thundercrack rang out and the children found themselves on the ground. Behind them lay the wagon, its front wheels missing.

Flora was crying. Joseph was numb. Some of the workers clustered around them and asked if they could walk. Flora and Joseph moved their arms and legs carefully, as if they were made of delicate glass. When he was on his feet Joseph began to cry, too. They were alone. Flora took his hand and began to run with him on the sidewalk to a spot fifty feet away where another crowd had gathered, and they pushed their way through a forest of legs until they saw their uncle sitting up and shaking his head. His hands were covered with raw red stripes from the reins, and he opened them when he saw the children. They jumped into his arms and he held them close.

"It's all right," he told them. "We're all all right."

He rocked them and kissed them and told them everything would be okay. The workers brought them some water and after ten minutes had gone by helped them to stand. All three of them were stiff and their limbs hurt but they were walking. Soon they began to smile, and even chuckled a bit. It was a strange day, Joseph thought.

The horse was found soon after. He had run back to the shop.

"Joseph? Are you awake?"

It was Flora, staring at him from the doorway of his room. Joseph threw back the covers and she came in and got onto the bed. She took the sheet and blanket from him and wedged them under her chin as she lay down.

"You cold?" Joseph asked.

"Just chilly."

They hugged and Joseph rested his head just below hers, pulling the covers down just a bit.

"Is that better?" he asked.

"Yes. Thank you."

Joseph settled in, and felt his sister's hand on his shoulder, rubbing it gently, and her breath rustling his hair. He closed his eyes.

"Joseph?"

"Hmm?"

"Do you hurt?"

"A little. It ain't bad. Just on where I hit the ground, pretty much. How about you?"

"The same. It's not as bad as I would've thought."

"Huh-uh."

"But Joseph?"

"Yeah?"

"I've been thinking."

"About what?"

"We should go to church tomorrow."

He raised his head to look at her.

"But Uncle Les said we didn't have to."

"I know."

"Then why would you wanna go?"

Flora did not answer. In a few seconds Joseph lay down his head again.

"I've just been thinking," Flora said. "What if it didn't turn out? What if we'd been really hurt? What if we died?"

"We didn't."

"But what if we did? Then what? God knew we weren't going to church. If we'd died, then what would've happened? We'd never of had a chance to say we were sorry."

"I'm not sorry."

"Don't say that."

"I'm not sorry. I ain't gonna lie. God doesn't like it when people lie, does he?"

"No."

"Well, then."

Flora began to rub his shoulder again.

"Does he like it when people miss church?"

"It's just one day."

"That's why we have to go. It makes a difference. If something happened and I hadn't gone, I don't know what I would do. What would happen? What if I couldn't go to Heaven?"

"You'll go to Heaven."

"How do you know? What if I made God really angry because I missed church?"

"You'd miss it if you were sick."

"But I'm not sick. I'm just not going. I'm not going for any other reason than you don't wanna go. God knows that. It scares me."

"Then go. I won't stop you."

"What about you?"

He blinked several times and gave a heavy sigh.

"Uncle Les said I didn't have to."

"So you're not going?"

"If I don't have to go I'm not going."

"But–"

"If you wanna go so bad, you go. I'm stayin' home."

"What if something happens?"

"Nothing'll happen."

"How do you know that?"

"Nothing *has* happened."

"What about today?"

"Nothin' happened. We're fine."

"We could've really been hurt."

"But we weren't."

Flora waited a moment.

"I think God did that to make us go to church tomorrow."

"No…"

"I do."

"God doesn't do that."

"How do you know? He can do anything. The Bible says so."

"Sure he can."

"So why wouldn't he do that?"

"I don't think he would hurt us to get us to go to church."

"That's just it. We didn't get hurt bad. It was to scare us."

"No. It didn't happen on purpose. It just happened. That's all. Things like that just happen. They happen all the time."

She frowned.

"I'm still going."

"That's fine."

"I don't want God to think I wasn't listening to Him."

"He wouldn't think that."

"I'm going, anyway."

"Do I have to?"

"No. I think you should, but I don't make you."

"You won't tell, will you?"

"God would know anyway."

"What about Mother?"

Flora thought for a bit.

"I won't tell her."

"Thanks," Joseph said. He looked up and gave her a kiss on the jaw. They smiled and Flora closed her eyes. She could feel her brother's heartbeat, and he could feel hers. The bed was warm now, soft and safe. Flora's breathing began to slow. Her head and arms felt heavy, and her thoughts started to blend together.

"Flora?"

She said nothing.

"Flora?"

"Yes."

"I'm sorry. Were you asleep?"

"Almost."

"I'm sorry."
"What is it?"
"No. It's all right."
"Tell me."
A full minute passed before he spoke.
"Do you think I'm bad?"

Ada Brady watched the girl throughout the service. She was impressed. Although she sat by herself her attention never waned. She looked at the reverend the entire time, and really seemed to listen to him. Given the option most children, if they were by themselves, would have flipped pages in the Bibles or the hymnal, or made little toys using the trinkets in their pockets.

Flora left first, once the service had finished. She did not rush, just walked at a normal pace to the exit, never hinting she might be glad it was over. Ada stayed back a while, until most of the congregation had filed out. The sun was radiant, and Ada squinted as she came out of the building after shaking the reverend's hand.

"Hello."

Ada stopped walking and looked back to see Flora standing near a large tree in the churchyard. The girl smiled and took a step forward.

"Hello," Ada said.

"Since we'll be going the same way for a bit, I thought we could walk together."

"Do you know who I am?"

"Yes. Do you know who I am?"
"I do."
"May we walk together?"
"Of course."
They walked half a block before Ada broke the silence.
"You must be a very good little girl to come to church all by yourself, especially since you mother is out of town."
Flora's cheeks felt warm.
"No. I just thought that I would."
"And that isn't being good?"
Flora said nothing.
"I noticed your brother wasn't here."
"Uncle Les said he didn't have to go, so he stayed home."
"That's boys."
"If he didn't have to go he wouldn't. That's what he said."
Ada nodded.
"You still come," Flora said.
"I like to."
"But no one makes you."
"No."
"You like it, though? Really?"
"Sure. I feel when I sit there and pray that I'm really talking to God, that He can hear me. And it's quiet. Peaceful. I don't get much of that."
"How do you mean?"
"Never mind, sweetie."
"With all the kids? I know they can be loud."
"Yes, that's part of it. I just meant that it's a relaxing time for me."
They walked a bit more.

"It's hard work, isn't it?" Flora said.

"Yes. But all real work is hard. That's why it's work."

"Do you like it?"

"Yes," Ada said after a second had passed.

"Even though it's hard?"

"Yes. Even though it's very hard. But all of us join together at the Home and do our share, and then it's not so bad."

"Can I help?"

"No. I'm sorry, dear."

"Why not?"

"I don't think your mother would like it." She seemed agitated. "I'm not even sure I should be talking to you."

"It's okay. She's not home. And I won't tell."

"The rest of your family, though. They would miss you, and then they would want to know where you were all day."

"I guess they would."

"Mm-hmm." Ada nodded. She seemed more at ease now.

"Is there still something I could do? Without coming to the house? Maybe something I could do in my room or at school, and my mother would never have to know."

"I'm not sure."

"Oh, please. I want to help."

Ada sighed.

"Let me think about it. Will you be at church next Sunday?"

"Yes."

"All right, then. Meet me outside next week like you did today and maybe I'll have something for you to do."

The week was torture. It felt like a month, and Flora had trouble concentrating on much. Her senses dulled. She was unable to listen, slow to speak, and asked repeatedly by the adults she knew if she were feeling all right.

On Sunday she came to church with her brother and uncle, who had to tell her more than once to quit looking over her shoulder, and put his hand on her knees to keep her heels from bouncing on the hardwood floor.

When the service ended Flora left the building with her family. They were at the sidewalk when she said she left something behind, and told them to keep going.

"We can wait," LeWald said.

"No, it's all right. I'll catch up."

"Okay, but make sure you do. Lunch'll be waiting for us when we get home."

Flora nodded and went back through the crowd of people still emerging from the building. She stopped at the entrance to the sanctuary. It was almost empty, and Flora did not see Ada anywhere. She looked for about fifteen seconds, then turned back. There Ada stood, waiting for her at the double doors at the front of the building. Flora ran up, panting, and apologized.

"I was with my brother and uncle," she said.

Ada smiled and put her hand on Flora's shoulder.

"Calm down, you'll make yourself sick."

"I'm sorry. I didn't wanna miss you. It was all I could think about all week long."

Ada's smile fell a bit.

"So what is it?" Flora asked. "What can I do?"

Ada sighed.

"I thought quite a bit about this, I really did. And I think the best thing you can do is to be a normal little girl. Be happy. Play with your friends, play with your brother. Go to school and learn. You're too young to think about this kind of work. So many children aren't as fortunate, and if they could, they would trade places with you in two seconds."

"But that's why I want to help them."

"If that's really what you want, then you should talk to your mother about it. I don't feel it's right for me to give you chores."

"She won't do it, either."

"You won't know unless you ask. If she says no, you can always ask again later on."

Flora's lip began to twitch as if it were being tickled by a hair. She looked toward the street at the passing wagons and carts. A single automobile weaved through them and most of the horses either jerked to a stop or reared up a bit.

"Please don't be mad at me," Ada said. "I really do think it's the best thing for you."

Flora looked her in the face.

"I'm not happy," she said. "I won't pretend. I'm not a baby."

Ada smiled again, but it was different this time. The corners of her mouth were turned down and wrinkles appeared by her eyes.

"You're so young," she said.

Breakfast already was cooking when Ada Brady got out of bed that next Saturday. She could smell the vague sweetness of the oats as they bubbled in the pot. It was not an appetizing smell. They were stale and tough, which required them to be heated longer than usual and left them with the appearance of masticated paper. Ada washed and dressed herself and left her room. Closing the door behind her she was hit by a new smell, sharp and warm and pleasant. It was meat. Bacon. Ada went down the stairs, through the hall – crowded with children, who smelled the food, too – and into the kitchen. Stepping inside she saw the girls readying the meal. With them, holding a fork over an open skillet, stood Flora. Flora watched Ada with a look of defiant satisfaction.

Flora left for home early in the afternoon smelling like an uncleaned griddle. Her legs were stiff and her hands were freckled with tiny red grease burns. It felt good, and she smiled without realizing it. When she arrived at the house she skipped up the front steps and opened the door. Her mother was waiting for her on the other side, and Flora stopped, her hand clutching the knob, the look of happiness frozen on her face except at her eyes.

"Come to my office. Now," Mrs. Baker said.

Flora did. The house seemed empty. If the rest of the family were in, they were silent. Mrs. Baker sat at her desk and Flora stood watching her.

"How does it feel to be a thief?" Mrs. Baker said in a flat voice.

"Don't blame Miss Brady. It's my fault."

"I know that."

Flora nodded and lowered her head.

"So you want to work, do you? All right, then. Scrub all the floors in this house. I should have you do that all the time. Then

I wouldn't have to pay anyone. You wouldn't like that, would you?"

"I'll do whatever you ask, Mother."

"Do this, and get started now. You know where the buckets are."

It took Flora the rest of the day. Mrs. Baker watched from the hall as she completed the last of the rooms. Flora's back was to her. Her shoulders were hunched and she moved like a crooked old woman as she dropped the rag into the bucket of water.

"What do you think of working now?"

Still on her knees, Flora turned and faced her mother.

"What can I do next?"

Mrs. Baker frowned. She thought for a moment.

"Eat something. Then get to bed."

It was April when things began to change for George M. Shelley. While he was on a business trip to Portland, Maine, John B. Lawrence, the chief clerk from the office of the assessor and collector of water rates, told a story. Testifying before a council committee, Lawrence said Shelley had owed the city about four thousand dollars. The funds, Lawrence said, were borrowed by Shelley from the office's collections. Lawrence said William J. Baehr, the city treasurer, had carried a twenty-five hundred dollar check from Shelley in lieu of cash, and that a further sixteen hundred dollars' worth of checks could be found in the cashier's cage at the water office. Shelley finally paid what he owed the day Baehr died, Lawrence said.

"That's the story, gentlemen," he told the committee. "I am sorry I had to tell it."

Shelley told his own story about two months later, after he gave up his position in the office of the assessor and collector.

"I'm all right, as sound as a nut," Shelley told a reporter from *The Star* in the office of the Scottish Rite Temple at Fifteenth Street and Troost. "No, I don't need anything, thank you," he said. "Thank you."

The previous day Shelley filed a voluntary petition of bankruptcy in the federal court, disclosing debts unsecured in excess of seventy-two thousand dollars. The paper said he had at times made one hundred fifty thousand dollars a year, owned one hundred thousand acres of farmland and more than sixty pieces of rental property, with a rental income of twenty-five hundred dollars each month.

"Sit down and I will tell you how happy I am this morning," Shelley told the reporter. "I am the happiest man in Kansas City. The burden is off my shoulders. I am free of the slavery of debt."

Shelley sat in a swivel chair and placed his thick elbows on the armrests. He smiled beneath his heavy mustache, and his eyes glinted like those of a man much younger than his sixty-one years.

"Yesterday I was relieved of the burden I have been carrying for five years. Five years ago we had a disastrous fire on Delaware Street, and this was followed by the failure of business concerns in various states, whose paper had been endorsed by me to the extent of two hundred thousand dollars. I've been trying to pay.

"Pay, pay, from morning 'til night. For five years every cent has been sucked up like a sponge until at last the debt has been growing faster than my ability to offset it. I have slept on a wooden cot at the store on Wyndotte Street, my living has cost me forty-five cents a day at cheap restaurants, I have dressed simply – almost shabbily – but the debts were getting ahead of me. A part of the time while I was assessor and collector of water rates I received two thousand dollars a year, and part of the time I received three thousand. Every cent of the money – every cent, mind you – has gone to pay debts. I have not taken a cent of it. Pride money, it was. In five years I brought the debt down from two hundred thousand to seventy-two. I could have become a voluntary bankrupt years ago, but I wouldn't. But now I'm getting old. There's no use denying it. I just couldn't do it any longer. I had to be free. I've pinched and pinched and saved, but I couldn't catch up. I'm too old, I guess. It was too heavy. I had to give way.

"The worst thing that can happen to a man is debt. There is no slavery so cruel as the slavery of debt. The advice I would give to my son, or to any friend, would be, 'Never endorse paper under any circumstances for anybody in the world.'"

Shelley gave a shrug and let out a peculiar laugh.

"I am happy today," he said and nodded. "Now I can begin again. True, I'm sixty-one, but I am in full possession of every power. A man can begin again, you know – even after forty-two years – and do something, and if I can regain standing in the community, no man is going to lose a dollar because of me, not a cent. I will pay it all. So, I am starting new today."

He rose and walked around the desk, not looking at anything in particular.

"You know, before ten o'clock this morning I had a dozen telegrams offering me both money and merchandise. Three of them have telegraphed me that they've mailed my cancelled notes to me. Then in addition to that I have been congratulated over the burden. Scores of brother Masons have tendered help. But I don't want anything from anybody."

Shelley stopped behind his chair, put a hand on its back and gazed out the window.

"Down at the little store on Wyandotte Street I have the names of perhaps thirty thousand men who owe me money – notes aggregating one million six hundred thousand dollars. I lent money to everybody, almost."

He shook his head, and a dull smile appeared on his face.

"I started at nineteen. Now I'm sixty-one."

He was silent for a while.

"I'm free this morning," he said once more. "I can begin again."

Marie LeWald clutched the reins tight as the wagon turned onto Brooklyn Avenue. It was about six o'clock and the sun hurt her eyes. She blinked and raised one hand above her forehead. Along the side of the road was an automobile, the driver of which stood at the front of it turning furiously on the crank. Seeing it, the horse stopped and took a few steps backward.

"Come on, now," Marie said and slapped the reins against its back.

The horse stopped moving altogether and began to shake its head back and forth as if it had water in its ears.

"You stubborn old..."

Marie whipped at him with the reins but he did not move. Soon the man with the automobile stopped turning the crank and hopped into the driver's seat. He pulled some levers, which prompted a powerful bang from the exhaust pipe, and at once the horse was off. There was no time for Marie to react. When they reached Seventeenth Street, about a block away, the horse veered into the gutter. The wagon hit the curb and sent Marie hurtling through the air.

The bed was soft, but as Marie lay on it all she was conscious of was pain. Her knee was dislocated and her arm was broken. Her face was bruised and there was a deep cut across it. She felt like she had been run through a thresher. The heat of the room made her itch, but LeWald tried to help by blotting her forehead with a cold wet sponge. Marie smiled and winced at the same time as he attended to her.

"What else can I get you?" he asked.

"Nothing."

"Some water, maybe? To drink?"

"All right," she said, nodding.

He lifted a glass to her lips and she swallowed just a bit, and groaned when she lay her head back down.

"You should have let the doctor give you something."

"I'll be fine."

"That's right," Mrs. Baker said from a nearby chair.

LeWald started, having forgotten she was in the room, and frowned without caring whether she noticed.

"There's nothing a doctor can do but set a bone," Mrs. Baker said. "Not when you have faith in God."

"Faith or not, my wife is in pain."

"If you allowed her to take that medicine she soon would become a slave to it, do you know that?" Mrs. Baker rocked in her chair. "Morphine, Demerol, it's the work of the Devil. Prayer is the only real medicine anyone needs. What you really should be doing is getting a different horse and stop bothering with all this talk about medicine."

LeWald patted Marie's head with the sponge. She closed her eyes and smiled in a way that made it look like she was cringing.

"You would give it to your children, I'll bet," LeWald said.

Mrs. Baker continued to rock. "I certainly would not. To them least of all. Not to anyone in my family – including you."

LeWald dipped the sponge in a bowl that sat on the bedside table and wrung it out until just a trickle of water was left. When he put it to Marie's head her eyes popped open.

"It's true, Les," she said. "Pray to Him and know the truth. Julia's right."

"You see?" Mrs. Baker said. "Your wife knows."

Marie nodded and shut her eyes again. LeWald returned the sponge to the bowl.

At three minutes before ten in the morning J. T. Chafin was given entry into the Home, where he was met with the sight of several dozen children standing to meet him. They were arranged in rows like a choir, with the small ones up front. Behind the children was an assortment of young women, some of whom held babies and others who merely stood at attention. At the side of the room was a large fireplace choked with wood and radiating heat. After she closed the door Mrs. Baker sidled up to Chafin and extended her arm toward the group.

"This is our family," she said.

A short stout man, Chafin removed his glasses, which had fogged up when he came inside, and wiped them with his scarf. Once he replaced them he took off his hat. His hair was thin, and the static pulled it up and out so that it fell onto his forehead in a long curly strand. Some of the younger children smiled and one laughed and covered her mouth. Embarrassed, Chafin quickly brushed it back with his palm and turned to Mrs. Baker.

"I-I wasn't expecting this," he said. "Are you this formal every Saturday?"

Mrs. Baker laughed and moved to take his coat, but Chafin shook his head and raised his left hand. He was timid, like a mole. Easy to manipulate.

"You're going to be working with us, so I felt you should meet everyone at the same time," Mrs. Baker said.

"Yes, I see."

"I'm only sorry the entire board couldn't come today."

"Yes. Well." He turned to the group and gave a shy nod. "Hello. Good morning."

"Good morning, Mr. Chafin."

They answered at the same time, and the noise startled him. He took a step back and then forward, as if he were swooning, and turned his hat in his hands. He cleared his throat and looked to Mrs. Baker.

"Is there someplace we could speak that's perhaps a bit more, er, private?"

"Certainly. We can retire to my office."

"Ah. Good."

Mrs. Baker turned again to the others and smiled.

"Thank you, everyone. When I conclude my meeting with Mr. Chafin I'll see to the rest of you. Until that time I want you to go about your regular activities."

At once the group relaxed and without talking spread to other parts of the house. When the room was for the most part empty Mrs. Baker gestured for Chafin to follow her.

"I would like to thank you, Mr. Chafin, for your assistance," she said as they moved down the hall. "And the board, too, you must thank them."

"Certainly. It's a worthy cause."

Mrs. Baker stopped at an open door and waited for Chafin to pass through. He refused, insisting she go first. "God save you," she said with a curtsy before entering.

The office seemed to double as a kind of generalized workroom. In addition to the simple desk piled with papers, along the walls stood tables holding fabrics, boxes and tools.

"Forgive the mess," Mrs. Baker said as they sat. "We utilize every inch of space that we can."

"It's no trouble. I like to see it. It means you're busy."

"Oh, it does. But that doesn't mean it's easy."

"Perhaps, though, once this incorporation process is finalized you'll have more time to focus on the Home's work." He jumped in his chair as if he had gotten an electric shock. "What I mean is, you won't be so focused on the business end of it. You'll have more time for the children and the Home itself. I hope you didn't misunderstand."

"I know what you meant. That is my hope."

"Very good."

"I want to have some additions built onto this house. We need the space, as you can see. That's one project I need to initiate."

"Yes, gladly – I would be glad to help you. If everything goes well – or rather, better than it is now – perhaps you could get a new house. A bigger one."

"That would be a great help."

"Yes."

"I want so to expand the work. More people need to know the plight faced by these children."

"I can help with – that is why the board appointed me."

"What must I do?"

Chafin took a sheaf of papers from his case and referred to them as he spoke. When he did he was like a different man. Apart from the occasional hiccup his stammer had gone, and he was able to maintain eye contact for more than three seconds at a time.

"Now, then. You've never been incorporated before, is that correct?"

"Yes," Mrs. Baker said, somewhat taken aback by his sudden change in demeanor. "This is the first time."

"Very good. Before you sign the agreement, before I take it to the judge, I need to be sure you understand what is required of you. Once the board takes control of the Home, you will turn over all of your bank books, your records, your trust funds to us. If there is any document pertaining to the running of this institution, you are required to give it to me. Do you understand?"

"Yes, sir."

"Furthermore, you must provide me with all of the collections and donations that you and your solicitors receive as they come in. They will be put into your account, from which you can draw as needed to purchase supplies, materials, et cetera. If you make a withdrawal, you must do it through me, and also provide me with any documentation regarding the purpose of that withdrawal."

"Yes, sir."

"Failure to comply with these requirements will result in legal action against you and against this institution."

"I understand, sir."

"I repeat. They *will* result in legal action. Not might. Will."

"Yes, sir."

Chafin smiled and nodded.

"All we need now is your signature."

He left the office by himself with his case at his side. He fastened the top buttons of his coat as he moved down the hall, and took deep breaths to prepare himself for the oncoming blast of cold air.

"Sir?" a voice said behind him.

Looking back, Chafin saw a young woman with a glove in her hands.

"You dropped this," she said as she approached.

Chafin felt his pockets and shook his head.

"Thank you, ma'am. I must have – It must have fallen out of my coat."

"You would have missed it outside," she said as she handed it to him.

"Thank you so much," he said and pulled it on.

The woman stayed nearby, looking like she wanted to ask a question.

"Can I help you, miss?"

"Brady."

"Miss Brady, yes."

"I'm the overseer here."

"Yes, I know."

"Is it true, sir?"

"Is what true?"

She lowered her voice to a whisper.

"That you'll be running things from now on."

While he did not whisper back, he spoke much quieter than before.

"No, no it – is that what you heard?"

Ada did nothing to answer him.

"Can you hear me?" Chafin asked.

"Yes, sir, I can," she whispered.

"No, I'm not running anything. I'm just – well, I'm something of an overseer, you could say. Like you. I'm keeping track of the accounts and all that sort of thing. No, I'm just – Mrs. Baker, she's the – Mrs. Baker's still running things. I'm just here to make it easier for her."

Ada glanced over her shoulder.

"Is anyone helping you?" she asked.

"No. Do I need it, do you think?" He smiled. "I've done this work for a long time. I'm a professional."

"Where have you worked?"

"With all sorts of – charities, the city – the gamut."

"How about with Mrs. Baker?"

"No. I don't – I've only met her today."

Ada nodded, thinking.

"Why?" Chafin asked. "What is it?"

"Nothing." She added one more thought before she left him. "Be careful."

Mrs. Baker pulled the box toward herself, over the leather desk protector, and wiped it clean of fingerprints before she opened it. She popped the lock with a small silver key and lifted the lid with a gentle touch, taking care not to jostle it and perhaps disturb its contents. The papers inside the box expanded as if they were awakened by daylight until they rose four inches over the opening. There was so much information – names, dates, monetary figures – and it was only she who understood how it all fit together. This puzzle was her masterpiece. One of them, anyway. Let other women concern themselves with such chores as cooking and housework. She was a businesswoman. The papers before her were success. They were control. Mrs. Baker did not even begin to sort them, or even take one note out of the box. Instead she simply watched them and marveled at how she was able to keep it all straight in her head, something a board of directors would never be capable of doing. They could never understand the significance of it all, even if she tried to explain it. It must remain like this, she thought. Unconscious of the smile on her face, she closed the box again and locked it.

The shop was empty again. The number of customers had dwindled since Enbody left, and there were no more than four or five each day. Judge Hazell still was not paid off, as Mrs. Baker had insisted that she be responsible for Enbody's payments. LeWald kept a stack of letters from Hazell in the bottom drawer of his desk, and made feeble replies each time a new letter arrived. Mrs. Baker would not discuss the situation. She said she knew what she was doing, and for LeWald to stop worrying. It made him feel like less of a man. LeWald smoothed his hands across the envelope, feeling the corners of the money it contained. Next to it was the paper with the list of names and amounts collected that Mrs. Baker had given him. He examined her handwriting, so careful and clean, like the examples in a penmanship manual. So easy to copy.

From beneath the counter he fetched a bottle of ink and some paper. Dipping his pen he transcribed the names of the solicitors. When he had finished he scanned the numbers and thought. Two dollars less for each? Three? Four? It would hardly make a difference. There were so many bills to pay, and not just from the judge.

LeWald replaced the pen and put away the ink. Then he crumpled the sheet of paper and threw it in the wastebasket, leaving the rest on the counter. The door to the shop opened and LeWald looked up with a smile, which fell immediately. It was only Chafin.

"Mr. LeWald."

"Hello."

"What are you, um – how are you today?"

"Very well."

He said nothing further.

"You have the, er–?"

LeWald took the envelope and the paper with the figures and handed them to Chafin, who examined them and moved his lips as he read.

"Is this everything?"

"It's what I was given."

"Of course. Would you – that is, could you speak to Mrs. Baker the next time you see her? She never seems to be around when I call on her."

"She's a busy woman."

"Yes. I only think that – no, I know. She must report to me. She must stop using you as her courier. This was not our agreement."

"I wouldn't know anything about that."

"Well. If I had known it would become permanent I never would have agreed to pick – to get the money and figures from you the first time. This is not what we discussed, and I don't think she realizes the legal, uh – ramifications of how she is doing business with us. With the board."

LeWald shrugged.

"How do I look?"

Mrs. Baker held out her arms and made a complete turn. The dress fit well, with no sagging areas. It was made especially for her with exquisite dark fabric that had the texture of velvet. Soft, warm, but not too heavy – perfect for spring and fall, and even winter with the right coat. A summer day like this one was a bit oppressive, but the dress was new and had to be shown off. There was a matching hat, as well, but she was not wearing it.

"It's quite nice," Ada Brady said from her chair.

"For fifty dollars, I should say it's more than quite nice – it's quite a bit more than quite nice."

Mrs. Baker ran her hands over the material, luxuriating in it with her eyes closed before she opened one of the bottom drawers of her desk. With both hands she lifted a tall bundle of magazines tied with two long pieces of white string.

"This is what I've brought you here to talk about," she said as she loosened the knot and took a magazine from the top of the pile. "This is what the children will be responsible for selling when they return from the farm."

Mrs. Baker handed the magazine to Ada. It was small, about eight pages, with a photograph on the cover of the Joseph

Walter Home and the children in rows on the porch and the lawn. So this is why it had been taken, Ada thought. The words "Mother's Appeal" were written in big letters above the picture.

Ada looked at Mrs. Baker, who watched her like a contented cat.

"Selling?"

"Yes. We need to raise more money."

"But the children will be doing this? What about school?"

"They'll continue on with that." Mrs. Baker stood and walked quickly around the room and moved her hands like windmill blades. "But after school and on Saturdays they can carry these around the city and sell subscriptions. That's what I want you to work out. Make a list of the children and organize them into small groups, who would work together most effectively and all that sort of thing. Then you can decide where each of those groups can go to make their rounds. You know them all, you would know better than anybody where they can best succeed in that regard."

Ada flipped the pages and scanned the columns, noting how many times Mrs. Baker's name appeared.

"What about your solicitors?"

"They'll continue as they always have. They're part of the reason I've had to establish this little book, God save them. They've been so successful that we've got more children than we can – oh, of course, you know all about it. No one knows better than you."

Mrs. Baker knelt beside the chair and placed her hands on Ada's knee.

"I appreciate it so. We all do. We couldn't function without you.

Mrs. Baker said it as one long brisk sentence. After a beat she stood again and went to the window.

"Get to work on that schedule today. I want to see it before the children return. You may leave now."

Chafin stood at the counter sipping his lemonade and checking the time. She was ten minutes late. It was his third glass, and it was less than a quarter full. The druggist pointed to it and raised his eyebrows.

"Can I get you another?"

"N-no, sir."

"Hot out?"

"Sir?"

"The way you've been taking 'em down. Thought it might be hot out."

Chafin shook his head. The bells above the door chimed and he saw Ada Brady come in. She moved toward him with an apologetic look and clenched fingers.

"I'm so sorry."

Chafin waved his hand and shook his head.

"I – it's just fine," he told her, and when he realized he was wearing his hat he quickly pulled it off.

The druggist nodded to Ada.

"You here to cash a check?"

"No, sir, I'm not. Why do you ask?"

"I know you work at Joseph Walter, so I thought I'd find out, save you the trouble of asking."

Chafin put his hat back on.

"Excuse me, but do you often cash checks for that institution?"

"Two or three every week, just about."

Chafin nodded and put his glass on the counter.

"That was something I was g-going to ask you about," he said to Ada.

The two of them went to one of the small wooden tables that lined the wall. Ada sat first, followed by Chafin. He took out some small sheets of paper and a dull pencil from his coat and used his thigh and hand as a makeshift writing desk so that nobody would notice. Ada watched him, mute. Soon he looked back to her.

"You know what you want to tell me, don't you?" he asked.

She nodded.

"Then go ahead. Please."

Ada took a few slow breaths. Although her voice was quiet when she began to speak, her tone was urgent, and she focused on Chafin's hand as it flew across the pages.

"We need food. Since they've come back from the farm the children have had nothing to eat but bread, milk, potatoes and hominy – and not enough of that, either. No fruit whatsoever. Their clothing is disgraceful, you've seen that. It's all unwashed cotton cloth. Almost none of them have shoes, and the little ones run around like a pack of shirttail boys. Which is fine for now, but I dread to think of what it will be like when winter comes. I've asked Mrs. Baker about it again and again, but all she'll say is that she has the situation under control, that she orders all the supplies the children need."

"Do you know anything of the money?"

Ada shook her head.

"Has she bought any more new dresses?"

"I don't know."

Chafin continued to write.

"What do *you* know about the money?" Ada asked.

"As much as you, I would suppose," Chafin said, still writing. "They don't give me enough to pay the bills. There's a four thousand dollar mortgage on the Home, but that's only half the debt. Nothing is paid off, not the gas, the furnishings, the telephone. Mrs. Baker sent me to see the milkman last week. He's threatening to stop his deliveries because she owes him twenty-five dollars. I don't want to worry you, but the grocers are making the same kind of talk."

He put his things on the table and rubbed his eyes beneath his glasses. Lowering his gaze, he blinked and stared at Ada.

"I told Mrs. Baker that we had to work out a plan to keep the home from going under. She said she wants to wait until her divorce is finalized, as if that has anything to do with it."

"Have you spoken to the board?"

Chafin nodded.

"What do they say?"

"They quit."

Ada said nothing.

"Even though she signed the papers she wouldn't turn over the company to them," Chafin said. "They've heard stories about her, the same kinds of things you've been telling me. And they decided they could not work with her. If they had known any of this months ago they never would have gotten involved in the first place."

"Will anything come out of that? Because she signed the papers?"

"No. The board wants to be as free of her as I do."

Ada felt queasy, and she looked away from him.

"I am sorry," he said. "Th-there's nothing I can do to keep the Home going. It would take a miracle." He paused. "I do have one other question. I don't wish to offend you, but I have to ask."

Chafin picked up his pencil as she gave him her attention once more.

"If the police were to come, would you be arrested for anything you've done?"

Mrs. Baker clutched the girl's tiny hand as they walked to the railroad station. It was two blocks away, and the noises of it could be heard like a thunderstorm building in the clouds. The girl was four years old, the mother had said, and she had red hair and cheeks that glowed as if she were always out of breath. She trotted alongside Mrs. Baker, who held the girl's belongings in a bundle under her other arm.

"I wish I were you, going on a big trip like this at your age," Mrs. Baker said.

The girl smiled and laughed but said nothing. She was too excited to form any words, and so she nodded, and Mrs. Baker smiled down at her in a way that made her feel protected.

The station seemed like a palace, with rows of shiny benches and clean slatted floors. There were people everywhere carrying bags and slips of paper, talking to one another or lining up at a counter and giving money to uniformed men.

Mrs. Baker bent over and straightened the girl's collar, and then took her by the chin.

"Now, listen, dear. I have to get our tickets, so I want you to sit over there on that bench and wait until I come for you. Do you understand?"

The girl nodded, too giggly to say anything.

"All right, then," Mrs. Baker said and nodded herself. "You be a good girl while I'm gone."

The girl all but ran to the bench and hoisted herself onto it. She sat with her knees together and her ankles crossed, with her hands folded in her lap. Her back was rigid and she stared straight ahead, like an adult. Her mother would be proud of her.

Mrs. Baker glanced once more at the girl before she left, making sure she was out of eyeshot. She passed through the entrance of the station walking fast, but not so much that someone might take notice of her. She was just another traveler in a hurry to find some place to stay. That was all. She did not look into the faces of those she passed. She rarely did so anymore, unless she was working. She was different than other people. She was smarter, cleverer. She knew. They did not.

When she reached the park she found an isolated corner and sat on a small white bench beneath a tree. She took the bundle in her lap and undid the string that held it together. The contents were meager: Two plain dresses, some socks and underthings, bits of green hair ribbon. Tucked in the middle of it all was a folded envelope, and Mrs. Baker pulled it out, leaving everything else in disarray. She tore it open and pulled out a small stack of bills. Twenty-three dollars total. She counted it twice and slipped it into her own bag.

Mrs. Baker tied up the bundle again without folding the clothes, so that when she was finished it looked like nothing more than a sack of rags. Which it now was, she thought. Standing, she let it fall to the ground, and nudged it under the bench with her foot, and quietly crept away. She walked along the sun-drenched path and was met by a young man and woman in good clothes who were pushing a baby carriage. Mrs. Baker stopped to coo and asked them if they had ever heard of home conserving.

She knew, she told herself as they gave her their answer. She knew.

On the last day of September fifty-four boys moved into the new site of the Boys' Hotel, which was located at the corner of Admiral Boulevard and Highland Avenue. According to the *Kansas City Star* the rooms were equipped with "neat iron beds, and new bed linen. There is a rug and a chair for every bed, and each boy has his own individual locker or wardrobe." The rooms were designed to house one, three, four or five boys.

"Two boys constitute an organization," Dr. E. L. Mathias told *The Star*. "They will conspire, hatch up schemes and execute them where no other member would. With three or four, there can be no such intimacy, for they act as checks upon one another."

Although not completed at the time of the big move-in, pool tables and a gymnasium were being set up, along with furnishings in the lobby and office. Regardless, the boys could not have been happier with their new surroundings.

"Yes, sir," one of them told a reporter. "This place cost somethin' like fifty-thousand bucks, but we wouldn't take a hundred thousand for it right tonight."

Three days later Chafin filed a petition asking that the Joseph Walter Home children be taken in charge by the juvenile court. The request was granted. A hearing was scheduled for Friday, the sixth.

The man climbed the steps of the house on Askew Avenue and knocked on the door. It was late afternoon on the fourth day of October. There was a chill in the air, refreshing, invigorating. Soon a uniformed woman appeared at the door.

"How may I help you, sir?"

The man removed his hat and held it to his chest along with some papers he was carrying.

"I'm here to see Mrs. Julia Anna Baker, please."

"I'm sorry, sir, but she's out shoppin'."

"What about Mrs. LeWald? Or, for that matter, Mr. LeWald? Are either of them at home?"

"No, sir, I'm afraid not."

"Do you have any idea when they'll be back?"

"No, sir. What's this about?"

"My name is James Gillham. I'm a probation officer, and I'm here to deliver subpoenas to all three of them, Mrs. Baker and Mr. and Mrs. LeWald. Are you absolutely sure they're not in?"

She shook her head.

"You could get into a lot of trouble if you lie to me, do you know that? You would be breaking the law if you did. Now, are they in or are they not?"

"No, sir, they're not, I swear."

Gillham nodded and put on his hat, and took a step closer to the door.

"And you're sure you don't know where they are?"

The girl's face began to turn red and her breathing became shallow.

"I really don't know. Maybe they're at the Home. You know, the Joseph Walter Home. Maybe Mrs. Baker's there, at least."

He put his hand on the frame of the door and leaned forward.

"I've been by there already. A few of us were. The juvenile court is taking charge of that place – for now, anyway. Someone filed a petition against them for mismanagement, and there's a hearing set for Friday."

"I'll tell Mrs. Baker when she gets back."

"No. I will."

The girl pulled in the door a bit.

"You can't come in."

"I'm not asking to."

He stood back and looked over the front yard. The girl stuck out her head a bit and watched him, but did not open the door any further.

"I'm waiting here if that's all right with you."

The girl said nothing. Gillham watched her a moment, then turned his back. A chair stood in the front lawn and he walked to it and sat facing the street with one hand on his knee and the other holding the papers. Without saying anything else the girl went back inside the house and shut the door.

In the chair Gillham took deep breaths. The cool autumn breeze made him feel good and he closed his eyes and let it wash over him like pure water. Soon he heard a soft tapping behind his head, and blinking, he turned around to see a young boy watching him through one of the front windows of the house. Gillham stared back. The boy waved. Gillham waved, too. Soon the boy opened the window, a strained expression crossing his face as he did.

"Hello," the boy said when the window was raised.

"Hello."

The boy settled himself in the window, resting his elbows in the frame and staring down at Gillham.

"Whatcha doin' here?"

"I'd like to see Mrs. Baker."

"She isn't home."

"I know. I'm waiting for her."

"You gonna arrest her?"

"No, son."

"Mm."

The boy stood, closed the window and left.

Gillham returned to the Baker house as the sun was beginning to set. He wore a wool coat and warm gloves, and swung his arms as he walked. He was met in the doorway by the girl he had seen earlier, who came out of the house when he started up the walk and waited for him with arms crossed to protect herself from the falling temperature. She was no longer fearful. Her nose was turned up and her lips shut tight.

"She's not here," the girl said when Gillham reached the door. "Neither are the others."

"Have they been back since I left?"

"Yes, and now they're all gone again."

"You wouldn't know where they went, would you?"

"No."

"You do know that–"

"I'm not some stupid little girl, you know. I don't have to tell you anything if I don't want to."

Gillham smiled.

"No, you're right. You don't have to say anything. But out of politeness, do you think you might be able to let me in on when they're coming back? It's getting cold, and I don't want to wait out here all night if I don't have to."

The girl sniffed and wiped her nose with the knuckles of her left hand.

"Saturday."

"I beg your pardon?"

"Saturday. They'll be back Saturday."

"You don't need to shout, I can hear you. Any idea of the time they'll be in?"

"No."

He nodded.

"You remember their hearing was set for Friday?"

"I guess they didn't care."

"So it would seem."

He turned up his collar and rubbed his hands together.

"There's nothing else I can do," he said with a shrug. "Thank you for being so helpful, miss."

She cursed him and went back inside.

Gillham could see the house from up the block. He watched it from the time the light of the sun was reflected in the windows. He stayed there watching all through the morning. He saw children walking to school, wagons in the street, sometimes an automobile, people on the sidewalk, but no one entering or leaving that house. That was his job. Waiting. He knew they were there. They had to be. Better to stay where he was than approach at the wrong time and scare them into holing up inside any more than they already had. As he stood there he wondered how many hours of his life had been spent this way.

The door opened around noon. Three of them came out, a man and two women. One of the women was in the lead. Gillham smiled and cleared his throat as he watched them come up the sidewalk toward him. He ducked behind a large tree that grew near the curb and removed the papers from his coat. He held his breath. He could hear their voices, faint and chittering, but growing louder. Soon he heard their footsteps, too. He cleared his throat again and adjusted his collar, and then they were about ten feet away he stepped out in front of them.

"Mrs. Baker? Mr. and Mrs. LeWald?"

The trio stopped short. The woman in front raised her chin but said nothing. The one in back grabbed the arm of the man and gasped.

"Yes?" she said.

The first woman could not hide her irritation. Still silent, she frowned at the second woman. Gillham handed the second woman one of the papers.

"Mrs. LeWald," he said, then handed another to her husband. "Mr. LeWald."

Then he held the remaining paper out to the first woman.

"Mrs. Baker?"

With reluctance, she took it.

"It's a disgrace – a travesty. Something to which my associates in the realm of legalities would refer as railroading."

Judge O. C. G. Phillips held his clenched fists below his chin and rolled his eyes to the ceiling. Mrs. Baker sat before him in a light-colored dress, at the edge of one of the elegant chairs in the hotel lobby, listening in rapt attention.

"Kansas City is a cesspool of corruption," Phillips said. "It's obvious to an outsider such as myself, since these men have no compunction against hounding such a pious lady until she's been stripped of everything – money, property, name, dignity…"

"And I have no money."

Mrs. Baker held a white lace handkerchief against her cheekbone. Phillips looked at her and gave a reassuring smile.

After he resumed speaking he stood and began to pace with his hands clasped behind his back.

"It pains me to say it, but it's a good thing. The curs would stop at nothing to wrest it from you. You won't care to hear this, I'm sure, but your best option would be to flee this den of vipers as one would a burning building. You can't be safe as long as you're within the wicked borders of this city."

"Where would I go?"

He grinned, still moving.

"It so happens that there stands in Oskaloosa, Iowa, a vacant hotel. It's not as posh as the one in which we currently find ourselves, but it's got sturdy walls and clean floors, and all the space an effort such as yours would require. Conveniently for you, it so happens that I myself am the owner of this establishment."

Mrs. Baker stroked her chin as she thought.

"Please consider it," Phillips said. "Oskaloosa is a good town. Its inhabitants are kind people who would be sure to press you to their collective bosom. For my part, I can explain your situation to them, lest they take seriously any of this malarkey with Kansas City's rotten legal system."

"Rotten or no, I still have the hearing on Friday."

"Have you acquired legal representation?"

She shook her head.

"I haven't the money."

"Then I shall accompany you to the hearing. You will require a man such as myself who can guide you through the inner workings of that morass of entanglements comically known as the legal system."

Mrs. Baker wiped her dry eyes.

"God save you," she said.

The hearing was held in the juvenile court and concerned the alleged destitute condition of the children. It lasted the entire afternoon, much of the time being given over to the gossip of neighbors and cries of financial doom from Chafin. But before much of that line of testimony could be given, Judge E. E. Porterfield announced that he would not accept any information regarding the misappropriation of funds. That was a matter for the criminal court, he said. Phillips did the best he could, defending Mrs. Baker's work in what the *Kansas City Star* described as "one of the most oratorical the juvenile court has listened to for some time."

Near the end of the proceedings Mrs. Baker was allowed to stand before Judge Porterfield in her own defense. Marie sat at the table beside her and held tight to her hand.

"If you take these children away from me you rob me of my life. I cannot live without them."

There was a catch in her throat and she clamped her free hand on her mouth and took a few deep breaths. Calm once more, she continued.

"Judge, my life is wrapped up in this work. I have never been happy. Everything has gone amiss with me. My first husband is gone and my second husband turned out a drunkard, but my heart always – even when I had a baby of my own in my arms – has been with these little ones out there at the Home. If you take them away, you kill the very best in me. I might as well die."

On the final word the sobs escaped her throat fast and loud. Marie stood and held her sister and cried, too, and Phillips stood and put his hands on the shoulders of both women while sadly shaking his head and clucking his thick tongue. Only after Judge Porterfield banged his gavel three times did the women quiet down. He sighed before he spoke.

"It's impossible to reach a definite decision in this case. There's too much conflicting testimony. For this reason, I will allow Mrs. Baker to continue in her role at the Joseph Walter Home under one condition: You will have to submit to a daily investigation, which will be carried out by Mrs. Agnes Odell and Dr. Laura Hulman."

At the table Mrs. Baker and Marie stood and hugged.

"Ladies. Please."

They sat, swallowing their cries, and held hands.

"This is a case of the future rather than the past," the judge said. "We are concerned with the question: Will the children be provided for from time to time? To me the future of the Home looks very dark, but I am willing to give you people a chance. I must say, however, that we do not intend to see those children mistreated."

Chafin resigned from the board the next day. "While I was secretary, Mrs. Baker was only a collector," he told *The Star*. "She is now president, and I will not serve under her. I believe it is only a question of time until the Home is closed because of debts."

Howard Hamilson was a difficult boy. Sixteen, ornery, heedless, he had been a fixture of the juvenile court since he was ten years old. But Dr. E. L. Mathias thought he had found a solution. An operation could be performed on his skull that would release the pressure on Howard's brain, Mathias said. Howard had a dent in his skull the size of a dollar that was about one half-inch deep, *The Star* reported. This dented portion would have to be cut away and replaced with a silver plate. When the pressure was relieved, Howard's behavior would improve, Mathias said. He had seen a similar case years earlier. Howard waited at the Missouri Training School for boys at Booneville as his father made the final decision.

"It is a serious condition," Mathias told Howard's father. "I don't want you to consent to it until you have consulted several surgeons. Take a day or two to consider it thoroughly after you have received the advice of several good surgeons. Then if you think it necessary to operate we will bring the boy back here for the operation or have it done in Booneville."

Ada Brady led Dr. Hulme through the hall to the room where the washing was done. There were a few large metal tubs sitting on tables and a couple of wooden folding chairs. Mounted to one of the walls was a single roller towel, brown with dirt and smelling of mildew. Dr. Hulme took some notes with a pencil as she examined it. She was tall and pale, with long slender arms. She had glasses with round silver frames and hair that was wound onto the top and back of her head, almost like a halo.

"Is this everything?" she asked without looking up from her writing.

"Yes?"

"How often is this changed?" Dr. Hulme asked, indicating the roller towel.

"Once a week."

"And this is to be used by all of the children?"

"Yes, ma'am."

Dr. Hulme stopped writing and looked at Ada.

"I've been told by several teachers that your children are routinely sent home with lice, as well as ringworm. Is this true?" She did not wait for an answer, and quickly added, "Of course it is – why should they lie?"

Ada nodded.

"Where do you keep the linens?"

"On the beds."

"The linens that aren't being used, I mean."

"We have no other."

"Miss Brady, don't you think your children would be less susceptible to these types of ailments if their home maintained proper levels of hygiene?"

"Yes I do."

Dr. Hulme took in the answer, then nodded once.

"And what about food?"

"They've eaten breakfast and lunch."

"What did they eat?"

"For breakfast, oatmeal."

Dr. Hulme nodded as she wrote.

"And milk?"

"Sometimes."

"What about today?"

"No."

"And lunch?"

"Boiled potatoes and bread."

"With or without butter?"

"Without."

"What will they have for supper?"

"We'll see."

When Dr. Hulme finished writing she motioned to Ada.

"Bring me to the kitchen, please. I'd like to make an inspection of its conditions."

They smelled a warm, hearty aroma of cooking before they entered. Ada held the door for Dr. Hulme, who passed through and found a table filled with women, each of whom had a full plate of thick, rare beefsteak, as well as stewed tomatoes and fat slices of bread. The women drank full glasses of milk, and spoke and laughed as if they had not seen the others enter. Dr. Hulme looked again to Ada.

"These are solicitors," Ada said. "Most of them. Some of them just work here in the house."

"Doing what? Certainly not cleaning."

Dr. Hulme walked around the table, watching them. At one point she moved in close and lifted a piece of bread from a serving dish. It was still warm from the oven, moist but firm. She sighed and put it back, then wrote something down. When she saw Ada watching her, she said only one word.

"Butter."

When the inspection had concluded Ada and Dr. Hulme went to the porch. A light wind was blowing, and Ada realized she never noticed how pleasant it smelled outside the house.

"You have some improvements to make, obviously."

"How soon?"

"The sooner, the better. Even if you can't fix some of the big things right away you should start work on what you *can* fix. I'll be by each day to see that it gets done."

"How bad was it? I know it was bad, but compared to some of the other places you've seen…"

"It would be inappropriate for me to give you information about other homes I've visited."

She began to walk down the front steps.

"Yes, I know, but–"

Dr. Hulme looked back.

"Miss Brady, these children are underclothed and underfed. The sanitation in this house is nonexistent. There is a grievous lack of basic care, or even interest on the part of the management. Frankly, I don't know what else to tell you."

"They'll shut it down, won't they? The city?"

Dr. Hulme sighed.

"Miss Brady, have you ever visited another children's home?"

"No."

"I didn't think so."

We knew he was mad. Of course we did. But these things happen so gradually you hardly notice. By the time they really manifest themselves, it's too late, and it seems you're the last to realize the truth. I don't like to think of it. I prefer to recall what he used to be. When he began his work in Chicago, father worked night and day, preaching, praying, healing and editing his newspaper. He worked so hard that he wore out two or three private secretaries and finally broke down, mentally and physically. I suspected he wasn't in his right mind when he began planning Zion City. An idea like that is not the product of a sane mind. I spoke to my mother about it, but she refused to hear me. She wanted to believe as much as his followers did. When he started his claims of being the reincarnation of Elijah, even she had to acknowledge his mind was failing him. But what could she do? What could any of us do? Anyway, it's too late to do anything now, if anything could have been done. He's long dead. I wish I could have stopped it. All of it. Zion City. The

New York tour. The funeral of my poor sister. It haunts us, my mother and I. She's had a breakdown now, too. She's at Battle Creek, in the sanitarium. I'm all alone now. It's difficult. The past is simply irretrievable.

Mrs. Baker stood at the full-length mirror and adjusted the sleeves of her new dress. It was a lighter color than most of her other clothes, a cool shade of blue with ornate beadwork across the chest and lace at the cuffs. It was a week before Christmas and the snow sat thick and heavy outside, which cast a blinding whiteness into the house. Mrs. Baker checked her hair and smiled. It was perfect. A knock came at the front door and she listened as one of the girls answered it. She waited until she heard Judge Phillips' voice to leave the room, which she did while holding her hands as if she were preparing to hug somebody.

"Judge, it's wonderful to see you."

"And you, Mrs. Baker," he said as the girl took his coat.

In her office a fire crackled and they stood on opposite sides of the desk, smiling and chatting. Mrs. Baker had closed the door when they entered, and she seemed in no hurry to sit.

"I wish to extend my congratulations on the conclusion of the investigation by offering you a piece of good news," Phillips said.

"We've had so much already. Since the case started people have been so kind. Our donations have increased – we have more friends than I realized. The average man and woman recognize the Lord's work when they see it."

Phillips nodded.

"They certainly do."

Continuing to smile, he came to her side of the desk and stopped when he was a few feet away. Mrs. Baker imagined she felt the warmth radiating from his body. It made her dizzy and she closed her eyes, raised her chin and waited. She heard the scratching of chair legs across the floor.

"You may want to sit down," Phillips said.

Mrs. Baker opened her eyes. Phillips had pulled out her chair. She blinked a few times, then sat and watched him as he stood next to the desk. He took a stack of folded papers from his jacket and balanced a pair of glasses on the end of his nose.

"I don't presume to take credit for any of this, but it does appear to have come about as a result of the articles I've been writing on your behalf. Please bear with me a moment as I read this."

Mrs. Baker nodded.

"'My attention has been called to the efforts and goodness of Mrs. Julia Anna Baker, founder of The Home Conserving Association, for sometime past, and have given attention and close observation to the successful manner and successful agreement of The Home and its splendid results' – He goes on like that a fair bit. Please allow me to get to the meat of this. 'I propose as a gift to the association, to-wit: A forty-acre tract of land, lying and adjacent to the city of Ostwatomie, Kansas, for the sole purpose of an additional home, such as Mrs. Baker is seeking to establish in your city. I ask your pardon in advance for any seeming egoism in mentioning the offer and gift, but as it evidences my sincerity and earnestness on behalf of The Angel of Mercy and the good cause' – and so on and so on. Ah – 'The site and tract of land that I am offering to give to Mrs. Baker for an additional home represents the very best efforts and days of young manhood, a place upon which shall be built a home has been moulded and shaped by the storms of centuries, and is situated on an elevation many feet above the Pottawattomie Valley.' Listen to this, now. 'Over and beyond is the Osawatomie State Hospital for the Insane, casting its gloomy grandeur to homes unseen and hearts that, though broken, beat on.'"

Phillips removed his glasses and stifled a grin.

"I believe it should be easy for you to comprehend why I must advise against your taking up this man's offer, generous though it may be."

Mrs. Baker sat back in her chair and let out a wild laugh. Phillips joined her and wiped the corner of his right eye.

"I do think, however, that you should at the very least communicate with him. Investigate the property for the mere fact that it will allow you to say you have had this offer. I'll see if I can get his consent to run his letter as a column in The Daily Herald. It can only strengthen your case with the people of Oskaloosa, especially if they believe this is the best offer you've had."

Phillips moved forward and returned the papers and his glasses to his jacket. He stopped two feet short of Mrs. Baker, watching her with a nervous smile.

"Mrs. Baker, I've been meaning to speak to you regarding a certain matter for some time now."

She sat up in her chair. Her body tingled with anticipation.

"Yes?"

"I was wondering if I might change the manner in which I refer to you in my commentaries."

She sat there, frozen, the feelings muted. Her face stiffened a bit and she said, "How do you mean?"

"Well, I think it would behoove you to be aligned not only with the Joseph Walter Home, but with the very idea of motherhood itself. When I refer to you as Mrs. Baker, people most likely imagine a stern, officious type with no warmth to her whatsoever. The proverbial old maid. The schoolmarm. If I were to refer to you as *Mother* Baker that image would be eliminated instantly. A name like that projects humanity, love, fond memories in the heart of the reader. This is a name one can trust."

Mrs. Baker nodded slowly.

"Yes…"

"Also, it would automatically paint your detractors with a negative color. Who would dare to go after a mother? To go after *the* mother? A woman who loves all children as her own, who provides them with shelter, with food and most importantly, with love? No one but a cad would dare to criticize that woman."

The smile returned to Mrs. Baker's face.

"I think it's a splendid idea."

Phillips leaned against the desk and tugged at his collar. His neck looked as if it were sunburned and beads of perspiration gathered on his forehead.

"I was hoping you would. But, I had no way of knowing whether that would be the case. Some people would refuse to be portrayed in anything but the most basic fashion. Modesty forbids them, and you madam, are the paradigm of modesty."

"Everything you said is the truth, though. That is how I feel about the children. They're mine – all of them. They're my own."

"Yes, yes," Phillips said, growing excited. "That is exactly the type of thing you should be saying."

"I feel it," she said with a shrug.

"Wonderful."

He pushed back on the desk a bit further until he was sitting on it partway. He hitched up his left leg and scratched his knee and did not set it back down when he finished.

"Thank you so much, Judge Phillips. I can't begin to describe what your help means to me. And to my children."

"I've done nothing, really, except act as a reporter. You've done all the real work."

Mrs. Baker stood and she listened, and stared at his raised knee.

"Thank you," she said and set her hand just above it, not too far up his thigh.

Phillips closed his mouth and stared into her eyes. He held his breath, seemed afraid to move. Mrs. Baker started to pull her hand away, but he grabbed it and held it in place. With his free hand he reached out and felt her breasts, then ran his thumb across her cheek. Then he put both feet on the floor and began to unbutton his trousers.

"Lock the door," he told her.

It was Saturday and Flora arrived before breakfast. In the kitchen Ada stirred oatmeal in a big pot that was less than half full. She nodded good morning to Flora, who went to the cupboard and brought down the stacks of bowls. There were about twenty in all – somewhat fewer than the number of children in the Home. They ate now in shifts, without the dishes or utensils being cleaned in between. There was no milk today.

Ada and Flora heard them outside long before they were ready to serve. Bare feet scuffling against the floor, hushed, agitated voices, pushing and shoving near the door. When it was opened at last the children made little hops and reached out for bowls and spoons, and banged into each other in a manner approaching panic. They ate and asked for seconds and frowned or even protested when they were turned away, and the next group came forward and ate while those who already had their turns watched with undisguised jealousy. Sometimes one of them would ask for bread or milk, and Ada would apologize to them. None of them ever looked at Flora, even if she was serving. They made it a point not to.

When the food was gone Ada led the older children out of the hall to where the magazines were kept. Stacks of them were organized in bundles tied with white string, laid out on a table like dishes at a banquet. With a small blade Ada cut the string of one bundle and gave ten magazines to each of the older children with a reminder that if they returned with fewer than ten, they would need to have the money with them. Each child also was expected to take a little one along to wave a small white pennant with the words "Mother's Appeal" sewn on in black letters. Each time Ada sent the children out, just before they left, she told them she was sorry.

Ada returned to the kitchen to find Flora wiping the bottom of the pot with a wet cloth.

"I thought they would be getting more food from now on," Flora said.

Ada sighed and shook her head as she entered the room.

"I don't know what to tell you."

Flora continued to wipe, and Ada went to the table, where she sat and rubbed her eyes.

"How is your brother?"

"He's being punished."

Ada looked at her.

"What is it this time?"

"Being fresh to Mother."

"What did he say?"

Before she could answer, a shuffling sound was heard at the kitchen entrance, and Flora and Ada looked to see a little girl standing there. She had thick blond hair that fell to her shoulders, and round cheeks. Her eyes were green like jewels, and one of her hands played at her mouth, working her bottom lip back and forth. Ada stood and walked toward her while Flora watched from the sink.

"Celia, is something the matter?" Ada said and squatted down so she could speak to the girl face to face.

"I didn't get breakfast."

"Oh my goodness."

Ada picked up the girl and brought her to the table. She put her in one of the chairs and patted her shoulders while Flora scooped out what little oatmeal remained in the dirty bowls and put it in a single one. The oatmeal just covered the very bottom of the bowl, and seeing it made Flora's stomach hurt. She grabbed a spoon and took both to the table. The girl was a fast eater. In ten seconds the bowl was empty.

"I'm still hungry," she said.

"Is there any more food?" Flora asked.

"Some bread and milk, and that's for lunch."

"We have to find something."

"There isn't anything."

"But she's hungry."

"Flora, they all are."

The girl ran her finger inside the bowl and licked it.

"I'll go back to our house and find something. Maybe I can get it out without Mother knowing."

"No," Ada said and got up from the table. "You'll just get in trouble again. I'll find something. Stay here with her while I'm gone?"

Flora nodded.

"I'll be back as soon as I can."

When she had left, Flora sat at the table next to the girl. She had cleaned every last bit of food off the bowl and her spoon, but she continued to lick them.

"What's your name?" Flora said, hoping to distract her.

The girl lowered the bowl a few inches so that her nose and eyes peeked out over the rim.

"Celia."

"That's a pretty name. You're a pretty girl."

Celia gave the bowl a final lick and set it down. Her cheeks grew darker and she tried not to smile.

"Where are you from?" Flora asked.

"Kansas City."

"Really?"

Celia nodded and adjust her position so she was turned toward Flora.

"I live with my grampa. He said I have to stay here for now, but he's gonna come and visit me."

"That's nice. How long have you been here?"

"Since Tuesday."

"That's a long time."

Celia nodded again.

"Do you live here, too?" she asked.

"No, but I come here to help sometimes."

"Where do you live?"

"With – I live in Kansas City."

"That's where I'm from!"

"You're right, it is. You're very smart."

Celia gave another shy smile, clutched her hands together and moved her shoulders. She looked right at Flora.

Marie stood back and watched as the photographer arranged the children in rows on the lawn in front of their house. There were ten of them, all from the same family. O'Brien was their name. There were more, but these were the ones she was taking. They were the youngest. When they all could be seen the photographer went behind the camera and draped the black sheet over his head. None of the children smiled. After a bit the photographer threw back the sheet and nodded to Marie.

"That's all, ma'am."

"Thank you very much."

Then he looked to the sidewalk, where a small crowd had gathered to observe him while he worked.

"That's all, everybody!" he shouted to them. "Come on down to my studio tomorrow and you can see the finished print!"

Marie clapped her hands together four times and the children came toward her.

"Now listen to me. Our train leaves in an hour and forty-five minutes, so I want you to wait in the yard here where I can see you until our wagon arrives."

They answered with nods and a few words and then dispersed to play in small clusters nearby. Marie stood watching them until a man's voice addressed her from behind.

"Pardon me, miss?"

She turned to see a handsome young man holding his hat. He had a nice smile and straight teeth, and he wore a suit that was well-cared for, but out of fashion.

"Yes, sir?"

"My name is Litten. Rev. Charles Litten. I was wondering if I could ask your name."

"I'm Mrs. Marie LeWald, from the Joseph Walter Home. It's an institution in Kansas City that helps families and children in need." She pointed to the ones on the grass. "These children have no mother, poor things, but for the ones that do, we see that they aren't permanently separated."

"That sounds like a worthy cause," Rev. Litten said as he put on his hat.

"Oh, it is. Home conserving, we call it. It's an idea of my sister's. Julia Anna Baker. Or rather, Mother Baker. That's how she's known to all the children who come under our care."

"Forgive my questions..."

"Not at all. We have time."

"Does your sister take these children into her own home?"

"Ideally, she would, but she's not got the space for all of them. She purchased a home in Kansas City not far from her own. It's a wonderful place. It's three storeys high, with a basement, too. The rooms are large and the furniture is new. It's gas-heated in the winter, and gas-lit all year round. There's art on the walls, and music everywhere. We have two pianos and an organ, and even a phonograph. But most importantly, we have love. That's what truly makes a home."

"Yes, I quite agree."

Rev. Litten watched the children as they gamboled about on the lawn.

"Isn't it a shame, though?"

"What is that?"

"I was thinking isn't it a shame how these children have to go all the way to Kansas City when the rest of their family will remain here."

Marie sighed and nodded.

"Yes. It seems to go against our idea of trying to conserve homes, doesn't it? But there is hope."

"Oh?"

"Right now, Mother Baker, my sister, is in the process of acquiring another home, right here in Iowa. Not far from here, actually – in Oskaloosa."

Rev. Litten nodded, still watching the children.

"When that comes to pass, it is our plan to bring those children, along with any others from Iowa, back to their home state – and the others who come from close by. So really, their being transplanted to unfamiliar surroundings is only temporary."

"Do you have many Iowan children?"

"Not at present, but when people hear we've taken some in, it isn't long before more suitable cases present themselves."

"I can think of a few."

"Can you?" She checked her excitement. "It's terrible, isn't it? But I do cherish the thought of being able to help some of them."

Both were silent a few moments. It was late in the afternoon, and shadows from tree leaves danced around like tiny pinwheels.

"Would you be willing to help us? Someone in your position would know how necessary a cause like ours is."

LeWald made no attempt to hide his disgust. He leaned on his workbench and shook his head, grunting as if he had a stomach ache.

"What is it?" Marie asked.

"You were takin' money, now you're taking children, too?"

"I was never good at raising money, you know that."

"I said taking. And I thought that was because you had a conscience."

She ignored him.

"We've been taking in children from the beginning."

"*You* haven't."

"Not personally, no, but we need to help them."

"How? With what? If your sister's got money, she's not spending it on those kids. You know that better than anybody – at least you should."

"Don't attack my family. It's bad enough to see the lies about her in the papers. I don't want to hear them from you, too."

He turned to her and held out his hands.

"Marie, you've been in that house."

"Stop it. Stop it."

"I know you're not blind. I hope you're not stupid."

"And don't you attack me, either. You're just jealous, that's all. We've made a success of ourselves and here you are, a failure in your empty shop."

LeWald picked up one of his tools and hurled it against the wall. He threw it away from his wife, but she jumped and screamed. She did not move from her place, though, and stared at him with her jaw out, breathing through her mouth. LeWald watched her and put his hands back on the workbench. His shoulders were relaxed and his elbows were slack. His anger had gone. When it looked like Marie would not speak again, he shrugged.

With a sigh Marie came to where he was standing and held his arm and put her head on the back of his neck.

"I'm sorry," she said.

He was silent a long while.

"I wish you could see me working now," Marie said. "I'm so happy. I've discovered what I'm good at – finally – and it isn't raising money. It's finding children who need our help. I can't describe how it makes me feel. I know it's been hard for you to keep this place open, but things will work out. I'm sure of it. If you continue to work hard you'll find what you're best at, too, and then we'll be so happy."

"I won't find it here."

She stood upright and took him by the shoulders.

"Fine. Sell the shop. I know you hate it here. Use the money you get from it to do something you want to do."

"No. I mean here. In Kansas City."

"Les..."

"I'm never going to find anything else to do as long as your sister is around, and neither are you."

Marie shoved him hard, which only served to push herself away from him. She crossed her arms and turned her back like a child on the verge of a tantrum.

"Anything either of us is doing is what she wants us to do," LeWald said. "It has been from the very start. Let's break it off, let's start our own lives. We can go anywhere. Just you and me." He approached her slowly, as if to keep from startling her. "Can you think of that? Both of us together, alone, with nobody else around to tell us what we gotta be doing? It's never been like that since we got married."

His hands snaked under her still-folded arms, past her crooked elbows, up until they reached her shoulders.

"You remember what that was like? You and me, all by ourselves? Can you? I barely do, it's been so long. I want to get that back."

"Where would we go?"

"It doesn't matter. We can go anywhere, like I said. It doesn't matter where it is as long as you're there."

He placed a warm kiss on the side of her neck and breathed in the scent of her hair. She pressed her back against him and felt his trousers tenting out.

"What if we went to Wisconsin for a bit?" she said.

"Yes," he said, kissing her again. "Anywhere, anywhere."

"We could stay with my parents."

He released her with a groan and began to stalk around the shop.

"No, goddammit! Not with them, not with anybody!"

Marie stayed in the same place and watched him, her anger building.

"Have you got a complaint against my parents, as well?"

"You missed the whole point of what I was saying."

"What's wrong with my parents?"

"Nothing."

"Then why can't we stay with them? Did you not pay Papa back that money you owe him?"

LeWald felt an instant stabbing pain in his stomach. The furniture was still not paid off. The judge, either.

"Yes, I paid him back."

"Why can't we stay with them?"

LeWald stopped pacing and took a breath.

"I want us to be by ourselves."

"We're by ourselves now, and I'm not too fond of it."

"It would feel like a prison with them around all the time."

"I wouldn't know how that feels."

There was no perceptible change in his appearance, but his voice came out as a low rasp.

"You better go. I've got work to do."

He walked to where his tool fell after he had thrown it. He placed one hand on the wall for balance when he leaned over to pick it up. When he was standing again he found he was alone. He dropped the tool and went to the window.

Joseph tucked all of the magazines under his arm except for one, which he held out to passersby on the boulevard as he said, "Mother's Appeal, help the children," in the most monotonous way possible. Few of the adults he saw even looked at him. His mother had him wear one of his oldest shirts. It was several sizes too small and could not be buttoned up all the way, and there was a red sauce stain on the chest that made it look like he had been stabbed. His breeches were old, too, with one of the knee clasps having been torn away. They were the worst clothes he owned. He always sold in them.

"Mother's Appeal, help the children," he said to a well-dressed man.

The man was plump, with a white mustache and gray spats. He stopped and gave Joseph an indulgent smile.

"What is this in regard to?"

"Joseph Walter Home, sir, over on Askew Avenue."

He held out the magazine, and the man took it and flipped the pages.

"What is it, exactly?" The man's thoughts were elsewhere.

"It's a home for children and their mothers. Children, mostly, if their mothers and fathers are in trouble and can't take care of them, if they're sick or something. Or if they're out working someplace. They bring their children to the Joseph Walter Home, and the Home takes care of them. That way the children don't hafta go off to some orphanage."

"Do orphans live there, too?"

"Some do, yes, sir. But most of them have parents. Or one parent, at least."

The man looked over the top of the magazine.

"Do you live there, boy?"

"Yes, sir."

"With your mother?"

Joseph made a show of hanging his head.

"I'm one of the orphans."

"I'm sorry, son, I didn't know."

He closed the magazine and reached into one of his pockets. As he pulled out a big coin he glanced at the cover again. He turned the coin in his fingers as he read, lines appearing on his forehead.

"Wait a minute, now... Joseph Walter Home... Wasn't there a problem there of some kind? Did I hear that? Some issue to do with how it was run?"

"I wouldn't know, sir."

"You live there – how could you not know?"

Joseph thought for a second.

"I'm just a boy."

It was the best he could come up with. The man had stopped listening, anyway.

"Yes, that's right, it was the Walter Home. I'm sure of it. It was a big to-do with their funds being mismanaged. I think that's what it was."

Joseph shrugged. A few seconds passed and the man returned the coin to his pocket.

"I'm very sorry, son," he said and gave Joseph the magazine. He walked away as fast as he could.

"Tight bastard," Joseph said under his breath after the man was gone.

Everybody seemed to ignore Joseph after that, no matter how loud he talked or how high he held the magazine. After another hour or so he stopped trying, and simply enjoyed being outside. It was sunny and warm, not hot, and it felt good to walk. He went along the edge of the street and put one foot in the gutter, kept the other on the sidewalk, bobbing up and down every alternate step. Ahead of him a block or two was a crowd of children. There were not from the Home, and not from his school. They had nice clothes, and despite the distance Joseph could see how clean they were. They were watching him. He knew it. As they drew closer they lowered their voices, but every so often he could make out a word like "trash" or "poor." He ignored them.

Soon they were on the same block. The words had stopped, but the children continued to giggle as if one of them had told a dirty story. There were five of them in the group, three boys and two girls. They looked to be about Joseph's age, nine or ten. None of them pretended they were looking anywhere but at him. Joseph looked past them all as if they did not exist. As they went by, one of the boys spoke.

"Are your parents dead?"

The giggling recommenced, but Joseph kept walking.

"I'm talkin' to you," the boy said. "Your parents are both dead, ain't they?"

Joseph took his foot out of the gutter so he could walk faster. Soon there was a boy at his left and another at his right. He felt a shove from behind, but it was not hard enough to make him stumble.

"Don't touch him, he's filthy," the boy on his right said.

"Yeah, look at him," the one on his left said.

A voice came over his shoulder. It was the first boy, speaking almost at a whisper. He picked at Joseph's shirt with a stick.

"You use this old rag to wipe your ass?"

The other boys laughed. There was no sound from the girls.

"Naw," the boy at his right said. "He just messes his britches and lets 'em go."

Joseph's face grew hot. He said nothing.

"These the only clothes you got?" the first boy said.

"They're just the best," the boy on the right said.

"Hey, kid," the first boy said.

Joseph ignored him.

"Kid. Hey."

The boy flicked Joseph's right ear.

"Hey. I'm talkin' to you."

He flicked the ear again.

"I wanna ask you somethin'. Hey."

Flick.

"Hey."

Flick, flick.

"How'd your parents die?"

Flick, flick.

"How'd they die?"

Flick, flick, flick.

Joseph brushed his ear.

"They ain't dead."

"What you say?"

"Says they ain't dead," the boy at his right said.

"They ain't, huh?"

Flick, flick.

325

"Then where are they?"

Flick.

"If they ain't dead, then where are they?"

The girls began to giggle.

"What's that? Did he say something?"

"Nope," the boy on the right said.

"Nah."

"Hmm," the first boy said. "Maybe they ain't dead." He waited a second. "Maybe they just got rid of him."

Flick.

"Yeah, left him on somebody's doorstep," the boy on the right said.

"Yeah."

"Or threw him in the trash," the first boy said.

The girls laughed openly now, and the boys joined in. It was jeering, exaggerated, and it made Joseph want to cover his ears. He was shoved again and he tripped, and dropped one of the magazines. He bent over to get it, but was pushed again, and the first boy came forward and pinned it under his foot. Joseph righted himself and looked at the boy. He was the only one who had stopped laughing, and he stood on the magazine with one knee out and his arms crossed, a smug smile on his face.

"Give it back," Joseph said.

"Look, he can talk after all," the boy said.

The others laughed more and crowded nearer, forming a ring around Joseph.

"Give it back."

"Give it back," said one of the girls in a high-pitched mocking voice.

"When you talk to me, you say please," the first boy said.

Joseph sighed. The other stopped laughing and now began to goad him with cries of "Do it" and "Go on."

"Please."

"Please what?"

"Please give it back."

"Hmm." The boy brought his hand to his chin, pretending to think while he ground his heel into the paper, tearing the cover and smudging it with dirt to the delight of the others.

Joseph rushed forward and used his shoulder to push the boy into the gutter. He leaned down and picked up the magazine and began to shake it off. Before he could add it to the stuck under his arm the other boy returned and punched him in the face. The blow was hard, but missed doing much damage because Joseph's head was down. Instead of making direct contact with his eye or his nose, it only brushed them, with most of the force going to his cheekbone.

The others cheered and applauded and the boy took a step back and grinned. Joseph watched him a moment and then, without thinking, rushed forward and punched him square on the nose. The boy stumbled and fell on his back, and the others went quiet. His face dripped red as if something inside of him had broken. He began to wail and got on his knees while his fingers shivered around his face. The other children went to him and tried to help him stand, but his legs were like noodles, and he curled forward into a ball. They were still trying to help him when Joseph began to run.

He had gone seven blocks before he stopped. He panted and brushed the sweat from his eyes and smiled. He could have kept going. He was not tired at all. Nearby was a clock tower and he looked at it. The time was just after three, and he had to be back home before the hour was up. He had not sold a single magazine, and doubted he could sell one, much less all of them. And one of them was ruined. His mother's voice echoed in his head with talk about wasted money and failure. He felt like crying again.

As Joseph walked back toward the house he started to notice the ache in his cheek. His skin was hot, and it felt like it was being filled with air. He stopped at a store window and looked at his reflection. His cheek was red and puffy. Quite noticeable. It might bruise after all. He continued to think and to watch himself, his gaze drifting down to the unsold magazines, then back up to his swollen face.

"Mother!" he shouted through tears as he opened the front door. He ran a few steps as if he did not know where he was, his arms flailing around his head. "Mother!" he called again, his voice catching on the last syllable.

Mrs. Baker's footsteps thundered down the hall.

"What is it now?" she called out in an annoyed voice. She stopped when she saw him. His clothes were dirtier than before and the bruise on his face was dark and shiny. Without thinking Mrs. Baker went to him with her arms out, but stopped short of actually touching him. "What have you done?"

His words came out in a long moan.

"Some kids came, and they pushed me down, and when I got up they hit me, and then they took all the magazines!"

The moaning continued, although he did stop speaking.

"Why did you let them do that?"

Joseph yowled as if she had hit him.

"I didn't! They snuck up on me, and there were so many of them."

Mrs. Baker sighed and lowered her arms to pat his shoulders with the tips of her fingers.

"All right, stop crying. It's all right. Go upstairs now and clean yourself up."

Joseph sniveled and wiped his nose with his arm.

"Don't do that, it's disgusting. Get in the bath."

Still crying, although more quietly now, Joseph began to climb the stairs. When he was midway up he looked down at Mrs. Baker.

"I love you, Mother."

She nodded and waved him away.

"Yes, yes, go on."

Joseph made crying noises as he went up the rest of the stairs, into the hall and then the bathroom. Catching a glimpse of himself in the mirror, he panicked. He wondered if she noticed he was smiling.

Rev. Litten noticed Marie sitting in the pew when he was midway through his sermon. He kept speaking but looked into her eyes, and paused when she smiled at him. When the service was over they met at the front of the church and shook hands, and he introduced her to his wife, Ida.

"What brings you back to town?" he asked.

"I'm speaking to the city supervisors about the status of the O'Brien children."

"Is something the matter?"

"No. We only think it right when we take children out of a community that we keep everyone updated as to their progress.

My sister thinks it best to do so in person. Letters can be so impersonal."

"My husband and I have such regard for the work you do," Mrs. Litten said.

Marie smiled. "It's really my sister's doing. She's the one who founded the principle of home conservation."

"And what a beautiful idea it is."

"Yes," Rev. Litten said.

"You should have heard the way Charles spoke of it after he met you. It's wonderful what you're doing for the O'Briens. Their mother would be so glad if she could see."

"I should think that she can," Marie said, "and that she is."

The Littens invited Marie to their small home for lunch, and walked the short distance in about five minutes, the two women linking arms in front and Rev. Litten following. The meal was simple, and Marie assisted Mrs. Litten in washing the dishes when it was over, while Rev. Litten went to the sitting room, reading and smoking his pipe.

"I wish there was something more we could do for you," Mrs. Litten said as she scrubbed a plate.

"You've done so much already."

"In terms of your work, Mrs. LeWald."

Marie nodded and dried some forks.

"It's wonderful what you're able to do," she said again. "Charles would never say so, but I think he feels a bit jealous."

"Don't be silly," Marie said and put the utensils in the drawer.

"I'm not," Mrs. Litten said and handed her a plate. Her voice was almost a whisper. "He's quiet about it, but I don't think he feels he does enough. He puts such a strain on himself.

He has a bad heart, you know. But he became a reverend so he could serve people. Even though he does serve them, it amounts to talking to the same few groups of people week after week. After two or three years, what else can there be?"

Marie set a plate on the counter and Mrs. Litten handed her another one to dry.

"But you – you can go anywhere you're needed, right away, a different place each week. That must seem very tantalizing to Charles. I don't think he would want to travel around all the time, necessarily, but I do know he wants something more than he has now." She stopped washing a moment. "A wife knows these things."

"I understand," Marie said.

She held the towel by two of its corners so it spread out like a flag. It was wet, almost transparent, and cool to the touch. She waved it a bit, as if that would help it to dry.

"You know we're trying to set up another house in Oskaloosa."

"Of course."

"My sister is looking for somebody to run it. Would you and Rev. Litten be interested?"

"Do you mean that?"

"I would have to discuss it with her first, but I think she would agree to it. You would be at the home quite a bit of the time, one or both of you, but you would go out some, too, either to speak about our work or to find more children who need help. You would both be suited to that perfectly."

Marie led Rev. Litten past the main staircase of the Joseph Walter Home. They went slowly, and he observed everything as if he were visiting an art gallery. Most of the children were still out.

"My wife sends her apologies," he said.

"I understand. I hope her mother feels better."

"Thank you."

Marie went from the front room into the main hall, but Rev. Litten lingered there, his hand scratching at his chin. When she saw he was not following she went to his side and waited.

"Didn't you tell me there were pianos?"

"Yes. I did. But – those had to be sold. My sister is very close to making a deal on some property, and she needed the funds to be at her disposal."

"That's too bad."

"It is, but they can be replaced. Would you care to see the washroom?"

"Certainly."

"Follow me."

They walked the length of the hall, Rev. Litten at half the speed of Marie, who would stop every few feet to let him catch up.

"I'm sorry I've not been able to give you a definite answer," he said.

"That's no problem." She looked back at him and smiled. "There's plenty of time yet."

Marie entered the room and raised her arm to show him in. Rev. Litten went to the wash basin and looked inside. It was dry, with a white crust at the bottom. He took the handle of the mangle and turned it. The action was hard but smooth, and he nodded. On a shelf above the basin was a cake of lye, and the smell of it made his eyes burn. He nodded again, looking at Marie, who remained at the door, which was now closed.

"Very good, very good. And this is it? Everything is washed out of this room?"

She nodded. "Every stitch of clothing and every piece of linen."

"How often is the bedding changed?"

"I'm afraid I wouldn't know. You'd do better to ask one of the girls."

"My wife had told me to ask you. If we were to run the home in Oskaloosa she wants to keep it at the same standard as this one."

"Of course." Marie went to the table and stood beside him. "Has she been away very long?"

"Only a week or so."

"That must be difficult."

"No, not very. I'm usually pretty busy. I only feel it when I'm home at the end of the day and she's not there. I've no one to talk to. It's peaceful enough that I can get my work done, but it's so very empty."

Marie nodded and ran her hand along the table toward his. If he noticed he made no indication.

"I should think that would be difficult."

"It is. But it won't last much longer, God willing."

He looked away from her as he spoke but did not seem to focus on any object in particular. Thinking now, he smiled and adjusted his glasses. Marie inched toward him. Then, still without noticing her, he went to the door.

"Come on," he said. "Show me the rest of the house."

He twisted the knob, but when he pulled it the door remained shut. He pulled again, but it only jiggled in the frame.

"It's the lock," Marie said, coming to him. She put out her hands to touch his arm, but Rev. Litten turned the lock with a snap and opened the door.

"Strange," he said and looked at her now.

Marie stopped walking and folded her hands at her waist.

"It's faulty," she said.

"Hmm." Rev. Litten clicked it a few times, oblivious to anything else. "You should get it fixed."

"Yes, I've been meaning…"

He stepped into the hall and motioned with his arm for someone to come over.

"You – I'm sorry, what is your name?"

"Ada Brady."

"I beg your pardon, Miss Brady. Something appears to be the matter with this lock. The door was closed, and it must have turned by itself."

He twisted the lock a few more times. Ada looked at Marie, who stared at the floor, and then at Rev. Litten.

"Perhaps it's a bit loose," Ada said with uncertainty.

"You're probably right," he said. "But someone should see about fixing it – you don't need one of the children getting trapped in here."

"Yes, sir." She looked again at Marie, who was red-faced. Her hands were folded in a prayer-like manner, and her nails were pressed hard into her skin. Ada cleared her throat. "Mrs. LeWald?"

She said nothing.

"Mrs. LeWald, should I get someone to fix this lock?"

Marie waved one of her hands in annoyance. "Of course you should, if it needs to be fixed." Then she smiled and joined them at the door. "Come with me, Rev. Litten. You must see the rest of the house."

"Certainly." He smiled at Ada. "Thank you, Miss Brady."

"Thank you, sir."

Marie talked and talked as they went back down the hall and up the stairs. Ada turned the lock several times with no problems, and then went back to work. She heard Marie's voice the rest of the afternoon. She did not stop talking until Rev. Litten had left the house.

The house stood at the corner of Ninth Avenue and Eleventh Street in Oskaloosa, large and angled so that if seen from above it would have looked like a fat backwards "L." That area of town was not built-up, so the home was surrounded by several acres of open land. Judge Phillips said it would be perfect. Like the house in Kansas City, it was three storeys high, not including the basement. The rooms were spacious, and there were dozens of tall windows to let in sunlight.

"It's breathtaking," Mrs. Baker said as she joined Phillips on the front lawn.

"That it is, my dear, that it is. And ideally suited to your purposes, I think you will find. Not far from here is a quaint little residence to be used by – I forget their names at present."

"The Littens."

"Yes, the good Reverend and his wife. I take it they have accepted your offer?"

"He'll preach his last sermon in Glenwood on the fifth of September."

"Splendid. And now, the house."

Mrs. Baker loved it, walking quickly from room to room, her excited voice echoing in the empty space. The floors were sturdy and the ceilings were high, and the walls were covered with clean paper patterned with sprays of flowers. The second floor was much the same, and Mrs. Baker scurried about the rooms looking in the corners and at the ceilings for cracks and water damage.

"Do you really believe we can afford it?"

"Yes, as long as I'm present to help broker the deal. The people of this community respect me, much as they'll come to respect you, and I can ensure you that you'll get it for a fair price."

He stood watching her from the entrance of the room. She was a few paces from a pair of windows, looking out onto the back yard and the grove of trees that grew at its edge. She had her hands folded at her chest.

"I'm so glad," she said almost under her breath.

Phillips grinned and walked up behind her. She heard him and looked at him briefly, smiling as his hand found her waist. She turned back to the yard and surveyed it with a joy that made her glow.

The articles of incorporation for the Home Conserving Association of America were filed at Oskaloosa midway through September, with signatories listed as Julia Anna Baker,

O. C. G. Phillips, Mary Magdalene LeWald, Charles W. Litten and Ida B. Litten. A deal on the home itself was closed several days later, although some work had to be completed before the children could move in. About sixty of them would go. The Home at Kansas City could barely hold them all, with Marie's recent gatherings. In the two weeks before the place at Oskaloosa was ready the Littens spent most of their time at the Joseph Walter Home. There they would sit, deep shock visible in their faces as they observed everything that went on there. On occasion Mrs. Litten would lean close to her husband and reassure him, "Ours will be different."

LeWald stared at his workbench, doing nothing, until his trance was broken by an envelope that landed near his lap. He looked up to see his wife standing above him, her mouth open to reveal her bottom front teeth. Her face was red, and she panted as if she had been running.

"I didn't hear you come in," LeWald said.

"Liar."

Her voice was hoarse and quiet.

"Honest, I didn't."

"You said you paid him back."

LeWald went silent.

"And you borrowed more than you said, too. What did you do with that money? What did you spend it on?"

"Keeping this place open."

She snorted and shook her head.

"Why would you lie to me?"

LeWald stared at his fingers as they silently drummed the surface of the workbench.

"I was ashamed."

Marie began to stalk around the shop like a big cat.

"I suppose that's why you didn't want to stay with them, isn't it? I suspected as much. It's very nice to pretend you have ideals, isn't it, and say you don't want to owe my father anything when you certainly well do owe him. You owe everyone. You owe my sister, you owe my father – is there anyone else?"

"Your sister still owes the judge. I couldn't get the money for him off what your father gave me."

She ignored him.

"Did you take any of the money my sister had given you to hand off to that secretary?"

"You know I wouldn't do that."

She all but ran to him and thrust her face into his, her voice rising in pitch until it cracked.

"How? How do I know? You've done nothing but lie to me through our entire marriage!"

"That isn't true."

"Maybe it isn't, but that's how it feels."

He reached out to put his hand on her shoulder, but she slapped it away. He grabbed her by the wrist and stood, drawing back his other hand, but she hit him again and he let her go.

"You're such a bully," Marie said. "You take from anybody who's weaker than you, isn't that right? That's all you've ever done, it's all you know how to do. If you don't get what you want you just take it."

As she spoke LeWald turned his back and slunk into the corners of the shop, with Marie following and giving him an occasional slap on the shoulder. He put up his collar as if he were in a rainstorm and tried to focus on walking.

"Except it's not taking with you, is it?" Marie said. "You think it's something that's owed you. You're not stealing at all. That's how criminals think."

"I didn't steal," he said, turning his face toward her just a bit.

"No, not you. It was owed, just like I said–"

"What it was, was a loan."

"It was not."

"It was."

"It most certainly was not. Other people pay back a loan. *You* steal money and then call it a loan later on."

LeWald wheeled around and glared at his wife. She stopped inches from him, so close he could feel her breath.

"And how am I supposed to pay it back?" he said. "With what? Tell me that."

She spat the words.

"By selling this place and getting out of our lives. But don't worry, my sister can take care of that, too." Marie shook her head, her mouth still open. "You were such an idiot to think you could ever run a business."

LeWald made a violent growling noise and ran back to the workbench. He grabbed a hammer and used it to smash everything that could be smashed. When he was done he realized that he was alone. He was tired. His lungs hurt. His face was wet. When he had calmed down he dropped the hammer and left the shop.

Joseph sat on the front step of the house. The sun was down. His mother was away and Flora was inside doing her homework. His own homework sat up in his room, unfinished. Up the block he heard the sounds of a horse and wagon, and he straightened his back and prepared to stand. As the cart drew closer he saw it was Aunt Marie, and that she was riding alone. Joseph got up and went to her, calling out before she had even turned in toward the shed.

"Where's Uncle Les?"

Marie jerked the reins and the horse made an abrupt stop, grunting as it did.

"He's gone."

Her tone was hard, and Joseph stopped moving. When he spoke again his voice was higher than usual, and had an air of forced friendliness to it.

"Where to?"

Marie threw down the reins and began to dismount.

"I don't care, and neither should you."

She stood now, both feet on the ground, and put her hands on her hips. Her eyes were cold and her jaw set as if she could not move it without pain.

"He's gone, and he's not coming back," she said. "Forget about him, do you hear me?"

Joseph nodded.

"Yes, ma'am."

"Good. Now help me with the horse."

Celia shifted in Flora's lap so that she could hug the older girl. Flora's dresses were clean and Celia loved to run her small fingers over the fabric and hum to herself. It was quieter again now that the others had left the house to sell magazines, although there often still were at least a dozen children in the home at a time. Soon Celia felt Flora's body tense. Her legs went stiff like they had turned into wood. Flora removed her hand from Celia's back.

"Miss Brady?" Flora said with a hint of dread.

Ada came up behind them.

"What is it?"

Flora said nothing but Celia felt her move, and heard her sleeve rustle.

Ada let out a sigh. "I knew this would happen." She came around and looked at the girl with a false smile. "Celia, we've got to wash your hair."

"Is it dirty?" she asked as Ada took her hand from Flora's dress.

"Yes it is, so we've got to clean it, all right?"

She began to lead the girl out of the room.

"Is Flora coming?"

"Yes, she's just going to heat up some water. Flora, use the two big pots we've got in the bottom cupboard."

"All right."

The water was very hot, but Celia allowed them to dunk her hair in it and to pour it over her head when Ada had finished scrubbing. That was the worst part, the scrubbing. Celia felt like someone had tied a cord around her head and was jerking it quickly back and forth. After they had wrapped her in a towel they put her in a chair so she could talk to Flora while Ada pulled a comb across her scalp. The teeth of the comb were very close together and Celia's head was pulled back each time it caught a tangle, but she was a good girl and never whimpered. Ada pulled the comb three times the length of Celia's hair. Flora watched Ada and pretended to listen as the girl talked. Ada held the comb up to her face and stared into it for a long while before she set it down and sighed. She put her hand on Celia's shoulder, where the towel was resting, and Celia looked back at her and smiled.

"Darling, I'm afraid we're going to have to give you a haircut."

A look of panic crossed Celia's face and she jerked her head to watch Ada, and then Flora.

"It won't hurt," Flora said in what she hoped was a reassuring voice and patted Celia's knee.

Celia looked again at Ada. "But why? Why?"

Ada moved next to Flora, and squatted so she could look into Celia's face.

"You have bugs in your hair. They're not dangerous – you don't have to worry about that, you don't have to be scared. But they're not good for you and we have to get rid of them."

"Can't you just pick 'em out?"

Ada shook her head. "There's too many, honey. Your hair is so long, it gives them too many places to hide. We would never get them all. I'm sorry."

Celia began to squirm and pant.

"But you can't do it."

"Darling, we have to."

"You'll be fine," Flora said. "You'll feel so much better when it's done."

"No, I feel good! I don't hafta get my hair cut!"

She got up and hid behind the chair, placing her hands on its back.

"Celia, you don't want the other children to get them, do you?" Flora said.

"I don't care!"

Ada stood and began to come toward Celia, but she backed further away, dragging the chair with her.

"Please do this for us…"

"I can't!" A fat tear plopped onto her cheek.

"Come, now."

"Why can't you, Celia?" Flora asked.

Celia's chest heaved as she spoke, and her words came fast and slurring.

"I can't! My grampa loves my long hair. I sit on his lap and he pets it and tells me it's just like my mommy's. You can't take it!"

"It'll grow back," Ada said and crept forward another step.

"No, no, he can't see me without it! Please, don't cut it! I'll be good! I promise!"

Ada took another step and Celia bolted, screaming toward the door. Flora jumped up and knocked her chair to the floor, and got in front of the little girl in time for Ada to scoop her up under one arm. Celia shrieked and cried and kicked her small legs while Ada wrapped both arms around her waist to better hold her. Flora stood watching, silent.

"Flora," Ada said above Celia's cries. "Get the scissors, please."

She did not move. It was as if she were in a trance.

"Flora, please get the scissors. I can't do it myself."

Flora nodded once, then went to the door of the washroom. When she opened it she saw a handful of children watching from the hall. They looked right at her, their faces tense with hate. Flora ignored them. She walked to the kitchen and opened a drawer. The pair of scissors gleamed in the light. They were enormous. They seemed almost a foot long. Flora took them out and brought them into the hall, where the other children remained. She went into the washroom and shut the door, then locked it.

Ada sat on the chair and held Celia, who continued to scream, between her legs. She held down Celia's arms, too, so that it looked like she was giving her a full-body hug.

"Flora, you'll have to cut it – I don't think you can hold her."

"I can't do it."

Celia bounced occasionally. She looked like a trapped animal.

"You have to," Ada said. "If I let her go we'll never catch her again."

Flora stood watching. Celia's face was deep red and so bright it looked like she would faint.

"Come on, now," Ada said.

Flora sighed.

"All right."

She came closer, raising the scissor blades so they pointed at the ceiling. Celia bounced again and Ada strengthened her grip so she could not move much at all.

"What do I do?"

"Take a few strands of her hair at a time and clip them. We can even it out and make it shorter as you go."

Flora's hand trembled as she gathered one of Celia's tresses in her fingers. The girl looked into her eyes and pleaded until she ran out of breath.

"No, no, no, no, no–"

She made the first cut. Celia screamed as if it had been taken out of her flesh. Flora held the strand of hair and looked around, unsure of what to do. Ada nodded toward a corner of the room, where a bucket sat next to an old mop.

"Put it in that."

Flora took the bucket and set it near Ada and Celia. She let go of the strand of hair and it floated down as if on a gentle wind. Taking another strand, Flora snipped and dropped it over the bucket, and repeated the action again and again. Soon the bucket was a quarter of the way full and Flora had to begin cutting close to the girl's head. All the time Celia screamed and cried. She was so loud she made Flora's head ache. She placed her hand on the girl's skull and raised the hair. She cut, let it fall, cut, let it fall. When she drew her hand away, Celia looked at her, face drenched with tears.

"I hate you!" she screamed.

Things have to change. Things have to change. Ada repeated it to herself as she walked to Mrs. Baker's house. Conditions needed to improve. It was what was right for the children. And there was the matter of Rev. Litten and Mrs. LeWald. Ada knew what she saw.

She arrived at the house just as Judge Phillips was leaving it. He saw her and waved, and he called out, and the excitement in his voice made Ada feel bad for him.

"How are you, Miss Brady?"

"Very well, sir, thank you."

"What brings you here this morning? Nothing amiss, I hope?"

She thought before she said anything.

"No, nothing. I'm here to make a report to Mrs. Baker, that's all."

"I'll leave you to it, then," he said and went to his car. "Good day!"

"Good day to you, sir."

Phillips' driver held the door of the running auto for him. When Phillips got in he slammed the door and trotted to the front seat. As they pulled away Phillips tipped his hat to Ada. She nodded in return.

Mrs. Baker was surprised but not upset to see her. She brought her to the office and spoke in a lively voice about Oskaloosa, the new Home and the judge. The office had changed since Ada had last visited. There were more pictures on the walls, and expensive-looking bookends on the shelves. Mrs. Baker was better-dressed at each meeting, and looked somehow younger, too, as if success functioned as a kind of sustenance to her. Her skin was smooth, with a healthy color, and her hair was shiny and free of white strands. Watching her carry on made Ada feel very old.

When Ada was finally able to break in, she was hesitant.

"Now that everything has begun to settle down, I wondered if you might possibly consider making changes with the Home here?"

The smile was fixed on Mrs. Baker's face. She did not sound angry.

"How so?"

"Well. The investigation has been over a long time now, but as much as I can see it's not any different than before."

"Precisely. There was nothing wrong with it."

"But what about the food? And the children's cleanliness? They still have–"

"It's your responsibility to make sure those children stay clean, Miss Brady. Yours. I'm not about to go chasing them all over creation to wash behind their ears. I have bigger concerns. If you're unable to do the job you were hired to do, perhaps you aren't as qualified as I had hoped."

Ada knew the matter was closed.

"There is one other issue that has arisen which does concern you. It's a question of morality."

Mrs. Baker became very interested, leaning forward in her chair and tilting her head.

"What do you mean?"

Ada contemplated how best to say it.

"It's the type of thing that could damage your reputation if the public were to find out about it."

Mrs. Baker's eyes grew wide. She got up from the desk and closed the door. Then she came back and resumed her same position.

"What is it? Speak quietly."

"It concerns two people connected to your association. They are very high-reaching, Mrs. Baker."

Ada watched her. She was frozen.

"It has come to my attention that they are having an illicit relationship—"

Mrs. Baker jumped from her chair and began shaking her head.

"No evil. No evil, no evil."

She walked toward the window and repeated the words.

"I have to tell you what I saw."

Mrs. Baker snapped back toward Ada, a look of terror on her face.

"No evil, no evil."

"Will you not listen to me?" Ada said and rose.

Mrs. Baker no longer spoke, but she continued to shake her head. Ada watched her, then went to the door.

"I'm tendering my resignation. I'm going to pack my things now."

She left the office. Mrs. Baker did not stop.

Flora and Joseph sat together on the train as it rattled its way to Carroll, Iowa. It was freezing, and they sat pressed against each other under a blanket, their hands interlocked, breath steaming onto the window to be hardened into frost. There were ten children in all, along with Rev. Litten, Marie and Mrs. Baker. It was their first performance, and they were told in the weeks leading up to it that they would sing, and they practiced the same song each day. Most of the appearance would be taken up with speeches by the adults. None of the adults were around. Mrs. Baker had reserved a private compartment for them.

"How much longer?" Joseph asked.

"I don't know," Flora said. She turned in her seat to look at the others. They were spread out in a few rows, all bundled into little groups to ward off the cold.

Celia was on a bench by herself. She had not spoken to Flora since the haircut, and she would look at her with seething anger when they were in the same room. Her hair had filled out some, but it was short enough that it could have been mistaken for a boy's. She wore a dress that was a bit too short, and the skin on her legs almost looked blue.

Flora stood and walked into the center aisle of the car.

"Where you going?" Joseph said.

"I'll be right back."

"Hurry up."

Flora stood near Celia, who looked at the frosted window.

"Come on."

She did nothing.

"Sit with us or you'll freeze."

Celia looked at her with a blank face.

"You don't have to sit by me. You can be next to my brother. Come on."

The girl stood, mute, and went to sit next to Joseph.

"Let her sit by the window," Flora said.

"But that's my seat…"

"You can't see out of it, anyway, with all the frost, so move."

With a grunt, he did, and threw back the blanket to let her in. Flora sat, too, and they all brought the blanket up to their chins. They were quiet for several minutes, until the warmth had spread.

"Are you warming up now, Celia?" Flora said.

Celia looked away.

"Ask her is she all right," Flora told Joseph.

"She heard you. She's sittin' right here."

"I know that, but she's not talking to me just now."

Joseph shook his head and rolled his eyes.

"Please, Joseph, just do it."

He sighed and turned his head to Celia.

"You all right?"

Celia nodded.

"She's fine," Joseph said.

"I saw."

"Then why'd you ask?"

Flora looked at her brother.

"Check her fingers."

"Hmm?"

"Check her fingers and see how cold they are."

"Why don't you check her fingers?"

"Because I don't wanna reach over you. Now stop being such a pain and check her fingers."

Joseph nudged Celia.

"Gimme your hand."

She did.

"Well?"

"They feel cold."

"Rub them with both hands, then. You've got to get the blood flowing."

"I ain't gonna rub her hands."

"I can't do it."

"I don't wanna do it."

"You have to."

He gave an annoyed sigh.

"For gosh sakes, you only have to do it a minute or two – just enough to warm her up."

"Fine. Here, gimme your hand again."

Flora heard the sound of furious rubbing. Celia watched Joseph, who pretended he was somewhere else.

"Now the other one," Flora said.

"Yes, ma'am," Joseph said sarcastically. The same noises were audible for another minute or so, and then they came to an abrupt stop. "That enough?"

"Yes."

"Good." He shifted on the bench, then jerked his arm three times.

"What are you doing?"

"She won't let go of me."

"I guess she likes you."

"Well, I don't like her!"

"Don't be such a baby. Just let her hold you."

"No!" With a grunt he pulled his hand away. "If she wants to hold hands so much, let her do it with you."

"She won't even sit next to me."

"She's got no choice now. I gotta go." He stood, which pulled the blanket off all three of them. The girls' arms went around their torsos and they made sharp inhalations. Joseph stepped over the fallen blanket and Flora pulled it over herself and Celia.

"Where are you going?"

He gave her an exasperated look.

"Oh. Hurry back so you don't freeze."

"No."

He walked to the other end of the car and disappeared into the restroom.

Flora adjusted the blanket so it was pinned between Celia's shoulder and the bench.

"Are you okay now?"

Celia looked at the window. Flora watched her.

"If your fingers get cold again put them between your knees. That or sit on them. That's what I'm doing."

Celia did not speak, but Flora felt her move. She smiled, and scooted closer to the little girl, and listened to the sounds of the train and the other children.

Dewey held the air rifle close to his chest. The barrel was smooth and cool, with a soft finish. The stock was worn, and he ran his finger across it and grinned. He felt different holding a gun.

"How long you had this?"

Danny looked up from his bed, on which he was stretched out fully-clothed except for his shoes, with a book on his chest. He was fourteen, and his voice cracked when he spoke.

"I don't know. Four years maybe."

"Since you were my age."

"Yeah, I guess."

Dewey lifted the rifle to his shoulder and lined up the sight.

"You ever think of gettin' a new one?"

Danny was reading again.

"Nope."

"You still use this one?"

"Yup."

"You use it a lot?"

"When I can."

Dewey aimed along the wall. The paper that covered it was filled with vertical dark and light green stripes, and he stopped on every other one and tickled the trigger.

"How much it cost you?"

"I don't remember."

"Was it a lot?"

"I saved a long time for it, yeah."

Dewey held out the gun so he could see it end to end.

"I wish I had one like this."

"Start savin' up."

Dewey looked down the sight again.

"Can I use it some time?"

"Long as I'm there, too."

"Sure, sure. When?"

"I'll let you know."

Dewey moved the gun until it was pointed at Danny's head, by his left ear.

"Got any rounds?"

"In a drawer."

"Any in the gun?"

"I don't keep it loaded."

"Good," Dewey said and pulled the trigger. Danny looked at him, his mouth hanging open in shock.

"Sorry," Dewey said. "I'll put it up."

He went to the shelf and put the rifle in its holder. He turned around and grinned.

"I didn't mean nothin' by it."

He noticed Danny's book had fallen open on his stomach and all the pages had shut. Danny's eyes were open, and so was his mouth.

"You okay?"

Dewey approached him carefully. When he was a foot away he noticed a streak of red, like a narrow ribbon dribbling out of Danny's temple.

The group arrived in Des Moines two days after the Carroll performance, staying that night at the Y.M.C.A., and planned to attend a conference the next day at the Methodist Episcopal Church. They all entered the church together, with Mrs. Baker holding the door for the children. Marie came through next, and then Rev. Litten held the door so he could enter after Mrs. Baker. When they all were inside Mrs. Baker went to a table with three men seated behind it.

"I am Mother Baker – Mrs. Julia Anna Baker – of the Joseph Walter Home of Kansas City. You will find me on the schedule of today's presenters, along with my children."

She raised her hand to indicate the crowd standing behind her.

"Mrs. Baker," said one of the men. "We've been trying to contact you."

He glanced at the other two men. One of them gave a wan smile to Mrs. Baker, while the third pretended to sort some papers.

"My children and I will be at the Y.M.C.A. for the duration of our visit. If you wish to find me the people there will assist you."

"Yes, I did find that." He stood and gave a short sigh. "Would you consent to speak with me in private for a moment?"

"You may speak to me here."

The man bit his lips, then straightened his posture.

"Well, then. I am truly sorry you've come all this way. I've been trying to reach you the past few days, but I was never able to connect."

"What is it? What's happened?" She raised her voice and Rev. Litten and Marie began to creep nearer until they stood beside her. Flora watched from the group of children. Her stomach began to ache and she held Celia close.

The man was direct. "We are withdrawing our invitation. We will not allow you to address this conference."

Mrs. Baker sputtered a few half-words that sounded like the beginnings of questions.

Rev. Litten broke in. "For what reason? You should be obliged to tell us now that we're all here."

"We have received some disturbing information about your home."

"What information?" Mrs. Baker all but shouted.

The man was never less than polite.

"I believe you know," he said.

"They're lies, any negative things you may have heard. I can assure you of that. My home, my staff, myself – we're all above reproach. Anything you've heard is nothing more than vicious gossip."

"Forgive me, madam, but the Kansas City Board of Public Welfare doesn't make it a habit of engaging in attacks on worthy charitable organizations."

"Lies. That's what they are. That board is at the mercy of organized charities and home finding organizations. I've been attacked by them from the beginning. I'm not afraid of their games. Let them try and stop me."

"Regardless of what you may think, we take these allegations quite seriously. You will not be speaking here, and that's the end of it."

Mrs. Baker looked at the others, then back to the man.

"What about my children? Are you turning them away, as well?"

"We would be against anything we thought might further your work."

Mrs. Baker ranted all the way back to the Y.M.C.A., and continued to shout as they entered the building. Once inside she fell silent, but her jaw was clenched and she looked as if she would start up again with the slightest provocation. As they passed the front desk the man behind it got up and ducked into a nearby office. Soon another man emerged. He was better-dressed than the first, and he raised his hand and waved to Mrs. Baker and called her name. She ignored him, but Rev. Litten stopped.

"Could you get her attention, please?" the man asked him.

Rev. Litten called her, but she kept walking and he jogged over and stood in front of her.

"What is it?" she said.

"That man wants to speak with you."

She glared at him, and did not change her expression before she turned back. The man had come around the desk and was waiting there with his arms crossed. Mrs. Baker let out a growl and went to him.

"Yes, sir?"

He was curt in his reply.

"We're revoking your permission to stay here. Pack your things and get out."

Mrs. Baker straightened herself, watching him with a defiant smile.

"Certainly, sir."

The Kansas City Times referred to Danny as "a boy of ill-fortune and tough luck." He had no parents and his aunt did not have the money to bury him. The Boys' Hotel had been his home for years, but it was low on funds, too. Even though the Juvenile Improvement Club had just raised seventy-five hundred dollars for its maintenance, it still operated at a deficit. The boys did what they could, offering what money they were able to spare toward his funeral until Judge Porterfield made them stop. It was not right, he said, considering half of them were without winter coats. Dr. Mathias called for other volunteers. Eventually Danny's former employer, the Irving-Pitt Manufacturing Company, came forward. They gave eighteen dollars. Along with anonymous donations, that made thirty-five. Soon the Carroll-Davidson Undertaking Company offered to foot the total bill. The boys paid for the flowers. The Times reported the other money probably would be used for a memento to be placed at the hotel in Danny's memory.

Mrs. Baker, Flora and Joseph returned home to find Judge Phillips in the parlor. He stood as they entered, and greeted them without his customary smile.

"Judge, this is a surprise." Mrs. Baker forced her voice to a higher pitch. "To what do we owe this pleasure?"

"I heard about your reception in Des Moines." He motioned toward a newspaper on the table near the chair where he had been sitting. "I need to discuss some things with you."

"It's all lies. You know reporters."

"I've heard from more than reporters."

"Who?"

"From Miss Brady, the former matron of your Home."

A stillness fell over the room, which was accentuated by the ticking of the clock on the wall.

"More lies, I can assure you."

"I need to discuss some things with you," he said again. "Immediately."

Mrs. Baker nodded.

"Go ahead. I'm waiting to hear what you have to say."

Phillips moved his lips and took a deep breath through his nose before he spoke.

"Mrs. Baker, perhaps it would behoove you to dismiss the children before I commence to describing the reports I have received."

Mrs. Baker did not move.

"Children, go to bed."

They left the room and went upstairs to a vent at the base of the wall at the end of the hallway. There they sat without taking off their coats, listening and hugging their knees. Mrs. Baker and the judge went to the office. His voice for once was too soft to be understood, but Mrs. Baker's grew more agitated until it bordered on hysteria. Even after he left and the children went to their rooms they could hear her cry like a mother who had just watched her child die. After that night she never spoke of Iowa, or of the judge, again.

The Joseph Walter children, fifty of them, arrived at the Orpheum Theater forty-five minutes before the show was to start. Most of them had never been to a theater before, and it was quite impressive. Built of red brick, it was like a monument, with windows arranged in diagonal rows on the façade and a tower almost like a steeple jutting out the top. Colorful posters lined its face at the ground level, which was sheltered by an ornate overhang that looked like something off a palace. The interior was even more elaborate, with thousands of padded seats, columns, murals and a vast deep red curtain hanging over the stage. Eventually the children were shepherded to a row near the front, where they filed in and took their seats.

Joseph was the first to go in, and he walked as fast as he could until he reached the seat at the far end of the aisle. He sat and stretched his legs and took in his surroundings as the others came up behind him. Soon the chair to his right was filled and he felt pressure from someone moving the armrest.

"I'm sitting next to you."

It was Celia. Her cheeks were pink and it looked like she was trying to keep from smiling. Flora sat in the next seat and giggled with the back of her hand to her mouth. Joseph ignored them both.

"Have you finished your letter?" Flora asked after a few minutes.

Joseph was confused.

"To the Elks Club, the thank-you letter," Flora said.

Joseph leaned back in his seat.

"Nope."

"But Mother said if you didn't write one you couldn't come."

"You gonna tell her?"

Flora said nothing. After a few seconds Joseph's stomach began to gurgle. His face was hot and his eyes stung. The fun was gone. He glared at Flora, and he could tell that she felt bad.

"I'm sorry," she whispered.

Joseph shook his head and looked back toward the stage. After a few seconds passed two hands were on his right arm and a head pressed to his shoulder.

"What are you doing?"

"I love you," Celia said.

"For Pete's sake. Get off."

He tried to pull away but her grip was firm.

"Let go, will ya?"

"Just let her be," Flora said.

"Or what? You'll tell Mother?"

"I said I was sorry."

Joseph put his hand between his arm and Celia and attempted to pry her off.

"Come on, this is stupid."

She did not budge and soon he collapsed in his chair, defeated. It was his punishment. She held him all the way through the show, and continued even as they left their seats and went back up the aisle. Then, suddenly, when they had reached the lobby, she let him go.

"Grampa!"

An old man squatted with open arms near the door. He had a long white beard and thin limbs. His clothes were old and frayed. Before the others could stop her Celia ran to him and jumped onto him and hugged him around the neck, almost knocking him to the floor. He put one knee on the ground to steady himself.

"How are you, darlin'? You're gettin' so big."

"I miss you, Grampa."

"I miss you, too."

Flora and Joseph came up and watched. The man noticed them and pointed.

"These your friends?"

"Yeah. That's Flora, and that's Joseph. I'm gonna marry him!"

Joseph turned to leave, but Flora held him by the arm. The old man grinned.

"Is that so? He's a little bit older than you, though, ain't he?"

"I don't care."

"That true, boy? You gonna marry my little girl?"

"No."

"Why not? What's wrong with her? You some kinda snob?"

Flora laughed and Joseph rolled his eyes.

"Will you please lemme go?"

"You two kids live at the home, too?" the old man asked.

Celia let go of his neck and slid to the floor, but continued to lean against him.

"No, they live in a house with Mother Baker. They're her kids."

The old man's smile dropped and he nodded. His voice became flat and unfriendly.

"Your mother here today?"

"No, sir, she's not even in town," Flora said.

"Where's she at?"

"Fundraising, but I don't know where."

Celia tugged at the old man's coat.

"Grampa, how'd you know I was here?"

His features softened again and he smiled at her.

"I saw it in the paper, sweetheart. Said you were gonna be here."

"Said *I* was gonna?"

"Well, you kids. It said the Elks were payin' for your tickets. I wanted to see you, so here I am."

"How come you haven't come to see me at the house yet?"

He thought for a second, unsure of whether to hold back. He glanced at Flora and Joseph and took a breath.

"Their ma won't let me."

Celia stared at the others, looking as if she had been slapped.

"Why? What'd I do?"

"It's nothin' you did," the old man said.

"Then why?"

He shrugged.

"She won't say."

Celia buried her face into his chest and held onto him. His anger was visible now as he looked at Flora and Joseph.

"Your ma do that a lot? Keep families apart?"

"Prob'ly," Joseph said.

"If I had money I'd get a lawyer. But I barely have enough to live on, so what can I do?"

Flora and Joseph edged a bit closer.

"Maybe we can talk to her for you," Flora said.

"You just said she ain't home."

"When she gets back."

The man shook his head. "I been talkin' and talkin'. What you think *you* can do?"

Neither of them knew what to tell him.

It was morning near the end of May when Judge Porterfield and Dr. Mathias brought two "movie experts" from Chicago to the various charitable organizations of Kansas City. George L. Cox and C.W. Hutton were their names. Their first stop was the Boys' Hotel. Porterfield and Mathias stood on the porch with some of the boys while Hutton aimed the camera at them and turned the crank for thirty seconds. They also shot footage at the First Congregational Church, the Girls' Home near Fairmont Park and the Clay County hills. They took scenes the next day, too.

"Someday we will show them their pictures," the men said. "It will mean one more cheerful evening for them at least."

Mrs. Baker threw the paper so hard that it hit the far wall of her office. She should have been in those pictures, standing surrounded by children, with their smiling little faces all focused on her. She would have been the highlight of the reel. It was no wonder she was not included, or even aware of it until after the film men had gone. It was Mathias' doing, his and Porterfield's. They were trying to break her. They were in cahoots with the home-finding organizations and the charity groups. Jealousy. Deviousness. It was shameful.

She rose from her desk and walked to the fallen paper. Bending over, she picked it up, and as she walked back to her seat she tore it in half once, lengthwise, and dropped it into the trash. It felt gratifying, but she could still not help thinking. She could have used the publicity. After the Oskaloosa home was closed the children returned to Kansas City. She found there were so many – more than a hundred – that she had to buy her biggest house yet. It was on 3500 E. Ninth. It was beautiful, and it would have looked so grand on a motion picture screen.

The Littens were gone. They could have run the new Home if they had wanted. Mrs. Baker made the most generous offers she could think of, but they were not swayed. The liars had gotten to them, too.

Marie was all she had left.

"What do you mean by that?" she asked.

"I've been abandoned by everyone," Mrs. Baker said. "People hear rumors and take them for the truth. They think I'm a fraud. They say the most awful things about me. You're the only one who has stayed true."

Mrs. Baker stood by the window as she spoke. The drapes were open less than an inch, and she looked outside as if she were in hiding. Marie watched her from the desk.

"I have to," Marie said. "You're my sister."

Mrs. Baker glanced back at her.

"But you do believe me, don't you?"

"Of course."

Smiling, Mrs. Baker returned to the desk and sat across from Marie.

"Forgive me," she said. "I've been betrayed so many times. It's difficult. But it can't be with you, can it? Ever since you came to me, whenever I thought I was losing faith, I just had to remind myself of your loyalty to home conserving, and to me. Then I always felt better. You're my strength."

There was a sense of desperation in Mrs. Baker's voice. Marie had never heard it before, and it frightened her.

"You do believe in me, don't you?" Mrs. Baker asked again.

"Yes," Marie said. She cleared her throat. "Yes. I'll say it as many times as you need."

Mrs. Baker nodded, and returned to the window.

The possums were back. Maybe they were raccoons. Mrs. Floyd was unsure. She never caught them, but she knew they had been there. Each time she went behind the house to bring something out to the garbage can she found the lid either askew or on the ground, and shredded bits of whatever she had thrown away littering the area. She tried everything to prevent it. She tied down the lid, put bricks on it. Nothing helped. It probably was raccoons. They were smart.

She carried out some potato peels wrapped in newspaper and put them in the can. It was almost full. Easier to tip over. She frowned and thought a bit. Then she noticed the fence. It was made from long wooden rails that were held in place by posts stuck into the ground about five feet apart. She noticed the rail in the middle was just about level with the lid of the can, perhaps a bit shorter. She pressed all her weight on the lid, forcing it down as far as she could. Squatting, she pulled out the bottom rail of the fence and let it flop onto the back lawn. She pushed the can under the fence, banging it with her hip until it was wedged in tight.

It was past lunchtime when she heard the noise from the kitchen, thick scraping metal and the rattling handles. Mrs. Floyd pulled a broomstick from the closet and was almost to the door when she thought of the time. It was too early for raccoons.

Still clutching the broomstick, she crept onto the back porch and looked out on the alley. Surrounding her garbage can was a trio of children, the oldest of whom appeared to be about ten. Joseph Walter children. It was easy to tell. They had been the in neighborhood about a month. They had tugged the can out from under the fence and thrown the lid on the grass. They dipped in their hands and took out what they found. What they could eat, they ate. They did so without shame.

Mrs. Floyd returned to the kitchen and got three big red apples and brought them outside.

"Children!"

Instead of running, they ate faster, reaching in up to the shoulders, bringing rinds and fat to their mouths and chewing fast.

"Stop eating that, now."

Just one of them, the smallest, took out his hand. He checked it, licked his palm, then wiped it on his shirt.

"Look what I've brought you," Mrs. Floyd said as she reached them. She held up the apples, and the children all but pushed the can away to get to them. It fell on its side and rolled a bit before the weight of the trash shifted and brought it to a stop. Mrs. Floyd gave them the apples, which they tore into with open-mouthed greed.

"You'll pick that can up when you're finished," Mrs. Floyd said.

They did not seem to hear her. They ate fast, grunting through their noses and slurping juice off their fingers and chins. They even ate the cores, although they did pull off the stems. When they were finished they stared at her.

"What do you say?" she asked.

The biggest one held out his hands.

"We need more."

Whenever Marie was in Jefferson City she stayed at the Central Hotel. It was the best. Four storeys tall, it was better furnished than any place she ever had seen, had electric lights throughout the building, bathtubs in each room and everything lined with polished oak. Staying there made it easy to forget she was working. Her favorite part was the basement, which served as the dining room. The tables were elegant, with beautiful dishes and silverware, and white linen tablecloths and napkins, and the menus were filled with foods she had never heard of.

She looked at her plate. It was breakfast. There were two eggs, sunny side up, a thick slice of ham, and toast with heavy smears of butter that melted and dripped across the rest of the plate. It looked so good she almost could not touch it.

Marie put the napkin in her lap and lifted the teacup. She blew into it and sipped, then set it back down. To her right was a bowl piled high with sugar cubes. Beside it lay a pair of silver tongs. She used them to put one cube into the tea, which she then stirred with her spoon. She took another drink and closed her eyes, holding the sweet liquid in her mouth.

As she opened her eyes again she saw an older man sitting across from her a few tables away. He was big and round, wearing what appeared to be a tailored suit. The coat was tan and the vest was done like a bright red and yellow checkerboard. On his head was a black bowler. He did not see her as he held his own sugar bowl in the palm of his hand and used his fingers to drop at least three cubes into his cup.

Marie's eyes went back to her plate. Picking up her fork, she used it to pierce one of the yolks. Immediately it spurted a great flow of yellow onto her ham, onto her toast. Before she cut into it again she doused it all with salt and pepper, even the toast. With her fork she cut a piece of the egg white, which she dipped again into the yolk and then brought to her mouth. Perfection.

As she swallowed she watched the man take a bite of his eggs. The piece on his fork was big and dangled in the air rather like a small fish at the end of a hook. The man stuck out his tongue and used it to guide the egg into his mouth, and then chewed with a loud smutzing sound. He had a mustache and beads of yolk clung to it like honey. When he had swallowed he ran his thumb and forefinger through the coarse hair, scraping it with his nails, which he in turn scraped on his bottom teeth.

Marie looked away. She wished she had sat someplace else. She listened for a moment as he continued to chew, then took another bite herself. After swallowing she picked up her toast, slid it through the yolk and munched. She sipped her tea. The food was so good nothing else mattered.

From his table the man cleared his throat. Marie decided not to watch him. She ate some ham, finished one of the eggs and sipped her tea.

The man cleared his throat again. Marie finished a piece of toast.

"Pardon me, Miss?"

It was the man. She looked at him and he wiggled his finger near his chin as he watched her. Marie was confused, but continued to watch him. Was he flirting? Eventually she went back to her meal.

"Miss?"

She looked at him, annoyed.

"Your chin," he said and wiggled his finger again.

Marie touched her chin and found a thick blob of yolk. She picked up her napkin and wiped until her skin felt raw, and then checked it with her hand.

At the other table the man smiled and nodded once.

"You got it," he said.

Marie looked at her food so she would not see him. She was no longer hungry.

Mrs. Baker sat at the head of the table and read the newspaper as she ate a piece of toast. Flora and Joseph sat across from each other farther down. Flora's plate was empty, while Joseph used a spoon to toy with his oatmeal.

"If you don't finish that you can forget about lunch," Mrs. Baker said without looking up.

"What about supper?" Joseph said.

Mrs. Baker took a bite of her toast and glared at him as she chewed.

"You're not too old for a spanking."

Joseph picked up the spoon and put it in his mouth. Mrs. Baker eyed him until he took another bite, then went back to her paper. Flora watched her and thought.

"Mother?"

"Yes."

"When do the parents of the Home children come visit them?"

Mrs. Baker looked up.

"How is that any of your business?"

"I was just wondering."

Mrs. Baker started to read again. She did not answer.

"You let 'em visit, don't you?" Joseph said.

Mrs. Baker glared at him again. He ate a spoonful of oatmeal and smiled.

"Why would you ask if I *let* them visit?"

Joseph shrugged, still chewing and smiling.

"I was the one who wanted to know, Mother," Flora said, trying to draw her attention away from him. "It's on a specific day, isn't it?"

Mrs. Baker checked her anger, looking back at the newspaper.

"Yes."

"What day?" Joseph said.

She did not look up.

"Visiting day."

Joseph took another bite of oatmeal.

"When's that?"

"Maybe I should send you there to live. Then you'd find out."

Joseph talked into his chest, dropping volume as he went on.

"Not sure I'd find out…"

Mrs. Baker threw the toast onto her plate, where it bounced and then landed on the newspaper. Her voice was like ice.

"What was that?"

Joseph shoveled down a heaping spoonful and shrugged.

"What did you say."

He pointed to his lips and mumbled, "My mouth's full."

"Swallow it."

He did.

"Now tell me."

He raised his index finger and drank some milk. Flora watched and sighed.

"That's better," he said after swallowing.

Mrs. Baker folded her hands on the table.

"Tell me what you said."

"I can't remember."

Mrs. Baker stood but did not leave her place at the table.

"But I think," Joseph said, "that it was something about living at the Home."

Mrs. Baker crossed her arms.

"Which was?"

Joseph's voice was quiet and slow, and he spoke through a half-smile.

"I'm not sure if I'd find out when visiting day was."

"Why would you say that?"

He shrugged.

"No," Mrs. Baker said. "You had a reason. Why else would you say it."

Flora thought she saw him blush.

"Well, how many times did I see my father?"

Mrs. Baker said nothing for a long while. Joseph scraped oatmeal from the sides of his bowl, unable to keep from grinning.

"Your father," Mrs. Baker said at last, nodding slowly. "Well, that's completely different. Your father didn't leave you *with* anyone. He just left." She moved toward Joseph as she spoke until she was right behind him. "The parents who leave their children with us at the Home want to see those children again. That's the difference. Your father left because he didn't want to see you again. He didn't want you to begin with. He was perfectly happy to live with Flora and me and provide for us."

"And the Home."

Mrs. Baker gave the back of his head a smack so hard that his face hit the rim of his bowl. He winced not from pain but because some dabs of oatmeal stuck to his eyelashes.

"Don't interrupt your mother," Mrs. Baker said without raising her voice. "I didn't have the Home then. We weren't even in Kansas City then. He's the reason I started the Home, because of what I saw after he left us, how difficult it can be for a young family without prospects. But I shouldn't say he left us, because he didn't. He loved us. He left you. Before you were born he would ask me to do terrible things. He would ask me to fall on a chair or sit in a bath of mustard water. Do you know that would do to an unborn baby? As if I could do anything like that. I thought he would change once you were born, that everything would be all right once he saw you. But it wasn't. He was gone within a month, and I haven't seen him since. I have heard about him, though. And he's dead. I told you that before. He's dead. So, don't think you can go and find him and get him to change his mind about you, because it can't happen. When I think of all I went through for you. Do you ever show me any respect? Are you thankful at all for the things that you have? No. You're a snide and wicked boy. Sometimes when I look at you I wish I'd listened to your father."

Joseph took a napkin and wiped his face clean.

"Do you feel bad now? That's how you make me feel. Whenever you do these things I feel like I'm going to cry."

Joseph turned around and looked right at her.

"I'm not crying."

She slapped his face hard enough to make his chair shift. He blinked a few times but his eyes did not even water.

"Keep this up, young man, and one of these days I'm going to give you away. I would do it gladly. I wouldn't think twice about it. I'm not telling stories, either. There are plenty of places that would take a little brat like you. Get fresh with them as you do with me, just once, and you would be sorry. They would fix you so you couldn't even think of doing it again. Try and remember that. It would make me very happy. Yes, your sister and I would be much happier if you weren't around anymore."

Joseph looked to Flora's place at the table. It was empty.

"Where'd she go?" he said.

"Probably she didn't want to see you behave like the spoiled little brat that you are. I've seen pigs with better manners."

She lifted him out of his chair by the ear.

"I don't want to look at you, either. Get upstairs and go to your room, and don't come back down until we leave for church tomorrow."

She gave him a shove toward the door, causing him to stumble. He caught himself and left the room without looking at her. He walked down the hall and turned at the stairs, which he climbed slowly, with his fingers batting the rails of the banister. Twenty-four hours with no food, stuck in his room. He stopped climbing and leaned over the railing to look around. He did not see Flora. With a sigh he climbed the rest of the stairs and went to his room.

Flora was there on his bed, waiting for him. Her arms were crossed and she clenched her jaw as she shook her head.

"What?" Joseph said with little inflection.

Flora sighed like a disgusted parent.

"She wouldn'a done anything anyhow," Joseph said.

Flora put her hands on his bed and leaned forward.

"Why do you always have to ruin everything?"

Joseph winced. His face scrunched up and his nose began to run. He rubbed his eyes with his sleeve, and when it came away Flora saw it was transparent. His voice gurgled when he spoke.

"Leave me alone."

He stood near the bed and waited for her to get off of it, but she sat and watched him.

"Get outta my room," he said in a voice that was almost impossible to understand.

When he finished talking he turned his back to her and went to the corner of the room. He rested his head where the walls came together and slid down until his chin was propped on his knees. Flora stood and came up behind him, kneeling. She placed her hand on his back, but he would not look at her. Instead he tried to burrow further into the wall. Up close like this he seemed to be shaking. Flora put her head where her hand had been and listened to the thumping of his heart and the shivery unsteadiness of his breathing. She felt like saying something but remained silent.

Marie sat in the elegant lobby of the Central Hotel pretending to read the newspaper. It was more than a half-hour before dinnertime, and the bed in her room was so inviting. The chair on which she sat was nice, too – high-backed, cushioned, soft – but the level of activity in the lobby would make sleep impossible. She considered lowering the paper to watch, but decided it would be unwise. He was still there. The man from that day at breakfast. She saw him come into the lobby by way of the main staircase and she hid behind the paper. She heard him sit in a chair across from hers and strike a match, which was followed by the aroma of sweet pipesmoke. She shook the paper in her hands to straighten it, but the top half folded down, revealing him, watching her.

"Hello, there," he said with a nod.

She nodded in return.

"I've seen you before."

She shook the paper again and put it between them.

"I remember."

"No, before that, even. You come here fairly often, don't you?"

She turned the page.

"I suppose so. Whenever I'm in town."

"I thought you did. That's good to hear. Good to know."

She all but dropped the paper in her lap.

"I beg your pardon?"

He seemed surprised by her reaction.

"I like to keep track of the regular guests," he said.

In a huff Marie folded the paper and put it on the table next to her chair. The man stood and removed his hat.

"Nothin' like what you think. I'm Col. Huegel. I own this hotel."

Marie was caught between a standing and sitting position.

"You–"

"Own it. Yes, ma'am. And proudly."

Slowly she stood to her full height.

"Oh... I'm sorry."

"I'm not. It's the best place in town. Best in the whole state, if you ask me."

Marie smiled, still a bit embarrassed.

"Yes. Oh, yes, I quite agree."

"Please, sit down."

"Thank you."

She sat once more with her hands folded on her knees and her heels joined under the chair. Huegel put his hat back on and took his seat, too, crossing his legs. He raised his pipe.

"You aren't bothered by this, are you?"

"Of course not."

"Some folks are. And I wouldn't wanna offend one of our regular guests. We depend on you. Once someone stays here, they usually stay again. That's how we like it."

"It is a beautiful place."

He smiled with pride.

"We like to think so."

"And you're right about it being the best hotel in the state."

"You like it here?"

"Oh, very much."

"Stay in a lot of hotels, do you?"

"Yes, I do. For my work."

"What is your work?"

"Home conservation."

"Sounds interesting."

Marie spent several minutes explaining the idea and describing the Home. Huegel gave careful attention and stroked his chin with the thumb of the hand that held his pipe. When Marie finished speaking Huegel smoothed his mustache and puffed the pipe, but no smoke came out. He fiddled with his vest to get his matches.

"You take donations, don't you?"

"They enable my sister's work to continue."

Huegel struck a match and held it to the bowl of his pipe. Rings of smoke lifted above his head as he puffed. When it was lit he shook the match and tossed it into an ashtray.

"I'd like to help."

"Would you really?"

"Sure I would."

"We'd be so grateful to you."

"I'm not doing it for that. It's for my wife – at least partly."

"I didn't know you were married."

"I'm not. Not anymore. She passed on not too long ago."

"I'm so sorry."

He shrugged a little, as if he were not sure of what to do. His smile was wistful.

"It's something she would have wanted, I think."

"I know how you much feel. My husband is gone now, too."

"Oh, no. When did he pass?"

Marie hung her head a bit.

"About a year ago."

"Just about the time of my wife, I'll bet. You have my condolences."

"Thank you."

He was thoughtful as he drew on his pipe.

"I can't imagine what it musta been like for a young lady like yourself. It was hard on me, but I'm an old man."

"No, you're not."

"I didn't say that so you could flatter me," he said with a grin. "I'm an old man. I don't feel like one, but that's what I am. I've got the hotel here to keep me busy, but every morning I wake up and see my old face in the mirror and think, 'Who is that?'"

"It must be wonderful to wake up here every day."

"You really like it here?" he asked again.

She nodded.

"I do."

"I'm glad of it. I thought I'd seen you here before. We have lots of regulars, but with so many people in and out it's hard to tell sometimes."

"I love it. I'm always sad when I have to leave again."

"That's how we want it. It means you'll come back."

"I will. You can rely on that."

Mrs. Baker gave only a bit of her speech before she was interrupted. The woman to whom she was talking was young and looked wealthy, and Mrs. Baker let her break in.

"I know all about home conserving. I read about it in the paper."

"I hope the report was accurate."

"As do I. It's a wonderful notion."

Mrs. Baker smiled and thanked her.

"Do you know Rev. Litten?" the woman asked. "Know him personally, I mean."

Mrs. Baker's nostril's flared as if she had smelled sour milk. "Rev. Litten?"

"I believe that was his name. The Litten Home was what the article was about. That's how I remembered it. Is that right? Litten?"

"Excuse me, I must leave."

Mrs. Baker put the magazines under her arm and walked away as fast as she could without running.

George M. Shelley stood in front of his small dry goods store and looked up and down the street. There had been no customers for the past hour and it was only two o'clock. He sighed and returned to the store. As soon as he was inside a woman came in behind him, and he whirled around and gave her his best smile. Perhaps she would buy something.

"How may I help you today, madam?"

"Are you Mr. Shelley?"

"Yes, that's me. What can I do for you?"

The woman drew herself up and spoke with absolute seriousness.

"My name is Mrs. Julia Anna Baker, and I am the mother and founder of the Joseph Walter Home. I understand you are the secretary of the city's public service committee."

"Yes, I am, but–"

"It pains me to have to inform on someone's unsavory practices, especially if they work in the same field as I. I would do anything to help children, and I feel nothing but goodwill toward those who do the same. But there is one establishment in our beautiful city that I cannot condone. I've been the target of unjust criticism in the past, but in this case criticism is more than warranted. Are you familiar with the Litten Home? It's located on Independence Road."

"Forgive me for asking, Mrs. Baker, but why come to me?"

"You were the only committee member whose name I knew."

He glanced at the door. They were still alone.

"Why seek out the committee at all? If this place is as bad as you say, why not go to the police or to the board of public welfare?"

She shook her head and lowered her eyes.

"I had thought of that myself, but unfortunately, sir, they're prejudiced against me and my work. If I went to them it would be a guarantee that nothing would be done. You have no idea how corrupt this city can be."

"Well..."

"And so I thought of your board. I'm something of a public servant. Caring for needy children is a public service, is it not?"

"In a way, I suppose."

"Then it's perfect."

"But, Mrs...?"

"Baker."

"Mrs. Baker. About that board, it's an orphan itself. It's been all but abandoned by its members, except for me, and there's very little I can do for the benefit of anybody by myself."

"I see."

"I understand your plight, and I wish there was something I could do, but I've no idea what that would be."

She nodded and shut her eyes.

"Home conservation was my idea – mine alone. They've stolen it, and now their home is being conflated with mine in the eyes of the public. What can I do? I can't let them continue."

Shelley nodded and crossed his arms.

"I wish I could tell you."

Mrs. Baker's case against Rev. Litten went to court before Justice Welch. She charged him with improperly diverting to his own pocket eighty-one hundred dollars donated to the Joseph Walter Home by subscribers. "How else could he manage to open his own home so quickly?" she asked whenever she spoke of it. Mrs. Baker said Litten never was able to provide her with a satisfactory accounting of what had been done with the money. Both the Rev. and Mrs. Litten testified the funds went toward the maintenance of the Home. Mrs. Baker added that Litten held his own needs against those of the children, that he ate separate from them and got better food. Again the Littens refuted her. Justice Welch agreed with them and dismissed the charge.

Later that week Mrs. Baker again sued Rev. Litten via the circuit court for the amount of eighty-one hundred dollars. The Littens were giving the children of their home breakfast the next morning when they heard a knock at the door.

"Good morning, Ida," Mrs. Baker said from the porch.

"Mrs. Litten to you. What do you want?"

"You've heard the news, I take it."

Her voice was stony.

"We were informed last night."

"It was in the paper this morning, as well."

Mrs. Baker took a copy of *The Star* from her bag and held it out for Mrs. Litten to see. A small item was circled in red pencil: "SUE PREACHER FOR $8,100."

"Sometimes their reporting does manage to be accurate. May I come in?"

"No."

"I must speak with your husband."

"He won't."

"Ask him. Perhaps he'll surprise you."

"No."

"Then I shall wait until he does."

Mrs. Litten closed the door in her face. Mrs. Baker returned the newspaper to her bag and looked out at the street. The air was humid and it smelled like steam. The door opened again.

"What is it you want?" Rev. Litten said. "It's not enough to sue us, you have to come to our house, too?"

"May I come inside?"

"No, you may not."

"I must speak with you."

"I don't care to hear anything you have to say."

"Regardless, I must speak."

Rev. Litten gave a short sigh and stepped out of the house. He shut the door, keeping one hand on the knob. His face was wet and his skin had a greenish tone.

"What."

"You and your wife have been quite short with me this morning. Are you under some kind of distress? Is it your heart that's giving you trouble?"

Rev. Litten pushed the door open again and began to go inside.

"Don't leave now," Mrs. Baker said quickly. "I know what it is. Money, is that correct? You have none."

He stopped and watched her.

"You would never be able to pay eight thousand one hundred dollars, isn't that so?"

"I didn't take that money from you."

"That isn't what I said. I said you wouldn't be able to pay. Tell me if it's not so."

"You know the answer to that question. Unlike some overseers, when my wife and I receive donations we spend them on the children. That's as it should be."

"God save you."

He ignored her.

"We have nothing," Litten said. "You'll never win this case, and even if you did we would have nothing to pay you."

"And how will you pay your attorney since your win is so assured? They don't work for nothing, you know."

"Get away from my house."

"After you *win* this case, I'll sue you again."

"For what?"

"Slander."

"It's not slander if it's true."

"Another legal victory. Congratulations to you. How are you going to pay?"

Rev. Litten felt a sharp pain in his chest.

"I will take you to court as long as I have to," Mrs. Baker said. "I will do whatever I feel is necessary. I will not, will not ever stop until you have nothing left. You say you have nothing now? Wait and see. I will destroy you."

She watched him with a friendly smile. He looked like he might throw up.

"What do you want? Besides money, what do you want?"

"Leave town. I don't care where you go, but I don't ever want to see you again."

"What about the children?"

Mrs. Baker continued to smile.

"There are other homes…"

Mrs. Floyd left the bucket on her back porch. It was nearly full. There were apples, bread and hardboiled eggs. She looked around as she set it on the top step. There was no one in sight. She thought about calling, but felt bad as soon as it entered her head. They were children, not animals.

She heard them once she was back in the house. The bucket scraped on the wood and the handle rattled against the side, and there was the pounding of their footsteps as they came to it. Mrs. Floyd crept to the door and watched as they sat in a circle, devouring what they found. There were three of them. They looked like brothers. They had dark hair that was cropped very short and large grown eyes. Their clothes were disgraceful, soiled and worn. The two oldest wore overalls and filthy shirts, and the youngest wore nothing but what appeared to be a long nightshirt. They did not speak as they ate, they just brought greedy handfuls of food to their mouths and chewed until Mrs. Floyd thought they would pass out for lack of breathing. When the food was gone they licked their fingers and ran their hands in the bucket in search of crumbs.

Mrs. Floyd held the doorknob firm. They were still so hungry. Like the last time. Slowly she bent her knees until she was crouched behind the door, and locked it without making any noise.

George M. Shelley lived in his shop now, in a little room toward the back. In the room was a bed, a small stove and all the clothes he owned – one extra suit in addition to the one he had on. Nobody came in to buy anymore. If they did pay him a visit it was to collect a debt. Mainly he was alone. His wife had died years earlier, in 1907. Shelley sat near the front window hunched over his ledger and staring at the figures. It was no good. He took off his glasses and dropped them on the paper. He felt very old.

The door opened, allowing a wave of February cold inside the already chilled room, and Shelley pulled his collar tight around his neck and shielded his face in the crook of his arm. When the door was closed again he relaxed.

"Mr. Shelley," a big voice said. It was Oldham. His body matched the sound of him, and the heavy winter coat he wore made him look even larger, almost like a trained bear. Shelley noticed a diamond stickpin. Landshares or not, Oldham still looked like a smalltime gambler.

"Charley. How are you?"

"Never better. Same for you, I'm sure."

Shelley spoke with a weariness more suited to a common laborer than an elder statesman.

"What do you want, Charley?"

"Mr. Shelley, can you let me have that two hundred an' sixty dollars you owe me?"

Shelley let out a sigh.

"I know times are tough," Oldham said. "Hell, they get that way for everybody sometime or another, don't they? But things'll work out long as you stay honest. And that's what you've done. I respect that, Shelley, I truly do. When folks heard I'd lent you money they said I was crazy. Said I'd never see it again. But I told 'em, I said, 'That Mr. Shelley's a man of his word.'"

He gave a devious smile.

"Shoulda heard what they said when I told 'em just how much I lent you."

He laughed for a few seconds, by himself. Then he clapped his hands and rubbed them together.

"So? Whaddyou say? You have my money?"

Shelley could not look at him.

"No, I don't. I can't pay you."

"You're really gonna do that to me now? After all I done for you? I just told ya what I said to all them people, and after that you sit there and say no. Just like that."

"I didn't say I wouldn't. I said I can't."

"No difference at all, Mr. Shelley. No matter how you put it I still don't get my money."

"I don't have the money to give you."

"That ain't my fault. So your business didn't work out. That ain't my fault, either. Might not even be yours. Sometimes things just don't work out, no reason at all, they just don't. Plain and simple. Just the way things are sometimes. That's life. But I want that money. I got a right to it."

"But I tell you I don't have it."

Oldham threw up his arms with an enormous shrug.

"You're the third man who tried to collect from me today," Shelley said.

"You tell 'em all the same thing?"

"That's all I can tell them. It's the truth."

Oldham shook his head and made a small gesture toward Shelley.

"See, it's things like that that give you a bad name."

Before he realized what he was doing Shelley rushed up to Oldham and punched him in the face. The force of it was not enough to make Oldham even stumble. In retaliation he wrapped his arms around Shelley and held him close.

"Stop this foolishness," Oldham yelled. "I'm the best friend you got, Mr. Shelley. The best friend you got!"

Shelley struggled to break free but Oldham's grip was unshakeable. Then another rush of wind passed into the shop. Shelley heard a man grunt and then a loud thump like someone hitting a block of wood with a baseball bat. Immediately Oldham released Shelley and fell to his knees clutching the top of his head. His hat was off and the sparse red hairs stood on end. Behind Oldham stood Max Gilsey from the shop across the street. In his hand he carried a rod like a police baton.

"You okay, Mr. Shelley?"

Shelley nodded, too surprised to speak.

Gilsey plopped Oldham's hat back on his head, took him by the shoulders and pushed him until he was out of the shop. Once outside Gilsey let him go and Oldham stumbled along groaning until he came to a stop against a post. Gilsey walked back to his shop without showing the slightest concern.

Shelley stood watching from the door of his shop. People in the street began to come near, some attending to Oldham, others following Gilsey. A pair of young women stood away from the scene. Their eyes were on Shelley. One leaned against the other and whispered in her ear. Shock registered on the woman's face and she covered her mouth with her hand. Lowering it again two seconds later, Shelley heard her faint voice ask, "Was he really?"

Turning away from them all, he went back inside his shop. He locked the door, picked up his ledger and hid in the back room.

It was warmer now, but the snow was only halfway melted and water flowed in streams on the roads and dripped like rain off the eaves of houses. Mrs. Floyd brought the bucket to its usual spot but did not set it down. There was no place to set it that would stay dry. She went back to the house and left the bucket outside the door, which she kept open so she could hear the dripping through the screen and enjoy the wet smell.

Near ten o'clock she heard a sound near the door. Going to it, she saw the three boys. She did not usually speak to them, but now she went over and addressed them from inside the house.

"What are you doing out of school?"

Only one of the boys acknowledged her presence. He stared at her, chewing and blinking his large green eyes.

"Teacher sent us home."

"You can't all three be in the same class."

"We ain't. She met us out front of the school. Told a whole bunch of us we couldn't come in."

"Why is that?"

The smallest boy looked up and shouted with a full mouth, "We got lice!"

"All of you?"

"Us three do," the first boy said.

"What about the rest of you?"

He shrugged and got an apple from the bucket. He took a big bite and chewed as he spoke.

"They sent most of us back today. They been sendin' more every day since Monday. Kid was sittin' in school and the boy in back of him, he's a Kraut and he points at the kid's head and yells, 'Loose!' Since then they been sendin' us home. We got some skin thing now, too, they said. They looked down our shirts to see our backs."

"Have they washed you?"

"They don't wash you at school!" the youngest one said.

"She means at home, stupid," the first boy said and slapped his shoulder.

"Have they?" Mrs. Floyd asked.

"They ain't washed us in a long time. They don't make us, either."

"I like it!"

"They ought to make you."

The boy stood and threw the stem of his apple as far as he could.

"They can't make me do nothin'," he said.

Mrs. Baker went with caution to the front door. From the walk she saw a piece of paper tacked to it. As she drew closer she realized it was not an official notice, but an item someone had clipped from a newspaper. She ripped it off the tack without reading it and went inside. The maid came in and saw who it was and curtsied.

"Are the children home, Kathleen?"

"Yes, ma'am, they're upstairs."

Mrs. Baker took off her hat and gave it to the maid.

"Make the chops for dinner, before they turn."

"Yes, ma'am."

"I'll be in my office."

Mrs. Baker read the clipping as she went down the hall. The article was not dated, and it was not clear what newspaper it was from. It was not very long, but the main headline was done in thick capital letters: "THE TELEGRAM'S TALE." The headline below it read, "Chief of Police Hammil of Kansas City Says Home is Unworthy of Charity." Mrs. Baker did not close her door before she went to her desk. She read on carefully.

"For the past week two well dressed women have been approaching citizens of Moberly with an appeal for help from the Joseph Walton Home for orphans."

Mrs. Baker rolled her eyes. Why was it so difficult for reporters to get the name right? At least this time the mistake appeared in a slanderous article.

"The two solicitors have winning smiles and, it is said, almost invariably received a contribution from the person approached.

"However, certain Moberly people have been stung so often on similar pleas for aid that they appealed to Chief of Police Hinton to learn whether or not the Joseph Walton Home was worthy of support or any orphans were being sheltered by that institution and would be benefitted by the contributions given there."

Mrs. Baker scanned toward the bottom of the article.

"And this was the answer which was received:

"Joseph Walton Home not considered worthy by United Charities here, proprietress run out of Joplin and forfeited bonds in several cities in Minnesota – H. W. Hammil."

There was more, but she did not read it. She crushed the paper in her hands, packing it into as tight a ball as she could. Then she threw it away. Standing, Mrs. Baker adjusted her hair and walked to the kitchen.

The maid faced the stove and melted butter in a skillet.

"Kathleen."

She jumped and turned to Mrs. Baker with a hand on her chest.

"My goodness, ma'am, I nearly burned myself."

"Was anyone here this afternoon?"

"Ma'am?"

Mrs. Baker gave an exasperated sigh, and spoke in a loud slow voice.

"Were there any visitors while I was gone?"

"No, ma'am. No one's been here but the children."

"Have you been out yourself?"

She shook the skillet to spread the butter, which had begun to sizzle and pop.

"No, ma'am, I ain't been out all day."

"Didn't hear anyone, didn't see anyone."

The maid shook her head.

"Did the children speak to you? Did they say anything?"

"Nothing they never said before."

"How long were they here before I came home?"

"Half an hour, I suppose."

Beside Kathleen on the stove was a sheet of butcher paper, on top of which were three thick pork chops. Without looking away from Mrs. Baker Kathleen picked them up one by one and set them in the skillet. They made a sound like rushing steam and the room began to fill with light-colored smoke and the warm good smell of cooking meat. Mrs. Baker stood in silent thought.

"Is something wrong, ma'am?"

Mrs. Baker blinked twice.

"Beg pardon?"

"Is something wrong, ma'am? Did I do something?"

Mrs. Baker thought another few seconds.

"No. But keep your eye out."

"Who for?"

"Anyone."

Kathleen was a good cook. When they were set on a plate the chops looked as dry as a piece of wood, but once they were speared with a fork or a knife the juice flooded out hot and clear onto the plate. She was unsure of the word for it. "Sear," Mrs. Baker said. And there were greens with butter and lemon, and fresh cold milk. Flora and Joseph devoured theirs and asked for seconds. Mrs. Baker had not cleaned half her plate. Slowly she tapped the side of it with her fork and stared into nothing. Flora stopped eating to watch her. Joseph watched her, as well, between bites.

"Mother?" Flora said.

She put down her fork.

"Hmm?"

"Are you feeling all right?"

Mrs. Baker used her tongue to work a string of meat out from between her molars.

"Did you children see anyone today?"

"Course we did," Joseph said.

Before Mrs. Baker could look at him Flora interjected, "How do you mean, Mother?"

Still working her tongue, Mrs. Baker picked up her fork again.

"When you came home from school, where did you go?"

"Upstairs, to our rooms."

"Immediately? You didn't laze about the parlor? You didn't wander in the halls? If I'm not home I expect you to know what's going on here. If people come to the door I expect you to tell me about it. You're my eyes when I'm not here."

"Did someone come?" Joseph said.

"Don't be a pig. Swallow before you speak."

"Mother, what are you talking about?" Flora said. "Were you expecting somebody?"

"No."

"Did somebody come? We didn't hear the bell."

"What did Kathleen say?" Joseph asked.

Mrs. Baker dug her tongue as far between her teeth as she could. The piece of meat came loose and she chewed it at the front of her mouth and then swallowed it.

"She said she didn't hear anything or see anybody."

"Then there must not've been anyone," Joseph said.

"How would you know?"

Joseph froze, his fork stopped a few inches above his plate.

"I don't know nothin'."

"About what?"

"I don't know."

"Mother, what are you talking about?" Flora asked. "Did somebody come? We're sorry if we missed something important, but we didn't hear anything. Honestly."

Mrs. Baker looked at Flora.

"The only reason you didn't hear anything is because you weren't supposed to."

"I didn't hear nothin' 'cause I was takin' a nap," Joseph said.

"That's right, Mother, I saw him. I looked in his room. He was sleeping until you came home."

Mrs. Baker continued to watch her daughter.

"You're sure?"

Flora nodded.

Mrs. Baker thought a long while. She picked up her knife and cut off another bite of her chop. She put it in her mouth and chewed.

Mrs. Baker opened her closet and went through her dresses. Against the wall hung the oldest one. Heavy and black, it was one size too small. The elbows were worn thin and strings dangled in greasy clusters from the hem. She removed it from the hanger and slipped it on, and then, holding her breath, did up the buttons. She went carefully to the mirror and looked at herself. It was startling, an unwelcome vision from the past. Had she really once appeared in public this way? She was different now. These rags seemed so out of place on her – her innate elegance showed through no matter what she wore. It must have always been that way. Why else would she have felt so dissatisfied?

She arrived at the utility office near ten o'clock and announced herself to one of the secretaries, who showed her to Mr. Scott's office. He looked up from his desk with a businesslike smile and held out his arms as an invitation for Mrs. Baker to sit.

"How can I help you today?"

"You know very well," she said in a fluttery voice. "You shut the gas off at the Home. How could you? Don't you have a heart?"

Scott swiveled in his chair, a smirk on his lips.

"It's because I have a heart that I waited to turn it off until after springtime came."

"And what are we to do now?"

"Pay your bill, I suppose."

"If only that were possible."

There was a catch in her voice on the last word and she opened her bag to get an old handkerchief, which she used to wipe her eyes.

Scott's demeanor was unchanged.

"You don't have to pay it all in one go. We could work out a series of installments – whatever you can afford. But we will not restore your service until you've caught up on your payments."

"How could you do that to children?"

"I'm surprised you didn't bring one along to make me feel guilty."

"They're in school."

"Are they really?"

"And the little ones wouldn't want to come all this way."

"Their little legs would get tired, I guess."

Mrs. Baker frowned and returned the cloth to her bag. She blinked her dry eyes several times.

"There is really no reasoning with you, is there?"

"I am being reasonable, Mrs. Baker." He stood and went to the window, looking out with his hand folded. "If you pay, the city will provide a service. If you don't pay, you can't expect to get that service for free." He looked at her over his shoulder. "There's no law that says we have to provide you with gas. Plenty of homes go without it, and they make do."

"They don't have more than a hundred children to care for."

Scott chuckled.

"Your argument might be more convincing if you had missed a payment or two on your own home's account."

Mrs. Baker glared at him but said nothing.

"It is difficult to care for a hundred children, I'll grant you that. It's much easier to look after yourself. Isn't it?"

He continued to look at her and grinned.

Mrs. Baker stood and went to the door.

"Come and see me again if you can scrape together the money you owe us," Scott said before he turned back to the window.

Mrs. Floyd watched the Home twice a day. It was when the children were fed – once in the morning, once near lunchtime. They stood in lines for a small amount of bread and some milk. There were not enough cups for all of them and they would be handed back and forth from child to grown-up without being washed before each refill. She did not know if they were fed in the evening. If they were, she never saw it. She told herself it was done indoors.

Their clothes grew worse all the time. They had become actual rags, most of them. She doubted they were ever washed. They probably would fall apart if they had been. She knew the children never were washed. Anyone could see that. They were becoming like animals, stopping everyone they passed in the street to beg for food, continuing to root through garbage cans. Some of them would squirrel what little food they found in the bushes and come back to eat it later.

Everyone in the neighborhood talked about them and gossiped about what might be going on in the house. The women who worked there were no good. The street buzzed with stories of late-night visitors. One doctor said if he saw one of the Joseph Walter children it was always an ordeal to get the Home to take them back. If parents brought their children there to stay, they usually took them back soon. A mother had once gone up and down the block informing everybody that it had taken two days to get her daughters' heads clean, and that her youngest daughter's new shoes had been stolen.

Mrs. Floyd continued to feed them. There would be more all the time. They waited for her and clustered around her in a frenzy when she came out of the house, even when she had no food, and cried and pleaded with her to bring them some. She tried not to go out much.

In March *The Star* reported the juvenile court "was being made a dumping-ground for feeble-minded children." It was written that Dr. Mathias began to investigate the problem the previous October, and that while the school board thought feeble-mindedness would be confined only to "certain parts" of Kansas City, he discovered such children could be found everywhere.

"In Kansas City's eighty public schools are between four hundred and six hundred children of defective mentality," Mathias said. "Most of them are in the second grade. Some advance to the third grade. A few get into the fourth grade. But the work beyond is too much for them. They drop out of school eventually without anything having been done for them. They become drags on the wheel – the boys grow up unable long to hold any job and drift into the unemployed criminal class; the girls, those that marry, bear children with inherited feeble-minded tendencies."

Mathias went on to say, "The first thing we will do will be to ascertain exactly the number of feeble-minded and worse in schools. Then we will classify them. The idiots and imbeciles have no place in the schools and will be weeded out. The feeble-minded we can help, and we will set about doing so.

"The ways of training are three. A special school may be selected, special classrooms in each school may be set aside, or the St. Louis plan may be adopted. The last is to rent a private residence in a neighborhood where ten to twenty defective children reside, install a teacher or two, and coach the children. The children can be taught domestic science, housework and so forth, and so pulled along to more difficult things.

"The best way to describe feeble-minded child so everybody will grasp the conception is to say he grows into a young man, if the defective is a boy, a young man who cannot hold a job. Such individuals pass muster in the world; folks just say they're rather stupid and let it go at that. But when it comes to working on their own initiative, they fail. An employer will say, 'I've got to show that fellow how to do everything,' and he'll discharge him. They continually need supervision.

"So our plan will be to teach the defectives self-reliance and confidence by giving them tasks they can do and gradually increasing the difficulty of the task. As it is now, in school, the defectives flunk continually, are mocked and obtain no belief in their ability to do anything. After years of that in school, of course, they fail in life. We will try to put backbone in them, and I believe it can be done."

A month later it was announced the school board was seeking a teacher "who is an expert in the work with defectives," and that special classes would be organized once that teacher was found.

Superintendent of schools J. I. Cammack told *The Star*, "Our idea is to begin in a small way and work out the plans as we go along. We probably will set aside a room in one of the regular school buildings for the first class. Into this we will put these pupils we know to be defective, and as others are found we will extend the work. The ideal condition, and the one that we hope for eventually, is to have a separate building for defective children where they may be trained without interference.

"We have experimented along somewhat the same lines for some time in our ungraded classes. These, however, are for retarded children principally. The whole plan is in line with the idea of getting away from fixed, arbitrary grades and teaching children as individuals, not as groups. The defective classes, for example, will not have more than fifteen in them, so that the teacher may pay particular attention to the problem each child presents."

"Special school training for defectives is not new," Mathias added. "Boston has had it for sixteen years and it has been adopted by cities all over the country. England has made mental surveys, not only of the schoolchildren, but of their population, to determine the number of feeble-minded.

"It was found that one in every two hundred forty-eight persons in England was either feeble-minded, an imbecile or an idiot. In every place where investigations have been made, the percentage of mentally defective schoolchildren has ranged from one of two-point-five. There is every reason to believe that the same holds true for Kansas City.

"It is this class that keeps our juvenile and police courts busy. Probably twenty-five percent of the children who come to the juvenile court are defective. This class also furnishes us with many of our hoboes, immoral women and public charges. The proper training of such persons is a wonderful aid in enabling them to be self-supporting instead of a burden on the community."

Mathias went on, "There is no definite dividing line between the defective child and the one that is merely retarded. The range of intelligence from the genius down through the average intellect to the profound idiot is a gradual change from one class to the other. It is impossible to say where one leaves off and the other begins.

"Defectives are about equally divided among all classes of society. They crop out in the higher ranks as often as they do the lower. The cause can generally be traced back in a person's ancestry. One thing we know is that two mentally defective persons have never produced a normal child. Under our present laws, however, this class is free to go on begetting its kind for the state to take care of.

"The delinquent girl very often is a defective. She has the body of a woman and the mentality of a child. Without training and supervision she has little chance to withstand the temptations she meets.

"The Prodigal Son probably was a defective. With him it was a matter of satisfying his stomach. There are many of his type living now.

"The matter of caring for these persons is just being taken up. The work in the schools is only part of it. There are eight thousand defectives in Missouri today who need instruction and care. The state is caring for four hundred seventy-two. The work has scarcely begun."

Marie's wedding was small. It was held in Jackson, away from the Home and away from the hotel. She wanted it that way. Mrs.

Baker was one of the few guests, along with a couple of Huegel's friends. Even though it was July and there was no school, Flora and Joseph did not attend. Neither did any of Huegel's grown children, who were to meet their new stepmother after the honeymoon concluded.

The reception was held at a restaurant downtown. When the meal was over Huegel and his friends went to the bar to talk and smoke cigars. Before he left he gave Marie a shy kiss on the cheek, which made her blush. She smiled as her eyes followed him out of the room.

"I'm very happy for you," Mrs. Baker said when they were alone. Her voice was flat.

"Thank you."

Marie took a drink of champagne and scrunched up her nose. Mrs. Baker held a small glass of water.

"The house will seem empty now that you're gone."

"No it won't. I'm always away – we both are. You won't even notice it."

"I will. I know I will. I'll miss you terribly."

"I'll miss you, too. And the children. Please, do thank them for their letters. They were so thoughtful."

"I made them write them."

"Still."

"And I practically had to stand over Joseph to make sure he would finish his. How that child ever became so helpless I'll never know. That's his father all over."

Marie smiled.

"See, now? You won't have time to miss me. You'll be too busy."

Mrs. Baker sipped her water.

"But of course we'll see each other," Marie said.

"Once you're settled, I know."

"Every holiday I want you to come. I've decided. You and the children. Christmas, Thanksgiving, Easter. The hotel is so beautiful. It would be the perfect place for us all to be together."

"I know what the hotel looks like. I've stayed there."

"Of course you have. Then you know."

Mrs. Baker nodded.

"I just said I did."

"And the other thing, so many groups meet there. Women's clubs, fraternal organizations, all sorts. If they're looking for speakers I could tell them all about home conservation. It would be perfect. Or you could come and do it. You're a much better speaker than I could ever hope to be."

Marie finished what remained in her glass. The bottle sat nearby and she emptied it into the glass. The fizz rose to kiss the rim, and she leaned in to slurp some of it up in case it overflowed, and she giggled when she sat back and wiped her lips.

"When will you return to work?"

Marie smiled but her eyes were sad. She tilted her head as she looked at Mrs. Baker.

"That will be my work from now on."

"Living in a hotel? That doesn't sound like work to me."

"Speaking. So many different people pass through each week – can you imagine how many of them I can reach?"

"No. How many?"

"As many as I can."

Mrs. Baker looked toward the bar. Through the door the booming laughter of Huegel and his friends came through, and she did not hide her distaste.

"Julia…"

"What?" Mrs. Baker said, turning her back on the noise.

"I can't live on the road anymore. I'm married now."

"You were married before."

"Yes, and it didn't work out."

"Don't blame the Home for that. You married a criminal, no one forced you into it."

Marie picked up her glass and took a slow drink. She did not put it back on the table.

"It's as if you don't remember what I told you," Mrs. Baker said.

"I remember."

"And it makes no difference, I take it."

"I've made up my mind."

"Definitively?"

"Yes."

Mrs. Baker gave a nod.

"Very well."

She stood.

"I must go."

Marie stayed sitting.

"Have a good trip."

Mrs. Baker watched her a moment. Her face was blank. Then she left the restaurant. When the door closed Marie drained her glass. The bubbles traveled happily down her throat to her stomach, and she felt warm. Closing her eyes, she smiled and hugged herself. Everything seemed bigger – noises, smells, feelings. Her heart raced. She opened her eyes, breathing slow. Soon she got up and went to the bar to join her husband.

The car was beautiful, shiny and black with four doors and a canvas top that could be folded up and back for comfortable riding on sunny days. Houston Matthews came to the station in it to pick up Mrs. Baker, and escorted her out to where it was parked with her bag in one hand.

"Oh, my gracious," she said.

"You like it?"

"God save you, sir."

Matthews blushed and deposited her bag in the back seat.

"You wanna drive it?"

"May I?"

"It's yours, you don't have to ask."

On the road to her hotel Mrs. Baker smiled so hard her face hurt. She felt the power of the engine through the steering wheel and it made her body tingle.

"What do you think?" Matthews shouted over the noise.

"It's wonderful! It's going to make my work so much more convenient!"

"More what?"

"More convenient!"

He grinned and nodded.

In the hotel restaurant they sipped iced tea near an open window. The air was stifling but Mrs. Baker seemed unaware of it. Positioned so she could see outside, she never looked away from the car, even as she spoke to Matthews.

"You don't know how much this means," she said.

"Sure I do. That's why I did it."

"I travel so much, you'd be astonished. I'll still have to take the train sometimes, for longer journeys, but if it's not too far, I won't even have to think of it."

"Where were you just now?"

"Jefferson City."

"That's a fair distance."

"Yes, but it's not terribly far. With an auto I could have driven there and made stops along the way. It's perfect for my needs."

"It's a bit farther to Kansas City."

"It is, but that means there are more places to stop. To be honest, what I'm looking forward to most is the solitude."

"You don't get much time to yourself, I'd bet."

"I surely don't. When I'm alone in the car I'll have a chance to think."

The terrain grew hillier the closer she drew to Kansas City. The heat was bad and when Mrs. Baker thought of Marie it became unbearable. When she reached home her dress was soaked through. She parked in front of the house and a small crowd, both children and adults, gathered and asked questions. Her own children were not among the onlookers. Mrs. Baker smiled and said a few words and waved her hand before her face, begging off all questions and talking of her need for water. She was on the sidewalk when she noticed a paper on the front door, tacked there just like the first. It was not a newspaper clipping but a circular printed on a press. At the top it said in fat black words, "Warning Against Fake Charity." Mrs. Baker walked quickly to it and read:

"The public is hereby warned against certain women who have been soliciting funds in various parts of the state for a so-called orphanage in Kansas City, Mo., known as the Walter-Baker Home or the Joseph-Walter Home, of which Mrs. Julia Anna Walter-Baker is the manager.

"The character of this organization is such that the Associated Charities of Kansas City have refused their indorsement as being unworthy of support. It is well known that Mrs. Baker and her associates, a few years ago, were compelled to leave Duluth as running a fake charity and were afterwards refused indorsement in Wisconsin for the same reason. Sometimes these women solicit for the Minnesota Children's Home Society claiming to take the place of our regular representatives. We take this means to warn the public against these people as having no authority from us or connection with us.

"To avoid being imposed upon in regard to the Walter-Baker Home write G. F. Damon, Gen. Sec., Associated Charities Kansas City, Mo."

Mrs. Baker dropped her bag and turned back to the street. Most of the people were still clustered around the car, although a few were watching her with undisguised curiosity. Mrs. Baker tore down the leaflet and went back down the walk, shaking it at the group.

"Which of you did this! Tell me right now!"

They were confused, even startled by the outburst. They said nothing, and they did not leave.

"You're all innocent, I suppose? Is that it?"

Some of them began to slink away, but most remained standing in mute befuddlement.

"I'm here to face my accusers! Can't you face me? I will answer every accusation in this paper! It's slanderous! It's obscene trash, lies, all of it, not one word of truth!"

Her face grew red as she spoke. Her knuckles were white and bony as she continued to flail her arms. She looked to the gathering and lowered her voice.

"If any of you have read this, you can be sure it's untrue. If you don't believe me you can come to the Home and see! Not one word of truth can be found in this paper, not one. Tell me now, who left this?"

Most of the people had begun to walk back to their homes, and those who remained stood fidgeting.

"I see, I see!" Mrs. Baker yelled. "Whoever left this is not only a liar, but a coward, as well! I tell you they should be afraid of me, whoever it was! What's in this paper is libelous! It's slander! I'm going to bring it to my attorney, and when we find out who left this filth we'll file a claim against them! That's exactly what we'll do! We'll win, too! The Lord is with me! I am not afraid!"

By this time everyone had gone. Mrs. Baker stood in the middle of the road, her chest heaving, a froth building inside her mouth as if she had been running. From her bedroom window Flora watched as her mother came back to the house swinging her arms like a giant ape. Flora knelt by her night table to avoid being seen. Then she opened it and brought out her box. Around her neck dangled a small golden key strung through a chain. She used it to unlock the box, which she then opened. There were five circulars left, all of them different, all from separate writers. She counted them twice, smiling.

Celia faced the side of the house as she ate, holding both hands to her mouth as if to hide the bread. It was dry and crusty and she swallowed it fast so that it stuck in her throat. She got in line again and waited for milk. The other children slurped and took their time while those who were not drinking hopped from foot to foot like they had to go to the bathroom. A cup was put in Celia's hands. It had not been rinsed, and there were tongue smears on the rim. Flora came up with the milk bottle and started to pour. When the cup was not quite halfway filled one of the matrons shouted, "Stop! That's too much!" The matrons were all old women now. They were always angry.

"Sorry," Flora said without meaning it.

"That has to last," the matron said. "How are we supposed to make it stretch for all these children if you give them as much as they want?"

Celia drank what was in the cup before she could be stopped. Flora saw and smiled with her eyes.

"Answer me," the matron said.

"I don't know," Flora said. "Maybe you should get some more."

"You know very well there isn't any more. Keep your eye on it next time."

"No."

The matron had begun to turn away. She froze. Celia's cup was empty and the matron grabbed it from her. She held it up and put her finger to the side, about a third of the way from the bottom.

"This is how much they get. You know that."

"I don't care what you say. It isn't enough."

The matron approached Flora with an arm raised, threatening to strike. Flora's reaction was not far removed from boredom.

"What do you think my mother would do if you hit me?"

The matron glared and took the milk away from Flora. She moved on to the next child without saying another word. Celia watched Flora and ran her tongue along her upper lip, making smacking noises.

"I'm sorry I couldn't get you more," Flora said.

"It was good."

Flora looked sad.

"I like it when you come to see me," Celia told her.

Flora stared across the yard. She did not seem to have heard.

"I wish you could stay here all the time."

Flora looked at her now. She smiled and took Celia's hand, swinging it a bit. As they watched each other a man's voice called out from the alley.

"Is that my big girl?"

Celia looked up and immediately pulled out of Flora's grip. "Grampa!" she shouted as she ran. He stood a bit beyond the yard and wore a smile that made his eyes wrinkle. He bent over to greet her and she leapt into his arms, almost knocking him down. He held her, though, and she nuzzled into his neck and he closed his eyes and told her how he loved her.

Flora stayed by the Home, watching them. They spoke, but it was too quiet for her to hear. Celia began to wriggle in his arms and he set her down, and she ran to Flora and grabbed her hand.

"Come on!" she shouted, dragging Flora toward her grandfather.

By the time they reached him his warmth had gone. He tipped his cap to Flora and said a curt, "Good afternoon."

"Hello, sir. I'm sorry I couldn't help you."

He shrugged.

"Grampa's gonna take me to live with him!"

"That's wonderful, sweetheart. When?"

"I wish you hadn'a told, Celie. I didn't want her to know."

"It's all right – it's wonderful, like I said. When are you taking her?"

He shook his head as if a bug had flown in his ear.

"No. No, no, no. I can't say. I don't trust you."

"I understand that. But I can't do anything to stop you, if you're taking her. Don't worry about what my mother says."

Celia looked back and forth from Flora to her grandfather.

"Take her any time. It's the only way you'll get her back."

Celia took his arm and began to pull.

"Come on, Grampa, let's go!"

"I'll keep watch for you," Flora said. "But honestly, I don't think anyone will notice."

The man picked up Celia and held her. She swayed her legs at the knees and smiled into his face.

"That ain't the way it's gonna happen. I never stole nothin' in my life. I ain't gonna start now."

"It's not stealing – she's your granddaughter. If anything, my mother stole her from you."

He shook his head again.

"No. It ain't right. There's ways, you know. There's ways."

"What ways?"

"That's what I've been told."

"By whom?"

He did not answer.

"Who, Grampa?"

He smiled at Celia and gave her a kiss on the forehead. His beard tickled her skin, which made her close her eyes and giggle.

"It's the courts, isn't it?" Flora said.

The man looked at her now. He wanted to talk, but bit his lip.

"I ain't s'posda say."

"They've tried it before, you know."

"Yeah. They tell me it's different this time."

"What's different, Grampa?"

He looked trapped. Flora patted Celia's knee.

"Honey, you can't tell anybody what we've been talking about," Flora said. "You've got to keep it a secret, all right?"

She nodded slowly.

"Don't say you'll go back to your grandpa. Don't say anything about courts. Just pretend, can you do that? Pretend everything's normal, like a game."

"That's right, Celie. You can't say nothin' about it."

"I won't," she whispered.

"Good girl."

He gave her another hug, then set her down.

"I better go now, but I'll be back soon, all right?"

She giggled again and nodded.

"Okay. Now you be a good girl and go play. I gotta talk to your friend."

When she had gone Flora walked the length of the alley with him.

"Do you know when it's happening?"

"Nope. It's comin', though. Before the end of the year."

"That's still months away."

"They wanna get as many people to talk as they can."

"They won't have to look hard."

When they reached the end of the block they stopped walking.

"Sorry about before," the man said after a while.

"It's all right. I don't blame you. If I were in your place I wouldn't have wanted to talk to me, either."

"And I'm sorry about your ma."

She looked at him.

"I am, too."

The food Mrs. Floyd set out disappeared faster each day, and there always seemed to be at least two children lingering at the back of her house. If she tried to get rid of them by giving them an apple, more would show up. Some would even sit and wait for her on the back porch. It had to stop.

After the sun went down she brought the bucket in the house and did not put it back out. She checked before she went to get it, making sure none of them were out there. The next day she behaved as she had before they came to the neighborhood. She gave her husband his breakfast and after he went to work she cleaned the house. She gathered all the rugs and dragged them out back, then went inside to get the beater.

When she returned, a pair of boys were in the alley. She knew them. About ten years old. Filthy, ornery and nasty. They were troublemakers. She went to the rugs as if she had not seen the boys.

"Where's the food?" one of them said.

Mrs. Floyd picked up one of the rugs and began to swat it.

"There is none."

"Yeah there is."

The first boy came forward, trying to look tough.

"No, there's not," Mrs. Floyd said without looking at him. She flipped the rug over and began to beat the other side.

The second boy stood beside his friend and kicked up some dirt with his toe.

"Why?"

"Because there isn't any more."

She laid the first rug on the porch railing near the door, then picked up the second.

"But you ate today, dintcha?" the first boy said.

Mrs. Floyd kept to her work.

"Sure she did," the second boy said. "See how fat she is?"

"Yeah, she's like a pig. She's even got the nose."

Mrs. Floyd beat the rug harder.

"Keeps all her food to herself now."

"Don't need it, though."

"Yeah. Big old sow."

"Or a dog."

They began to laugh. Mrs. Floyd glared and held up the rug beater.

"If you boys don't run on home I'll use this on you!"

"Go ahead and do it, see who cares."

"You'd never catch us, anyhow."

"'Cause you're so fat, you can't run fast."

Mrs. Floyd dropped the rug and marched toward them. They kept laughing as she swung the beater and they darted out of the way. They circled her, taunting and grunting, until finally she swung the beater like a baseball bat and cracked the second boy on the face, hitting him square on the nose. He fell to the ground and groaned as he made contact with it. No bones were broken, but the blood started to flow and he whimpered more out of surprise than pain.

"She hit me!"

His friend came to look at him and Mrs. Floyd picked him up by the waist and cracked him a few times. He kicked his legs and squirmed but she had a tight hold on him. When she finished she let him go and he fell in a pile next to his friend.

Mrs. Floyd went back to work. The boys lay on the ground for a few minutes, talking so she could not hear. When they stood they walked slowly until they were right behind her house, on the opposite side of the alley. They sat in the grass, watching her. The second boy wiped the blood off his face with his sleeve. They said nothing more.

When she had finished Mrs. Floyd gathered up all the rugs. She glared at the boys before she went back inside. Still watching her, the brats. She went from room to room putting the rugs back in their places. Once most of them were laid down she peeked out one of the windows. Finally the boys had gone. She smiled and gave a single nod. There were three more rugs to put upstairs, and she hoisted them under her arm and began to take them up.

She heard the crash as she reached the second floor, the unmistakable sound of breaking glass. She dropped her bundles and ran back downstairs to find shards of crystal like pebbled strewn across the floor in the front parlor, along with a few large rocks. Growling, Mrs. Floyd went out the front door and looked around. She saw no one, but far up the street she heard the receding echo of boisterous laughter.

It was December and still the notices were showing up. In the beginning Mrs. Baker would pray and eventually begin to forget about them, and then a new one would arrive. There was no forgetting now. The notices confused her. They came from everywhere, but each told the same lies, which she would then have to explain to the people she met. If they would speak to her.

She drove the car carefully up the icy street toward her house. She nodded to the people she saw, but they never looked at her anymore. They had been poisoned against her. As she drew closer to the house she saw a man with a sheaf of papers under his arm. He went up the walk toward her front door. She knew it was him.

Mrs. Baker deployed the brake and skidded past the house. No matter. She parked and jumped out of the still-running car and ran like a chicken on the ice to the man, whose back was turned.

"Sir! What do you think you're doing?"

Startled, he stopped walking and looked back at her.

"Pardon me?"

"Who are you?" she said, moving slower so she would not fall. "What is the meaning of this?"

"Are you Mrs. J. A. W. Baker?" he asked.

"Of course I am, and I demand you stop this harassment! I'm a law-abiding citizen and I can have you arrested!"

"You're the proprietress of the Joseph Walter Home? That Mrs. Baker?"

She came to a stop before him, her breath fogging out like smoke.

"You know very well who I am. How dare you! I'm a good woman, and I run a legitimate charitable organization. It's the others you should go after – it's all a money game to them."

"I don't know what you mean, ma'am."

"The devil you do! Six months I've been harassed by you! Now that you're caught in the act you pretend to be innocent, but you'll not fool me. I can see right through you."

"Ma'am, I–"

"Let me see those papers!"

He handed her the file and she looked at the top sheet. Immediately she tried to give them back, but he stepped away. She was being charged with neglect.

"You'll be expected in court December tenth," the man said, adding with a tip of his hat, "Good afternoon."

Mrs. Baker tallied the figures three times and began to do it a fourth when the maid appeared at her office door and knocked on the frame with a timid hand.

"Ma'am?"

Slamming her pen on the desk, Mrs. Baker looked up and bared her teeth.

"What."

"There's some people for you."

"Send them away."

"They're right here in the hall, ma'am."

Mrs. Baker stood, mute, and trudged to the door. She took the handle and moved back to slam it when the Huegels stepped into view. She froze.

"What are you doing here?"

"What are *you* doing here?" Marie said. "We've just been to the courthouse and your attorney said you're not coming."

"He's right. I'm not."

"But why?"

The maid continued to stand nearby. Mrs. Baker waved her arm and the maid nodded and left.

"Why not?" Mrs. Baker said as she went back to her desk. "They've already decided I'm guilty. What's the good of sitting with them while they slander me? I've done that enough in my life. I've taken enough abuse. No more."

Marie and Huegel had entered the office. Huegel offered a chair to Marie, but she continued to stand.

"You've got to fight them," she said.

Mrs. Baker sat in her chair and leaned forward on the desk.

"No. I have witnesses who will testify on behalf of my work, but I'm not going to do it myself. Those lawyers are wicked. They take what you tell them and twist it into something ugly and false, and soon you find you're defending against their impression of you, not what you actually are. I've wasted too much time with those people. I'll not waste any more."

Marie stood next to her husband and gripped the chair he held for her.

"I'm so sorry, Julia."

"I'm used to being attacked."

"I am sorry, though."

Mrs. Baker's posture slackened and her voice became soft.

"Please, sit down. Both of you."

Marie came to the front of the chair and sat. When she had settled herself, Huegel sat, too.

"How long were you there?"

"All morning. Until they broke for lunch."

"What did they say?"

"You know what they say."

"It was awful," Huegel said. "Railroaded from the first."

Mrs. Baker nodded at him.

"Who testified?"

"Teachers," Marie said. "A couple of them. A doctor, too."

"Shameful," Huegel said.

"We looked for you, but we didn't see you anywhere, so as soon as they broke we approached your lawyer. He said you were here, and that you didn't plan to attend."

"He was right," Mrs. Baker said.

"But you are going to come sometime, aren't you? You can't just sit in your office."

"I'm not sitting. I'm working. I have a magazine to publish."

"Can't that wait?"

"No."

A silence fell over the room. Huegel cleared his throat.

"What if we went for you? We'll go to the hearings, and then at the end of the day we'll come back and tell you what happened. We could talk to your attorney if you want to say anything to him. Maybe we could get you a different one if he doesn't work out. I'd be willin' to do that. I have the money. I'd do it for you. I'd pay anything."

Mrs. Baker watched him.

"Marie thinks the world of you. I guess you know that already, but she does. Talks about you all the time, talks about your work, and your home. Not all sisters are like that. But I agree with her. Personally, I never did like it when they go after people that won't defend themselves. Let us do it. We'll be there for you."

Mrs. Baker took the sheet of figures from her desk and crumpled it into a ball, which she threw in the wastebasket.

Dr. E. L. Mathias filed the charges, which asked that two boys, Willie Taylor and Willie Skinner, be made wards of the court. Mathias said the boys were delinquent because of neglect and the mismanagement of the Home. He soon called for the custody of ten additional children and filed more charges related to their neglect.

A good part of the second day's testimony was given over to written statements. There was one from the former mayor of Joplin, C. W. Lyon, who wrote, "Many complaints have been made that the inmates were poorly fed," and that the city was "compelled to furnish transportation to mothers and children who did not find the home as Mrs. Baker represented it." Rev. E. P. Savage, superintendent of the Children's Home Society of St. Paul, wrote about Mrs. Baker's jail sentence in Wisconsin. Even Chief Turner from Duluth wrote in.

By the end of the day Savage had filed ten more charges against Mrs. Baker.

"Please, ma'am. The judge said these children can't be brought into the courtroom. Take them home."

The matron raised her nose at the bailiff and motioned to the sea of little faces swarming around her.

"These children are at the very center of the case," she said. "You must let them in."

The bailiff was young, but his eyes were marked with deep lines like grooves scraped into a piece of clay. His tone was firm, but civil.

"Ma'am. You cannot enter. There is no discussing it."

The matron looked around her. People had to slow down and zigzag through the crowd if they wanted to pass through the hallway. Most of them just took the stairs to avoid it altogether.

"If we can't go inside we'll wait in the hall until we *are* admitted."

The bailiff nodded. "Okay, thank you," he said quickly as he closed the door.

The matron stood a moment, blinking, then looked around for a bench. Flora and Joseph had flanked her at the door and Celia was wedged under Flora's arm. The matron said she wanted them there because they were dressed better than the others. When she found a place to sit she left the children where they were without saying another word. Joseph put his head against the door and covered his other ear.

"Can you hear anything?" Flora said.

Joseph pushed harder against the door, closing his eyes.

"Anything?" Flora said again.

Joseph opened his eyes and stood up straight.

"The wood's too thick."

They backed away from the door, but it was hard to move with so many children around. They pressed against each other and shuffled about looking for some place to go, but all they could do was stand and wait. Sometimes the doors would open and a new witness would enter the throng, often bundled in winter clothes, and then clumsily maneuver their way out of the building. Each time the door opened the children would squeeze closer together so that they felt their shoulders touch. After the third time Joseph felt a frantic pair of hands at his side and he looked down to see Celia pinned by several others against a wall. Her face was red and wet and she reached for him saying, "Help me, I can't breathe!"

Joseph leaned over and picked her up and she hugged him around the neck, shivering like a frightened animal. Flora was there, too, and she stroked Celia's back as the girl whimpered.

"Don't let her hair touch yours," Flora whispered. "You'll get lice."

Joseph thought a moment, then held her even closer.

"It's all right," he said. "You'll be okay."

The door closed and the crowd relaxed again. Flora looked to see who had come out. It was Ada Brady.

"Wait here, I'll be back," Flora told her brother.

"Where would we go?" he asked, annoyed.

Ada saw Flora at about the same time, and they waved to each other and pointed to the stairs at the end of the hall, which they worked their way toward with their arms lifted like someone trudging waist-deep through a pool of water. They descended the stairs before they embraced. They held each other a long time.

"How are you? How is school?"

"It's fine. I miss you."

"Oh…"

Ada took Flora's face in her hands and smiled.

"You're getting so pretty."

Flora hugged her again, and Ada allowed herself to be held.

"How did it go?" Flora asked.

"Very well."

"What did you tell them?"

"Everything I know."

"Did you hear anyone else?"

"A few people, yes."

At last Flora stepped away.

"How do you think it'll turn out?"

"Honey, I really can't say. They aren't exactly singing your mother's praises in there, but it's not really anything that hasn't been said before."

Flora nodded.

"How are you?" Ada said and rubbed Flora's shoulder. "Are you really all right?"

"Yes."

"I know it's difficult, but things will calm down again. Maybe they'll be better when all of this is over."

"Where do you live now?"

"I'm still here. Still in Kansas City, although I might be moving soon. I haven't decided yet, but I might go to Colorado for a while to stay with my sister's family."

Although her head was raised, Flora looked down. Her eyes were halfway closed. When she spoke her voice was high-pitched and quiet as if she were on the verge of tears.

"Can I go with you?"

Ada let go of the girl's shoulder.

"You know I would like nothing more. But it's not possible. Your mother would never consent to that."

"We won't tell her."

Ada sighed.

"I can't."

She bent her knees so she could look into Flora's eyes.

"You'll be able to leave her someday, but right now you're still a young girl."

"I'm fifteen."

"Yes. You're a young girl." She paused. "I'm so sorry."

"It's all right."

A voice called to them from the hall.

"How dare you!"

Ada jumped, but Flora gave no reaction.

"Mrs. LeWald," Ada said.

Marie and Huegel came up to them, with Marie all but spitting in Ada's face as she spoke.

"After all my sister did for you, this is how you repay her? By telling lies?"

"I told no lies."

Marie snorted, and Huegel shook his head while he made a sour face.

"What would you call them?"

"Everything I said was the truth. Were you in the courtroom, Mrs. LeWald? I didn't see you there."

Marie drew herself up and squinted as if she were staring at the filament of a naked light bulb.

"My name is Huegel. Mrs. Huegel, to you. This is my husband."

"I had no idea. Congratulations."

"Flora, please leave us to deal with this woman."

Flora waited to move.

"It's all right, darling, we won't let her bother you anymore," Marie said.

"She wasn't bothering me," Flora said.

"Such a brave girl. Joseph, would you kindly bring our niece back upstairs while I deal with this traitor?"

Without a word Huegel lifted his elbow for Flora to take. She looked at Ada, frozen to the spot. Soon Huegel took her arm himself and guided her to the stairs. Flora watched Ada the whole time.

"Come on," Huegel said.

Ada nodded and Flora joined him. Ada watched them as they climbed the stairs. Flora's head was still turned toward her. They looked into each other's eyes until Flora and Huegel reached the next floor. When they were gone Ada looked to Marie.

"I hope you're proud of yourself," Marie said. "Those people upstairs might have believed your story, but we know the truth, don't we?"

Ada brushed a strand of hair from her forehead.

"Does your husband know about Mr. LeWald?"

"We have no secrets."

"Then you've told him about Rev. Litten?"

"I don't know what you're talking about."

"It's a shame you didn't hear my testimony, then."

Marie stiffened.

"Get out of my sight."

"No."

Ada stood in place and crossed her arms. After ten seconds had passed Marie huffed and started up the stairs.

Mrs. Baker greeted the men from *The Star* with a warm smile and brought them into the parlor. There were two of them. Both carried pads of paper, which they used for furious scribbling, one taking notes and the other making sketches of Mrs. Baker as she spoke in a musical voice.

"Where shall I begin, gentlemen?"

The reporter smiled. "I'm sure you know what you wanna say, Mrs. Baker."

"I do, but I don't know what will be of use to you."

"You say what you want. I'll use what I need."

"That's what I fear."

The comment hung in the air a second before Mrs. Baker allowed herself a chuckle. The men joined her and soon they all relaxed. Mrs. Baker put her elbows on the armrests of her chair and touched her fingers in a shape like the peak of a roof. She closed her eyes and turned her head down, deep in thought. When she opened them again she lowered her arms and began.

"I started my charity work in 1899, in Minneapolis, Minnesota. I was married to Joseph Baker then – that same year, in fact. He was a follower of Dowie and wanted to found a religion along those same lines. That also is why we were married without a legal ceremony. If people asked us about it we told them we considered ourselves man and wife in the eyes of God.

"Ten months after my marriage my first child was born, and when the baby was only a few months old my husband deserted me. Alone in the world with my baby, I saw the sufferings of widowed mothers and I conceived the plan of starting a home for them, which I did. Shortly afterward my husband returned and took over the management of the home, which was then at Duluth, Wisconsin. He conceived the plan of sending out solicitors to get funds to keep the house alive. At his command, after he had beaten me repeatedly, I went out with my baby to collect money for him.

"While collecting at Hudson, Wisconsin, charged with obtaining money under false pretenses, I was tried and sentenced to six months in jail. I appealed the case and while awaiting bond was placed in jail. In the meantime my husband had again disappeared and my father took the mothers and children in the home to Alma, Wisconsin, where he lived. The superior court reversed and remanded my case for a new trial and I was released on bond. Later the case was dismissed.

"My husband appeared at Alma after I was released from jail and once more forced me to collect money. By this time I had two babies, both too young to be left at home, and I took them with me. Everywhere I went I was hounded by the Children's Home Finding Society, which sent pamphlets broadcast, telling of my arrest in Hudson.

"After travelling through several states I reached Joplin, Missouri, with only a few cents. There I heard my husband had once again disappeared, this time with another woman. I talked with several persons in Joplin and told them of my plan for starting a home so the mothers might live with their children in order that they would not be separated. I obtained the aid of a few and started my home in a small cottage. After I had been there a short time I brought the children from Alma, Wisconsin, to the home.

"Before I left Joplin and came to Kansas City in 1903 I had built up a large home with about forty children. By that time I felt I was able to broaden my work and so I came to Kansas City. I started my first home here at 2610 Cleveland Avenue. We were there several years before the house, which I bought, was sold under mortgage. We then moved to the old Hicks home at 3500 East Ninth Street, where more than one hundred children are living.

"My plan is to keep families of children together, and if their father or mother is living restore them when the parent is able to care for them. In the home now are four families of six children and many smaller families. The home is absolutely non-sectarian, the children going to any Sunday school they desire. The Protestants are sent to the public schools and the Catholics attend the parish schools."

Mrs. Baker looked to both men. The fingers of one hand were clenched as she raised it.

"Gentlemen, my life is wrapped up in this work. No court in the world is great enough to break down the principle I follow. Even when I am dead I feel sure the home will continue to grow and prosper, caring for any children who might come to it asking for aid.

"The home is now maintained by the Mother's Appeal, a magazine owned and operated by the Baker Corporation of which I am president. There are no solicitors for the home anymore, but we have several traveling agents getting subscriptions for the magazine."

Mrs. Baker fell back in her chair, silent. She looked tired, and wiped her face with a handkerchief. When she saw the men from *The Star* were waiting for her next comment she smiled.

"You do believe me, don't you, gentlemen?"

When the story appeared in the next day's edition, the main headline read, "FRAUD OR ANGEL, WHICH?"

Union Station's waiting room was crowded, but the information bureau was empty. Mr. White sat at the desk and rubbed his hands together. Then he opened the bottom drawer and took out his bottle for a nip. He savored the burn and rubbed his stomach. As he screwed the cap back on the door opened and he quickly hid the bottle and shut the drawer again.

"How can I help–?"

When he looked up he saw no one.

"We need to know something," said a little voice.

White stood and saw two boys not older than six standing before his desk. They looked like brothers, about one year apart.

"What can I do for you gentlemen?" White said with a grin.

The older boy shook White's hand in a businesslike fashion.

"I'm Ray Bergstrom, and this is my baby brother Lloyd. How can we get to the Joseph Walter Home?"

White glanced at the copy of *The Star* on his desk.

"Where are you from?"

"Pleasanton, Kansas."

"Did anybody bring you here?"

"No, we came all by ourselves. Our ma fixed it so we could go to the Joseph Walter Home. Our pa died and she couldn't feed us all. So, where is it? We wanna get there by dark."

White considered his options.

Joseph stood against the school building out of the wind. He rested the back of his hand on the wall, the bricks of which seemed somehow harder in the cold. He watched the other boys run, and the girls who stood in little groups talking and hugging themselves. He wished vacation had started, but he was glad he was not home.

About ten yards away a cluster of three boys and two girls stood openly watching him. He knew them from that day years ago when he was trying to sell magazines. As they stared one would speak and the rest would laugh, and they never stopped looking so he knew they were talking about him. He stared past them but refused to look away. After a few more comments back and forth the group began walking toward him. He would not move. Their wealth was visible to everyone. Their winter clothes were new, and without patches. The girls carried muffs.

"Baker!" one of the boys shouted. He was Darren Welch, their leader. He was the same age as Joseph, but a head taller, and he had broad shoulders. His cheeks were red and his black hair made him stick out against the white background. His nose was crooked.

Joseph looked into his eyes without saying anything.

"When's your ma goin' to jail?" Welch said, prompting a chorus of derisive laughter from the others.

"She ain't goin' to jail, and it's too bad," Joseph said.

"Sure she is, they got her place in the courts every day."

"It's juvenile court, not criminal. You can't send a grown-up to jail out of juvenile court."

One of the other boys, Leroy Nelson, snorted.

"You're just sayin' that. They'll cart her off for sure. My pa says they shoulda done it a long time ago."

"Your pa's a smart guy," Joseph said.

"And they're gonna, too."

"'Fraid they can't."

"Bullshit," Nelson said, accenting the second syllable.

"What's wrong with you, Baker?" Welch said. "You think you're better than everybody? Well, you ain't. Your ma's a crook."

"I know she is."

"Think you're so goddamn smart, too, you just say whatever I do. Goddamn pansy."

"Where you think he'll go when they take that bitch away?" Nelson said.

"With his pa, prob'ly," Welch said.

Nelson smirked. "Naw, not him. He ain't got one, my pa read it the other day."

"Ran off. His ma was too ugly for him."

"She sure was," Joseph said. "He *is* dead, though."

The children crowded around him so he could not move from the wall, but he made no attempt to get past them.

"You think you're funny or somethin'?" Welch said. "You're just actin' like an asshole, that's all you're doing."

"Goddamn crybaby," Nelson said.

"I'm not crying."

"Goddamn smartass."

"I hope they throw that bitch in jail for twenty years."

Joseph gave a weary sigh.

"I wish they would, but it's juvenile court. Even if they find against her she can't go to jail because it's not criminal court."

"They oughta have it the other way."

"You're right, but that ain't how it is," Joseph said.

When he finished speaking Joseph crossed his arms and glared at the others.

"I know how it is," Welch said. "I've been readin' it. Your ma's nothin' but a goddamn cheat and a crook and a liar."

"I know that," Joseph said.

"She's a whore, too, that's what I read," Nelson said. "Men come to their house all hours of the night, that's what the paper says, and you know what that means."

"Can't be every night, 'cause she travels," Welch said. "But I bet she's got other guys she sees outta town."

The girls blushed and wore mean smiles. One of them hid her mouth. Nelson saw it and he looked back to Joseph.

"If they're still comin' to his house when she's gone, maybe they're seein' his sister."

Joseph's eyes burned.

"'Course," Welch said. "You know all about his sister."

"Sure, everybody does."

"I know plenty guys that've been with her."

Joseph pushed himself off the wall and took a step away from the group, but Welch shoved him back.

"Don't get mad about it, everyone knows," Welch said. "The girls here, their mothers say they can't talk to your sister 'cause she'll give 'em a bad name."

"Better'n what she gives the men she sees," Nelson said.

The others laughed, and Joseph pushed himself off the wall again, only to be shoved back. The others closed in further so he could not do it again. Despite this, he did not feel threatened.

"You better talk to her," Welch said. "Next time the cops come around they'll be takin' your sister, not your ma."

"Shut up about my sister."

"Hey, it's all true. Ain't it."

"Said so right in the paper."

"The paper never said that."

Joseph realized his voice was higher than usual, and it squeaked on the first word.

"Did so, I read it myself."

"Me, too," one of the girls said.

"We all read it," Welch said. "Everyone knows."

When Joseph spoke again his words came out in a whisper.

"It's not true."

"Is so. They can't put nothin' in the paper that ain't true."

"It never said anything about my sister."

"Sure it did," Welch said. "We all read it, didn't we?"

The rest of them all but shouted their agreement.

"I'm not gonna talk about something nobody even wrote," Joseph said, his voice beginning to quaver.

Welch grinned.

"You sound like you're gonna cry. Don't he?"

"Sure does, the pansy."

"Go on, cry for us."

Joseph took a breath. His eyes no longer itched, and his pulse slowed. The others started leering at him, but he felt nothing. He smiled.

"Smartass," Welch said. He barely finished the word before he gave a kick aimed at Joseph's shins that swept his legs from under him. Joseph watched from the ground as the others laughed with each other and walked away. He was suddenly cold again. Bits of snow like frozen gravel were caught in his collar and he grimaced as he stood and ran his finger over his neck. He felt something bat against his side and looked to see Pauline, a girl from his class who had not been with group, wiping snow off his coat. She was little, with thick red hair stuffed under a blue cap.

"Did they hurt you?" she asked.

Joseph stared at her for a second and then shook his coat to get the rest of the snow out.

"Naw."

Pauline stopped brushing and rested her hand on his arm. She looked into his face. "I'm glad," she said, then stood on her toes and gave him a quick kiss on the cheek. She smiled and ran away.

Three days before Christmas, Mathias amended his charges against the Home to include ten more violations by the management. The next day Mrs. Baker's attorneys made their only statement, which was that if the decision was made against the Home an appeal would be filed. The appeal would question the constitutionality of the juvenile court, the lawyers said, because the court deprives persons of their freedom without trial by jury.

It was Christmas Eve. The hearing would start in thirty minutes and already the courtroom was packed. LeWald found an open seat in the back row next to the aisle, and he got into it without taking off his coat. At his right sat a boy of about seventeen, who kept looking at the entrance. He wore work clothes, which hung loose on his thin frame, and each time he moved the seats would creak.

"It'll be a while yet," LeWald told him. "This stuff never runs on time, especially on a day like today."

"You ever been to one of these before?" the boy asked.

"I know how it works."

The boy turned to the front of the room.

"Have you been here at all?"

"I just got into town," LeWald said. "You?"

"When I could. If it wasn't the holiday I wouldn't be here. I have night classes. Lots of the same people come every day, though. They don't have anything to do with it, they just want to watch."

"That's normal. Some people, that's all they do, come to the courthouse and watch the show. Usually there's not so many, though."

"I've been talking to some of 'em. They really want her to go down."

LeWald looked at him, unable to stifle his grin.

"Oh, yeah?"

The boy nodded.

"Lotta people testify against her?"

"Oh, sure."

"What'd they say?"

"They all say about the same thing. That the kids don't have food, they don't have clothes, she's got all the money. Mrs. Baker, you know."

"Yeah, I know."

"She's got it all, and doesn't give the kids anything. She's just the same as she ever was."

LeWald was surprised.

"You know her?"

The boy nodded a single time.

"I wouldn't be here if I didn't."

"How do you know her?"

"I stayed in her house once with my brother and sisters."

"When?"

"Oh, a long time ago. Everything they say about her is true, too, believe me. I could tell you a few stories. It's nothing you haven't read, though, if you've been following it in the papers. The kids have nothing, she has all the money. I know it's true. I saw where she lived. I snuck out one day and saw her house. I was just a little kid, but even I could see where the money went. She caught me, too."

"What happened?"

The boy turned to LeWald. His face was grim.

"Nothing happened. She didn't know who I was. Those kids all look the same to her, and they each have a price tag around their necks."

Mrs. Baker's attorneys entered from the side door and LeWald and the boy watched as they went to their table.

"That's too bad," the boy said.

"What is?"

"I was hoping she'd be with them. I've been coming every day this week and she hasn't shown up."

"You wanna see her?"

"Just once."

"What would you do if you did?"

The boy shrugged.

"I hadn't really thought about it."

Mathias entered the courtroom and took his place near the right front.

"Who's that?" the boy asked.

"I don't know."

"Not him, I know him. I mean over there."

He pointed toward the seats behind the defense table.

"That woman up there. She keeps looking back at us."

"You sure?"

"Mm-hmm. Wait a second, she'll do it again. There, see? You know her?"

LeWald swallowed.

"No."

Huegel held Marie's arm.

"Dear, what's so interesting back there?"

"Nothing," she said and turned back in her seat.

"You don't worry about those people. They're just here for a show. Buzzards, that's all they are. Ignore 'em. That's what I do."

"I'll try."

Judge Porterfield entered the courtroom from his chambers and everyone rose.

"You may be seated," he said as he sat down himself.

For a moment nothing was audible but the creaking of the benches and chairs, and then a hush fell over the assembled crowd.

"I have something for you," Flora said as Celia ran to her. Celia jumped into her arms and hugged her tight.

"What is it?"

Flora felt Celia's warm breath on her neck and looked about for a place they could go that was not overrun with children. She put Celia down and took her hand.

"Come on."

Together they went to the back of the house, to the washroom, and Flora opened the door. Celia went inside and Flora entered, too, and locked the door. The room was lit by the fading glow of the early-setting sun.

"Close your eyes and hold out your hands," Flora said.

Celia listened, and soon felt the weight of what seemed like rubber balls. Waxy in texture, they gave a bit when she applied pressure to them.

"You can look now."

Celia opened her eyes and squealed with delight.

"Oranges!"

"Merry Christmas."

Celia held one out to Flora.

"No, they're both for you," Flora told her.

Celia dug her finger into the rind of one and tore off a piece. Juice dripped out like water from a leaky faucet and she put the orange to her mouth and squeezed, slurping and giggling. Then she stuck two fingers in and ripped the orange in half and began to pull out sections and gobble them down.

"Do you like it?"

Her mouth full, Celia only nodded.

"Thank you," she said after she swallowed.

"You're welcome. When was the last time you had an orange?"

Already eating again, Celia shrugged. Soon it was gone, with nothing remaining but the halved peel, which looked like a pair of small bowls. Celia clutched the other orange to her chest like a squirrel with a nut.

"Are you going to eat that one, too?"

"In a minute."

"You can't wait too long. Someone else might want to come in here."

"They can wait."

Someone knocked on the door.

"You see?" Flora said. "We'll be out in a minute," she called.

"Who's in there, please?"

It was a man's voice. Neither girl recognized it. Celia ran behind Flora and gripped her dress. When Flora opened the door she saw a clean-shaven man with fair hair.

"Yes?"

"My name is Dr. Mathias. I'm chief probation officer of Kansas City."

"Hello."

"I'm here to collect Celia Young."

Flora pivoted to reveal the smaller girl.

"This is her," she said and gave Celia's back an encouraging rub.

Mathias held out his hand.

"Come with me, young lady."

Celia cowered, and Flora stroked her shoulder.

"It's okay. He's going to take you back to your grandfather. Aren't you?"

Mathias smiled and nodded.

"That's right, miss."

"You see? Isn't that good news?"

Flora bended over and gave Celia a big hug. She picked her up and turned to Mathias.

"They found against her, then?"

"Yes they did, miss."

"What'll happen now?"

"We're taking twelve children tonight, and we'll figure out what to do with the rest next month."

"I'm glad."

He nodded.

"I am, too, miss."

Then he tapped Celia on the back.

"We have to go now, young lady."

Flora set her down and gave her a kiss

"Be a good girl."

Celia nodded.

"I love you," she said.

"I love you, too."

Mathias held out his hand and Celia took it with her free hand, the other still clutching the remaining orange. Flora watched as he led her down the hall and out of the house. When they were gone she closed the door to the washroom so she could be alone.

"What are your plans now?"

Mrs. Baker put down her teacup. Shelley sat facing her in the next chair with both hands folded in his lap. A fire crackled in the fireplace and the room was filled with a white light from the snow outside.

"I haven't made any," Mrs. Baker said. "It's funny. I've been up against adversity before, but this time – I don't know. If they hadn't taken all the children I would still have something to work for."

"You've got your own children."

She moved her eyebrows up, then down.

"They don't need me. Not like the others did. I do have another case pending."

"What about?"

"Judge Hazell's widow says I owe her some money. Something about payment for furniture. It's ridiculous. She doesn't know what she's talking about."

Shelley took his cup from the table and held it on his knee.

"You know, I've been through hardships, too, but things seem to work out, usually."

"Usually."

Shelley took a sip.

"I read the papers," he said. "Not everybody was kicking you. It seemed like there was a lot of good and bad."

"Truth and lies."

"All right. But it wasn't all lies. That's what I'm trying to tell you. People spoke in your favor every day. I read it myself, and I know I'm not the only one who did."

Mrs. Baker stared at the fire.

"And you do too still have something to work for. What about that magazine of yours? They didn't take that away from you, did they? They didn't take away your right to publish it."

"No…"

"No, they didn't. In the times I was down I wish I'd had something like that to fall back on. It would've kept my head above water."

Thinking more, Mrs. Baker looked at her teacup, then back to the fire.

"Lots of people still read it, too, I'll bet. Don't they?"

"They do."

"Nearly ten thousand, isn't it?"

She raised her head to look him in the face.

"We have sixteen thousand paid-up subscribers."

"In addition to the ones who buy it on the street."

"That's right."

"How many issues a year?"

"We had eight in 1915."

Shelley smiled.

"Do you know what that is?"

Mrs. Baker shook her head.

"That's power."

Mrs. Baker nodded slowly, and a smile grew on her face, too.

Baker wiped the lunch counter. It was after two and most of the customers had gone. It was hot and the front and back doors were open to create a cross-breeze through the room. Baker sighed and wiped his graying hair with his palm. At the front door he heard the clicking of a woman's shoes on the floorboards, and he turned toward the direction of the noise.

It was her. He smiled.

"'lo, Julia."

She walked up to the counter but remained standing.

"That's rather forward, considering," she said.

His smile turned to a smirk.

"Sure. How are you today, Mrs. Shelley?"

"I'm well, despite this heat."

"Selina and me, we wanted to thank you for helping us out."

"I would think that should have been the first thing you said."

"It was. Practically."

She looked around the café.

"You want to sit down?"

"Not over here."

"At one of the tables, then."

She went to a table against the far wall and sat facing the entrance. Baker followed, but as she was sitting she waved her hand so he would scoot over and give her an unobstructed view of the door.

"Kansas City's nice," Baker said after a moment. "It's big, too, after South Dakota." He cleared his throat. "The girls like it a lot."

She looked at him and he stopped talking for a few seconds.

"How's Mr. Shelley?"

"He's well."

"Kind of an old guy, isn't he?"

"He's healthy. He's quite youthful. He seems younger than you."

"I work hard."

"So does he."

"It just wears on me, I guess."

She raised her eyebrows.

"Some things don't change," she said.

Baker looked to the front door but no one had entered. He put his hand on the table and looked at it as he drummed his fingers.

"How are the kids?"

"They're grown up now."

"But how are they?"

Mrs. Baker spoke as if doing so was a chore.

"Flora's a dream, of course. She helps out whenever she can with whatever she can. I've never had a second of trouble with her."

"My girl."

"No she isn't. You gave her up."

"What about Joseph?"

She gave an exasperated sigh.

"He is an unholy terror."

"He's seventeen."

"Yes, he's seventeen, and he's becoming impossible. I've never been able to control that boy."

"Let him go, then."

"That's very easy to say. How would that reflect on me and my work? 'My mother says she loves children, but she booted me into the street.' He would adore being able to say that to everyone he met."

"Maybe I could talk to him."

"That's not our arrangement. What could you tell him, anyway? You're the last person in the world I would want talking to him."

"I know."

"If he were to come in here now he wouldn't even know who you are. You would be a stranger to him. You *are* a stranger to him. I want to keep it that way."

"I wasn't gonna see him, so forget about it. Is that why you came here today? To tell me to keep away from him?"

"I'm here because you asked me to come."

"You've never in your life done anything because someone asked you to."

"It's why I'm here today. Now tell me what you wanted."

"To say thank you."

"You could have done that in a letter."

"That's not the same."

"No, it's better that way. I wouldn't have had to drive all over town to find this place."

"You knew exactly where it was. You're the one who told me about it."

She said nothing.

"I guess I wanted to see you," Baker said.

"Why?"

He shrugged.

"See how you look. Hear your voice. I don't know, it's been a long time."

"Here I am. What do you think?"

"You're beautiful."

"And you're an old man."

"I know." He grinned. "Hear anything lately from Herman Thorp?"

"No." Her eyes suddenly grew wide. "Why? Have you?"

"No," Baker said, laughing.

Mrs. Baker allowed herself to smile.

"I haven't thought about him in ages. He's dead for all I know, in which case it doesn't matter." She shook her head. "What makes you think of him now?"

"I don't know. I hadn't for a long time, same as you. It was like I'd never met him. Then he just came to my head, I guess, when I was getting this place ready, and before long I couldn't get him out. You know, if it hadn't been for him you never would've met me."

"Curse him."

Baker cackled and she smiled.

"You never would've started in business, either. You might not have come to Kansas City."

"Do you want to write him a thank-you letter, too?"

"I'm just saying. It's funny how things work out."

She rolled her eyes.

"Don't get sentimental. Even if you and I hadn't been introduced I don't know that I would have stuck by him. I hate mining camps and I hate restaurants. Working in them, that is."

"I was just a horse to ride away on, then."

"That's right. If it wasn't you it would have been somebody else. But as I said, it doesn't matter. It's done, so let it be."

"I suppose so."

Baker checked the front door again. The engine of a passing car backfired like a gunshot.

"You want to see Selina?"

"No."

Baker watched her. There was a mystified look on her face.

"I guess that would be uncomfortable for you," he said.

"A bit."

He nodded.

"I had better go," she said.

She stood and left the table.

"Already?" Baker said. He rose and followed her to the door.

"I have work to do."

"Sure. I understand. Thanks for stopping by."

She passed through the door and onto the sidewalk.

"Come back any time," he called after her.

She looked back at him for a while, as if she had remembered something. Baker waited for her to speak. Instead she stared into his face a few seconds more, and then moved on.

Dec. 1935

Dearest Celia,

Of course I remember you! How could I not? You say you think of me as your older sister, and though I agree, I sometimes think of you as my first child. I do have children of my own now. Two of them, and a wonderful husband, but when I take care of my children I often think of you, and I always wondered what had become of you.

Life has been kind to me. I met my husband, Earl, after high school, and we were married 10 years ago. Where has the time gone! We have two lovely children, Ruth and Ada, and are also taking care of Joseph's daughter Linda, who we love as one of our own.

I know you had quite a crush on him when you were a girl, so I hesitated to write this, but felt that I must. I do love him – he is my brother, after all – but he is such trouble. It's better when he isn't around. He started marrying girls when he was 16. I don't know how many it's been now, and I'm not sure he does, either. I don't even know if he loved any of them. He just marries them. Then after a brief while, they either get divorced or the marriage is annulled. Perhaps if our father hadn't left things would be different. Who's to say? There are things we will never know.

I do miss him. I believe he's in Florida. It's strange – a day before your letter arrived I was thinking of that time on the train, the three of us, and how cold we were. I know Joseph was just pretending when he said he didn't like you. I'm sure you know it, too. That's how boys are.

I prefer to remember him as a boy. We were so close – we had to be – and now I feel like I don't know him. I remember once when we were young, he was upset and I told him not to worry. I told him that when we grew up we would be happy. You never can know how things will turn out – especially at that age – but I feel like I failed him.

You asked about Mother. It's more than a year now that she's been gone. I don't know if you had heard, but she was remarried to a man named George Shelley. Earl and I lived with them all that time after we were together. Mr. Shelley was an old man, and he died already some time ago after he fell on the stairs in front of his office. It was winter and he hit his head.

Mother worked until the end. Although she did try a few times, she never opened another house, for which I am thankful. Instead, she lived for her magazine. I'm not sure how long she was sick. It wasn't like her to complain about that sort of thing, and she never saw doctors, either. All I know is that one day the pain in her stomach became so great that we had to call for one, so it must have been very bad. He told us it was cancer, and there was nothing he could do. I had noticed she was losing weight, but she always said she felt fine. Her last months were agonizing. She refused all medicine. All she did was pray.

After she was gone I got rid of the old magazines, threw them all down the incinerator. Joseph never came.

These things are sad. I don't like to think of them. It's why I thank God for my husband and for my girls, all three of them. And now, with your letter, it's four! It makes me so happy.

You must come and see us! We would love to have you, for as long as you want to stay. It's so important to me, dear. You're all I have left who remembers. Will you come? Don't wait. Do it soon, darling. Our time is so short.

Please write soon.
<u>*Love always.*</u>
Flora

A Note on Sources

This book could not have been written without historical accounts of the life and actions of Julia Anna Baker. The following are just some of the newspapers and magazines whose archives contributed to the research involved in telling her story: *The Bemidji Pioneer, The Carroll Times and Carroll Sentinel, The Daily Capital News, The Duluth Evening Herald, Everybody's Magazine, The Jefferson City Post-Tribune, Leaves of Healing, The Minneapolis Journal, Mother's Appeal, The Kansas City Journal, The Kansas City Star, The Kansas City Times, The Mills County Tribune, The New York Times, The Ogden Standard Examiner, The Oskaloosa Daily Herald, The Pella Chronicle, The St. Louis Republic, The Saint Paul Globe, The Salt Lake Herald* and *The Salt Lake Tribune*.

The Minnesota Historical Society, The State Historical Society of Iowa, The State Historical Society of Missouri and the Yankton Community Library also made invaluable contributions.

Finally, special thanks also go to Ruth Sarar, Brian Gulbrandson and Katie Hoeck.